THEY CALLED HIM MARVIN

A History of Love, War, and Family

Roger Stark

With the Letters of 1st Lieutenant Dean and Connie Sherman

SILVER STAR
PUBLISHING

Silver Star Publishing
3942 Krause Ct.
Washougal, WA 98671

Printed in the USA by Gorham Printing

Cover Design: Kathryn E. Campbell
B-29 "Limping Back Home" digital art courtesy of Kenneth Walker

Editors: Barbara Fandrich and Leah Wegener

ISBN: 978-0-578-85528-8

To those who gave their all.

They shall not grow old as we that are left grow old;
No, age will not weary them, nor the years condemn.
At the going down of the sun, and in the morning,
WE SHALL REMEMBER THEM

—Robert Laurence Binyon

Preface

IF YOU SHOULD EVER get an invitation to a dinner party put on by Judy Sherman, by all means go. Jump at the chance. You will not be disappointed.

It was at such an evening event that I first heard of Dean Sherman. His son, Marv, and I were in conversation and somehow the fact that he had never known his father came up. I asked him to tell me more. The story he told me is the story found in this book. I felt an instant urge and without really thinking about it, I asked Marv if I could please write the story.

I went in search of details to understand what happened to Lieutenant Dean Sherman. Marv obtained his father's service record, and had in his possession the letters he'd written home. I went to the National Archives and spent a week looking through the military records there concerning Dean and his crew. Also in the Archives were the War Crimes Trial Transcripts, detailing the charges and the judicial actions brought upon his captors. The internet is a wonderful help in looking into the past and many, many sources were researched.

The results are on the following pages.

This has truly been a life-changing experience for me. It was a story that demanded to be told. Often inspirations came in the night or early morning hours that required me to get up and go to the computer to record them. I often felt Dean looking over my shoulder. Research fell into my hands that I was not looking for, nor had I known it existed. What I am trying to say is that there was something greater than myself directing the writing of this history.

I, like many who will read these pages, was surprised by some of the details that were revealed in the research. I did not know we dropped napalm extensively on Japan's citizens. I had no idea the Japanese labelled captured B-29 crew members as War Criminals, denied them POW status and rights, and beheaded hundreds of them, most without due process.

The atrocities on both sides were staggering.

The comfort comes from understanding there is a power greater than ourselves, that this life is but a flash in our existence and that for most all of us, the story will end well.

WHEN YOU ARE OVERSEAS
THESE FACTS ARE VITAL

Writing Home

THINK! Where does the enemy get his information—information that can put you, and has put your comrades, adrift on an open sea; information that has lost battles and can lose more, unless you personally, vigilantly, perform your duty in SAFEGUARDING MILITARY INFORMATION?

CENSORSHIP RULES ARE SIMPLE, SENSIBLE. They are merely concise statements drawn from actual experience briefly outlining the types of material which have proven to be disastrous when available to the enemy. A soldier should not hesitate to impose his own additional rules when he is considering writing of a subject not covered by present regulations. He also should guard against repeating rumors or misstatements. It is sometimes stated that censorship delays mail for long periods of time. Actually, mail is required to be completely through censorship within 48 hours.

There are ten prohibited subjects!

1. Don't write military information of Army units — their location, strength, matériel, or equipment.

2. Don't write of military installations.

3. Don't write of transportation facilities.

4. Don't write of convoys, their routes, ports (including ports of embarkation and disembarkation), time en route, naval protection, or war incidents occurring en route.

5. Don't disclose movements of ships, naval or merchant, troops, or aircraft.

6. Don't mention plans and forecasts or orders for future operations, whether known or just your guess.

7. Don't write about the effect of enemy operations.

8. Don't tell of any casualty until released by proper authority (The Adjutant General) and then only by using the full name of the casualty.

9. Don't attempt to formulate or use a code system, cipher, or shorthand, or any other means to conceal the true meaning of your letter. Violations of this regulation will result in severe punishment.

10. Don't give your location in any way except as authorized by proper authority. Be sure nothing you write about discloses a more specific location than the one authorized.

CONTENTS

CONTENTS

About This Story

We can't know exactly what was said in the recreations in this story. Some scenes come directly from documents in the National Archives, family histories, and other sources; some scenes are dramatizations but they are based on historical research; and the sixty-seven letters in the book were written by 1st Lieutenant Dean Sherman and Connie Sherman.

Chapter 1

The Story Begins

STANLEY CARTER started all this.

He was just a kid, a student at South High in Salt Lake City, Utah. A Mormon boy, as are many in the region, and a member of South's ROTC program; in fact, the student commander of the Army ROTC at South. His duties occasionally took him to the Fort Douglas Army Base a couple of miles east of the city.

Entry to the base included the obligatory stop at the guard house, a box of a place parting the road at the fort entrance. Bookended by road barriers normally open and standing at attention during the day-light hours, visitors on foot such as the bus-riding Stanley Carter were invited to enter the building and make themselves known.

On this particular Saturday afternoon he presented his credentials to one Private Dean Harold Sherman, military policeman. Stan handed Dean his papers with the greeting, "Hello, Private Sherman. How are you doing today."

The army blouse, complete with stark white name tag and chevrons of rank prominently displayed, made such identifications easy.

Dean studied Stan's papers and without looking up, asked, "So, Stanley, are you heir to the Carter's Little Liver Pills fortune?"

The question humored Stan. "That would be nice, but no such luck. I am just a high school kid with definitely not rich parents.

"How about you, Private Sherman?"

"Me? I am just a Montana ranch hand that came here for Basic

Training and am now OJT with the military police."

"You're new to these parts then?"

"Been here a couple of months."

"Do you know anyone in Salt Lake?"

"Other than military buddies, not a soul."

"Well, you know me now."

"Yeah, I guess I do know one person from Salt Lake now."

Stan wandered off to fulfill his post duties but he couldn't stop thinking about the affable military policeman. After completing his errands, Stan went looking for Dean and was glad to find him still on duty, shuffling papers in the guard house.

"So, Dean, I have been thinking," Stan said.

"You probably shouldn't do too much of that," kidded Dean.

"You're right. It gets me in trouble all the time. Dean, I want to help you with your problem of not knowing anyone in Salt Lake."

"What exactly do you have in mind?"

"Tomorrow I am going to my girlfriend's house. Come with me. She would love to meet you, and then you will know two people here."

Since his social calendar for Sunday, a non-duty day, was incredibly bare, Dean answered, "I could be talked into that."

"We are going to meet up at church and then go to her house."

So, there was that thing Mormons are known to do—veil an invitation to attend church so that it seems entirely harmless.

By the end of church the following day, Dean would actually know three people from Salt Lake City. This came about because Stan's girlfriend, Carol Woffinden, happened to be the best friend of Constance Avilla Baldwin, who also just happened to attend the same Waterloo Ward of the Mormon Church, who also did not have a boyfriend, and who was also more than happy to make a visitor feel welcome.

Dean innocently walked into all of this.

Mormons have a special interest in non-Mormons, or Gentiles as they call them. You see, a Mormon is never far from, or without, his missionary zeal. If you're not a Mormon and you're going to hang out with a Mormon for very long, you're going to get zealed. For Dean Harold Sherman, it was to be a life-altering dose of zealing.

The Backstory: 12 March 1922 Was Back Before

Back before he joined the army or flew airplanes or fell in love with a girl named Constance.

12 March 1922 was the day Dean Harold Sherman drew his first breath, kicking and screaming into consciousness as the newly born do. A man child, born to William Fred Sherman and Kathreen Williams Sherman in the city of Lewistown, in the county of Fergus, in the state of Montana, USA. He was not born at home as his five siblings were; complications made the hospital a more prudent choice.

Soon enough he would see the Gilt Edge family ranch and soon enough realize his family of origin had issues and that life comes with challenges. But understand, the only misgiving he ever voiced about his start in the world was his middle name. The moniker came at the absolute insistence of his father, no discussion required, a common approach for Bill; so, even though it met with healthy resistance from his mother, the name was given.

Dean wholeheartedly agreed with his mother.

Connie would tell their grandchildren, in an effort to help them understand the grandfather they never knew, that Dean often said, "I am no more a 'Harold' than I am a horse or a cow or a chicken. The 'H' in Dean H. Sherman should stand for 'Happy'—that is a middle name I could live with."

31 March 1925

On this day, Constance Avilla Baldwin was born to a mother with the exact same name, Constance Avilla Baldwin, whose husband was Claude Leslie Baldwin, in the city of Salt Lake, in the county of Salt Lake, in the state of Utah, USA.

The doctor, after the fact, no doubt went home from his shift thinking it was a typical delivery, but Constance was not a typical baby. She did not cry. At least she did not cry the way most babies cry.

She did make crying noises, but often they were like a gentle, haunting, tonal wail, delivered in sustained notes that approached the sound of an ancient saxophone.

Dispersed in her wailings were occasional small musical interludes, several-note melodic moments, often triads. She would start at the root of a chord and move to the third and then to the fifth, perfectly pitched. On rare occasions of extreme displeasure, she would also add the seventh or the octave.

This led her mother to brag that she was the "baby that came out singing." Often, she would add her prediction, "She is going to be an entertainer."

In truth, Mother was right. After coming out singing, Constance never stopped. She became a contralto in the Mormon Tabernacle Choir and entertained in Community Theater venues throughout the Salt Lake Valley for much of her life.

28 June 1939

On this date, the Very Long Range (Heavy) Bomber, the B-29 Super-fortress, was born in the city of Washington, in the District of Columbia, in the state of Maryland, USA. The conception was a result of intensifying world hostilities and a modest effort of the American military to be prepared for what might be coming.

This baby was a big one. Ninety-nine feet long. Wingspan 141 feet, weight (empty) 65 tons. Notably she had thousands of miles of wire, over fifty-five thousand parts, and was held together by a million rivets. She was designed to do one thing—fly over an ocean and bomb an enemy.

It was a premature birth.

The B-29 jumped a couple of engineering generations. Design never got all that far ahead of production. So blatant were the problems that the final step in producing a brand-new B-29 became sending it to a modification center in an effort to repair the many flaws that actually flying the plane revealed.

The first deployment of B-29s was in the China-Burma-India Theater. Five of the early arrivals fell out of the sky while doing no more than flying. No one realized they weren't designed to fly in India's 120-degree heat. Hundreds of other flaws were found in this same trial-and-error way, causing planes to be lost, and crews to be lost. (Craven)

Engine fires were a special problem. The fire suppression systems were simply inadequate and worked less than 20 percent of the time. Quite unfortunately, wings failed quickly, folding in half soon after an engine caught fire.

In the end, the B-29 obliterated Japan's major cities, burning them down to the sidewalks by firebombing. The 29s blocked navigation in their harbors by mining, and forced the Japanese unconditional surrender by dropping two atomic bombs on its citizens.

Back to January 1941

Army life isn't like normal life. It can take some getting used to.

However, every buck private thrown into a barracks full of shavetails quickly understands the normal goings on. It is a gaggle of army manboys, not quite soldiers, not long from their mothers' apron strings, thrown together by luck of the draw, absent of reason, as is the army way.

For Dean Harold Sherman, age eighteen, lately of Gilt Edge, Montana, newly assigned to Fort Douglas, it was indeed a new building, new barracks' mates, but with his history of military service, he realized it was also the same old same old.

Same old two-story, wooden-frame barracks, complete with army green roof. Same old army issue bunks, barely passable for sleeping, equipped with the same old foot lockers, themselves veterans of many soldier users. Same old pungent barracks fragrance, the stench of cleanliness that hangs in the place, the residue of a thousand soldiers mopping the army tile floor. The same cream color walls colored by paint the army must have bought by the trainload. The same old disappearance of self, absorbed by a forty-eight-man organism, without a face and only the name of Company B. Personal privacy replaced with a half-dozen porcelain toilets, arrayed in the open, perfectly aligned and fastidiously cleaned awaiting the public conduct of personal business.

The building was filled, like every US Army barracks, with the harvest of America's families, one-half of the nation's most valuable commodity, the male members of the next generation. These American boys were rowdy, reckless, full of wonder and curiosity. They sought adventure, with bravado, patriotism, and testosterone. They were volunteers to a man. They came to the army in the years before World War II. They didn't need to wait. Some would become men of oversized destiny, charter members of the "Greatest Generation."

At that moment, they were blind to their future greatness, to the tremendous challenges they would rise to meet. Right now, they were mostly concerned with the present moment, and if duty and time allowed, the consumption of alcohol and the meeting of girls.

Dean was well-prepared for this world.

He had come to the army by way of the National Guard unit based in Lewistown, Montana. He joined up in November of 1938 at age fifteen. He participated in summer camps and week-long winter tours until his high school graduation in 1940. In the fall of that year, he enlisted in the Regular Army.

Dean liked the army, but he sometimes missed Gilt Edge. Located in central Montana, it was more a ghost mining community than anything else. Sitting like a boulder that rolled off the east edge of the Rockies and landed on the Great Plains, Gilt Edge was one of those places you don't get to without some determined effort.

The large and bustling Sherman Ranch, run over an ex-gold mine, was at the end of a long, meandering gravel road that forked off the tar road leading to Lewistown. The sprinkling of families that lived on the road were tough people.

They had to be.

Dean's father bragged to anyone who would listen that "the farther up the road you go, the tougher people get," always making a point that the listener knew his ranch was the last one on the road.

Dean was born over in Lewistown, the Fergus County seat. He graduated from the county's high school, where he was a bit of a track star, in the class of 1940. By all accounts he was handsome, as the Montana Shermans tended to be, and was never very far from a grin. Slightly built at five foot ten and one hundred forty-five pounds, he felt keenly eager to establish his place in the world.

He had an extraordinary maturity, no doubt in part derived from being the man of the house as his mother wandered through three marriages. He was elevated to part-time confidant, parent and caregiver, forcing him to be "grown up" at a young age.

He held a great determination, of unknown origin, to live his life well. A certain sense of foreordination abode in him, that he had been selected to experience an extraordinary life, that he had great "doings" inside of him.

In this assumption he was correct. What he did not realize was that he only had 1,575 days of life left. Fifty-two and one-half months—four years and some change.

19 January 1941: The Meeting

To say Dean's first visit to a Mormon Church was transformative would be an understatement.

Stan Carter's girlfriend, Carol, immediately asked her best friend Connie to join their threesome. Few men have been smitten in the way Dean Sherman was on that day.

Those first few moments of introduction ventured toward the un-earthly. Their initial eye contact held for them an intimacy neither had heretofore experienced. They didn't feel like strangers. They held an odd curiosity about one another, as if they had come upon some lost part of themselves.

Dean would later describe the moment saying it felt like time was suspended, that they busied themselves getting acquainted, conversing, laughing, celebrating their new friendship, in a very lengthy conversation that had the flavor of two old friends reuniting rather than two strangers in a chance first encounter.

His recollection of the experience disputed the fact that there were no words spoken and the moment lasted but a few seconds.

In his days in Gilt Edge, Dean had a lot of girls that were friends. But he never had one he could describe in the one word, girlfriend. No one ever "clicked" for him. This particular Sunday, in this church he had never been to before, he felt himself "clicking" all over a girl who was a total stranger.

The worship service was conducted by a gentleman who very much reminded Dean of his father and led his mind back to Gilt Edge, wondering if Bill had gotten drunk last night. If he had, a very unpleasant day was likely in the offing. He had quit calling William F. Sherman "Father" long ago, a few months after his mother married him for the second time. It was her third try at marriage, and none of them seemed to work out very well.

He never could reconcile that. His mother was funny, warm, loving—all a son could hope for in a mother—but her choices in men fell to tragedy. Her misguided loyalty and sense of duty kept her bound to relationships that did not deserve her effort. Maybe she was just terrified of being alone, worried about how to provide for her children. It was beyond his understanding but it saddened him.

When Dean wasn't being smitten by Connie, he was being smitten by the sermon presented in the service. It was delivered by a Brother Wilson, a man of unusually large stature, meticulously groomed, whose penetrating eyes seemed to look directly into the souls of everyone, even those in the back of the chapel.

His message began, "Marriage between a man and a woman is ordained of God."

Dean liked that idea, He didn't know much about God but liked that He might offer his support to Dean's eventual marriage.

"It is our most cherished earthly relationship." Wilson drove the point home by saying, "Like the Lord, we have been commanded to love our spouse with all our heart."

This message was a new perspective, loving a spouse with all of one's "heart." He had seen marriage and family done another way. His father had married three times, twice to his mother, and his mother had married and divorced three times, creating a hodgepodge family dynamic full of hurt, anger, and uncertainty, along with many other things that fell short of the image this Brother was presenting. Dean had determined long before to do marriage differently from his parents.

There had to be a better way.

Perhaps this Brother Wilson knew the secret.

After services, the evening followed Stan's plan to go to Carol's house, except after gaining permission from Carol, Dean invited

Connie to join them. A pleasant evening of chatter and Monopoly ended with Dean walking Connie the few Salt Lake City–style blocks home. Home to a house at 567 Sherman Avenue. That was the beginning of a thousand jokes about how Dean Sherman found the love of his life on Sherman Avenue.

Dean ended the evening with an invitation to an upcoming dance at South High that Carol had mentioned, just in case he wanted to see Connie again. He did want to see Connie again—absolutely, he wanted to see her again—the fact of the matter was that he didn't want to ever stop seeing her.

Spring 1941: A Romance Blooms

The following account of Dean and Connie's budding relationship is in her own words from Connie's family history.

> "For Dean and me, that was the beginning of several months of mostly double dating with Carol and Stan, going to school dances, and to the movies, and such. There were also some church parties, and quite often Dean would ring the doorbell on Mutual night (Mormon midweek youth services) so he could go with me to Mutual. Sometimes he borrowed a car and picked Carol and me up after school and drove us home." (Sherman)

Dean became a very proficient car borrower. His MP work put him in contact with lots of cars and their owners. He especially liked the guys going on a temporary duty assignment. If they weren't taking their cars, Dean offered his services to watch after and take care of their vehicle while they were gone. Who better than an MP to protect one's motorized investment?

The new relationship was not without problems. Connie's parents were more than concerned that their very young daughter was dating a soldier. Connie understood and would sheepishly report, in the understatement of the month, "At that time servicemen had a rather bad reputation."

Dean countered with an afternoon visit to the Baldwin household, not to see Connie, but to visit with Mother Baldwin. As Connie recalled,

> "He visited...to get acquainted and try to assure Mother that he was a nice fellow, and not to worry that her daughter was going out with a soldier. He wanted her and my father to know that he would take good care of me." (Sherman)

Dean must have done a good job, but it probably didn't hurt that Father Baldwin had already had a dream in which he saw himself baptizing Dean into The Church of Jesus Christ of Latter-day Saints.

> "After that it was all right that I went with him." (Sherman)

1 June 1941: Mechanics School

Their first test of separation came seven months after they had started dating. Dean had signed up for Airplane Mechanic School and was ordered to Chanute Airfield in Rantoul, Illinois. Dean came in the afternoon to Connie's house to say his goodbyes.

> "I wouldn't kiss him goodbye. After a while Dean left and as I watched him walk up the street and disappear around the corner to catch the bus, all at once I knew I loved him and wished with all my heart I had given him that kiss." (Sherman)

Dean was a good and vigilant letter writer during his six months at Chanute, keeping Connie up to date with his progress. One of the fringe benefits of Mechanic School was that there were a lot of airplanes sitting around after the workday ended. One of the Mechanic School instructors was also a pilot and Dean charmed him into enough lessons that he became a proficient pilot. He racked up many hours of flying time, "testing" the work of the mechanics in training.

Dean was convinced the planes could never get too much testing.

9 November 1941: The Return to Salt Lake City

Upon graduation from Airplane Mechanic School, Dean returned to Salt Lake City, now assigned to the Salt Lake Air Base.

> "These were wonderful months for Dean and me. We went to school dances and the Tuesday night dances at the Coconut Grove. Coconut Grove was a huge beautiful romantic dance hall in downtown Salt Lake City; every Tuesday night was waltz night. Every other dance was a waltz—it was wonderful. We went to the movies often, and again he picked me up as often as possible after school, whenever he could borrow a car. We went uptown on the bus a lot of the times too. Dean was with our family for both Thanksgiving and Christmas dinners that year. There was a picnic in the canyon in the spring one afternoon, too." (Sherman)

6 December 1941: The Proposal

Across all lives, there are days and then there are DAYS. For Connie and Dean, 6 December 1941, was such a day. Of course, it was the eve of the attack on Pearl Harbor with the changes that would bring into their lives, but for this one more day, they were free of that reality. They set off on a quiet, intimate walk in Liberty Park.

This December Saturday, the weather gods looked kindly on these young lovers. It was a windless, bright sunny day, surprisingly warm for Salt Lake. They wandered as they most often did, to the south end of the island in Liberty Park Pond, to a rock they considered their own private place to be together.

To be together and alone.

And so, it was fitting that young Dean Sherman slid down onto his right knee, took Connie's hand, and asked if she would please become his wife.

This turn of events startled Connie—it was beyond her expectations. And while she knew Dean wanted her to say yes, she could not. Not because she did not love him—she had realized that the day she refused to kiss him goodbye on his way to Mechanic School—but because of her fear for her parents' reaction.

"Connie, you're much too young for such a commitment," spoken firmly in her mother's voice was all that was going on in her sixteen-year-old brain. It was hard for her to argue with that point. Love or no love, she knew she was still the age of a girl, not a woman.

Dean was persistent without being obnoxious. Over the coming weeks he continued to ask and on New Year's Day, 1942, the negotiations were completed with Connie accepting a wristwatch as a secret engagement present.

7 December 1941: Pearl Harbor

The motivations for Japan's sneak attack on Pearl Harbor were centered on gaining the resources and harbors found throughout the Pacific and Asian areas. Japan had already sent a million soldiers to invade China in 1937. They considered the British and American Navies the only deterrents to domination of the Pacific area.

They fully expected a "blue water war," one conducted far from their homeland, a war waged by their Navy that relied heavily on their superior battleships and aircraft carriers that were weaponized with excellent pilots and planes of war. The initial goal of the attack on Pearl Harbor was to annihilate the American Navy threat. They came very close, but not close enough.

Japan as a nation and as a people looked at life and war much differently than Americans did. They had barely pulled themselves out of the feudal age, and they disdained personal freedom and rising within the social classes. They were an obedient, compliant people.

The Japanese were convinced that because they were known as "the Land of the Rising Sun," they were blessed and favored above all other people of the earth, and that their emperor was blessed with communications from the gods.

The development of an Army and Navy Command responsible only to the emperor, unconstrained by oversight of parliament or citizens of the nation, resulted in Pearl Harbor.

Ten hours after the surprise attack, the prime minister of Japan, Tojo Hideki, gave a national address:

> *"I am resolved to dedicate myself, body and soul, to the country, and to set at ease the august mind of our sovereign. And I believe that every one of you, my fellow countrymen, will not care for your life, but gladly share in the honor to make of yourself His Majesty's humble shield.*
>
> *The key to victory lies in a "faith in victory." For 2600 years... our Empire has never known a defeat. This record alone is enough to produce a conviction in our ability to crush any enemy no matter how strong. Let us pledge ourselves that we will never stain our glorious history, but will go forward..."* (Hideki Tojo)

And so, Japan went forward, racing toward their first defeat, blind to the destruction they were about to bring on themselves, each citizen striving to be a *Home Front soldier* embracing their calling as a *personal humble shield* of the emperor. And for those that would become soldiers, there was no greater honor, no greater achievement than giving your life honorably for this grand cause. The contrary rule was also true— there was no greater disgrace than surrender.

8 December 1941: War!

> *"Yesterday, December 7th, 1941—a date which will live in infamy—the United States of America was suddenly and deliberately attacked by naval and air forces of the Empire of Japan."* (Roosevelt)

These famous words of President Roosevelt delivered to Congress and the American people the day after the Pearl Harbor attack are recognizable to nearly every American. They served as a preamble to the declaration of war with Japan.

If it was going to be a war of gods, the Americans had their own ideas about just whose side deity might be on: *"With confidence in our armed forces, with the unbounding determination of our people, we will gain the inevitable triumph—so help us God,* "Roosevelt concluded.

The Americans made a decision early on, that this war would only end with unconditional surrender. There would be no negotiations, and no repeat of the armistice of World War I.

With the declaration, the air corps immediately needed pilots and lowered the entrance requirements for pilot training from college grads only to qualification by test. It was a test Dean passed easily.

28 December 1941: Baptism

A baptismal font is a strange place.

It is something like a bathing spa in a walk-in closet. And when Dean descended down the font's tile steps, he was wearing a baggy, one-piece baptismal gown that had been worn a hundred times before, by a hundred people making this commitment. He reached to grab the steadying hand of Brother Baldwin, Connie's father, waiting for him in the water.

It was a simple ceremony and a straightforward commitment, consummated by prayer and culminated by the act of being immersed in the water and brought forth a new person, raised from being buried, as was the Christ.

Participation announced one's commitment to take the name of Christ upon themselves, thereby to be numbered among His disciples, committed to always remember Him and to be earnestly striving to keep His commandments.

It is not a one-way promise. The ordinance creates a covenant with God. It is a covenant, in that if one keeps his sacred vows, Heavenly Father promises the Holy Ghost, through the ordinance of confirmation, as a constant companion.

It is a strange religion; these are peculiar people. Dean began developing a belief, a personal testimony or witness, the very first Sunday when he went with Stan Carter to church and met Connie.

22 May 1942 to 6 February 1943: Becoming a Pilot

Making a pilot out of a soldier was no small thing. It was lots of ground school, lots of flying, even more testing, and at the end of a training module, the regular failure of one-third of the class of candidates. Instructors evaluated the surviving students and made recommendations for their next level of training. Orders would be cut accordingly.

The heavily testosterone-laden were herded into fighter pilot training. The coolheaded tended to be "Big Plane" candidates. It was solely at the discretion of the US Army. No soldier input was required. Dean made no secret he was interested in the biggest of the big, the B-29. He could, however, only hope for that assignment.

Dean's training gauntlet was accomplished in a baby-step tour of California. From Pilot Preflight in Santa Anna, to Pilot Primary in Tulare, to Basic Pilot in Merced, it culminated in Douglas, Arizona, with Pilot Advanced Training. The reward was his commission as a 2nd Lieutenant in the United States Army Air Corps.

While at Merced, Dean had mailed Connie an engagement ring. Their intention to marry no longer needed to be kept secret, Connie was turning eighteen and coming of age. Their hope and plan was that upon his commission on 6 February, Dean would receive leave and he would hurry to Salt Lake to be married. Of course, the army air corps had other plans and Dean was immediately posted to Victorville Army Air Base in California.

The army wanted him to help train bombardiers. Training was held in AT-11s, known in the civilian world as Twin Beeches, a rather long-lived product of Beechcraft Aviation Company. Dean was designated as an "approach pilot." He flew the plane around while an instructor tried to train a new bombardier.

Dean was granted leave without warning near the end of April 1943. He borrowed a car, called Connie to warn her to make what preparations she could, and started driving up the future route of Interstate 15 to Salt Lake City.

30 April 1943: A Date in the Temple

On 30 April 1943, 2nd Lt. Dean Harold Sherman married Constance Avilla Baldwin, who was one month older than eighteen, in the Salt Lake City Temple of The Church of Jesus Christ of Latter-day Saints.

It was the beginning of their eternal family unit.

They enjoyed a hastily arranged reception thrown together by Mother Baldwin on the 3rd of May and made their way back to California.

Dean had rented a cabin in Wrightwood, a mountain retreat area in the San Bernardino Mountains of Southern California. It was a community of summer homes that were largely being rented to servicemen and their wives during the war effort.

Connie described their time together in these words:

"As lovely a place as Wrightwood was, we only lived there for five-and-a-half weeks. On 14 June we moved to a motel in the small town of Adelanto, California, right on the Mojave Desert. The reason for the move being that it was much closer to Victorville Air Base, and so much better for Dean. After sometimes having to fly into the wee hours of the night, it was too hard for Dean to stay awake on the long ride home through the canyon to Wrightwood in the still borrowed car.

During the time in California, Dean took me on several trips to Big Bear Lake, Lake Arrowhead, Hollywood, and Long Beach, to name a few of the places. He also took me to visit Uncle Paul Williams in Los Angeles (a brother to his mother). On one of the visits to Hollywood, Dean bought a pair of swim fins and he always had a great time swimming with them when we were at the lakes and seashore. He was an excellent swimmer.

Dean took me for a couple of rides in an AT-11 while stationed at Victorville. He frightened me to death almost when he put the airplane on automatic pilot and then walked to the back of the plane and sat down.

Dean was rather inclined to being adventurous and a bit of a dare devil at times. His air force buddies said he could fly so low he could go under the telephone wires, missing both them and the ground. Surely, he didn't really do that though." (Sherman)

Chapter 2

Where is Burma Anyway?

THE UNDERSTANDING OF AMERICANS about the scope of World War II took a giant leap forward when a plane carrying Eric Sevareid, famous war correspondent, a voice and face every citizen who followed the war's progress knew, crashed in Burma. The rescue was a major news story, and a look into the future for Dean Sherman, airplane commander.

Flying from India to China through the Himalayan Mountains would come to be called "the toughest flying in the world." It became necessary when Chiang Kai-shek's Chinese National Army got cut off from their land and sea supply lines by Japan's occupation of Southeast Asia and eastern China.

It was important to America because if Chiang could occupy part of the million-man Japanese Army in the region, MacArthur could lead his army, and Nimitz his navy, to drive the Japanese out of the South Pacific. America was supporting the Chinese efforts with weapons, materials, and fuel, all delivered by being flown over "the Hump," a meandering path through the Himalayan Mountains between India and China.

The pioneer pilots were flying worn-out, hand-me-down aircraft with no air or ground support through the god-awfullest weather and mountains on earth. Because so many planes went down, it was called the Aluminum Trail. Pilots new to the job were told they could navigate by following the string of burning crash sites on the ground.

The air fleet of C-46s and 47s were crafts designed in the 1930s to facilitate the new-fangled method of travel by flying. They were twin-engined planes, called "Gooney Birds," or, in reference to a new Disney moving picture show, "Dumbos." The men flying the Hump called them something else—the rather poetic "Curtis Calamity" or the macabre "Flying Coffins." Whatever the name, the planes were never designed with the power or pressurization to transport heavy cargo in the world's tallest mountains.

President Roosevelt needed to know from someone on the ground if Chiang Kai-shek was holding up his end of the deal and not using American aid to fight the civil war he also had going on with a fellow named Mao Tse-tung. Eric Sevareid was chosen for the task and boarded a C-46, on Flight 12420 out of India, bound for China.

The plane had human cargo—not weapons and war supplies—some eighteen passengers, civilians, ambassadors, and army personnel intent on gaining intel about the military situation on the ground. They were served by four crew members.

The number two engine failed early in the flight and the pilot tried to return to India. Instead, it became necessary to give the abandon ship order. Twenty-two novice parachutists jumped out of the failing plane. Rather miraculously, twenty-one survived with only a broken leg or two.

Sevareid and ten others gathered about a mile from where their plane crashed and were spotted by a rescue plane that dropped some supplies with a note assuring that help was on the way. The next day medical help and guides parachuted in to prepare for the eighty-two-mile hike to the British offices at Mokokchung, India. The rest of the passengers, less the copilot who did not survive, were entertained by a village of nearly naked, spear-toting headhunters for a night before joining Sevareid's group.

It took ten days for a ground rescue unit of sixty native shotgun-toting porters and escort guards, led by two American soldiers, to arrive with the assignment of leading them out. Hiking around fifteen miles a day, walking trails better designed for mountain goats than a passel of survivors with a couple of men on stretchers, they arrived at the British outpost twenty-two days after the crash. They subsisted on mutton, cheese, and goat milk, and were glad of it considering the alternatives.

Heavy news reporting of Sevareid's adventure introduced America to the China-Burmese-India (or CBI) Theater of the war.

When Dean Sherman, B-29 airplane commander, arrived in India a little over a year later, flying the Hump was a little safer because B-29s were more powerful and fully armed and pressurized. But the route was never a cakewalk and continued to claim planes and crews for the duration of the war.

17 January 1944: Hobbs

After Victorville, Four Engine School at Hobbs Army Air Field was Dean's next posting.

Hobbs barely avoids being in Texas, sitting west of the state line a few miles, nestled in the southeast corner of New Mexico. The climate is designated as semiarid, meaning hot summers, mild winters, and less than sixteen inches of rainfall per year. This type of weather facilitates desert creatures and good flying days, allowing training missions almost every day.

Several "instant" airfields sprung up in the good weather climates of America. A lot of concrete and piles of lumber were thrown together by huge crews of working men and women.

The surrounding areas were seldom ready for the influx of thousands of soldiers-in-training and the staff it took to instruct them. It wasn't bad for single men. There was always a bunk somewhere for them. It was different for married couples. Orders to training often included rather strongly worded suggestions that wives not accompany their husbands.

That wasn't an option for Dean and Connie, and they always seemed to find a way to be together.

Dean set his sights on flying the big planes. The B-17s at Hobbs were not B-29s, but to get a jockey seat on a B-29, he first had to master the B-17. He mastered them enough that he served as an instructor on his graduation.

Connie had spent the Christmas holidays of 1943 with her parents in Salt Lake City. When she arrived at Hobbs on the Greyhound bus, she was whisked away by Dean in their "new to them" 1939 Chevy.

Dean's car-borrowing days were over.

Connie described the freedom of having their own vehicle:

> "After getting the car, Dean liked to take me and ride along the country roads and shoot prairie dogs, etc. He also liked to shoot rats at the city dump. Dean liked to follow every strange country road to the end just to see what was there. He would sometimes stop the car on the side of a desert road, get out, and poke a stick at and play with a tarantula that he had spotted while driving along.
>
> One time while living in Clovis, New Mexico, we went driving and came back with at least a dozen great huge turtles in the back seat of the car that he collected along the side of the road. We also visited Carlsbad Caverns National Park while in Clovis.
>
> Dean received his orders to report to Lincoln, Nebraska, to receive his further orders as to where he would go to B-29 School. We left Hobbs on May 13, 1944, for Lincoln, driving in the new car, arriving on May 15th. We took a room in a boarding house, and had a wonderful fun time in Lincoln. We were there two weeks and left May 28th, heading back to New Mexico...this time to Clovis, because that is where Dean was to take his B-29 training. We arrived in Clovis May 29th and found another motel to live in." (Sherman)

1 June 1944: Clovis

Cannon Army Air Field in Clovis, New Mexico, also sits near the Texas border just like Hobbs, but about one hundred thirty miles due north. It is where soldiers were sent to learn to fly B-29s.

Another of the nearly instant airfields of World War II, the structures were wood frame army buildings that became trademarks of the war effort. Twenty-four feet wide and forever long, they were the product of two thousand carpenters, many of whom, because of the demands of war, had never been paid to be carpenters before.

On the building project's first day, all carpenters were assembled and instructed by the project manager that job one would be for every man jack of them to build a set of sawhorses.

"I always want there to be enough sawhorses," he explained.

The twenty or so men that immediately went to work constructing their sawhorses—the men that actually knew how to build a sawhorse—were then each surrounded by a hundred men who didn't. The vast majority of the new carpenters tried to learn by watching, which was typical army on-the-job training.

Nevertheless, in a few months, the bare ground they started on was covered by a configuration of buildings needed for an army airfield, surrounded by thousands of yards of concrete shaped into runways, hardstands, and maintenance hangars.

The NCO Club sat in the middle of the offices and support buildings, a short walk from the enlisted men's barracks, next to the classrooms used for neverending ground school.

On this first night of June 1944, six near strangers sat around a corner table. The post was being flooded with new blood. A bevy of new B-29 crews were being formed. These six, about to become comrades, were collectively inching closer to combat. Each soldier at this table was worthy of entrance to the Noncommissioned Officers Club by virtue of the two stripes on the sleeve of his military blouse.

These corporals had been introduced a half day earlier at an assemblage for orientation. They were named the "Sherman Crew," designated to the command of a still unmet Lt. Dean Sherman, airplane commander. Most were not of legal drinking age, but the army calculated if you were old enough to join the army, old enough to go to war, and old enough to die for your country, you were old enough to drink alcohol.

And drink they did.

They drank toward oblivion, partly showing off to new friends, partly out of inexperience, and partly out of the recklessness of soldiers that would soon wander into harm's way. They had already taken a number, by virtue of their enlistment, in the lottery of death for airmen going into combat.

There were more questions than answers for them at this point. Gunners and radiomen, they were each fresh out of training in their military occupation, ready to become part of a crew. Some had been good enough students in their training that they had been selected as instructors for a while.

But now was their time. The war was calling. They now formed half of a crew of the greatest warplane in aviation history, the Superfortress B-29.

The night was spent chugging ten-cent beers and revealing themselves—places of origin, pre-army occupations, family histories, and "after the army what" stories. The beer loosened their tongues, diluted their fears, cemented their friendships, and spoke their stories.

"What do you hear about Sherman?" asked left gunner Carl Manson.

"He is from Montana is about all I know."

"I hope he is not full of himself. I have run into a couple of those kind of officers, and they can be real assholes," replied Manson.

Carl was from Long Beach, California, and was bilingual. Having a mother born in Mexico and growing up in a Latino neighborhood, his family and friends spoke more Spanish than English. He sometimes had trouble keeping his languages straight, especially after a few rounds of beer.

"What I want to know is who has a sister I can write to?" piped up Evan Howell.

Evan was the youngest man on the crew, still a teenager. He had been a wannabe welder at home, and had spent much of his youth sticking pieces of metal together with high voltage. He had hoped it would be his military occupation, but the army felt certain he would be a great central gunner, and made it so, effectively putting him in charge of the substantial firepower of a B-29.

"Who has a girlfriend I can write to?" said the rounder Ben Prichard. He was answered with a chorus of boos.

"How about you, Johnson? You're from Louisiana. I bet you got a real pretty Southern belle. Mind if I write to her?" pushed Prichard.

"I'd rather y'all didn't. We're married," drawled Johnson.

Jerry Johnson was good enough on the radio that he had served as a trainer at radio school. He and his wife, Hilda, hoped he would avoid going overseas and stay at the school, but the army thought differently. Jerry came from Ouachita Parish, Louisiana. He, like his father, worked in the vast natural gas field in the parish. He met Hilda at a high school sock hop and he was so smitten he never got over it.

"Where did you take gunnery training, Howell?" asked fellow gunner Ed Gentry.

"Vegas. Boy, that was an education."

"I know what you mean," interjected Paul Labadie, "Vegas takes some getting used to. I grew up on my father's freighter, sailing on Lake Huron and Erie. I hate the desert."

"I didn't mean the desert, Paul. I'm from Indiana. There aren't no girls in Indiana like the girls in Vegas."

"Hear, hear!" was a group reply.

"If you grew up sailin' in the Great Lakes, why aren't you in the navy?"

"When my dad dropped me off at the enlistment center in Detroit, he thought I was joining the navy," explained Labadie.

"Ohhh," groaned the group.

"When did he find out you didn't?"

"About a month into basic I finally wrote home."

"My dad would have killed me," noted Howell.

"I did hear there was some cussing and yelling when Dad read the letter, but he seemed over it when I went home on leave."

"My dad didn't say much to me, but my grandpa that fought in the Civil War told me not to trust any damn Yankees," said Ed Gentry, of Knoxville, Tennessee. No one could tell if he was joking or serious.

A student of architecture in his father's firm, six days after Pearl Harbor, Ed dropped to one knee and proposed to his childhood sweetheart, Heloise. After she said yes, he immediately proceeded to the army enlistment station. His small stature qualified him to be a tail gunner. He did, however, feel destined to design big buildings someday.

"Hear, hear! for the South," chimed in Prichard and Johnson.

"I just don't get that. The Civil War is over," announced Manson, the Californian.

"It may be over, but we aren't forgettin'!" volunteered Johnson.

"My justice of the peace suggested I might like the army. Six months in county jail or join up," said Ben Prichard, formerly of Harrisonburg, Virginia.

"What did you do?"

"Well, I joined up, dope. Why else would I be here?"

"No, what crime did you do?"

"Public intoxication, and I may have taken a police car for a ride without permission."

The group erupted. "You stole a police car?"

"Not for very long," was Ben's only defense.

"Last call! Last call! We close in five minutes," called the club orderly.

Corporal Carl Manson rose to his not-so-steady feet. His tongue was as drunk as the rest of him. Holding his mug high, letting it roam the air above his head, he declared, "Amigos, I propose a name for our august group, and a toast."

His audience cheered.

"To my new best amigos, 'the Corporalies.'"

The cohort of corporals rose as one. "To the Corporalies!"

The Corporalies were not the only ones getting acquainted that night at Cannon Army Air Field. The front-end occupants of the Sherman B-29 were meeting for dinner. The day's orientations and trainings had not facilitated much in the way of personal introductions. So, in Officers' Mess #4, seated under a window that revealed another building six feet away, the five people who would occupy the front of the Sherman B-29, four officers and a tech sergeant, broke bread.

None could have known that in a week less than a year they would all be swimming in Ise Bay, Japan, their B-29 shot down short of Nagoya.

The men from up front consumed far less alcohol than the Corporalies. For one, their airplane commander and bombardier were teetotalers, and the three others were still measuring this Lt. Sherman. They recognized immediately his response to the waiter when asked if he wanted a drink.

"No, thanks. I don't drink. Just water for me."

It was a night for first impressions, probably not a good night to get sloppy drunk. In spite of the lack of alcohol to loosen tongues and liquidate inhibitions, they were an open, gregarious group.

Tech sergeant Lloyd Miller, flight engineer, was a Missouri boy. He was twenty-five years of age, easily the oldest man on the crew. He would become the Corporalies' unofficial commander. They naturally gravitated to him like an adopted big brother; whether by personality or his maturity, the Corporalies sought his attention. He meant to make a career of the US Army Air Corps, and as things played out, he would.

Miller and 2nd Lt. Robert Orr, the plane's navigator, were the "lucky ones" sitting at this table. When they parachuted over Ise Bay, it was their good fortune to be picked up by a navy patrol boat, meaning they would be imprisoned in a navy POW camp and survive the war.

A rather ridiculous thought to think that they were lucky to go to Ofuna POW Camp (along with Louis Zamperini of *Unbroken* fame), there to suffer all manner of deprivations and beatings for serious breaches like talking to each other, but in the end, to be given the blessing of survival. Orr, the child of university professors, had grown up in Berkeley, California.

The fellow designated as copilot was 2nd Lt. Ted Reynolds, a "Green Mountain Boy" of hardy New England stock from Peterborough, New Hampshire. After their B-29 was shot down, Reynolds was injured badly enough that his captors sent him to a Japanese military hospital in Tokyo.

He, who had helped drop napalm on urban areas and other non-military targets, was killed when the American B-29s hit the hospital as part of a firebombing raid on Tokyo. The jailers released their countrymen and even the Koreans during the attack but reportedly made no effort to let American prisoners out of their cells when the incendiaries started falling.

The bombardier, 2 Lt. Norman Solomon, was from Norwalk, Connecticut. He was a Jewish boy and former used-car salesman who was blessed with the "gift of gab" and spent most of his time exercising it. He sported fiery red hair.

Norm's mother considered the red hair a curse. Neither she nor her husband had red hair, so naturally friends enjoyed questioning where the red hair came from, most often with a wink and a laugh, always to her great embarrassment. She hated the hair but dearly loved the little boy that grew up underneath it.

His other notable physical characteristic was his height. Norm was six foot four, and with his bright red hair he served as a homing beacon when they were out among the Chinese and Indian natives. He was hard to lose in such a crowd.

He became something of a landmark. When the crew was out sightseeing or shopping in native communities, they always agreed to meet up at Norm, wherever he was, at a designated time.

You just couldn't miss him, even in large native crowds.

12 September 1944: Orders and Letters

Dean was pushing the Chevy north on US Route 60 outside of Clovis as fast as he dared go. His mind was racing a good deal faster. The sun was trying to set in a frenzy of brightness that erased anything on his left side. He moved the visor to the door window for protection, irritated at anything that tried to slow him down.

Seeing a cop car at the East End Diner did slow the car down, but his mind kept right on breaking the speed limit.

He had big news. He was no stranger to racing home to reunite with his bride for romance, but now he knew their end-of-the-day reunions of passion were about over.

The trip from Cannon Army Air Field south of Clovis to their quarters usually took half an hour. Today he would be well short of that.

Dean hit the brakes hard as he pulled into their parking place, making dust billow and gravel fly. He was out of the car before it stopped moving.

The pregnant Mrs. Sherman emerged from the dust cloud to meet Dean halfway to their room.

"Hello, sweet boy. Welcome home."

"Mmm—you smell wonderful," said Dean with his mouth buried in her neck.

Chuckling, she answered, "Thank you. I am supposed to. How was the airplane commander's day?"

"Big news today."

"Yeah?"

"Orders will be cut shortly. We are headed to Kearney, Nebraska, to deploy from there."

"How soon?"

"Probably ten days."

"Ugh…" Tears were forming. "I don't…"

"Peaches, sweetheart, no tears. We knew this was coming."

"I know. I know. Still, I'm not going to like you being gone."

"It won't be for long. The Japs are on their heels."

Her grip on him tightened. "Dean, any long is too long."

"We need to make arrangements to get you and the car to Salt Lake."

"First, we need to talk about letters."

"Letters?"

"Yes," Connie ordered with some teasing. "You had better write a bunch of them."

"Ha! I will, I will, every chance I get. But if the army is as bad at mail service as they are everything else, it may not be very dependable."

"Alice says about two weeks for John's letters to get home. They do get bunched up though. Yesterday she got three."

"We should try V-mail. I'll grab some on the way home tomorrow."

"V-mail letters can't be very long."

"Just one page. We'll have to write real small."

"My love is too big to write small," Connie protested.

"You'll find a way."

"Honey, I am not comfortable with some soldiers microfilming my love chatter. They will be able to read my red-hot love messages to you."

"Humpf," Dean was grinning. "They'll be jealous and know how lucky I am. The microfilm instead of stationery saves a lot of weight."

"Well, I hope they are ready because I have a feeling my letters will be torrid. I am not going to hold back just because they are going V-mail."

"I hope not! You have my permission to be very, very torrid."

Laughing, arm in arm, they made their way into the motel. Dean removed his bomber jacket and cap and began to hang them up.

Connie was following his path. "One other thing I have been thinking about. Let's number each letter as we write so we know their order."

"You think I can keep track of that?"

"Well, the first one will be number one, the second, number two…"

"Ha! I get that part, Miss Smarty-pants. Just remembering which letter I am on might be a problem."

"For an airplane commander?" said Connie incredulously. "Why, I would think a command officer, a man of such accomplishment and organization, should have no problem numbering his letters."

Dean was humbled beyond more protestation, raising a hand as if to protect himself from the humiliation. He complied with a laugh, "Okay, okay, I'll do it."

It was a man promise. Sixty-nine times Connie sequentially numbered her letters perfectly. Dean, on the other hand, only numbered the first. The following fifty had no such designation.

15 September 1944: The Kiyoshis

North and west of Tokyo's Imperial Castle, Edo, in the lowlands cut by the Sumida River, spread the community of artisans and craftsmen known as Shitamachi. Densely populated, the wood and paper homes and shops began where each neighboring building ended. Weekends, it was more a marketplace than a neighborhood as thousands of Tokyo residents converged on the district to sample and shop the wares of the resident entrepreneurs.

Takana and Kigi Kiyoshi were typical of those that lived there, artisans first, gifted and hardworking. They were dedicated to the good of the order and to fulfilling their responsibilities in the community. This family did have a special notoriety, a proud samurai heritage and lineage. *Bushido* guided their daily lives.

Although samurai were abolished in the 1870s, a modified Bushido code remained a foundational piece of the Japanese social order. All were familiar with it and most generally tried to observe it. But this family earnestly personified the code and practiced its study and observance.

The tireless Kigi served on the board of the Community Council, coordinating with nearly two hundred Neighborhood Associations on distributing rationed food and clothing. She was a small, energetic woman, gregarious but thoughtful. Her relentless approach to life led others to follow Kigi's lead.

Takana was her opposite—tall, muscular, and quiet. Reserved might be the polite description. His children treated him as unapproachable. His life was practiced in a methodical, contemplative way, seemingly never in a hurry or frustrated by the turn of events. Just the qualities the head of the Neighborhood Association's Fire and Air Raid Defense effort needed. He often wore the distinctive fire captain's steel helmet, which sometimes embarrassed his children.

True to his samurai heritage, Regimental Commander Colonel Kiyoshi was part of the Japanese 18th Infantry Division that served with great distinction in the siege of Tsingtao during World War I. They fought alongside the British against German forces in Kiautschou Bay, China. His service resulted in lingering wounds that precluded his service in the current war.

The Kyoshi family included four children. The two sons were Reo, who would soon be entering the military, and twelve-year-old Riku. The twin daughters, Mio and Mei, were six years old.

The family resided over the shop where the Kyoshi parents plied their trades. Kigi painted elaborate landscape scenes for shoji, the Japanese room dividers. Her work was in great demand.

Takana made and sold firefighting waterguns of his unique design. The guns were in demand throughout the nation because of their volume and accuracy. The war and threat of enemy bombs had grown his business exponentially and he suddenly sold a lot of waterguns. He had begun looking for an assistant.

Made of bamboo, the guns were four inches in diameter and a little over three feet long. They operated much like a syringe. The gun was filled with water by drawing back the driving piston and sent toward the fire by energetically compressing the piston.

Takana was well-known as an expert with his watergun, a winner of several national competitions. His secret was in the bamboo and the sculpting of his handmade guns. He was known to roam bamboo forests for days at a time, always returning home with specially chosen bamboo stock in a relentless search for the perfect gun. The knowledge he did not share with anyone was his unique design of the gun's nozzle.

After the losses of the navy battles of Midway and the Coral Sea, the threat to the homeland increased exponentially. Citizens were charged with defending their own homes against the bombs. Water barrels and mini-reservoirs, maintained by the neighborhood association, were located throughout the community. Watergun and bucket brigades were organized to lead the defense against fires using the stored water.

There were professional fire stations in the community, Tokyo having one of the most modern and well-trained in the nation, but each citizen was expected to be the first line of defense for his own home from the threat of fire. Each neighborhood was organized for a volunteer response.

Of course, in Japan, volunteer firefighting was not volunteer at all. Societal pressure mandated that each household was expected to designate a member that headed up the family's defense and attended the bi-monthly assembly meetings that Takana directed.

Over the course of the war, the makeup of the assembly changed. Able-bodied men were in short supply, most conscripted into military service. Those that worked in factories were obliged to be part of that factory's civil defense and were unavailable to defend their homes. Takana's firefighting force evolved with the demands of the war and became made up of old men, young boys, and females of all ages.

On second and fourth Tuesdays, precisely at seven p.m., volunteers were expected to assemble at the water barrels just below Takana's house. (Those still trying to master techniques were expected to arrive at six thirty). A large red canvas with an elliptical target was hung on the second story of the home adjacent to the barrels. The fire drill was conducted with the feel of a military assemblage. The group created a semicircle around the barrels, each citizen assuming his assigned place.

Fukushima, a confirmed and aging bachelor, was often absent, being overcome by his sake. His absence was met with a standard amount of murmuring and negative judgment. No matter how many times he was absent, he was condemned verbally by those in the circle. This technique kept the others attending. No one wanted to be shamed publicly for their failure to do their part. Fukushima, after a certain level of sake intake, was often just past caring.

Yuasa Hajime, head of one of the richest families in the neighborhood, sent his manservant, a rather cheerful Korean fellow of distinctly large stature, who quite dutifully did his master's part. The circle did not murmur about Yuasa or condemn him out loud, but everyone was envious and all carried a special resentment for the wealth that allowed him to avoid their assembly.

Typically, after a short training lecture given by Takana, the drills began. The semicircle drew in close to the water barrels, as Takana's assistant loudly gave the order, "Fill!" followed by "Prepare!" directing each to aim. The drill session ended with a unison shout and the emptying of guns at the red target. This was repeated three times. Accuracy was important, and if Takana judged that not enough water was applied to the canvas target, the drill continued.

After the watergun training, the buckets were brought out and the semicircle reformed into a circle to facilitate training. Those near the beginning of the circle worked to empty the barrels by filling the buckets and passing them around the circle, the end of which tried rather vainly to fill the barrels. After the allotted time, measurements were taken to ensure that careless handling had not wasted water. Poor scores meant the drill would be repeated until losses were in the acceptable range.

The B-29: The Airplane

Before America entered the war, army generals ordered aeronautical engineers to sketch a design for large superbombers with instructions to "make them the biggest, gun them the heaviest, and fly them the farthest."

In December of 1903, Orville Wright is credited with the first powered airplane flight. It lasted about 12 seconds and covered 120 feet at the heart-stopping speed of 6.8 miles per hour. Forty years later the B-29 rolled down a runway with a wing span of 141 feet, able to fly over 350 miles per hour, with a range of 5,592 miles. From stem to stern, she was 99 feet long.

Aviation had come a very long way.

The B-29 should be listed as one of the wonders of World War II. It was such a great leap forward in airplane design and construction that some thought building and flying it was impossible. Not surprising, with such great leaps forward in technology, there were problems, unforeseen consequences, and design flaws that would plague the B-29 and her crews throughout the war.

Dubbed "Big Brother," the plane had its start in the vigilant mind of General Henry H. "Hap" Arnold as much as anyone. Arnold was an army pilot when you could count the number of army pilots on one hand. He grew up with the corps, eventually directing its growth. He foresaw the growing threats in Europe and Japan.

Some shared his fear that the US might have to bomb Europe without the benefit of bases in Britain, and everyone was worried about the unique problem that Japan presented. The problem was that American isolationism and the Great Depression worked against the development of a modern air force.

B-29 design or re-design was nearly simultaneous with production and testing. The B-29s were so advanced that some designers at Boeing were uncomfortable with the aircraft, feeling they were going too far forward into the technological unknown.

Mechanical issues would become the norm in the field. The 18-piston 2,200-horsepower Wright Douglas Cyclone engines were difficult to keep from overheating. On takeoff, for example, the race to get enough airspeed to cool the engines was a challenge. Once a fire started it was very difficult to put out; the carbon dioxide fire suppression systems were just not up to putting out fires fed by aviation fuel, oil, and magnesium engine parts.

Overhauls were scheduled every seventy-five hours of flight for the full engine, while the top five cylinders were replaced every twenty-five hours. Twenty-five hours amounted to two long-range bombing runs. Just getting the planes to the Far East required overhaul pit stops along the way.

General George C. Marshall would later explain that we needed a "new type of offensive weapon" that would present "a new problem" for the enemy and specifically their homeland.

The world held its breath as Britain withstood Germany's onslaught. We would not need to fly European missions off of our eastern seaboard. The attack on Pearl Harbor created a new compelling need for the weapon. It was now "our" war and we really needed a VLR bomber to reach the enemy.

We needed a B-29.

We needed a B-29 that was big and could fly higher, faster, and farther than anything else. The plane was pressurized, which allowed flying at 30,000 feet without oxygen. Designers created three pressurized cabins in the plane, one up front for the pilot and others flying the plane, a midsection that housed the gunners operating the plane's exceptional firepower, and a lonely tail section, sized for a single occupant, to manage the rear gunnery.

The compartments were connected by tunnels, creating the pressurized effect without having to pressurize the bomb bays. The plane utilized tricycle double-wheeled landing gear and a leap into the future—a computer-controlled firing system that allowed the .50 caliber machine guns to be controlled from several firing stations.

The workhorse B-17 had been named the Flying Fortress. This monster could be called nothing less than the Superfortress. (Gorman)

Chapter 3

Separation

DEAN'S IMPENDING DEPLOYMENT brought about big changes for Connie, as she later recalled.

> "None of the motels we lived in, in Adelanto, Hobbs, and Clovis, had a key to lock the door. That sometimes made for nervous feelings, but nothing ever happened.
>
> I was with Dean in Clovis until September 19, 1944. Dean had completed his B-29 training and was waiting for his orders to go overseas for combat duty. Daddy came to Clovis by request so he could help me drive the car back to Salt Lake where I would be living with my parents while Dean was overseas.
>
> I was four months pregnant when I left Clovis."

As the Chevy rolled north under the steady hand of her father, Connie wandered in and out of an awake state, alternating between daydreaming and dozing. She considered that this had all started with a "crush," a state that overtakes most adolescents from time to time— but hers was "king-sized." Adolescent crushes most often came with an expiration date. Her crush on Dean had not.

She had loved no one else. There were no other lovers for comparison, but she knew without doubt that what they shared was beyond remarkable.

She thought of her grandmother, the woman the family called "Mammy." Connie's first utterance to her grandmother, a failed effort to say her name, came out as "Mammy," and thereafter she was identified by it. She was known in their community as "the woman who never smiled," her face everlastingly frozen in a look of sadness. The look was perfected over a lifetime and was apparently untouched by the magical passion Connie found with Dean. Mammy had been married forty years when her husband passed.

She said "yes" to his proposal because he was a store clerk. For reasons of her own, she adamantly refused to marry a farmer, the vocation pursued by the vast majority of single men in the Salt Lake Valley. It was not that the farm boys didn't come around asking—just that she had already prepared a "no" for their proposals. When John announced he was *not* a farmer but rather a shoe salesman, his occupation won her over.

It was a functional relationship that created a family, extended the family genealogy, and weathered the test of forty years. On the second anniversary of his passing, Mammy felt reflective, and announced for the first time that she realized she loved John. The pronouncement had never been made to John or admitted to herself in his lifetime.

She missed so much.

Connie's own capacity for passion when she and Dean were romancing astonished her. Without direction, it would rise up and flow out of her. Connie was certain it was not of her doing, that it was Dean who made it so. She was of a mind there was no luckier woman on the planet.

She did sometimes wonder what he saw in her.

The euphoria of love has an opposite, and Connie was now about to get acquainted with it. The pain of separation is as far left on the negative scale as the euphoria of love is to the right on the positive scale. She descended quickly into the sadness produced by their separation and her abandonment.

As long as she didn't think about Dean being away, or of the fear of losing him, or of being alone, she didn't feel the sometimes overwhelming sadness. But this was a remedy that would not work forever.

20 September 1944: Going Home

As Daddy maneuvered the Chevy into its new temporary parking place on Sherman Avenue, Connie was not happy.

Her anger was not with her father or anyone else, but with the situation in which she found herself. Her life had been advancing, moving forward—courtship, marriage, living with Dean, starting their family. Coming to live in her childhood home as a married woman, with child, didn't feel like moving forward. It felt like the opposite.

"Go on in. I will get the bags," Daddy directed.

Connie moved up the three steps to her new, but old, front door. Standing in the biting cold November mountain air, she pushed the door open and was met with the rush of heat outward from an overstocked wood fire. She was wrapped in the fragrance of the Baldwin home, and the familiar aroma of baking bread and pies.

Close behind were Mammy and Momma. Rushing to her, they were a blast of their own. Their pent-up expectation of her coming was unrestrained.

"Mrs. Sherman!" Momma nearly shouted, while Mammy, her beloved grandmother, called, "Constance! Oh, Constance!"

She disappeared in the joint hug of these squarely-built women. They formed a statue of ambiguity. The love of her mother and grandmother tried to soothe her resentment of returning home. It was a standoff for now. She went limp in reaction to their imprisonment.

"We're so glad you're here," said Momma, realizing the exuberance was a bit much for a pregnant girl just off a long drive home. "Would you like to lie down and rest up from your trip while we fix dinner?"

Connie, unable to stop her welling tears, nodded "yes" and was ushered by the mothers Baldwin to her bedroom.

As the door closed behind her, her discontent again caught fire. Her childhood bedroom was as she'd left it, but it had shrunk—the proportions were all out of whack. She had passed into the adult world of womanhood, but this room was stuck in the past. It now felt like a child's playhouse, pulling her back toward adolescence.

The pink-painted walls didn't welcome her. Nothing in the room did. She recognized a picture from her sixth grade "Spring Festival," one of her childhood moments of glory when she had played the heroine. A guttural "humph," expressed her disdain.

She kicked at her doll collection occupying the floor, sending the dolls flying, trying to clear a path to the bed. Perhaps they were beloved companions of her youth, but now they were just in her way—impediments.

The pink walls, her doll collection, a once-prized canopy bed, and a Hall of Fame wall of childhood awards and achievements were perfect for a twelve-year-old, but that was then, and this was now. It felt like something was trying to make it seem as if the last four years had never happened.

"Oh, Dean...I don't want to be here. I don't want to be away from you," she said to a man a thousand miles away.

He did not answer.

There existed a three-member committee in Connie's head that maintained a constant stream of inner chatter for her consideration. The airplane commander's wife was dignified, wise, and benevolent. She loved to cheer and entertain others. She was a leader, with other wonderful qualities fully commensurate with a woman of her stature.

Nineteen-year-old Connie felt like she had her feet in two worlds. She loved being in love with Dean and starting a family, but often worried she wasn't "good enough," or ready to be an adult, and would at times testify, "Egads, I am still a teenager."

The inner-child-Constance was the product of the room she found herself in. She sort of wanted to grow up someday, but mainly existed in a world of child logic and fantasy.

The committee had been assembled and was definitely in session.

Connie-the-wife said, "You're fine. Look what you and Dean have. This incredible magical love—your souls are united. And by the way, when your bodies are united, well, need I say more? This time will pass quickly, and, oh, the romance at your reunion!"

Connie did acknowledge that their passion together was rather astounding.

Connie-the-teenager was struggling the most. "I miss Dean. I feel like part of me is missing. Thinking about the 'what-ifs' is driving me crazy. I am afraid. It makes me so sad."

This "sadness" was to be a fixture for the rest of Connie's life. She managed it well at times, but it also held the field some days. As time passed, her only defense would be to not think about it.

Constance-the-child-committee-member was checked out, avoidance her best offensive weapon. Her input was, "I need a nap."

The decision of the committee was to go with the suggestion of Constance. She lay down on the bed of her childhood, exhausted by her journey, and drifted off toward sleep.

In her short married life, she had experienced flashes of what it meant that a couple could become "one flesh." She knew the joy of the unification of souls and the passion of the unification of bodies. She felt complete in the comfort and sense of well-being that comes from approaching and achieving the unification of two souls in love.

And now the agony manifesting in her breast was the pain of separation that occurs when "one flesh" is divided, when one is ripped from the other and they become two again. She felt the screaming ache of her wounds and had precious little defense for it.

7 November 1944: Riku and a Sliver of Brightness

He was a scrawny boy. There is really no other way to say it.

Riku Kiyoshi was a long, wily, twelve-year-old, with a body that looked stretched over a skeleton three sizes too big. His knees, exposed by his constant wearing of shorts, looked fully grown, even though the rest of him obviously wasn't.

He didn't bother moving if he was not running, and his eyes saw everything, even when his parents were sure he couldn't. Mischievous, certainly, he was also blessed with the exuberance for life that his mother had, and found his joy in learning and being. And, oh yes, he had a smile that got him out of a lot of trouble.

His hair was cut short, his face dominated by his round, bright eyes and that disarming smile. Yet there was something not quite right. A lack of color, a hint of gauntness and emaciation, occasional fatigue—clues that whispered his body's haggard struggle. It could not grow like it wanted to. His physical development was being truncated. He was fighting atrophy.

Along with every citizen of Japan that didn't live in the Imperial Palace, Riku was struggling with malnourishment. Fostered by the imposition of rationing and the general lack of food, an out-of-balance nutritional diet became the norm. Japanese staples of rice, fish, soy sauce, miso, and sugar disappeared from markets early in the war. The citizens struggled to replace them with beans and rutabagas.

Everyone was hungry in Japan.

Riku had twin sisters, Mei and Mio, who were the bane or joy of his life, depending on the moment. He was often responsible for them, due to his mother Kigi's heavy schedule with the Community Council. Her responsibilities took her out of the home from early morning until late at night nearly every day. Riku was tasked with watching over the twins and taking them to school and back each day. That is, until they were evacuated.

The government began recommending the sending of young children to the countryside to live with relatives in December of 1943. By mid 1944, as it became obvious that the homeland was going to come under the bombs of the enemy, an evacuation order was issued by the nation's Cabinet. By the end of the war, 1.3 million children had been evacuated from Japan's major cities. Most were sent to live with relatives, but one-third were settled in group settings. Whole school classes were moved with their teachers and housed in temples, inns, or simply among the families of rural communities.

Mei and Mio were sent to a favorite uncle's home south of Tokyo for their safety. Uncle's home was deemed to be a safe place because there were no military sites or factories there. Riku avoided the evacuation because his parents obtained an exemption, owing to their heavy responsibilities in the community and Riku's essential help at home.

Riku believed himself special. His genealogy actually made that decision for him. He was descended from a nearly eternal line of samurai warriors. His grandfather often spoke to him of what that meant—that he was no ordinary boy; that he must live differently; and that there was destiny in front of him that he must discover.

To guide Riku, his grandfather fashioned a necklace of a samurai coin, minted in 1802, commemorating the Battle of Sekigahara of 1600 that led to the establishment of the *Tokugawa shogunate*, the last great shogunate in Japan's history. One of Riku's ancient grandfathers was a hero of the battle.

When the coin rattled on his chest, Riku remembered.

———

Riku and friend Yasou knelt, bare-kneed, in the dirt battlefield of their school exercise yard, playing wargames with wooden tanks. Their pretend combat zone was furrowed deep from the wear of hundreds of other boys fighting hundreds of other engagements, trying to win the war of the day.

It was a day November must have stolen from summer, the sun much warmer than usual in a cloudless sky, the kind of a November day most rare in Japan. It was the kind of day that would make an American general salivate at the bombing target possibilities. The general's bombing days, however, were not quite here, but the general was free to do reconnaissance.

The field Riku and his friend made war on was used more for military exercises than for a school playground, just as school was more a military training organization than it was a center for liberal arts education.

When a school pageant was produced, it featured soldiers, like buglers, charging into the enemy lines. Art works revolved around military scenes, and calligraphy was practiced in letters written to fighting soldiers expressing gratitude for their service. Teachers adopted a drill sergeant approach to teaching, hoping to begin the training of patriots that would obey orders without question.

Hours each day were spent in military education for boys and nursing training for girls, teaching each the glory of giving all for the emperor. Today's lesson was on a principle of *Hagakure* from the Bushido code—a samurai lives in such a way that he will always be prepared to die.

Riku had long ago, with his grandfather's help, made a sacred commitment to live by the code.

The boys' attention was buried deep in military strategy in the dirt. Silent in its approach, a low flying Tony, a Kawasaki fighter, delivered a blast like thunder as it passed low over them. They were each rocked, startled, to their feet, and their heads snapped to the sky. The unmuffled engine boomed across the ground as the plane fought for altitude. It was joined seconds later by another Tony and a Nick, a twin-engine interceptor the boys knew as *Dragonslayer*.

Though they were but children, they understood something unusual was happening. Riku took charge. "You count the Tonys. I will count the Nicks," he said, extending a finger with the passing of each plane. They were good at this. It was part of their daily military training. But they quickly ran out of digits for recording the count.

"Are those Zeros?" asked Yasou, pointing toward an approaching wing formation of a dozen planes. Zeros flew off of aircraft carriers and were rare in their sky.

"Yes. More than I have ever seen!"

The Zeros joined in the torrent of warbirds forming a scroll of planes moving away from them at more than 200 miles per hour, each one moving forward to make room for another in the parade in the sky. The roar of their engines crowded out every other sound and made their world shudder from the sound waves. While they quickly lost count of the number, history reveals nearly one hundred warplanes joined the chase.

The fighters were intent on gaining altitude, and were dedicated to the same destination northwest of them. Local bases emptied as every air-worthy fighter and available pilot was called to the air.

The stream of planes sucked people out of adjacent buildings. Students, neighbors, workers, and teachers gathered themselves around Riku's pretend battlefield, all looking upward to the northwest in curious wonder at this display.

And then the reveal: the stream of fighters created a giant arrow that pointed directly at a sliver of brightness—a distant sparkling airplane, pulling an exceedingly white tail across the sky.

A B-29, loaded with cameras, not bombs, was taking recon photos.

The spy was taking advantage of this extremely rare cloud-free day for planning future B-29 missions over Tokyo. It was the first American plane over the city since the Doolittle Raid in April of 1942.

The fighters gave their all, climbing at half a mile a minute, but even at full throttle they failed to gain on the Superfortress. As the glistening plane and its tail hooked hard to the right, leaving the sky and heading back home to Guam, the frustrated fighters peeled off and returned to base, leaving a silent sky to the gathered crowd once again.

Riku turned to his teacher. "What was it, Mr. Sazuki?"

"B-san, I think." The military and propagandists had been preparing citizens for the coming of the B-29.

"What does it mean?"

"I am not sure, but I do not think it is good."

20 November 1944: Not Happening

"Sir, can I talk with y'all?"

Lt. Dean Sherman knew without looking that it was Johnson trying to get his attention. He turned in the direction of the familiar Southern drawl of his radioman. Corporal Jerry Johnson and Dean formed a select fraternity as the only married men on the crew.

Johnson was a true son of the South from Louisiana. Within seconds of his speaking, his accent would confirm it. It didn't take a psychologist to see he was struggling. He was wearing his anxiety on the outside.

"Of course. What's up, Johnson?" Dean wasn't surprised by his radioman's apparent distress. They were in the last days of preparing to fly overseas, and everyone was racing to get all of the loose ends tied up.

"Sir, I need to transfer out," explained Johnson.

Dean stifled a laugh. He knew that wasn't going to happen to anyone who was able-bodied. "It's kind of late for that, Corporal."

"Yes, sir; I know, sir, but I just found out my wife is having a baby. How can I leave her, sir? I am the only family she has. I feel like I am running out on her when she needs me the most. I was an instructor in radio training for a while. Couldn't I go back there?"

As the corporal pleaded his case, Dean was thinking how familiar this sounded. No need for fabricated empathy—Dean was leaving his own pregnant wife; the corporal's struggle was his own.

Ignoring protocol, Dean moved beside Johnson and put his arm around his shoulder. "Jerry, this is about doing our job."

"Sir?"

"We are all here to do a job for our country. Do you know how to run that radio, Jerry?"

"Well, yes, sir, frontwards and backwards." Johnson didn't follow. He wasn't here about the radio.

"Jerry, operating that radio is the job you have been trained for. The most important part of your job is to come back home. You take care of that radio and the rest of us will do our jobs and you will be back here in time to see that baby born. Besides," Dean pointed out, "scuttlebutt is that Japan might surrender before we even get there."

That possibility made them both laugh.

Johnson contemplated while he laughed, working out things in his head. "Okay, sir." Dean's encouragement made sense.

He straightened himself. "Yes, sir. Thank y'all. Sir, I'll do my part." He offered a salute and moved out.

Dean returned Johnson's salute and while watching him go, mumbled, "Running out on a pregnant wife..." He was shaking his head and didn't bother to finish the sentence.

God knows, I need to listen to my own advice.

Dean returned to the matters at hand, getting his crew and plane ready to leave in the morning.

It would be a very long night.

21 November 1944: Wheels Up!

Airplane commander 2nd Lt. Dean Harold Sherman stood under the shelter of the giant port wing of his B-29, *Peach Blossom,* which by no coincidence was also his pet name for the angel who became his wife, Connie Avilla Baldwin.

His crew, ten air warriors that didn't have much need of shaving, stood in an orderly line before him, flight gear arranged regulation-style at their feet. It was 0500, 21 November 1944, a pre-flight inspection. They were parked on Smoky Hill Army Airfield in Salina, Kansas. They took up but a speck of the umpteen square miles of concrete that comprised this made-for-war airfield. It was early, wicked cold, and since they were in Kansas, the wind was howling.

They had assembled there out of patriotism, the whim of chance, the foolish belief of invincibility that empowers and blinds the young, and the undeniable gravity of destiny. The future was a secret to them, but the present moment was not. They knew the drill for pre-flight inspection—it was a routine cemented by hundreds of practice inspections and flights. Flying a B-29 was about following routines and checklists, doing things meticulously by the numbers. This particular morning it was no longer practice.

There would be no more training, no more elaborate efforts to create combat conditions. Flying into combat and facing enemy fighters while dodging flak from the ground was their new reality, the natural outcome of their training.

They had rehearsed over and over to make everything automatic and coordinated because a B-29 Superfortress was a complex flying machine that was beyond the ability of one man to fly. It demanded a crew that rehearsed and trained until they could do their jobs in their sleep. When they had that down, they learned to do someone else's job nearly as well.

All of this created redundancy, with the goal of meeting who-knows-what kind of emergency in combat while creating a command unit that acts as one being. This was what the air corps called "crew integration."

His men called him "the Old Man" behind his back as servicemen do, but this Old Man, their airplane commander, was not old. He was but twenty-two years of age. In most military units, command-level officers are separated from the men, kept free of familiarity, personal relationship, and attachments. It was easier to send men into battle and possible death that way. B-29s were different. When airplane commander 2nd Lt. Dean Harold Sherman sent his men into harm's way, he was seated beside them.

Here we finally are, thought Dean, as he inspected his way slowly down the line, looking over the crew meticulously. If they failed for want of equipment, he failed. There was no room for being forgetful. In a few days they would be halfway around the world.

He was checking their flight gear, stacked by the numbers at their feet—coveralls, boots, gloves, pistols, flak vests and helmets, parachutes, oxygen masks, and Mae West life jackets. He made eye contact with each crew member, giving his approval. He paused in front of radioman Johnson, and gave him a special nod and wink before moving on.

Two more airmen and the inspection was complete.

It was time for a few words, time for the airplane commander to command. He couldn't decipher what it was within him that made him commander material. He saw himself no differently than most of the tens of thousands of soldiers who sought the pilot's seat, yet he was one of the chosen few to survive the testing and training process. Whatever brought him to this cold, windy tarmac and this moment, it was the best part of himself. He was not afraid of it; he assumed it was his destiny manifesting.

He brought the men in close so the wind would not steal his words. They were huddled up like they were playing football, like boys their age should be doing instead of flying off to war.

"Men, harm's way is now on our horizon. We did not choose this fight. The Japs created this. What they have done demands our answer. I know you are making sacrifices to be here, we all are, but it is our lot—yours and mine—to answer for Pearl Harbor. We can honor and give meaning to the lives of our brothers who have died in this war by helping to bring it to a victorious end. We are well-trained and prepared for what lies ahead of us, we are flying the greatest airplane ever built, and God is on our side. Lids off for prayer."

They uncovered their heads. Dean acted as the mouthpiece, requisitioning divine protection and guidance, and praying for their collective safe return.

At the amen, Dean issued the order, "Miller, let's push through the props."

Engineer Miller scrambled into the ship to supervise the process.

Verifying all engines were turned off, he shouted, "Go on number one!"

The crew lined up two by two on the propellor on number one engine. Navigator Orr and bombardier Solomon led out. Each put a hand on the propeller and "pushed through" until it raised up away from them. Prichard and Johnson followed, pushing the next blade, as Orr and Solomon peeled to the back of the line. The scene repeated until they had pushed through four full rotations of each engine, and without another word, they picked up their gear and disappeared into the bowels of the plane.

Their new goal, the goal of every aircrew, was to get to 85 points. An 85 Adjusted Service Rating Score got you a ticket home. Measured another way, thirty-five combat missions would accomplish the same thing. Crews kept track by painting a neat row of bombs on the side of their ships, a bomb for each mission completed. A round trip over the Hump qualified as a combat mission, and was noted by painting a camel on the ship below the bombs.

Of course, the army could find ways to screw up the going home part. No one would be declared "surplus" until a replacement crew was on hand and the going home crew spent fifteen days training them.

There were a surprising number of rituals that were necessary to keep a B-29 in the sky. Pushing through the props was concerned with clearing oil that had leaked past the engine rings into the cylinder chambers, thus preventing busted or bent connecting rods upon engine starting. The Superfortress demanded attention to many such details.

The cockpit cabin bustled with six men trying to do just that—pay attention to details and get their stations ready for flight. All were arranged before instruments and controls. All had their part in making the bird fly.

Dean moved into the airplane commander's chair.

It sat on the port side of the plane. His console started at his feet with two oversized brake pedals. He straddled the yoke (or control column), a half steering wheel with which he controlled the plane. The column moved toward and away from him to establish the plane's altitude. His dashboard presented a few gauges and instruments arranged in four rows.

His job wasn't to stare at gauges and make sure everything was A-OK. That was why there was a flight engineer. But some instrumentation was vital to his flying the plane. Under his left hand the four control throttles for engine RPM rose up to a comfortable height. On his right side was an end table–type stand with switches and lights cluttering its top.

Copilot 2nd Lt. Ted Reynolds's station sat on the opposite side of the plane from Dean's. His console and controls were configured essentially the same, with a few less gauges and lights. The copilot was often an airplane commander in training. These two men were the conductors of this B-29 orchestra.

There was a seat in front of and about three feet below Dean and Reynolds, occupied by the bombardier. The B-29 had a wraparound glass nose where 2nd Lt. Norm Solomon was seated in the middle so he could direct the bombs to fall on the enemy. He also had responsibility for firing the two forward machine guns.

The great glass nose inspired the first description of flying a B-29 that Dean ever heard. Early on in his four-engine training at Hobbs, he asked what flying the "big one" was like. There was a lot of B-29 training going on, but no B-29s.

His seasoned instructor had answered this question before. He deadpanned, "Flying a B-29 is like sitting in your living room's bay window and flying your house."

On the Reynolds side of the plane, the engineer, T.Sgt. Lloyd Miller, sat back-to-back with him and faced a wall of gauges and controls. He had a set of throttles also for his part in starting the engines. He ran the airplane while it was in the air, allowing the pilot and copilot to tend to the details of flying. Perhaps his job's most critical moment was to announce, "All lights green!" as the B-29 rolled up to the line to take off. Takeoff was a risky venture when everything was perfect, and a malfunction somewhere could be deadly.

Radio operator Jerry Johnson's work station was also located on the starboard side, just behind Miller. Radio equipment was mounted over a work surface on the outside wall of the ship. Jerry was also the crew medic, had extensive first aid training, and maintained the crew's first aid kits.

Back on the port side, behind Dean, sat navigator 2nd Lt. Robert Orr. His navigator's table required the largest workspace in the cabin. Orr and Johnson spent a lot of time doing a do-si-do with the front gun turret, located square in the middle of their area. It was no small obstacle, being the base for four .50 caliber machine guns.

A ladder between the navigator's seat and the radio operator's station allowed crew members to access the tunnel that connected the other two pressurized sections of the plane.

The crew was working the pre-takeoff checklist, Reynolds intoning the item, and crew members supplying the response:

"Emergency bomb release?"

"In place."

"Emergency cabin pressure relief?"

"In place."

"Landing gear transfer switch?"

"Normal."

"Overcontrol?"

"Engaged."

"Landing gear switch and fuse?"

"Neutral—fuse checked."

"Battery switch?"

"On."

"Put-put."

At this point the copilot, Ted, radioed back to the tail gunner who was in charge of the put-put, a gas-fired generator.

Corporal Ed Gentry manned the tail gun on Dean's ship. He pushed the start button and the put-put roared to life. It would stay running until they were in the air. The put-put supplied electricity to power the systems and gauges on the ship until number two engine and its generator were on line. It was kept running until the ship was airborne as an emergency backup in case engine number two failed.

"Put-put is on," radioed Ed.

Ed's position, as one might suspect for a tail gunner, was at the back of the plane, and he was the lone occupant. It was tight quarters for even one. The space was six feet in height and had a little over four square feet of floor space. His battle station looked like a narrow farm tractor cab sitting at the base of the plane's tail. Two twenty-millimeter cannon protruded from the plane under his perch. He had a commanding 270 degree view of everything going on behind the plane. He also had two .50 caliber machine guns that he was responsible for loading and firing.

He was connected to the forward areas by means of man-size tunnels, capped off with pressurized doors. The compartmentalization served to protect the integrity of the pressurized areas of the ship in the event one area was hit by flak or enemy gunfire. On the long six-to-eight-hour flights, it was not unknown for Ed to crawl forward and play cards with the gunners to pass the time. The tunnels were also great napping stalls when flying long distances at lower altitudes.

More items of the checklist were waded through, and Dean called for the engineer's report. Tech sergeant Lloyd Miller responded, "Checklist complete. Ready to start engines."

Dean issued the "stand clear" orders and announced, "Start engines." He leaned to his window and flashed two fingers to the ground crew. That was their signal that the crew was about to start engine number two.

Engineer Miller started the engine.

A cloud of blue exhaust, a product of the prop push-throughs, fouled the air around number two. The process repeated in the order of engines one, three, and four. With the engines brought to life, the B-29 named *Peach Blossom* moved into position at the head of the runway.

"All lights are green," announced Miller. The tower's "go light" flashed, Dean's left hand pushed the controls forward, and the B-29 started racing down the runway, trying to get up to over 105 miles per hour to take off.

Only two of these air warriors would ever touch American soil again.

Chapter 4

San Antonio 1

SEVENTEEN DAYS after Riku's first encounter with the *sliver of brightness* pulling its white tail across the sky, B-sans came again.

Operation San Antonio 1 was launched from Guam, 1,600 miles away, by the Army Air Command. It was the first B-29 attack on Japan's capital city. Their primary target was the Nakajima Aircraft Company's plant in Musashino. One hundred ten *slivers of brightness* headed for Tokyo. Mechanical issues turned back seventeen of them short of their target.

The tactical results were pretty lousy. Clouds were an issue, but the jet stream caused the most trouble. Winds of 130 miles per hour could do that. Pilots and bombardiers had trouble with airspeed. Bombs dropped from five miles up were blown off course to land in unintended places. In addition, the enemy had enough warning to scramble 125 interceptors to greet the B-29s.

The Japanese evidently were taking Americans bombing the homeland personally. B-29s had been hitting the fringes of the Japanese Islands since June of 1944 from bases in China. Operation Matterhorn had launched a total of forty-nine missions, most against targets in Asia and Manchuria. Only nine times did they take on targets like Yawata and Omura on the southeast end of the homeland. The Japanese were forced to realize the Americans were coming, and now that the bases in the Mariana Islands were taken by the Allies, they would be coming hard.

The Japanese military tried its best to prepare. In the build up to the start of the war, the Japanese had trained their pilots exceptionally well, and their equipment was superior. But once they poked the "Sleeping Bear" of America with the attack on Pearl Harbor, their advantages were challenged and began to disappear with the great naval battles of the Coral Sea and Midway in May and June of 1942. By late 1944, their stocks of well-trained pilots were depleted and they were far short of serviceable airplanes. The war was eating up airplanes and pilots—of the twenty-five graduates of a 1937 class of the navy's Fliers School at Tsuchiura, only one would survive the war. (Sakai)

Riku was obediently standing by his desk, his right hand resting upon it, his classmates likewise. They stood nearly at attention with the discipline and formation worthy of a military unit. Their education had a decidedly military and nationalistic bent with an official ideology and a pedological strategy chosen to affect the students on an emotional level.

A lone, distant wail of an air-raid siren collected the attention of the class. The first siren was joined by another and then another. New siren sounds leapfrogged across the city, creating a siren choir as the home defense system tried to warn its citizens.

When students were dismissed, Riku was anxious to locate the B-sans. He searched the cloudy sky, but they were invisible to him. The home defense radar gave Tokyo eighty minutes of warning; the B-sans would not be visible for over an hour.

As time passed, Riku lost hope and turned away to go home, convinced that this was another false alarm or perhaps a test of the air-raid defense system. But the first echoes of flak bursts brought him back. Their black clouds clearly marked the area of the invading B-sans. The B-29s passing in and out of cloud formations became visible in the sky to the north of him.

Bomb shelters were being added to the school, a work hampered by the lack of building materials and construction workers with the skills to build the shelters. The Community Council had recently been tasked with the work, and called work parties each night to finish the shelters, but progress was very slow.

Riku judged his school was in no danger, and he lingered to watch, hiding himself from view so as to not infuriate his instructors that insisted all students enter the unfinished bomb shelters.

The B-sans again flew very high, but instead of a single plane as in his first sighting, they appeared in clumps of six to twelve planes, undaunted by the flak, flowing toward a target he could not see. Riku was certain he could see the bomb bay doors open but could not see the bombs dropping.

He could tell the bombing run was over when the B-san turned hard to the left, looking for the return route to Guam. He could also hear and feel the concussions as the bombs exploded—500-pounders left little doubt of their arrival on earth. Even at this great distance, the impacts were noticeable. The bombing parade went on for an hour and a half.

Riku raced home to tell his father what he had witnessed.

"Father, the B-sans came today!"

"Yes. They bombed the airplane factory in Musashino."

"Will they come again?"

"I am afraid so. The Fire Association was given new directives last week. We are to build more water stations and clear more lines for fire fighting in each neighborhood."

"Are they going to drop bombs on us?"

"I don't think so. We are peaceful people. We aren't close to any military targets. But we must be prepared to defend our house and neighborhood. You must do your part too, Riku."

"I will, Papa. Their bombs shake the ground."

"Yes, Riku, they are very powerful. Musashino is twenty kilometers from here."

7 December 1944: The Sudan

Unrelenting desert sand showed a green flaw in its otherwise perfect presentation on the horizon, the beginnings of Khartoum, Sudan, where the White Nile and the Blue Nile rivers converge. Norm Solomon, bombardier, spotted it first. He pressed his throat mic to his neck and announced, "Nile River ahead." His perch in the wraparound windows of the nose of the plane allowed him to see everything in a truly unique panorama.

Dean radioed the navigator, "Good job, Orr. Another perfect arrival. You may be getting the hang of this navigating."

Co-pilot Reynolds chimed in, "There is a first time for everything."

Bombardier Solomon said, "Even a watch that doesn't run is right twice a day."

They cracked wise with each other, camouflaging their true feelings as fighting men do. It wasn't the crude or arrogant high school locker room wisecracking, although none of them were very far removed from that, but more the teasing of brothers that love each other. No one took it personally. They were comrades in arms. The grotesque demands of war required that they literally put their lives in one another's hands.

The bombardier's seat was something akin to sitting on the edge of a cliff in a kitchen chair, feet dangling over nothingness—at times, 30,000 feet of nothingness. It took some getting used to, sitting there, suspended above the world as it passed under their great bird.

Initially, Norm didn't want to sit there. He started down the path to becoming a pilot, just like Dean. He had completed successful training at his Primary Training and Basic Flying schools. At Advanced Flying School he had washed out. He consoled himself that a full one-half of the class had a similar fate. When the army confronted him with a choice between navigator or bombardier training, he flipped a coin and said bombardier.

Norm was a bombardier who was fascinated with insects. He had been employed as a salesman at the local Ford dealership prior to the war, but had every intention of becoming a biology major at the University of Connecticut after his service. He never wasted time on being disappointed about not being a pilot, and saw his service as a government-financed bug expedition.

His specimen collection was about to grow exponentially.

Dean was focused on his landing. Altering the plane's altitude slightly, he allowed the rear wheels to gently come into contact with the runway.

The tires let out a screech and a belch of smoke from the contact. With a master's touch, he allowed the front of the plane to lower to the runway, the tires' "screech" the only indication they were down.

The crew never got tired of the magic of his landings, and co-pilot Ted Reynolds regularly took it upon himself to announce, "Smooth as glass," as he slid his palms across themselves.

He respected the artistry of Dean's landings because of his own jarring experiences at the controls. He had a good idea of just how hard it was to accomplish.

The ship was directed to the end stand R-34 on Baker runway. It sat at the edge of the green strip created by the Nile River. Fortunately, their quarters were in the "green" and felt about one hundred degrees cooler than the parking stand. The ship was due for some maintenance. They would be in Khartoum for a while.

Dean penned a letter Connie wouldn't see for three weeks.

7 December 1944, Anglo Egyptian Sudan

Good Evening Honey:

Here I am all tired from a big day's flying but can always find time to write you a letter. Sure hope we get a day's rest here. Could use it.

I sent you a small package from Gold Coast West Africa with numerous small items I thought you may like. It will probably beat this letter though, because they say the mail service is good. Sent some agate beads, a necklace and an ivory belt. The belt may fit now but you'll have to take out a couple of pieces later. Sure hope you like all those things, Honey; and let me know when you get them.

I have an alligator hand bag to send when I get time. It should be worth about three times what I paid for it. Would you like it?

We are parked at present on the mystic Nile valley. You can read about it in your Nile book. From here it is just a narrow green strip in the desert though. Would like to go crocodile hunting tomorrow if there are any around. I'll let you know.

The natives are still black, but different. They take off their shoes if any, kneel on the little rug and praise Allah. A fine way to get calluses on the knees I think.

Last night, when we stopped, I had the good fortune to find a record player and some more records. I played "Make Believe" by Guy Lombardo about five times. And other beautiful pieces like, "An Hour Never Passes" and "All the Things You Are." Also "I Love You Truly" and others.

And I'll have you know, I do love you, Honey, with all my heart, and am very lonesome for you this evening and every evening and every hour, too.

I guess it will be a few days yet before I get any of your letters. I sure am missing them too. Maybe I'll have a whole stack to read one of these days. There sure is a lot of desert, over which we flew, that looks like Eastern New Mexico and West Texas. Nasty stuff, only hundreds of miles of it with 90 miles between oases. Long time between drinks, isn't it?

I guess I've told you before, "War is Hell" and I'm believing it. I'm just eager now to turn around and be starting back.

When I do I'll sure be ready for lots of dancing and romancing with you, I guess you know!!

Goodnight Now, You Sweet Woman,

Dean

Ninety-degree days in December challenged Dean's internal weather clock, when two weeks ago the temperature couldn't get above freezing at Smoky Hill. He thought he knew about dry heat from training in places like the Mojave in California and Arizona, but this desert made those places seem mildly pleasant.

He had made fun of his town cousins when the tenderfoots came to the Montana ranch. When exploring this place, trudging through ankle-deep sand, trying to get to the top of a sand dune that only revealed that the sand dunes appeared to go on forever, he knew what it felt like to be out of his element. Visiting Khartoum wasn't exactly on his bucket list. He was only vaguely aware of the Sudan's existence before he landed his B-29 there.

But here he was.

On the third anniversary of Pearl Harbor, 7 December 1944, Dean lay under the protection of a mosquito net, on a bed that felt like the floor, in Sahara Desert heat that was on the edge of unbearable. He was in a restless search for a sleeping position that benefited from the noisy, wobbling overhead fan in his room. Sleep didn't seem likely to be arriving any time soon.

These days all of Dean's thoughts and contemplations, no matter where they started, flowed only one direction—toward home, back to Connie. He missed her, wanted to be with her, and wanted to share what he was seeing with her. Once she entered his mental musing, the thoughts proceeded to a predictable ending, a certain train station in Kearney, Nebraska.

On the platform of their separation, he held her like he knew this embrace would have to last for a while. His mind was trying to memorize what she felt like in his arms. She fit him like she had been sculpted by the Almighty with him in mind. He felt her body shudder in reaction to his embrace.

He raised his hand to her face and let his fingers slowly follow the contour from her temple to her chin. Her lips reached to kiss his fingers. He slid his cheek against hers. Only the growth of Junior disturbed the perfection of the embrace, or perhaps Junior was the perfecting of it.

The conductor called "All aboard!" The engine made that first "chug," announcing movement. The banging of couplings followed down the line as gaps closed while the platform speaker blared a message no one could understand. Steam and the smell of coal filled the air. He didn't like what all that meant.

"Take care of yourself and Junior. I will be back. I love you," said Dean. Their lips again came together.

"Dean, swear you will come back to us. You have to swear."

"I swear."

"You had better. I love you forever." She pulled away and stepped up onto the train. As she disappeared, Dean's heart fell out of him. His foreknowledge of this parting brought no comfort. His anguish pushed him down the platform, fighting to extend the moment.

He found her as she moved into a compartment. He leaned across the gap between train and platform, resting both hands on her window. His feet matched the train's tempo as it slowly accelerated.

Connie, attending to the details of entering her compartment, was startled when she looked up to find Dean at her window.

Her reaction inspired his finest grin. Trying to assure her one more time, he was shouting without words, "I love you, and I will come back soon!"

His heart was hemorrhaging. Connie made an attempt at triage, frantically trying to communicate her love through the window glass.

The train won the race at the end of the platform and pulled away, stealing Connie. As the train disappeared from his view, duty began to stir within him. He slowly straightened himself to the position of attention, placed his right toe behind his left heel, performed a precision about-face, and started marching smartly toward the airbase.

In less than ten paces he was in full airplane commander mode, his mind racing through his final checklist for his B-29, his men, and himself.

Dean would return again and again to this moment of memory, shared through a train's window, to savor and bask in Connie's message washing over him. He never stopped wondering if she understood his wordless message of assurance. And here, alongside the confluence of the Blue Nile and the White Nile rivers in Khartoum, Sudan, he wondered again.

Nine thousand miles away, Connie was lying on the bed of her childhood on Sherman Avenue. She was also having a restless time with not much hope for sleep. It was not the heat bothering her. She wasn't trying to sleep in the Sahara Desert. December brought the cold of winter to the Salt Lake Valley.

The baby was the source of her dissonance. She hadn't mastered the art of being pregnant and she was pretty sure that Junior hadn't mastered the art of being a baby. Neither of them could get comfortable. As was her habit, if her mind lacked direction it would automatically wander back to her final parting from Dean at an out-of-the-way train station.

On the platform of their separation, she held him like she knew this embrace would have to last for a while. Connie wanted to remember this and snuggled into his embrace, hoping it would be an everlasting protective shroud. She shuddered with the intensity of her love for

Dean and a parallel gratitude to God for sending him into her life.

As his fingers traced her face, she reached with her lips and softly, tenderly kissed them. She elevated to her toes and slid her face beside his. She noticed that the baby was complicating this kind of moment nowadays, a natural reminder that two was about to become three.

The conductor called "All aboard!" She hated what that meant.

Dean said, "Take care of yourself and Junior. I will be back. I love you," and their lips came together.

"Dean, swear you will come back to us. You have to swear."

"I swear."

"You had better. I love you forever."

She pulled away and stepped onto the train.

The conductor, Alvin, a veteran of the rails, had already made friends with her. He was especially vigilant about his passengers with child. Connie's pregnancy was no longer in doubt to anyone.

"This way, please, Mrs. Sherman." He beckoned to her.

He was a large man of color taking up most of the narrow train passageway. Her bags looked like doll luggage in his giant hands.

Connie trusted his face. It emanated a serenity, a kindness that few faces ever achieve, perhaps a product of serving others on the trains for nearly a lifetime. It pleased him greatly to serve her. There was an open single sleeper compartment and he situated her there.

While he put away the bags, she went to the window in hopes of catching one last glimpse of Dean. She was startled to find him in the frame of her window.

Instinctively she was aware the parting was wounding him and attempted first aid. Separated by glass, her options were limited. She could not touch him or kiss him; she could only offer her expression without words. She sent all she felt for him—her love, passion, respect, gratitude, and devotion.

She "read" his response to her, written over his loving grin, and knew he was trying to reassure her, "I will be back."

As the train separated them, she moved closer and closer to the window finally pressing the side of her face against the glass, desperately trying to never lose sight of him, but she did.

She fell back into the seat. A new reality generated a sudden dark uncertainty. *I'm alone. Really alone.*

The baby kicked at her.

"Okay, I am very alone and pregnant," she whispered, as she massaged the protruding mass that held her child.

It worried her some that the baby seemed to know her thoughts.

Connie's memory began to cloud her eyes with sleep. It was finally approaching. She adjusted her pillow. The memory had stirred her; she wanted to feel his arms around her, and in the blended world of dreams, wishes, and reality, she reached out to hold Dean.

Likewise, Dean's remembrance of their parting created longings deep within him. He ached for her, and sensing her desire, rolled over toward her, searching with his arms to draw her to him, forgetting for a time she was on another continent.

9 December 1944: No Mail

While Dean was living his adventure, flying the "big" planes, Connie spent the first part of six mornings a week staring at the mailbox for 567 East Sherman, the mailbox that refused to produce a letter from her husband.

The mailbox's betrayal wore on her. Whether it was just the loneliness, or the troubling what-ifs of not knowing he was safe, or maybe the demons of self-doubt that wanted to have her believe she didn't deserve him, she did not know. She just knew it hurt.

She had built an expectation that mail would come about three weeks after they parted. That seemed plenty of time for his mail to find its way home. It turns out that was naive. She had far too much faith in the US Army and Postal Service.

In the void, she comforted herself by making up and "receiving" imaginary letters from Dean.

My Dearest Peach Blossom,

Hello sweet girl, I sure have been thinking of you lots these days and wishing so much that I could be around to take care of you, and be holding your nice soft hands and giving you lots of moral support, and see your pretty face and look in your eyes and without saying a word, tell you millions of wonderful things that you mean to me.

You do too, Honey, mean so many wonderful things to me. All the wonderful things a beautiful girl can be and my best companion ever along with being the sweetest wife any guy ever could love. Those are just a few of the things, Darling, which make me love you more every day.

Dean

"Oh, what a beautiful letter, Dean," she would say, fully aware he had not written a single word of it. "So much love and romance. You somehow always say just what I need to hear."

Whenever she felt her feelings dip, she would write another letter. Sometimes, however, the dips were too deep. A made-up letter could not bridge them.

Her frustration and despair led to a fog of depression that could set in for days at a time, a toxic cocktail of loneliness, despair, fear, forlornness, and perhaps some anger at the unfairness of it all. In many years' time, with much reflection, she would develop some understanding, if not a cure.

But that was a distant hope. Now the demons were having their way. She slipped onto the piano bench. She moved it back an inch or two. *I have to move this bench farther away every day*, she thought, acknowledging the fact that Junior was growing.

She sat but struggled to play. The sadness was getting the best of her.

A single finger of her right hand struck a key. Her left elbow rested above the keyboard and held her head. She plunked at a tune and her voice followed. "Sweet hour of prayer! Sweet hour of prayer! That calls me from my world of care." She ignored tempo and sang, haltingly, "In seasons of distress and grief, My soul has often found relief…by thy return, sweet hour of prayer." The sorrow began to lift as she sang. With each verse she added more fingers and vocal support.

Like the light of dawn racing across a landscape chasing away the darkness of night, playing and singing the hymns chased the struggle out of her.

She sighed more relief into her heart. *I love this hymn.* Her fingers grabbed a few more pages of the hymnal and turned them. It fell open to "Nearer, My God, to Thee." The hymnal knew where the hymns were she needed.

Her face drew up into a smile as if she were seeing an old friend. Her left hand, without direction, came to the keyboard. She rearranged herself on the bench like she was trying to make her music teacher proud, and began to play and sing, "Nearer, my God, to thee, nearer to thee! E'en though it be a cross that raiseth me. Still all my song shall be, nearer my God to thee."

The tension continued to flow out of her neck and shoulders, down her arms and out her fingers as she played. She could feel the stress and tightness fleeing her body, the volume of stress startling her. She closed her eyes, let her body sway, and focused on letting it all go. She was on a quest to find the place of peace within her. Her fingers did not need her eyes to play this hymn.

Her brow furrowed at the thought of stopping. She was fully aware that her respite from her struggle was not permanent.

It was all complicated by her pregnancy. She was in her seventh month, her emotions rolled out and in like great ocean waves, her body generally tired from doing the work of supporting two. And Junior seemed to know when she was falling asleep because he would kick at her like he didn't want to be the only one awake.

Going into the fourth week with no mail from her husband deepened her disappointment. She had established a daily observation station by the front window, hidden by the drapes, protecting her from the odd person that masqueraded as their mailman. Here, she could observe his delivery for the day with the benefit of no personal interaction.

Not getting a letter was a progressive frustration. Today's disappointment sat atop yesterday's.

"It didn't take him long to forget about us," Connie said, making the baby part of the conversation. She was certain Junior understood.

"Looks like it's you and me against the world, kiddo," she said with the beginning of a smile, patting her tummy, trying to regain her emotional equilibrium.

A morning without letters would create a powerful sadness that would take the rest of the day to relieve. Momma and Daddy did their best to comfort her, but as the days mounted, that became impossible.

10 December 1944: Therill Hanson

On mail delivery days, Connie Sherman had to decide if she would hide behind the drapes or go outside to interact with the obnoxious man that delivered her mail.

She dreaded him. The drapes offered safety, but delayed her learning if there were letters from Dean in his bag.

Not looking was not an option, so most days she watched as the somewhat eccentric Therill Hanson, faithful mail carrier and distant relative of some sort, put mail in the box at 567 Sherman Avenue for the family named Baldwin and now for a Sherman that also lived there.

He came within a minute or two of exactly 10:06 a.m., six days of the week. His punctuality was his trademark. It distinguished him from other mail carriers. For reasons known only to Therill, it was mandatory that he was dependable. He loved to explain his punctuality. It became a ritual that Connie sought to avoid.

Therill, in the presence of any of his mail customers would retrieve his watch from its small pocket on front of his uniform, check the time, and say,

"Most excellent, I am right on schedule this morning. Being on time is important. People need to be able to depend on when their mail will arrive, especially in these times. I can't go to war, but I can help in this small way. I want people to be able to depend on me."

This unrequested explanation was lavished, verbatim, on anyone who dared be outside when Therill brought the mail. He had no filter to prevent him from presenting the dissertation over and over to the same people. Like Connie, many watched from the safety of their home to avoid him, causing Sherman Avenue to appear deserted around 10:00 a.m. each morning. There followed a small explosion of activity with folks coming out of their homes to check the mail shortly after they were completely certain Therill Hanson had passed by.

Connie was so anxious to get a letter from Dean that she had pushed it a few times lately and Therill had trapped her outside and delivered the full speech. Today was one of those days.

True to form, Therill immediately started fumbling for his watch and started, "Most excellent…"

Connie checked out, her eyes quickly glazed over, and her resentment simmered. She could recite Therill's speech for him, she had heard it enough. The echoes of her father's advice spoke up in her head. He often said, "Insulting the mailman, who carries your fate in his bag, is never a good idea." And thus, she endured.

Such an odd duck, she thought as he finished with "…want people to depend on me."

He was a short person, fully six inches shorter than Connie. She judged his face was the face of a man that no one would find handsome, his uniform looked as if it had been tailored to fit someone else, and his people skills—well, he just didn't have many people skills.

Therill could, however, organize one hundred letters for delivery faster than any other mail carrier in Salt Lake. He possessed a remarkable memory that allowed him to recite, in street order, every family he had ever delivered mail to. These were both perfect skills for a mail carrier. Hidden beneath that off-putting exterior, Connie would later learn, was more to Therill than met the eye.

Speech over, she could say, "Thanks for your service, Therill. We all appreciate it," thinking it isn't a lie when you are being kind. "Any mail for us today?"

Therill knew what she really wanted to know. "Sorry, Connie, none from Dean today."

Connie turned back toward the house with only disappointment. "Oh well, surely tomorrow."

She had repeated that sentence with diminishing hope and enthusiasm since shortly after saying goodbye to Dean in Kearney. She had started to wonder if it were true. She returned to the house not having to say a word to report to those inside, "No mail from Dean."

Chapter 5

The Same Damn Movie

WHEN DEAN and his B-29 crew left Smokey Hill, they knew their destination was Morrison Army Airfield in Florida. From there, they had no idea where they were going. After spending the night at Morrison, they were given a heading and a sealed envelope containing their flight plans, with the instruction to open the envelope an hour after getting airborne.

Secrecy was a priority. "Loose lips sink ships" was the popular reminder. The crazy part was, in spite of all the clandestine efforts, after ten stops and nearly sixty-two hours of flying, spread over twenty-two days, Tokyo Rose welcomed Lt. Dean Sherman and each crew member by name to the war the day they landed at Piardoba Airfield in India.

That was a real head-scratcher.

A pattern for the trip evolved—fly for four to eight hours, stop overnight, and get up and do it again. From Florida, they had followed the coast south to Natal, Brazil, and crossed the Atlantic to Africa. Jumping the ocean was eleven hours and fifteen minutes of flying. Then they had flown across Africa to the Middle East, and on to Pakistan and their duty station in India.

The trip involved two long stays—six days in Ghana, West Africa, and several days in Khartoum, Sudan, for maintenance of the airplane. At each destination, the crew would get cleaned up upon landing and head for chow. Their next interest was finding out what was playing at the movies.

In Puerto Rico, the crew was quite happy to watch the new release of *The Lady Takes a Chance,* starring John Wayne and Jean Arthur. Coincidently, when they reached British Guiana, the same movie was featured. Not to be deterred, the crew again enjoyed the film. When they got to Brazil and it was again the featured picture show, some murmuring occurred. The Corporalies were feeling cheated.

When they found the movie would also be playing at their fourth stop, they complained to Dean.

"Sir, ain't the army got any other movies?"

"We know the lines better than the actors!"

"We know John Wayne is going to eat the lamb chops because Jean Arthur cooked them for him, even though he is a beef man."

"Maybe there will be something new at our next stop," was the consolation Dean offered. But at each of their ten layovers, *The Lady Takes a Chance* was the featured movie. After crossing the Atlantic, the Corporalies showed signs of giving up on the movies.

But in Khartoum, the Corporalies, forced into the NCO Club by the searing heat and therefore "forced" to drink cold beer all day, had a terrible yearning, near evening, for a movie.

"Howell, go see what's playing at the movies tonight," ordered his fellow Corporalies.

By virtue of being the youngest, Howell was often the brunt of such requests, especially after three or four beers. He had given up protesting that he was the same rank as they were. In fact, as the central gunner, he was in charge of the other gunners in combat. But as the youngest of four boys at home, he felt a strange comfort in replaying the role with his combat brothers.

"And damn it, don't come back if it is *The Lady Takes a Chance!*"

Of course, he discovered that *The Lady* was indeed that night's special feature. On the way back to the NCO Club with the sad news that John Wayne was again eating those lamb chops even here on the edge of the Nile River, he met his airplane commander.

"Sir, they are playing that same damn movie here! Oh, sorry, sir. That same John Wayne movie is playing here. We are sick of it, sir! Ain't the army got any other movies?"

Dean could easily see that Howell was near to beer incapacitation by his puffy face, glassy eyes, and speech just a bit off. He took pity on his central gunner.

"Evan, the reason that movie shows up everywhere we go is that we have been tasked with delivering it to our final destination while allowing each layover airfield to use it."

Howell stared at his airplane commander as his cognitively-impaired brain tried to process. The light finally came on for him, a bit dim, but it came on. "Oh, sir. I see, sir. I'll tell the boys."

And off he wandered, not in the direction of the boys, but in the direction of his bunk, taking his comrades' threat to not return with bad news seriously.

12 December 1944: Letters!

The "surely tomorrow" Connie had been searching for finally arrived 12 December. Therill found two letters in the mailbag from the main post office addressed to one Mrs. Dean Sherman. He took it upon himself to bring the treasures to the door at 567 Sherman Avenue.

Connie was confused for a moment by his presence. Mailmen didn't come to the door unless they had a special delivery letter or perhaps a package. She glanced down at his hands. No package. But she did see two letters with handwriting she recognized.

"Letters from Dean!"

Her elation jumped out of her body. She grabbed Therill, hugged him, and planted a kiss on his cheek, her embrace and fragrance overwhelming him like a witch's spell. His words were startled right out of him. For the first time in his mail delivery career he was physically unable to deliver his speech glorifying dependability.

Connie was grateful, and told the dumbfounded man so, although he was unaware that some of the gratitude was for not having to endure his speech. She abandoned Therill on the porch and retreated into the house.

The incapacitated mailman was frozen on the stoop.

His trance was only broken by his internal alarm clock that would not allow him to fall behind schedule. Shaking his head to escape his paralysis, he turned and followed his smile to the next house.

Connie looked the letters over carefully, and arranged them by postmark date—a regular mail envelope dated 24 November 1944, and an official Postal Service airmail envelope processed 2 December 1944.

Just having the letters in her possession sufficed for a moment. She did not need to open them. The possession of them made her giddy and she hugged them to her breast like they were Dean himself. The waiting was over. The fears and doubts that had tormented her were, for now, vanquished. Her heart was settled.

While she was busy studying the letters, Momma and Mammy gathered around her. There was a knock at the door. A neighbor, Sister Butterworth, sensing the excitement, had come to hear the good news. "Letters from Dean today?" The neighborhood had been keeping track.

While it was true the letters were for Connie, it wasn't just Connie and Dean that were at war. The whole country was in this fight; everyone had a stake in it. Letters from "the boys" were nearly a community property. All rejoiced in them.

Likewise, everyone dreaded when the army vehicles rolled into the neighborhood delivering telegrams. People began to mourn even before they saw where the car went and what family had suffered a loss. No matter which individual had died or was missing in action, the entire community had lost something precious.

Connie excused herself and took her letters to her bedroom.

She chose to open them in postmark order. But her fingers weren't working very well. The seal would not give way, and in her frustration she overpowered the paper and tore the envelope in half, barely sparing the letter inside.

She settled herself with a deep breath and prepared to read. She was distracted by a strange hole on the first page—a rectangle, cut out about an inch and a quarter long and a quarter inch high, a few inches down from the top of the letter. Her first notion was that it was some kind of trick or game, and she held it up to her eye and looked through it, which revealed absolutely nothing. When she turned the page over, she realized the censors had been at work. One word was missing from the back page of the letter.

"Oh my! Dean said something he shouldn't," she said with a giggle. The letter again started shaking in her hands, as thirty-five days of anticipation returned to her all at once.

#1—23 November 1944

Darling Connie:

Good evening Honey! And how is every little thing your way? Sure hope you had a fine trip home without having to ride the coach. I had a fine trip with everything going well.

This being Thanksgiving here, was quite an enjoyable day. We had a fine turkey dinner, but not to compare with eating dinner at your house. Anyhow, it was good, and I was well filled and more.

Guess what else I've been doing, and since you couldn't I'll tell you. I went deep sea fishing with some of the rest of the crew, and had more fun. It was arranged, since we are here a couple of days waiting to get the ship and everything checked, and now not much to do. I had more fun than I've had in a long time. Anyhow eight of us had a small boat chartered for fishing. I even caught a fish too. It was an Albacore about 20 pounds. Altogether we got six, Ted got a 7 ½ foot sailfish, and one of the gunners got one about 6 feet long. We got one tuna of about 15 pounds, a 3 foot shark, and a mackerel.

I got some suntan and never got seasick either. More fun. Think we may go again tomorrow.

There are lots of [Redacted] growing around here, even on the post. We've eaten so many we are practically stuffed but still fun. I'll try to send you some if possible. I know you would like them because they sure are lots better than the store ones around there. Dale should have fun getting the husks off if you get some.

Don't imagine I'll be getting any mail for quite a while, but you can write anyhow and I'll have a pile all at once, more fun!

Now that I remember, could you get yourself an insurance policy for about $500 or $1000 for sickness and accidents? I think you should have it, and it would be a good idea. It wouldn't cost much, and you could make your Dad or Mother beneficiary, so if something happened we wouldn't be too short of money. Let me know when and if you do, Honey.

Maybe I'll get used to these censored letters pretty soon, at least I hope so, so I can relax and enjoy writing. Seems like I used to write dozens of letters without telling any military secrets, and now that they are censored I keep thinking twice before I write anything.

We had a few pictures taken after our fishing trip so when they are developed, and we get them, I'll be sending them to you. You can then see the big fish I caught.

Guess I've about run out of chatter for now Honey so the best thing to do is stop.

Take good care of Junior and then pretty soon you can tell me if it's Junior or Marlene. I had a funny dream last night about two a month apart. Oh the thoughts I think!! Don't you know?

For now goodnight Honey and remember how much I love you, because I do, lots and lots.

Love and Kisses,

Dean

As her eyes worked down the page, her heart traveled down also, from giddy elation to consternation, past annoyance, over disappointment and frustration, through resentment, to anger. When she came to the last words, she threw the letter on the floor, stunned.

This was not the letter of her expectations.

She felt cheated. She used her outside voice for a one-sided conversation. "Where is the romancing, Dean? The words of love?" she demanded.

"This is nothing but a travelogue!" Rocking her head side to side, stretching her face, she animated his words with great sarcasm. *"I had more fun than I've had in a long time."*

"War is supposed to be hell, or maybe the hell is only for the wives back home," she fumed.

The airplane-commander's-wife tried to take charge of her thoughts and stop her ranting. But she failed in her attempt at nobility. Her anger again took charge. She stopped trying to be a good wife, stopped trying to figure it out and just broke down, letting it all out, unleashing

[69]

thirty-five days of frustration, fear, loneliness, and worry.

Momma heard the sounds of distress and came near her door. "Is everything all right, honey?"

Irritated, she replied with an uncivil tone, "Yes, Momma, everything is fine."

Everything certainly wasn't fine. She went back to her tirade. "He is off on a lark, a fun trip with the boys, eating great meals, getting a suntan, fishing and catching exotic fish, and raving about some stupid, fabulous thing that is only a hole my letter. He barely asked about me and the baby, but took great care to lecture me about getting insurance."

"Insurance, of all things!" She grabbed up the letter and shook it at him as if he were sitting in front of her. "Insurance isn't very romantic, Dean!"

Fuming in her annoyance, Connie could hear Momma again approach her door. "I am fine, Momma," she repeated, firmly redirecting her back to folding the laundry.

I am not interested in what anyone has to say right now.

Connie surrendered. She rolled onto the bed and buried her sobs in the pillow. She began releasing a month of waiting without word from him. Thirty-some days of what-ifs that she had been exhaustively fighting off. Thirty days where the tribulations of sadness lurked in the shadows, doing their damage, never really leaving her alone.

In due time she did come to herself.

"My, that was a good cry," said the airplane-commander's-wife. Smiling at herself, she recovered the second letter and again began flushing with excitement and anticipation.

I wonder what he will tell me to buy in this one—probably adjoining cemetery plots! Connie "Happy" Sherman laughed.

Constance "Happy" Sherman is who I need to be.

She stopped for a moment, the letter and her hands falling to her lap, cocking her head as she looked into the future. This new realization was not a passing thought; she was making a right turn on her path to maturity. This was a foundational moment, an awareness of how to govern her future conduct.

"I am married to Dean "Happy" Sherman. I shall be Constance "Happy" Sherman, no matter what!" she declared in full voice.

And in a story with a happy ending, she probably would have been. She opened the letter and began to read again.

30 November 1944, West Africa

Good evening Honey:

This is about time I was writing to you, and as this is the first place I've had the time, I will.

Have been having a fine trip so far with no trouble at all, but have been rushed quite a bit.

I sent you some silk stockings from Brazil. Hope you get them before too long and Merry Christmas Honey. They didn't look quite the shape to fit your pretty legs but they may be OK. Let me know. I got me some brown boots there too.

We had a short stop in Puerto Rico, British Guiana and Brazil. Lots of water and jungle to fly over. Didn't look like a good place to land.

Had a nice swim at the beach at Natal. Water and sun were both warm and I got a nice sunburn. I may be to the beach here tomorrow if my back feels better.

The natives here are barefooted and black as tar babies with minimum amount of clothes.

The censors like short letters, so if there is only one page you'll know why. I like them long to you, Honey, so maybe I'll find some bigger pages to write on.

Has Junior kicked you out of your clothes yet? Feed him good with carrot juice and he will be good I hope.

I don't know if chocolate would keep very well, it's really hot and damp here. Something like a pound coffee can would be good tho, so if you have lots of extra send me some. I haven't found a shortage of anything special yet except love, and if you save my ration for me Honey I'll be happy. I just want you to know that I love you dozens and dozens.

Be good and go to church for me because I can't here.

If you care to, you could write Mother once in a while and tell her what's cookin'. I don't always have time to write two letters.

Goodbye for now, Honey,

Dean

She smiled, resigning herself to a new reality and expectation about letters from her husband. Freely applying forgiveness, she judged, "Dean, you did a tiny bit better with that one."

She went into the parlor to share the letters with the rest of the family.

The redacted word became a community puzzlement. As family and friends read the paragraph, they all registered their guess of what exactly it was that Dean was so impressed by.

Surprisingly, the puzzle occupied the minds of many. After days of considering, someone at the dinner table would hazard a new and improved guess. Neighbors arrived unsolicited, some they barely knew, announcing themselves with "I have figured it out." But no one ever did. Responding to Connie's question, Dean, in a future letter, would reveal that it was *coconuts* that they could not get enough of. The answer surprised everyone and spread through the community like a juicy piece of gossip.

12 December 1944: Piardoba Airfield, India

Piardoba Airfield, India, was home for the 770th Squadron of the 462nd Bomber Group. Located within the tropics in the Bankura district of West Bengal, it was some ninety miles northwest of Calcutta. Built by Indian laborers hired by the British, it was short on amenities.

The base was a hodgepodge of buildings thrown together out of desperate need rather than planning. Some Nissen huts were borrowed from the British and were similar to the Quonset huts known to the Americans. A couple of US cut-plywood prefabs showed up and were erected. There were even a couple of Italian prefabs, complete with bullet holes, liberated from Eritrea in Africa. They showed some wear but were serviceable.

Several hangars with overhead cranes provided shade for repair work. They were a steel-frame design with canvass covers. A lot of jerry-rigging was involved because of missing or stolen steel elements of the buildings.

The heat combined with the humidity to make the air feel so thick one wondered if walking were possible. The water was barely drinkable, there was no electricity for barracks lights, and refrigeration consisted of a wooden sawdust-insulated "icebox" that seldom had any ice.

When the darkness of night fell, flashlights were mandatory. On a cloudy evening, without the help of moon and stars, you could see about as far as a person who had just put his head in a bucket of mud. Dean learned that lesson when he fell into a foxhole on his way to the Officers' Club in the dark.

The barracks at Piardoba Airfield, called hutments by the British, were of the native "basha" construction. They had hard earth or concrete floors and bamboo walls covered with what passed for plaster, all under the shelter of thatch roofs.

Long narrow buildings, they were framed similar to the American pole barn style. Furnishings, other than rope mattress beds, were not provided. Furniture was fashioned out of whatever scraps of wood could be found. Ammunition cases and bomb cribbing made some pretty commendable tables and chairs in the right hands. (Craven)

One of the few perks of Piardoba was the availability of manservants. A young Indian boy showed up in their area the day after the crew landed.

"Who captain?" he wanted to know, and was directed to Dean.

"I Abdul. I be your bearer."

"Well, what exactly does a bearer do?" asked Dean.

"Shine sahib's shoes, sweep, keep a very nice order."

"What about laundry?" interjected Reynolds. None of them were very interested in doing that chore.

"Laundry yes, but more."

He had the crew's full attention by now. "How much for all?" questioned Miller.

"A rupee a week."

"For the whole crew?" questioned Miller, ever the haggler.

"Sorry, sahib. A rupee a week, each."

A deal was struck. A rupee amounted to thirty-five cents. For less than a couple of bucks a month from each of them, the rooms would be swept, beds arranged, shoes shined, and laundry taken once a week to his mother to wash over rocks in the river, all at very little cost for them, but a king's ransom for his family.

He was given the name of Benny, for his appreciation for Benny Goodman's music that he had somehow heard.

"Sahib know Benny Goodman?" he would ask every airman he met. Benny proved a valuable guide, translator, procurer, and companion. He was the one thing the crew hated leaving behind in India when they left.

The reason Dean and his crew were in India was a little thing called Operation Matterhorn. It was one of those brilliant ideas that looked great on paper but failed in the face of its implementation. There were probably a few too many cooks working the soup, which may have blinded their wisdom in their demand for results.

In military history-speak, the operation would later be given the kiss of death descriptive term "non-decisive." However, Matterhorn accomplished a great deal, even if not in bombing destruction. It did allow the Americans to drop bombs on Japan for the first time since Doolittle's 1942 raid, resulting in a major boost in morale for the Americans, and an ominous warning for the Japanese of what was coming. Learning how to maintain and keep the repair-loving B-29s in the air was another benefit.

On the first raid over the Japanese homeland, the seventy-five B-29s from the 462nd Hellbirds, that started out to bomb the Yawata Steel Works, could count their total direct hits on one hand. That lack of marksmanship didn't seem to matter; the outfit was given a commendation. What mattered was they got there and they "bombed the bastards." (Craven)

13 December 1944, Orientation

0800, 13 December 1944, New Arrival Orientation, 770th Squadron,
462nd Bombardment Group, Piardoba Airfield, India.

Dean and his officers crowded into what passed as the squadron operations building. They were among several new crews that had arrived in the last few days. The squadron was gradually inching toward full strength since they arrived in India in April and May of 1944. The standing-room-only crowd included all flight officer personnel of the 770th. The meeting would double as orientation and the welcome wagon.

Dean noticed several guys from his training days at Hobbs and Clovis as he scanned the room waiting on the arrival of the brass.

"Attention" brought everyone to their feet. In strode Major John S. Bagby, squadron commander. He quickly administered the "at ease." Bagby was the squadron "Old Man." Dean thought he looked anything but old. A baby-faced twenty-five-year-old, he looked to be one of the most junior officers in the room physically, but the brass on his collar and the emblems on his chest told a different story.

A native of Chester, South Carolina, India had given Major Bagby an enviable bronze tan and his brown hair was combed over with a sizable loft. He was slightly built and stood five foot eight. He also wore a grin that reminded everyone in Dean's crew of their very own commander.

He had gotten a pilot rating before war. After his enlistment, his flying skills moved him up through the leadership ranks quickly. He had spent several years as a trainer both in Basic and Four Engine programs.

The scuttlebutt Dean had heard was that he appreciated good flying and demanded a disciplined approach to the craft. This became verified as the newcomers spent hours in ground schools and "ride alongs" before taking off on a first mission.

"Gentlemen, welcome to Piardoba and India, and more importantly, welcome to the Hellbirds. The Japanese have given the B-29s the name *Jigoku No Tori*, literally translated as the Birds from Hell. It is our mission in the 462nd to be just that, and help bring this war to a close. Our motto is With Malice Toward Some. We are on a righteous mission here. We appreciate you new arrivals and wish you Godspeed. I will now turn this meeting over to XO Captain John Kozak, and he will shepherd you through the rest of the day."

Kozak was a man of few words, but he always started with some levity.

"Did you hear about the Red Cross worker that called into army command this week to report an occurrence of a tropical disease?

"'We've got a case of beri-beri here. What should we do with it?'

"The soldier had a quick reply—'Give it to the Hellbirds'. They drink anything.'"

The joke got to the funny bone of most everyone in the room. Several in the audience felt they had proven the punchline true.

Kozak continued, "I want to echo the welcome of Major Bagby. We will now divide into groups based on your air assignments. Airplane commanders and copilots will stay in this room while the bombardiers and navigators report to the Officers' Club. We will all convene at the Officers' mess at 1200 for a reception in the newcomers' honor."

That comment elicited a barrage of laughter and applause from everyone but the newcomers; they were not yet aware that the "reception" was lunch as usual.

As the room emptied, Dean sought out James Hanson. They had been in training together at Multi-Engine School at Hobbs.

"James, you old worthless dog! How are you?" They threw a bear hug on each other. Neither of them could stop grinning at the surprise reunion.

"I am just fine, Dean, just fine. How is Connie? By the way, how did you ever get that girl to marry you? You really married up, you know."

Dean smiled at the comment and didn't disagree.

Hanson was a newcomer also, arriving a day ahead of Dean. His plane had lost an engine coming in and was put into the 100-hour maintenance slot. It wouldn't fly for a week.

"So are you the Sherman in the lottery? I should have guessed that."

Dean snorted, "I don't think so...what lottery?"

"Some guys came by this morning selling shares on an airplane commander named Sherman who has never been heard to swear. Pick his first swear word and the pot is yours. The pot is over two hundred dollars."

"My men obviously don't have enough to do," said Dean, looking quite sheepish. "I will look into that."

"I hope you don't mind—I want to buy a hand, so if you were going to swear, Dean, what word do you think you would use?"

Dean's head fell in despair. With a shake of his head he suggested, "Shouldn't we be taking a seat?"

14 December 1944, Greenhorns

The night after their arrival in Piardoba, Dean and navigator 2nd Lt. Robert Orr made their way to the club to avoid sitting in the dark. They found an empty table and concentrated on not looking like the greenhorns they were. Orr grabbed a couple of sodas for them.

Lt. Homer Watkins took one of the empty seats at their table. He was from New Hampshire and was a bit of a down-easter, complete with a Maine accent and a very slow approach to talking. Watkins recognized Dean and his navigator as wild-eyed rookies, and assumed they had a lot of unanswered questions. He didn't mind doing a little tutoring; others had done it for him, and he was a good man for the job, if one had the patience to hear his slow-paced answers.

After the appropriate introductions and pleasantries, they got down to business.

"You men been to China?" Watkins asked in his slow-motion way.

Dean answered, "We are up to go in a couple of days. They are still tinkering on the plane. Number three engine has a fuel line leak."

"Well, you know, you won't be a'needin' to take Mr. Orr on that trip. Navigators aren't necessary," Watkins said in his most deliberate way.

Dean and Orr looked at each other and stepped right into it. "Well, no, we hadn't heard that. Why don't we need him?" asked Dean.

"It is the Aluminum Trail. So many planes have gone down in the Himalayas, there is no need to navigate, just follow the piles of scrap aluminum." Watkins delivered the punchline as serious as a man could be.

After a rather pregnant pause, Dean and Orr realized they were had, and they enjoyed a good laugh. They also registered a mental "holy crap," wondering what they were in for.

Watkins continued his deadpan. "The maps are useless, mountains are in the wrong places and elevations are inaccurate. The weather is challenging. It can turn on a dime. Updrafts can be huge. Thunderstorms are worse than any you have ever been in. It seems like being socked in is the norm. Other than that, it is a piece of cake.

"My last trip, the weather was bad going over. We were on instruments the whole way. We came back in bright sunlight and realized one mountain listed at 18,000 feet was at least 23,000 and had been on our flight line. I don't know how we missed it."

Lt. Oscar Hanson heard their conversation as he walked by, took a right turn and pulled up a chair. Part of the 793rd Squadron, he was on temporary duty at Piardoba. Hanson, like nearly everyone else in the room, was a man-child in his early twenties, doing a job that much older men of experience and expertise should be doing. But there were no such men, only these eager baby-faced fighters out to defend their way of life.

Hanson wanted to put in his two cents about flying the Hump. "We came back yesterday from China. Keep in mind you have to fly at 23 to 24,000 feet. We ran into a thunderstorm I thought was going to tear our ship apart. Tanks broke loose in the back and tore a pretty good-sized hole in the floor. At one point, the climb indicator said we were climbing at the rate of 4,000 feet per minute, even though my copilot and I had the stick all the way forward. We were dang grateful to land in one piece."

As Dean and Orr walked back to their barracks, Orr asked, "So are we better off knowing that stuff? Some of it scared me shitless."

Dean's nod was hidden by the darkness. "Well, I guess we know we need to be ready for anything."

Chapter 6

A Blubbering Mass

CONSTANCE SHERMAN was well into her final trimester of pregnancy. Each phase of the process brought new challenges. She was suddenly dealing with a whole-body tiredness that demanded solutions. She tried sleeping to satisfy the malady, but having the baby growing inside her did not make it easy to find a comfortable position for sleeping. If she was lucky enough to come upon one, it was never long-lived; either her body started aching from the pressures upon it, or the baby would be completely unsatisfied with things and demand a change in position. Her tiredness had a progressive nature and she never felt caught up on rest.

The growing baby started messing with her bladder, squeezing it, causing the frequent need to empty the organ.

"I feel like maybe I should just move into the bathroom," she would often say.

When she caught her full-length reflection in her bedroom mirror, she reacted with "I feel big and fat!" a rather new experience for the slender Connie. She possessed enough vanity that she was cognizant and concerned about how she appeared, not the rational cognition that pregnant women get a free pass on their size, but more the irrational judgment that this distorted body of hers looked awful.

She didn't much like living in it.

Her emotions were driving her crazy.

I don't even know myself, was often part of her inner chatter.

The additional hormones racing around her body, trying to nurture two lives, threw everything out of whack. Though she struggled to maintain Connie Happy Sherman, frustrations were magnified, she occasionally was mired in self-pity, and everything felt like it was a matter of life or death.

These collective issues caused the falling of many tears.

Sometimes I feel like a total blubbering mass.

A week or so before Christmas Eve, a struggling Connie managed, half-awake, to waddle into the living room.

With an "Ugh" she fell into the big old rocking chair, taking up residence. This was the very rocker her mother took comfort in while waiting for the arrival of Connie, and had been handed down from her own mother. Grandfather John had bought the chair for Mammy as she waited for Momma.

The grandfather clock spoke two chimes. This rocking chair gave the comfort needed at two a.m. to mothers with child. It freely gave up its comfort. When a mother of the future took refuge here, the chair faithfully knew how to offer up temporary respite from the ordeal.

The room was colored by the soft glow of the Christmas tree decorations. The fire in the fireplace had lost its life, but its brick shell still warmed the room. There was a relief, a sense of peace, in the combined elements of the room. She sat and rocked. Junior liked the rocking and was settling in, at least to the degree Junior ever settled in.

I don't think I have realized how tired I am. I never seem to be able to catch up on rest.

As she continued rocking, a serenity settled upon her, quieting her concerns and opening her eyes to a new understanding of this ordeal. Perhaps it was the power of the chair or perhaps a divine tender mercy, but whatever the source, there arose a sense of wonder at what her body was doing—the creation of life, the unquestionable outward manifestation of the love of Dean and Connie Sherman.

Her role in the process was humbling and filled her with an absolute gratitude. Armed with this new vision, the unpleasantness of not sleeping, the peeing every twenty minutes, and even the rollercoaster of emotions all lost their significance, and for a few moments did not matter.

The glow of a mother, normally only bestowed after delivery, took over her countenance.

Yes...yes, I am honored to do this.

In this quiet, divine moment, she came to be at peace with her ordeal.

The only interruption was the voice of her unborn son.

"Thanks, Mom."

18 December 1944: Suzy and Mary

Radioman Jerry Johnson and radar radioman Ben Prichard spent a long morning in ground school training. Instruction covered radio operation in the China, Burma, and India area of operation, one of those necessary but boring trainings soldiers have to endure. At lunch break, with less than a thirty-minute break, they decided to duck into the closest mess hall, the "Lucky 7," for a quick bite. They got in line. Nothing unusual. Mess halls are all about the same.

Breaking glass and the startling clatter of trays meeting the floor got everyone's attention. The action was taking place five guys ahead of them where two soldiers were backing away from the pile of food on the floor that had been their planned lunch.

"What the hell?"

The mess sergeant burst out of his kitchen. *He* knew exactly "what the hell." "Suzy! Mary! Leave the soldiers alone!"

Two thirty-five-pound leopard cubs, about five months old, were earnestly trying to clean up the mess on the floor. They seemed keenly interested in the meat.

Sgt. Emile Manara called to his girls again, "Suzy! Mary! Get over here," and with seemingly no effort they bounded over the serving counter into his arms. Two dining room orderlies immediately appeared to clean up the mess and resupply the food for the soldiers. It was obvious this wasn't the first time they had preformed the drill.

"What the heck?"

"Damn, just when I think I have seen everything."

"You guys haven't eaten in here before, have you?" asked the fellow behind them. "Those are Manara's pets. He has had them since they were ten days old. Everyone says he only lets them out when the food is bad. You would be surprised how fast the line moves when they are around."

Indeed, the line did move quickly and Jerry and Ben were back to training in plenty of time. (*Hellbird Herald*)

———

In April 1942, Lt. Col. Jimmy Doolittle had led sixteen B-25 bombers on a daring raid on Tokyo. The planes launched off a navy aircraft carrier, the USS *Hornet*. Since landing the bombers back on the *Hornet* was impossible, the flight plan was for the bombers to fly on to the friendly part of China after the raid.

The raid killed fifty Japanese, mostly civilians. Eight airmen were captured by Japanese forces. They were tried in Tokyo for bombing nonmilitary sites and killing "peaceable" people. All eight were sentenced to death, though five later had their sentences reduced to life in prison. The attack moved the Japanese parliament to pass legislation that declared that all captured crews from planes that bombed nonmilitary sites would be declared "special prisoners" and denied the privilege of POW status. The reward for being a "special prisoner" was death.

Hankow, China, located on the Yangtze River, was a major Japanese supply center, especially for fuel for its million-man China and Asia operation. It was the site of the largest Japanese airdrome in China. On 18 December 1944 it was also the target of a daylight raid for ninety-four of the B-29s of Dean's Twentieth Bomber Command. It was flown out of China a day before Dean and his crew came over the Hump.

The raid used incendiary bombs dropped from low altitude, in an effectual trial of the tactic. The results were stunning. Follow-up attacks by 200 B-25s of the Fourteenth Air Corps, a half hour after the B-29 attack, reported a ring of fire along the Yangtze with smoke billowing to ten thousand feet. Damage assessments reported a large percentage of the warehouses were completely razed, effectively cutting off Japanese Army supplies in the south.

One of the driving forces for the attack was Japan's attempt to launch attacks on the B-29s' China forward bases. This mission ended those attacks. The fires of Hankow burned for three days. General Curtis LeMay would use these results when he changed tactics from strategic bombing of military sites to fire bombing of Japanese urban areas.

When Dean reviewed the photos of the raid, he was impressed by the completeness of the destruction. He also noticed it lacked surgical precision. It wasn't just the military installations that burned. There was plenty of devastation intruding into the obvious urban and residential areas. Homes were burned and civilians were hit. He considered what that meant. *War really does stink.*

Hankow was not just a precursor for future American firebombing tactics. The raid also revealed how the Japanese were going to treat downed airmen in the homeland. Second Lts. Lester White and Henry Wheaton and Sgt. James Forbes took part in the Hankow raid and parachuted out of their damaged B-29 fifty miles north of the target area and were immediately captured.

The airmen, according to a *New York Times* newspaper report, were declared "special prisoners," paraded through the wintery streets of Hankow in only their underwear, beaten, kicked and reviled. Two of the men died from the treatment. The following day, the two corpses and the survivor were taken to a suburban crematorium, doused in gasoline and set ablaze. Yes, one airman was reportedly still alive when the fire was started.

The *Times* article was republished in *Stars and Stripes*, and there was not an American at home nor an Allied airman in the Pacific Theater that did not know about it.

19 December 1944: China Here We Come

Orders were issued: *19 December 1944. All available aircraft to the forward China bases.*

That meant a trip over the Hump, a chance to earn a camel.

And a chance to fly through the worst-rated weather in the world. The warm, wet weather of the Indian Ocean heading north travelled the same passes the army air corps was trying to fly. That warm air invariably met up with the much cooler air produced by the wicked altitudes of the mountains. The collision spawned gigantic and violent thunderstorms. Hemmed in by the towering Himalayas, the storms were only able to spread north and south in the passes and they could stretch on for hundreds of miles.

These monster storms always played a little game with airplanes. Unable to fly above or around, flying through the storm front was the only option. When returning from China, the leading edge of the storm forced those foolish enough to enter the pass, or those poor devils under orders, downward, hard. To avoid crashing into mountaintops, planes entered the slot of entry as high as possible, an unwanted and forced use of fuel.

Then the game began, at a point chosen by the storm. The strong downward pressure turned upside down and the plane, without pilot input, wanted to rise hard—5,000 feet in mere minutes. Even with both pilot and copilot using their full strength, the plane most often obeyed the storm. Some of the smaller DC-3s were forced to flip over. Stunt flying in a Himalayan thunderstorm is not advised. The reverse occurred when traveling to China.

If all that were not enough, there was the issue of hail, often softball-sized hail. Rudder controls, flaps, outer skin, and windows could all be seriously damaged or penetrated by hail. All of this and other dangers caused over six hundred planes to crash in the five-hundred-mile pass.

Dean had grown up on the east edge of the Rockies, had explored them on foot and horseback, and had lived at the foot of the Utah Wasatch Mountains. His flight training had him crisscrossing the Rockies, Sierras, and every other high spot in the southern half of the United States, but none of that, nothing, had prepared him for the Himalayas.

They had exceptionally fine weather for their first flight to China. Dean was trying to find words to describe what he was seeing, flying at 24,000 feet, halfway to China. The Wasatch would look like flatlands or maybe foothills compared to these monster mountains. The scale was so large that the plane felt as if it were flying in slow motion, a toy suspended against the larger-than-life backdrop and reference points.

All of the front cabin crew members were sitting in silence, awestruck by the massive, towering peaks they were flying through.

All except Lloyd Miller, flight engineer. He wasn't allowed to take his eyes off the gauges and instruments in front of him. They were the pulse of the airplane and required his constant attention. The difference between "all is fine" and "emergency" was measured in a few seconds. His job was to always be on top of any problematic changes.

Dean liked Miller, a few years older than himself, who had quickly gained Dean's trust. When they were picking up their plane in Kearney, an engine caught fire on one of their early flights. Miller fought the fire and Dean nursed the plane in for a landing. Their reward was a royal chewing out. Crews were more valuable than planes, they were told in no uncertain terms. The proper protocol for engine fires is to abandon ship! *Don't try to be heroes. The wings will fail!*

Dean had promised Miller he would give him a full description of their Himalayan passage, but he was having a real problem finding words that conveyed what he was seeing.

Turning to his copilot, he said, "Reynolds, you've got the plane."

Touching his throat mic, Dean said, "Miller, trade me places." Miller sat back-to-back with Reynolds, facing his set of gauges and instruments.

Miller wasn't sure what was going on, but was good at taking orders, and moved forward to take Dean's seat. Dean assumed the engineer's seat. He had crossed-trained at engineer, was a US Army-trained aircraft "repairman," and could stare at gauges as well as Miller could, at least for a few minutes. It was way easier to stare at the gauges than to find the words to describe what they were flying through.

As the Himalayas played out, Dean took back the commander's chair and dropped the plane down to 10,000 feet. The endless rice fields began to appear. The land was startlingly flat once the mountains were behind them. The crew was headed for A-7, one of four forward bases in China. They had flown out of the tropics into winter, and were greeted by a light snow cover on the ground.

What lay before them was a crude airport, Kiunglai (Qionglai) Airfield, China. If the crew thought the India base was primitive, China's forward base would convince them what they had in India was modern.

Kiunglai is an example of what a guy with a two-pound hammer, a wooden shovel and wheelbarrow, and a little hard work can do. Throw in a couple of baskets, a hoe, and invite 350,000 of your best friends over, and you can build an airport with a runway nearly two miles long, complete with fifty-two hardstands for parking B-29s.

Top layers of soil were excavated down nearly two feet with pick and shovel and removed in wheelbarrows. Then, round rocks were gathered from nearby rivers and tightly stacked. Rocks were hand-crushed into gravel, "poured" over the round rocks, and overlaid with a tar-like brew of water, clay, sand, and tung nut oil. The slurry mix was made in round holes dug in the ground, with workers dancing around, mixing it with their feet, looking very much like winemakers squishing grapes.

The one large "machine" used in construction was an immense, round compactor stone. Ten feet wide and eight feet tall, it was fitted with an axle and harness for four hundred coulees. They provided the horsepower to pull the great round stone from one end of the nearly two-mile runway to the other, over and over, to prepare the runway for the comings and goings of the 120,000-pound B-29s. The great machine had no brakes, and more than a few workers were crushed in the process of runway compaction.

Weather was calm and visibility clear as the tower gave permission to land. Everyone was glad at the thought of getting out of the plane after flying 1,200 miles, a little over six hours of flying time, through the tallest mountains in the world. All was proceeding as normal, the runway rising up quickly to the plane. There was a sizable group of apparent natives standing off to the port side of the runway.

Solomon announced, "Look, a welcoming committee."

Without warning, two of the welcoming committee ran onto the runway in front of their ship. "What the hell?" shouted Solomon.

Dean fully expected to hear a thump from hitting them. "Gentry, what do you see back there?"

Gentry, already looking after hearing the commotion on the radio, had caught view of the "welcomers" just after they cleared the starboard side of the plane. "Two little skinny guys running like the devil himself was after them."

That turned out to be nearly true. Dean's crew had flown out of the modern world and into the ancient world. The native folk were convinced demons followed them around and one way to exorcise them was to run in front of a car or truck and the demon, following closely behind, would be run over and be exterminated. Timing and speed were required, but occasionally, quite sadly, one of the skills was in short supply. When the B-29s arrived, they became the favorite demon killers in the area.

Welcome to China.

It would be hard to find more contrasting cultures than the remote, rural, poverty-ridden communities of India and China and the life in the United States that these crews left behind. Many had not previously traveled far from their homes of origin and very few had traveled abroad. Most of them carried a perpetual look of wide-eyed wonder.

Barracks in China were tents. Nights were cold. Beds, consisting of an air mattress supported by ropes, sleeping bags, and multiple layers of blankets, could almost make for a comfortable night. Cold mornings were challenging. Getting from the warm bed into the warm clothes of the day created some "chilling" experiences.

One advantage of China over India that most everyone appreciated was the availability of meat in the mess halls. The Chinese did not share the Hindus of India's reservations about eating the meat of the sacred cow.

20 December 1944: More Mail

Therill Hansen, the distantly-related cousin who delivered the mail, created a secret notification system for Connie. If he had letters from Dean, he would start whistling "Stars and Stripes Forever" a few doors prior to her house.

Connie knew him to be a very remarkable whistler, and thought it to be his only redeeming quality other than prompt mail service. He was good enough to be on the local radio once in a while. His father, also named Therill, and his father's brother, Merrill, were also known to be exceptional whistlers. They were remotely related to Papa

Baldwin and he enjoyed taking her to hear them preform. They had each learned to whistle two tones at once, so could harmonize with themselves.

They were popular entertainment at church and community gatherings, and in their grand finale, the brothers would whistle "God Bless America" in four-part harmony, always to a standing ovation.

Therill honed his whistling skills by hours and hours of practice as he trudged the streets around Liberty Park delivering mail.

Being the eccentric that he was, the "mail from Dean" notification system signal was so secret that he told no one of it, including Connie. She figured it out with Therill's next delivery, which he again brought to her door near the end of a rather rousing rendition of the grandiose "Stars and Stripes Forever."

Therill presented a bonanza of three letters!

"I appreciated your "Stars and Stripes Forever" this morning. It was marvelous," she said with a smile and a wink, acknowledging the secret code without mentioning the why of it.

This odd little man provided a small kindness that saved a few seconds of uncertainty and anxiety for her. Therill, for his part, was hoping for a repeat experience of the first letters from Dean he had delivered to Connie. But in this, he was disappointed. Connie took the letters, thanked him again, and disappeared into the house.

She looked at Therill quite differently after that. She even hung around the mailbox on occasion so he could deliver his speech glorifying his punctuality; his eccentricities didn't bother her anymore. War, it seemed, could make friends of people with nothing much in common.

Connie rushed past Momma to her room. Her expression and the three letters in her hands answered any question Momma had, for now. She dispensed with the inspection of the letters. She didn't care about their postmarks. They would be read a hundred times in the coming days, and the order didn't seem important right now. She quickly opened them and read.

13 December 1944

India, 770 Bomb Squadron, 462 Bomb Group, APO 220

Dearest Connie:

We arrived here a couple days ago, and have been quite busy getting settled. We had a fine trip and no trouble.

It seems to be rather comfortable here, warm but not hot, good food, and a fairly decent barracks. I've sure been missing you Honey and am getting more in love with you as the days pass if it is possible to love you any more than I have.

Hope this gets there by Christmas, and if so have a merry Christmas for me Honey.

Have an early day tomorrow, so will have to make this short. I'll find time tomorrow to write you a nice long letter.

Am set to go on the first mission tomorrow so best get on my knees and pray a while.

Best say goodnight for now you beautiful sweet woman and remember that I love you with all my heart. Take care of Junior for me too.

Love and Kisses,

Dean

15 December 1944, India

My Dearest Sweetheart:

Good Evening Honey! And it is a good evening to be writing you a nice long letter after the last rush job.

This may be a nice place to take you for a visit to, but I don't exactly like living here. It isn't so bad though.

The natives or Ghuks as they are called locally are dark but not as black as those in Africa. There's not much difference though. What they wear is a couple of rags, mostly around their head. Some of the Moslems wear a long sheet draped around them and a big turban. It isn't at all unusual to see some wearing a shirt, tie, coat and hat, and bare legged and barefooted. Quite a combination to be sure.

The food is good, with a few fresh vegetables, and fresh eggs once in a while. The Officer's Club is pretty nice, with plenty of easy chairs and desks to write you letters on. There is a piano, which someone has been playing all evening. It makes a pleasant noise too, only would give anything to be hearing you play instead.

We have been busy enough so far so the time goes fast. Have a little ground school and work on our plane to keep busy with. Haven't flown yet. As I told you, I missed the mission I was going on. We were an alternate ship and didn't go. All came back too, which makes everybody happy.

We have a nice bamboo and grass barracks to live in. Only the walks and floor are cement and stone. Hope the roof sheds water, but it probably won't rain until June. The plumbing is practically non-existent, but we get by. Nice cold water for showers and shaving. Maybe that's why I haven't been shaving too regular.

I have a pillowcase that I'll be sending you right away. Did the other packages arrive that I sent on the way here?

I got in a pretty good Squadron, all seem like nice fellows, so guess I'll get along OK. Might even get a rating after a few years.

I sure wish I had some of your nice sheets to sleep on. We do have air mattresses though and that is nice on rope springs.

I guess I sent my pajamas home, so I bought some today for seven rupees.

Seems funny how one gets to thinking in terms of the local money. I just about had the west Africa, pounds, shilling and pence figured out, with bartering with the natives there, and then Egyptian was pounds and piastres, which had me all confused again.

Rupees are paper and worth $.30. The largest coins are half rupees, and annas worth 2 cents. Makes quite a full billfold without being rich.

I'm sure lonesome for you, Honey, as always, and miss your wonderful company, sweet kisses, and passionate lovemaking. You sweet woman, I'm sure glad I married you, and it's best I did for Junior's sake, and for all my love too. Would really like to be hearing some of our favorite music with your nice hair on my shoulder and my arms around you here and there.

And a sweet mouth to kiss at our pleasure. I guess we'll just keep on having a honeymoon when we are together again for years and years.

This evening coming to the club I fell in a foxhole and got plenty bruised up. They are only 5 or 6 feet deep though so I can still write you.

Will stop this chatter now Honey, and dream about kissing you good-night in your little bed, with me there to cuddle and make big love to you.

Goodnight Darling,

Dean

(Editor's note: The following was a short letter on a V-mail form.)

15 Dec. 1944, India, 770 Bomb Squadron. 462 Bomb Group

Dear Beautiful Wife,

Missed the mission today in case you get my letter before this. They are keeping us busy with ground school and working on our plane (Peach Blossom) for a few days. Is warm like September here so that's nice. I can hear from here what's on at the out-door movie, so that helps. Haven't received any mail yet but hope it gets here pretty soon. Remember, I love you Honey, dozens. Don't believe any wild rumors either. More letters coming.

All My Love, Dean

And so, this was how the mail was going to be—a feast of three letters followed by two weeks of famine.

Chapter 7

No Assholes Here

THEY WERE SITTING on bags of sand, the fancy seats in the thrown-together amphitheater of the air corps base at Piardoba, India, waiting for the house lights to be turned down by night's darkness so a movie could be projected onto someone's sheets. Sweating from the heat that didn't give up even when the sun did go down, it did not matter they had seen this movie six nights in a row. It was something to do.

"You know what I like about this crew, sir?" asked T.Sgt. Miller of his airplane commander.

"No, Miller. What?"

"I just like that there aren't any assholes on this crew."

"Ha! I wouldn't have said it that way, but I think you're right. Just a bunch of good guys here."

"Yeah, even the officers," Miller straight-faced it.

"Even the officers, huh? If I didn't know better, I would think you're giving me a compliment, Miller. We are all just guys trying to do our jobs."

"Yes, sir, but it isn't always that way. We enlisted men see things, hear things. Some guys are really in the shit."

"Some officers do take themselves very seriously, don't they."

"Now that is some understatement. You know, sir, you're way too nice."

"Miller," Dean started, changing the subject, "you know I look to you to take care of the Corporalies. Don't let them get in too much trouble."

"Well, which do you want, sir?" asked a laughing Miller. "Do you want me to be your flight engineer or chaperone for the Corporalies? Given the way the Corporalies carry on, I don't think I will have time to do both."

CBI Mission #23: Mukden, Manchuria

Primary Target: Manchurian Aircraft Manufacturing Company.

The Secondary Targets: Shipping in the Port of
Darien or the South Manchurian Railway.
Target of Last Resort: Chenghsien Rail Yards.

Forty-nine B-29s answered the call to bomb Mukden and
the Manchurian Aircraft Manufacturing Company, builder
of aircraft used in training Japanese pilots. (Craven)

---

21 December 1944: 0300 Mission Briefing

Zero two-thirty is a pretty awful wake-up time on any day. Waking up at zero two-thirty on the eve of your first combat mission, after a night cut short by rampant pre-combat jitters, leaves a soldier to wonder if he were ever really asleep.

This was where the war got very, very real. This was the day a soldier got up to get shot at. The Sherman crew would be under the enemy's guns and flak, and who knows what else, in just a few hours.

The crew was quartered in adjoining tents dictated by rank. The canvas shelters offered little comfort in the jarring polar weather of Kiunglai. They lay fully clothed, encased in Arctic sleeping bags, and smothered with as many wool blankets as they could get their hands on. The weight of the blankets created the illusion of warmth, but not always the reality of it.

Gear was neatly stacked beside these lumps on their rope cots; evacuation to mission briefing wasn't going to take long.

All Dean had to say was, "It's time, guys," and his officers popped up.

"Ted, would you go get the Corporalies moving?"

Reynolds disappeared to the neighboring tent. He let out an

inadvertent weather report on his way—"Shit, it's cold."

His intention was to step inside the tent and wake the Coporalies, but when his fingers didn't appear up to the task of untying the frozen knots of the tent door flap, he gave up and just delivered his message: "Hi-de-ho, it is time to go" and a tent full of gunners and radiomen were moving.

As the officers escaped their canvas home, they merged with the Corporalies, best described as semi-conscious but reporting for duty.

The sky over them was stunning, so full of stars it was doubtful another would fit in the firmament. The crew became gawkers. Stars in this cold, dark, clear part of the world seemed larger than any they had ever seen.

The only hint of man-made light was the glow from the command center a mile away, the only sound, the crunch of the forests of frost beneath their feet. Their breath sent up plumes above them as they sauntered down the self-lighted path to the outermost edge of the tarmac. Awaiting them, a steam-belching deuce-and-a-half with a driver profanely demanding the heater do its f-ing job.

"Let's mount up, men," ordered Dean.

Jostling into place, Howell felt compelled to declare, "Holy shit, is colder than a witch's tit out here."

Hanson gave him an elbow to his gut. "What?" Howell reacted.

Hanson said nothing, just threw a nod toward Dean.

"Oh, sorry, sir."

Dean took no offense and laughed. "I don't have much experience with the breasts of witches, so I really can't confirm or dispute your comment."

The crew erupted in laughter. That was about as racy as they had ever heard their commander talk. His joke made things better, bringing a light to their eyes, uniting them in laughter and indirectly in purpose, these comrades "going over the wall" for the first time.

The mission briefing room was a welcome warmth after ten minutes on the deuce-and-a-half. It was an overcompensating heat, built by two huge furnaces on either end of the building and spread by a menagerie of fans. The room would hold the twelve crews that the 462nd would be sending out on Mission #23. Men were chatting in groups, inhaling coffee, while trying not to spend too much thought on what might be waiting for them in Mukden.

The front wall of the room was covered with a giant map of China and Manchuria. Reflective tape clearly marked the attack route to the rallying point, the target area, and the egress route for home. Pertinent items were identified. Heavy flak areas, most likely areas of enemy fighters, landmarks helpful for navigation, flight altitudes—these details were presented to everyone. Robert Orr and other navigators had met the night before and been given detailed navigational information.

The mission duration time was set at thirteen hours of flight.

Lloyd Miller and the other flight engineers were given flight plans annotated with times, temperatures, power settings, gross weights, and fuel calculations for the entire mission.

Next up, breakfast. Definitely not breakfast as usual. For the before-mission meals, cooks and servers went all out, offering unlimited quantities of everything—seldom seen bacon and sausage and steak filled their trays, and pancakes were stacked so high they listed badly. It was unspoken, this kindness; for some eating at these tables, it would be their last meal on earth. The courage that required was worth honoring with some extra bacon.

As a "parting gift," each crew member was given a brown paper sack lunch to serve as a mid-flight meal, and a pile of K-rations for snacking.

Miller, a confirmed coffee addict, hung back. He had a connection in the kitchen. His cousin, Ronnie Woodings, was one of the cooks. In his pre-war life, Ronnie was a chef at the fanciest restaurant in Kansas City, and until recently had a cushy job as private chef for a general at CBI headquarters. That gig ended quite abruptly one night when MPs rousted him out of his bunk, packed his bags and put him on a flight to Kiunglai, which was unequivocally the outermost, most obscure place in the realm.

Ronnie was tight-lipped about the whole thing, but Lloyd did know the story involved the general's favorite nurse who evidently enjoyed Ronnie's "cooking" too.

Lloyd gathered up the two-gallon thermoses of coffee and the fresh cinnamon rolls Ronnie had set out for him. There was some of the "why does he get two" catcalling, but Miller was long out the door and into the safety of the night before he could be challenged.

The plane's outside inspections were done by flashlight, and *Peaches* was the target of beams coming from every direction, mini-searchlights cutting up the dark as the crew worked quickly through checklists on every part of the plane. The crew lined up for inspection, also peformed in a quickstep rhythm, not lackadaisically but efficiently, without carelessness. The B-29 would refuse to fly at the worst possible moments for careless crews.

"Let's double-time through the props," ordered the airplane commander.

Orr didn't bother to wait for everyone to man their stations to start the engines, hoping to get the heaters inside of *Peaches* online. No one had a problem with that, as all were anxious for some heat. Even with all their cold weather gear it was chilly.

As Dean nudged the Superfortress off of the hardstand, ground control came on the radio. "Sherman, you're number three for take-off."

"Thank you, ground control. We are happy to be number three."

Taking off was a meandering process, jostling for a position in the order of takeoff, waiting, moving one plane closer, waiting. It was the enactment of the army grunts' favorite saying, "Hurry up and wait."

The waits were ended by the green light attached to what served as a tower. Each flash of green sent a B-29 down the runway and brought a new bird up to starting position.

As Dean and crew pulled up for their green light, they watched the tail of a B-29 lurch away from them and begin its fight for flight. It would take a minute or so for the lights to get small enough to say they were half a mile away. That would turn on the green light.

All eyes were on the flight control center.

"Green light," called out Reynolds. Looking toward his engineer, Dean responded, "All lights are green."

Dean pushed forward on the controls, demanding takeoff speed of the engines.

Mukden would take them farther north than any of them had ever been. North as in cold. Not China cold—Siberia cold.

The six or so hours to Mukden was uneventful. Dean kept the plane at 8,000 feet to conserve fuel. They would not be flying over any enemy territory, and Japanese fighters had stopped bothering them in these skies now that Hankow had been firebombed. They saw a half-dozen other B-29s in transit from their mission group.

Because planes took off at one-minute intervals, at 250 miles per hour, they were instantly strung out over four-mile intervals. The planes did not bother creating a formation for travel, which would be a waste of fuel and unneccesary with no possibility of enemy fighters. Each plane headed for the rallying point to form up there.

"Thirty minutes to the rallying point," Dean announced.

Time to get serious. Manson took charge of his gunners, firing off rounds, target shooting at nothing to make sure everything was operational.

"Lt. Solomon, sir, would you fire twenty rounds, please?" Manson reveled in his opportunity to order around an officer. Solomon didn't mind; he would purposely not fire the front machine guns until he got his orders.

Solomon always snapped off a "Yes, Corporal" as his part of the game before dutifully firing the rounds.

"Front guns check out, Corporal."

"Thank you, sir," ended their little charade that never failed to amuse everyone.

Navigator Orr was fine-tuning their course, getting them where they were supposed to be. Bombardier Solomon was checking his payload and then situating his sights. He needed to see the lead bombardier drop his load. General LeMay's new approach was to use specially trained lead navigators and bombardiers to bring the formation to the bombing point, and bombardiers would drop their loads when they saw the lead bombardier release his load. Today, that wasn't going to be easy.

"Is that *frost* forming on our windshield?" asked Dean incredulously. "What does the free air thermometer say?"

"Minus 51 degrees."

"Never had this problem in India," laughed Reynolds.

Dean was bringing the plane to 22,000 feet and looking for the lead plane to form up on. The outside temperature was overpowering the pressurized heating system that was supposed to keep the windshield clear in any conditions. Evidently these conditions were outside of design parameters. Frost was quickly taking over any glass area on *Peaches*.

The rallying point was over Darien Bay, a huge, white expanse of ice, covered with snow, slashed with a shipping channel that someone was working hard to keep open.

Reynolds first caught sight of their lead plane. "There he is at ten o'clock."

"There we go," said Dean as he began to maneuver into position as the formation was quickly taking shape. Lead planes were pretty easy to spot—they would circle the rallying point with their front wheels down.

Holding formation was going to be challenging. Although the weather was clear, and visibility a ten, their sight lines were being shrunk by the frost. Flying near a bunch of 120,000 pound planes, loaded with bombs, that you can't see, at 250 miles per hour, added another helping to their already full first-mission-anxiety plate.

When the eighth B-29 pulled into formation, the group set course for the initial point and the target. They could now see it, laid out in front of them. The city of Mukden was surrounded by an ancient wall, built to protect the city before B-29s roamed the earth. It would not protect them today.

To the right of the city rose a formidable black smoke screen, set on fire to obscure the location of the airplane factory. To the north, the smoke had a runway sticking out of it, verifying that below that smoke was indeed their primary target. To the south were rows and rows of warehouses, the unique Japanese-style warehouses built to store armaments and ammunition. The arsenal wasn't on the list of objectives for the day, but no one would get yelled at if a few bombs hit it. The army air force called that sort of thing a "target of opportunity."

"Initial point, mark," the lead plane announced by radio. That confirmed *Peaches* was at the beginning of the bombing run. Dean and his crew were about sixty miles out, some twelve minutes or so from dropping their first bombs on the enemy.

"You know, I started training for this moment two-and-a-half years ago, and finally today I get to kick some Jap butts," Reynolds volunteered.

"Let's just focus on doing our job and getting our butts home," offered the airplane commander.

As the eight-plane formation homed in on the target, the smoke screen continued to billow. The factory, with the aid of prevailing winds, was well hidden beneath the shroud.

Flak bursts began to appear above them. Inaccurate as they were, the concussions and exploding debris took their toll. It was hard not to flinch at flak exploding in the neighborhood of the ship. Some audible debris bounced off the plane occasionally, but the plane suffered no serious damage.

The B-29s created formations for self-preservation and bombing accuracy. A gaggle of eight B-29s could bring eighty .50 caliber machine guns to bear on a single target, a nearly impenatrable wall of lead.

The Japanese fighters had enviable flying skills, their tactics were brilliant, and their bravery and commitment to their cause could not be questioned. They knew that 800 yards, around a half mile, was about the range of the Superforts' guns. They often teased just outside of range.

They attacked in small groups. One technique involved a fighter making a head-on assault to draw the ship's attention, while another pilot or two would attack from the flanks of the B-29. Ramming was always an option for the out-gunned fighters. *Old Campaigner* was a casualty of ramming by an obsolete Nakajima Nate on this Mukden mission. Only radio operator Sgt. Elbert Edwards survived the crash. (Mays)

Bombardier Solomon announced he was opening the bomb bay doors, but was losing visibility to the frost. "I am having trouble seeing the lead ship. Can anyone help me out?"

Reynolds replied, "I have a view for now. I have never seen frost take over like this."

"Ever fly when it was minus fifty-one degrees outside?" questioned T.Sgt. Miller.

The question went unanswered as Reynolds was doing his best to be a second set of bombardier eyes.

Labadie, from his gunner's blister, announced, "*Belle Ringer* just let go." *Belle Ringer* was positioned on their port side.

"Maybe she has a clearer view than us."

"I can see a couple of others letting go," said Labadie.

Solomon deferred to Dean, "Should I let them go, sir?"

"Yes. If it's a mistake, we will all make it together," ordered Dean.

"Bombs away," announced Solomon. In just seconds they were gone.

The next order of business was to check the bomb bays to make sure the payload was away. Hung-up bombs presented a clear and present danger. The job fell to the radiomen, Prichard checking the aft bay and Johnson the forward bay.

"Aft bay clear."

"Forward bay clear."

Solomon noted, "Bomb bay doors closing." And with that, their work was finished.

Crossing Darien Bay, headed for home, the crew aboard *Peaches* was done with Mukden. But Mukden was not quite done with them.

Labadie sounded the alarm. "Jap fighter at four o'clock, 800 yards!"

Central gunner Howell turned everything toward the oncoming plane and sent a hail of tracers as a greeting. Tracers are a curious thing. They are of prime importance for aiming fire, but as they lose speed, they begin to twist and turn, rise and fall a bit as if they have a mind of their own. When six or eight sets of .50 caliber machine guns are unleashed on one target, it creates quite a light show, even in broad daylight.

The Japanese intruder, seeing what was being thrown his way, thought better of it and pulled up and out to go see if he could surprise someone else. A new wave of B-29s was forming at the rallying point. The fully-armed incoming bombers were superior targets to the expended *Peaches*. The new wave was now drawing all the attention of Japanese fighters.

As he pulled up and showed the crew his belly, Labadie gave the Japanese pilot a vulgar salute and wish, "Good riddance!"

"Not gonna miss him!" said Manson.

"So, that is what a mission is like," piped up Johnson. "Thirty-four more and we go home."

Navigator Orr set the course for home. Dean throttled back to the "sweet spot" air speed that was the most economical on fuel for the ride home. Orr tinkered with fuel mixture and prop controls, and started staring at head temperatures, his main concern for the immediate future.

In a day of many firsts, the crew would have their first opportunity to experience a common malady of war. It was called post-anxiety fatigue. It manifests after warriors indulge in the life-threatening games of battle. It doesn't help that B-29 crews have six or seven hours to anticipate enduring life-threatening situations and then get to spend a half hour or so in harm's way—harm's way replete with the sound effects and scenes of war, flak that might hit an engine, and bullets coming at them that might have their names on them.

The body and mind have defenses for such situations that sustain a soldier in settings humans should not have to endure. But when the threats begin to recede and a sense of relative safety returns, the body shuts down, seeking a time of regeneration. A feeling of fatigue demands to be attended to. It can make the six- or seven-hour trip home a struggle, especially for the pilot, navigator, and engineer, whose work is not done until they hit the end of their home runway.

Post Mission Analysis

The smoke screen employed by the Japanese was even more effective than that of the first attack due to an earlier warning and the construction of a number of new generating sites...the entire arsenal and aircraft factory as well as the airfield were effectively screened by the time the second wave of aircraft appeared... this smoke screen hampered bombardiers necessitating off-set bombing methods and prevented visual observation of bomb strikes. (Craven)

23 December 1944, India

My Dearest Connie,

Have finally found time again to be writing you a nice long letter. Have really been pretty busy these last few days which I'll tell you something about.

I recovered OK from falling in the foxhole but had two stiff knees for a couple of days. I have sure been keeping a good lookout since tho. The moon is a little help now so I can miss them OK.

Came very near having a white Christmas after all, but not here. Was in China for a few days and just got back. Flew over "the Hump" and back to the forward area. It was pretty cool there but nice. Seemed almost like home weather for a few days. There was no snow but plenty of frost. Sleeping in tents there was a little chilly, but had plenty of covers. Had a sleeping bag with my air mattress and a couple of blankets so it was almost as warm as your little bed, only rather chilly getting up.

Have been on one mission so far and it was a little rough. Have seen the red balls and spitting guns on the Jap fighters, along with the burst of flak. Believe me, it isn't pleasant. The Lord was with us, we didn't get a scratch. I asked a blessing on our ship like a new baby in church and will keep on doing just that.

You can probably read more in the papers than I can tell, so will let the war correspondents do that.

Honey, are you having a nice white Christmas there? I know I sure am lonesome for you and all the nice things at your house on Christmas. I imagine we'll have a nice dinner but it will be mostly from cans.

The food was very good in China. We had fresh meat and eggs and vegetables. And had a roast duck dinner once. It's seldom we get fresh meat here, so that was nice for a change.

No mail has come yet and it's getting rather monotonous checking. I'm hoping it comes for Christmas, but that's only a couple of days.

You sweet woman, I sure am missing your wonderful charms and fun with you. I can still dream of you tho. All the beautiful things about you, like your pretty hair, and soft cheeks, and peaches skin in great abundance. I would really love to hear your nice chatter this evening and whisper lots of nice things in your ear. My back needs scratched too, now that it's been peeling from the sun I've been getting.

Honey, don't ever forget for a moment that I'm in love with you with all my heart, and it will stay that way, because it's you, you sweet girl that I married, you and all our love, which shall never end.

Goodnight Darling,

Dean

26 December 1944: A Visit to the Temple

The stretch from Thanksgiving to Christmas and the New Year wasn't going well for Constance Happy Sherman. Seven weeks from her delivery date, she couldn't sleep, suffered from emotional surges of undetermined origin, felt like she had a herky-jerky watermelon inside her, and worried for and missed Dean. Sadness appeared and stayed for days at a time. Out of desperation more than anything else, she decided to visit the Salt Lake Temple. She and Dean had been married there; perhaps there were memories in the building that would comfort her.

The Salt Lake Temple was built of huge granite blocks dragged from the mountains by oxen, shaped by hammer and chisel by men and women who could barely scrape out an existence in the desert that is the Salt Lake Valley. The building of it occupied them, off and on, for some forty years. It was the anchor of their community and society. Its imposing five stories and multiple towers shouldered the task well.

Once inside the great building, the relief was immediate.

"I was right to come here."

Demons and fears departed her, falling away like unwanted scales, shed from her by the holiness of the place. The relief was startling; with each step, muscles relaxed, her back straightened, her neck and head rose. The constant weight of the burden had made her unaware of how heavy it had become.

There was a presence in this building. The being could not be found by visual inspection, although its power and intensity would have suggested it could be seen. Connie undeniably felt it in the deepest parts of her heart and soul and welcomed its comfort.

Much had been forgotten in her absence from the place.

More than quiet solitude, the building generated a sense of instant well-being, the comfort of safety from the demons waiting outside the doors. There came a powerful assurance that all was, and would be, well in spite of her fears, in spite of the reality of loneliness and a raging war that threatened what she held dear.

Well aware she was nineteen years of age, married, and about to have a child with a soldier husband flying into harm's way on a regular basis, she felt ill-equipped to handle it all.

I'm still a teenager for crying out loud!

The murals on the walls were both welcoming and comforting. She used the time to mentally recreate her wedding day and could see her unsure self hoping not to do anything "wrong," mother and grandmother on either side of her.

The session brought a flood of forgotten recollections, recollections that injected comfort. The peace was settling. It felt good to think of things that had not been thought of in a while.

Connie sought out the room where their marriage was solemnized. Immaculate and exquisite, she became an observer, a witness as she watched her mind reenact her marriage. The vision attacked her shoulders with a shudder and the assurance of well-being fell like it was pulled by gravity through her body. Her knees buckled and, involuntarily, she knelt at the altar, bowed her head in prayer, begging for the preservation of her husband and their family, pleading with a Presence, a God, that in this place, she could feel.

She put her hands on the altar as she had done during her marriage. She closed her eyes. Her remembrance brought Dean to the opposite side of the altar. She could feel Dean's hands take hers. They squeezed each other. She shuddered again as a divine assurance coursed through her body that her family would be forever.

27 December 1944, India

Dearest Connie,

I sure was all happy today when some mail came. I got ten letters this time. The latest, Dec. 6 from your mother. Boy, I was all smiles for quite a while. Since it came shortly after Christmas. It was like it was today and nice too. I guess the rest will be coming regular now. When you use the new address it should make it in about ten days.

Now to get you straight on what the censor cut out. It was coconuts that we had in Florida. Don't know why that was taken out. If anymore are cut up let me know and I'll tell you what's missing.

We did have a nice Christmas dinner, turkey, Virginia ham, and cranberry sauce with trimmings. The turkey was canned but was still pretty good. It sure could never come near being like having any dinner at your house, but it was nice for here.

It is nice and warm here, with cool nights so it doesn't seem a bit like Christmas. We heard some Christmas carols tho and there were some well-decorated trees around.

There are some Latter-day Saints here and have services every Sunday. But so far I've been busy when the time came. I'll be going the first chance tho.

Honey, I really do want to go thru the temple with you again at our first opportunity. I'm glad you went tho. And we'll be going together when I'm around again.

Honey, I sure am in love with you this evening as it always is. This beautiful moon reminds me of lots of wonderful times with you. I really do like all your nice ways and good looks and wonderful personality to be loving company with. I guess I'll just be dreaming of kissing your sweet lips, and more and more stuff that you know all about.

I know I'm always lonesome for you; but still the time goes fast and it won't be so long before I'll be seeing you again.

Guess your dental work is all done now. I'm glad too Honey. It's good news too that you are getting along so well.

Everything has been pretty quiet the last few days, so we're having lots of rest.

I had this L-5 today for some entertainment and fun for a while. I chased a few buzzards (kites) and had lots of fun. Sure would like to take you for a ride in it some time.

Have about run out of chatter for now, Honey, so will just be telling you that I love you always and more and more.

Be good to Junior too!!

All my love,

Dean

28 December 1944: Politics

This Pacific War, like the war in Europe, was only going to end with an unconditional surrender; there was no other political or military option. That course was set by the Casablanca Conference held in January 1943.

Roosevelt and Churchill announced the determination that the Axis powers would be fought to their ultimate defeat and unconditional surrender. The results of World War I dictated the policy. The Allies wanted no part of the Axis powers bringing war to the world a third time. An armistice, a negotiated settlement, was not going to be an option.

This was a point of miscalculation by the Japanese. As the war wore on and the outcome became obvious, they held the belief that peace could be negotiated, thereby achieving a much better outcome than an unconditional surrender. Their bargaining chip was the immeasurable losses the Americans would absorb when they invaded the homeland of Japan. They continued to fight even while there was tremendous suffering among their people, with no hope of winning the war. The atom bomb liberated them of their hopes about negotiating.

Bringing about the unconditional surrender with the minimum loss of American lives became the million-dollar, or perhaps billion-dollar, question. To the point, the development of the B-29 was labeled "the three billion dollar gamble." (Craven)

The various military entities—army, navy, and army air forces (soon to be air force) were anything but unified in purpose, other than defeating the Japanese. How to do that was up for debate, as far as the branches of the services were concerned, with each of a mind that *they* had the ultimate solutions.

The navy, under Admiral Nimitz, was quite certain this was a blue water naval war that required action across the broad expanse of the Pacific. Some sixty-four million square miles were involved between Hawaii, the Philippines, Australia, and Japan. His marines were able fighters on land and his ships were gaining control of the seas.

The army, led by General Douglas MacArthur, advanced the plan of island-hopping, starting in the southwest Pacific and ending in Japan.

The navy, of course, would serve as his soldiers' chauffeurs along the way.

Both the army and navy saw the air corps as a support entity that would help them advance their cause.

The army air corps wanted something else. Being convinced that a very long-range bomber with precision bombing capacities (the B-29) would turn the tide, bring Japan to its knees, and end the war, they wanted the army and navy to conquer territory within range of mainland Japan and they could take care of the rest. Decisive force could be brought to bear. (Gorman)

The problem with bombing Japan was always how to get close enough to bomb the hell out of her, when Australia, China, and the Aleutian Islands were just too far away.

The conflicting goals of the services involved some powerful egos. Everyone wanted to be the one that won the war. A navy adviser noted, "The interests of the Army Air Force and the Navy clash seriously in the Central Pacific campaign. The danger is obvious of our amphibious campaign being turned into one that is auxiliary support to permit the AAF to get into position to end the war."

The infighting in Washington D.C. was fierce. From all of this jostling and urgency, Operation Matterhorn emerged. It called for setting up bases in the British colony of India and forward bases one thousand miles to the northeast in China, from which B-29s could reach Japan.

President Roosevelt was the Matterhorn champion out of a loyalty to China's Chiang Kai-shek, having promised him support in his war with the one million Japanese soldiers occupying a good-sized piece of his country. Roosevelt felt that putting B-29s in India and China was keeping his word to the Chinese leader, and would help China survive and keep them in the war.

30 December 1944, India

My Dearest Sweetheart,

Good evening Honey, I sure am happy to be writing you this evening even if it is late. #5 and 6 came today. Your letters have all come in order so far and as all the letters have been coming to the shipping address, I can't tell if the V-mail is any faster. I think all the mail comes airmail anyhow. But that V-mail you wrote sure did have bundles of sweetness and love in it.

And if this paper will stand it I'll send back all I have, because you should know (so I'll tell you) that I love you , Honey, more and more all the time. I love all of you too, you know, your pretty hair and peaches skin, hot lips that are wonderful, and breasts like fountains of heaven along with other things about you that only practice can make perfect. And Darling you know we've had the practice, only I want years and years more.

I'm a lucky guy that I married you, Honey, and have such a wonderful woman waiting for me. I'm waiting for you too, until we can live our lives together in peace.

Thank you, Honey, for the nice Christmas card. I couldn't get any so I just wrote you a letter. The one came too from your mother and dad and I liked it. Give my greetings to Catherine and family (Greetin's). I didn't forget anyone, but didn't have the remembrances available.

I sent you another package today. It has a pillow slip and shoes in it. I sure hope you like that and can wear the shoes sometime. If you can't tho, trade them off.

I have been flying a little once in a while, just around here tho so far. It keeps my time up anyhow. I do need a log book so if you can find a small (or about the same size as the other), standard pilot's log book, I would like you to send that.

No Packages have come yet but imagine they will be coming before too long. I'm happy now anyhow that your wonderful letters are coming. Hope you love all the packages I sent, or at least pretty soon.

I got a Christmas card from Mrs. Johnson today, so I'll send you her address. Her name is Hilda. She is expecting. They hoped that would keep him stateside but we know how that goes, don't we Honey. Mrs. J. W. Johnson, 600 So. 85 Place, Birmingham 6, Alabama. Hope I can have better luck with the pictures than you did. I'll let you know when they are fixed.

> Goodnight, Darling Connie,
>
> Hot love and kisses,
>
> Dean

Chapter 8

The Doctrine

WARS ARE FOUGHT in many locations.

Some don't involve hand-to-hand combat, but rather clashes of minds and egos hidden deep in government buildings far from public view or the battle's front. They are imaginary war games, battles of war planners, most often generals or others of high rank, or long-tenured bureaucrats that hatch out policies, strategies, and battle plans.

The grunts who later live out their strategies in the real-time world of bullets and exploding shells generally come to the conclusion that these sequestered-away experts (in grunt language, "bastards") "don't know their ass from a hole in the ground."

But it is the best system we have.

One example of the system's folly was "The Doctrine for Strategic Bombardment" to guide the use of the B-29.

"Bombers, because of the speed, range, and altitude [and] limitations of pursuit planes, would always prevail. [When early results of the war in Europe showed the vulnerability of bombers because of the advances in pursuit design, the Americans amended their assumption to say that well-armed bombers or "Superfortresses" would always prevail.]

"High altitude bombing would overcome ground defense systems and the lower altitude fighters.

"Precision bombing could target and destroy critical war effort infrastructure that would eliminate the enemy's ability to make war. [Planners eliminated the idea of directly attacking enemy populations as unnecessary, thinking the will of the people would disappear with the destruction of the war infrastructure.]

"The precision necessary could only be achieved by attacking in daylight hours."

In the end, all the tenets of the Doctrine for Strategic Bombardment were ignored as the realities of the war became obvious. Had they been followed, serial number 44-69966 would very probably not have gone down on 14 May 1945, but also the war would have progressed much differently.

Design and technology advances allowed the B-29 to be the weapon of choice to fulfill the Strategic Bombardment Doctrine. Pressurized cabins allowed the aviators to be comfortable flying at 30,000 feet, easily above the pursuit of enemy fighters. Newly developed bomb sights and radar technologies allowed for the possibility of precision when delivering payloads.

The B-29 was a Superfortress because of its gunnery and the use of computerization to aim and fire. The ten .50 caliber machine guns could be fired from several locations and coordinated on one target. The 20 mm cannon, mounted in the tail, gave the B-29 an extraordinary calling card for enemy fighters.

The air corps desired to move from being the support arm of the military to the strike force that would end the war. The resultant doctrine of high-altitude, daylight, and precision bombardment was the goal and standard. But war is never simple or easy, nor does it like to follow the plan. In fact, the new technologies of the B-29 brought uncertainties, unintended consequences that "complexified" the problem rather than simplifying it. The Japanese responses and the personal and inter-service rivalries further added to the complexity. (Gorman)

The theorists got it much more wrong than right. High-altitude bombing didn't work very well over Japan. Precision bombing was negated by many of the same issues that neutered high-altitude bombing. But a job needed to be accomplished—the Japanese needed to be driven to unconditional surrender.

One of the greatest errors in theory of the think tanks and warmakers was their expectation of what that would take. There was a pronounced lack of understanding of Japanese culture and the nation's citizens' commitment to their "holy nation" and their emperor, and their resultant ability to bear hardship.

Jan 1, 1945, India

Dearest Sweetheart,

Good evening Honey, I sure am lonesome for you this evening as always! I can dream tho of loving you and kissing your sweet lips and lots more of what you like, lots of, and me too!

Yesterday was payday as you may know, so for a while I had lots of money, but as you see you can take care of some of it for me. I forgot where I put the bank envelopes so you can take the money up and the account book at the same time and get things fixed straight. I hope you don't need the money but can be saving it for me. Do you have enough to take care of Junior and everything? There also will be a $100 war bond coming pretty soon. Let me know when it comes. See if you can get me some more of these bank envelopes and send a couple please.

I also paid our income tax. I guess the statement should have come to you, but it was in one of those window envelopes and your address was out of sight so I got it and paid it, which makes us all happy.

I'll see if I can get my cable address right away so when there 's some big excitement at your house you can let me know. I've heard the cable takes about as long as a letter but we'll see.

Guess what? So I will tell you. Our crew had a big time today making ice cream. We got a freezer and had some powdered ice cream mix. When we put it all together and cranked for about an hour we had ice cream. It was good too. Only we didn't keep track of things too close and it was a little rich. Tasted more like rich malted milk, but it was good anyhow, and will probably be making some more pretty soon. It was fun anyhow.

Haven't had much excitement here lately but I imagine we'll start working again pretty soon. I'd just as soon rest but I guess you'll be hearing what we do a lot sooner than I could tell you. I'm still glad you like the silk stockings. Why don't you try them on and tell me how they feel. As I said, they didn't look like quite the right shape for your pretty legs, but I hope they are anyhow.

Oh, you beautiful woman. I sure have been thinking of you lots today, and thinking how wonderful you are, and how wonderful it would be to be with you now and forever afterward. I guess you know I could sure make you happy now, the best ever and ready for a good night's sleep. It would be fun to cuddle with you for hours and hold you in my arms and go to sleep with you in kissing range!

Isn't war hell?

Goodnight Darling,

All my love and kisses,

Dean

5 January 1945: Matterhorn

Operation Matterhorn immediately identified the shortcomings in the strategic planning for the B-29s.

In December 1943, the building of airfields in India and forward bases in China was undertaken. Thousands of Indians labored to construct four permanent bases in eastern India around Kharagpur. Meanwhile, one thousand miles to the northeast, across the Himalayan mountains, 350,000 Chinese workers toiled (with only the benefit of hand tools) to build four staging bases in western China near Chengdu By April 1944, eight B-29 airfields were available in Asia.

In June of that year, attacks on Japan, originating from the airfields in India, with refueling stops at the forward bases in China, began, sort of. Due to mechanical issues, distance, weather, and the difficulties of logistics on such an enormous undertaking, actually dropping bombs on the enemy didn't happen very often.

Subsequent analysis indicated that the XX Bomber Command was only free to use 14 percent of its B-29s against the Japanese. The others were used as ferry tankers keeping the B-29s supplied with fuel and bombs

At their peak, XX Bomber Command could manage only two sorties per month per aircraft, with only half of those sorties directed against the main islands of Japan, not a tempo that would bring the enemy to their knees.

General LeMay commented, after the war, "When ordered to fly a mission out of China, we had to make seven trips with a B-29 and off-load all the gas we could, leaving only enough to get back to India. On the eighth trip we would transport a load of bombs, top off with gas in China, and go drop them on Japan if the weather was right. Then we'd start the process all over again. So the logistical situation was hopeless in China." (Craven)

Admiral Nimitz was directed by the Joint Chiefs of Staff to invade the Mariana Islands of the Central Pacific in Operation Forager to provide air bases within striking distance of the Japanese mainland. Saipan, Tinian, and Guam (a US possession before the war) were roughly 1,200 miles from Tokyo. The fighting was intense, but construction engineers arrived even before the battles were over and began building and expanding airfields.

Tinian, with its four runways, would, for a time, be the largest airport in the world. On 12 October 1944, the first attack was launched by the newly created XXI Bomber Command.

One of the results of taking the Marianas was that the Imperial Japanese Navy sortied in response, gathering to attack the US Navy fleet supporting the landings. The resultant Battle of the Philippine Sea (the so-called Great Marianas Turkey Shoot) on June 19 and 20 of 1944 inflicted heavy and irreplaceable losses to Japan's carrier-borne and land-based aircraft.

Like Operation Matterhorn, B-29 raids from the Marianas were not without difficulties. The attacks against the Nakajima aircraft plants in November 1944 that were witnessed by Riku from his schoolyard, were typical of the first attempts at precision bombardment against Japanese industry from the Marianas. The raid was cancelled five times over a two-week period, due to poor weather over the target.

Of the 111 B-29s that participated in the eventual attack, seventeen aborted before reaching Japan and six were unable to bomb because of mechanical difficulties. The attacking bombers encountered winds of 120 knots, while overcast cloud layers obscured the target area. Of the eighty-eight airplanes that bombed the area of the plant, thirty-five had to do so by radar. In the end, only forty-eight bombs fell in the factory area, damaging 1 percent of the building, 2.4 percent of the machinery, and injuring or killing 132 people in the factory complex. Two B-29s were lost over the target. (Robertson)

The weather over Japan definitely favored the home team. Precision high-altitude bombardment was not possible in the jet stream winds. Bombs were just plain blown off target when dropped from more than five miles in the air. Cloud cover also negated accuracy or even eliminated the ability to drop bombs. Weather was so poor, especially during the winter, that there were sometimes only three or four good bombing days a month. (Gorman)

In the jet stream, problems were manifest in both directions. Planes flying with the high-level winds would have so much increased air speed they blew by targets. Planes flying against the winds greatly reduced their range, using precious fuel they needed to get home, and saw their actual ground speed drop to pedestrian levels, leaving them more vulnerable to attack. On one mission, flown upwind to increase bombing accuracy, aircrews even reported flying backward along the ground, as wind speed exceeded their true airspeed.

The end result was that this magnificent airplane designed for precision bombing from the safety of 30,000 feet, beyond the fighters and ground defenses, could not accurately hit the proverbial broad side of a Japanese barn from that altitude.

These early results were difficult for air crews and generals. Many logistical and design issues had been resolved, some at the cost of crew lives, but there was, as one historian put it, just not much to show for the effort other than a lot of men had lost buddies.

11 January 1945, India

My Dearest Sweetheart,

I just got a whole stack of mail that has been collecting for me for the past few days. Have been in China since my last letter and am about to go there again before I can write another. China is where our forward base is and we sorta commute between here and there.

Was on one more mission, which you probably have heard about. It was rough too but I am back and waiting for the next one.

I sure was happy to get your letters, Honey. Ten and eleven are missing yet but they should come soon, twelve came yesterday.

I do enjoy myself in China when I'm not too busy doing something else. Had a look through one village that is near our base. I bought a rabbit skin hat and some chopsticks.

The place looks just about like any pictures or descriptions I've ever heard of China, only when actually seeing it, it doesn't seem quite real. Seems like a play or something, only temporary. I don't see how people can spend a lifetime living like that.

Have narrow crooked streets, crowded, and all the small shops open to the street. It's winter but they wear their straw hats, and some are barefoot or with grass sandals. It doesn't seem to be because they are so poor, but they just don't mind. They lead their cows and pigs thru the streets and thru the crowd, others carrying baskets of vegetables and such stuff. Everybody who isn't carrying some merchandise of some sort carries a little basket with a charcoal fire to keep their hands warm.

I sent you a Chinese bill in one of my letters and maybe some more in this if I remember. They are only worth a few cents.

Honey, I hope you make out with the money OK. I hope you put that money order in the bank, because I can send you some more. How much was the dentist bill? I'll pay that extra when you let me know, so you don't have to take it out of your check. Do you have any in the post office now?

Our tithing is or will be $40 for a couple months and more again pretty soon. I'll send you some more money, but just remember that we have to save some too, because when this job is over we'll probably get by on a lot less for a while. Remember you used to get by on a lot less.

I want you to have all you need, Honey. I know I can save it here because there is nothing here much I need to buy but when you are getting most of it, you need to help too.

I guess I missed your Christmas letters (they haven't come yet). Hope Sharon gets over the chicken pox right away. Boy, how kids do carry on and get into trouble!!

I'm glad you got the package, Honey, and hope by now you have the alligator purse with a picture in it.

I guess my letters from the Nile must have been heavily censored. The place where we stopped was where the White and Blue come together.

I managed to grow quite a beard while I was in China. It has been over a week growing now and is doing well. I'll get next to a razor pretty soon I think. I also got a cold which I hope I get over. I'll love to give the quick cure tonight.

Boy there I go writing pages and pages, but I still have hundreds of things to say, Honey, which can hardly be put on paper.

I know I'm in love with you more than ever if possible, and know you are the most wonderful woman who ever happened to me. I'm sure glad I married you, Honey, but what could I do, and I like it too. All the sweet things that are you and just for me, and for us. Just keep sweet like you are always for me, and I'll be around to make you happy again forever, Goodnight, Darling!

My love and kisses,

Dean

PS My song flute makes a good noise that even someone else can recognize!

12 January 1945: Some Mail

It was but a one-letter day on Sherman Avenue. With Junior's arrival but weeks away, the ordeal was nearly over. Letters from Dean renewed her spirits as Connie entered the home stretch.

Winters in the Salt Lake Valley are often described as harsh. This day could define harsh—a consistent wind falling off the Wasatch Range, cutting through layers of protection without any respect. The wind carried a cold that could freeze anything.

A bundled Therill Hanson, whistling mailman extraordinaire, ever faithful, ever on time, rendered "The Stars and Stripes" in surprising form considering the conditions. Connie had trained her ears to be listening at 10:06 a.m. for the Sousa march. Sadly, there was silence more days than not.

But today it was rendered. The sound propelled Connie, immediately full of anticipation, to waddle to the door without remembering the blast of winter that waited for her.

She recoiled at the frigid welcome of the open door, accepted quickly Therill's offering, sent him a smile and a thank you and retreated into her room to read.

14 January 1945, India

My Dearest Sweetheart,

Greetings, Honey, and since I have plenty of time on my hands (which I will explain) I'll go on with this chatter.

Right now I'm enjoying all the comforts of confinement and having nothing at all to do, except eat sleep and write you long missiles of chatter.

This morning when about ready to depart for China again, I fell from the ladder entering the ship and broke a bone in my right foot. It isn't bad and doesn't hurt much but keeps me confined to the limits of crutches and a wheel chair which I have at my disposal.

Maybe the angels or someone else didn't want me in China, anyhow here I am, enjoying all the comforts of the hospital. I expect a cast to be put on my foot but so far it hasn't been done. Maybe they are waiting for it to stop swelling. It is only a slight fracture so as yet isn't bandaged but it isn't good for walking and probably won't be for a few days at least.

Right now a cold is bothering me more than my foot so when I get over the cold I'll be happy again.

We have a radio here and all the swell music has me in the mood for romancing with you, Honey. You sure would be nice company now to nurse me and chatter with. In fact I think it would be wonderful to cuddle with you now for hours and make hot love to you, you sweet woman. Maybe Junior wouldn't like the hot loving tho but I would and I'll bet you would too.

Honey, I sure do love you tonight as always and am thinking of a beautiful girl with pretty hair, sweet lips, and peaches skin and lots of wonderful experiences.

Am thinking of a wonderful woman and when we went through the Temple together and lots of things that it meant to us. That was where I received the greatest blessing of my life and Honey, you did too. I hope to be able to go thru with you many more times before too long too.

I can dream of an adorable girl who is mine that night and from then on and still. Honey, you are the one who keeps my life bright and interesting and who the plans and dreams of the future are for.

I am being treated well here and getting along fine, Honey, so don't worry about me. Just take good care of yourself like I would if I were there and be happy for both of us.

I will close now and dream of you while listening to some beautiful stateside music. Sure is wonderful.

All my love and kisses,

Dean

As Connie's eyes came to the bottom of the page, she was gob-smacked—*fell from the ladder while entering the ship.* She stared at the words, trying to assess how this would change things for her husband.

So Dean will be in the hospital when I am. The thought made her smile. *Too bad it's not the same hospital.*

The news brought comfort. Pilots don't get shot down if they are safe in the hospital. The idea of him hurting himself climbing into the ship had never crossed her mind. She worried about flak, Japanese fighter planes, and mechanical problems, never something as simple of a misstep. *Although he did fall in that foxhole.*

She glowed; the knowledge he was out of harm's way brought a sense of comfort that surprised her.

As her delivery date grew closer, she would occasionally feel a sense of relief that the ordeal of pregnancy was nearly over. By the same token, she would then be reminded that the ordeal of delivery and its unknowns lay at the end of pregnancy. And beyond that, the greatest unknown—she would be taking a baby home to nurture, raise, and teach. That would go on for a while, but she would always be this child's mother. Forever.

So a red-blooded American officer, completely healthy except for a small bone in his foot that limits his mobility severely is cooped up in an army hospital, thousands of miles from home with nothing but memories of his new wife and their times together. What would you expect to happen?

Dean, for his part, composed the Love Letter Trilogy.

15 January 1945, India

Good Evening Sweet Woman,

Can I come and make love with you tonight? Right now? OK! Lay down, I want to talk with you.

I guess that is a terrible thing to say tho, now, with anything so wonderful so far from possible. But I will be thinking of you and be remembering lots of wonderful things about you, Honey.

I know I sure would like to go dancing with you tonight and any night and have lots of fun romancing with you. And we will go to Cocoa Nut Grove too. It can be easily arranged if we really decide to do it.

I have a nice big cast on my foot now, the left one, only most of it is on my leg and not the foot. It is all from my toes almost to my knee. That's for a support tho so I can walk on it. I've been learning to walk on it pretty good today and it goes just like a wheel on one side, there is a rocker block under my foot. My foot doesn't hurt at all so I feel like I'm just wasting time.

I got out for a while today. There was a USO stage show featuring Lilly Pons and Andre Kostelanetz and some others. It was an excellent musical show and I liked it a lot. I heard a lot of beautiful music, which was nice for a change.

Only we have lots of good music here with the radio. We get rebroadcasts of all the popular programs. Last night I heard Hit Parade, I think it was from a couple of weeks back tho but it was really nice.

Your letters #7 and #10 came the last few days. They get rather mixed up with the mail situation. I hope mine aren't so mixed up because I keep forgetting to number them. They are dated anyhow.

I'm glad Ruth wrote to you. She said she was going to Montana in January so maybe she is there now. Maybe you should make her some baby clothes. She will be needing them soon, too, you know!

Honey, I will be happy for a girl or a boy, too. Honey, I'll like what ever cooks, so you can know that you won't have to trade a girl off unless you can get a nice mean boy. But maybe there should only be one meany in the family and you can't get rid of me. I'll be happy Darling for what ever is given into our care. Have Grandpa B do the blessing, maybe after two or three I'll learn that too. Guess we'll have to get busy to think of some new names! But whoa!!! What's the hurry??

I rather like Larry for a boy's name too and Anita, Elaine, or Eloise for a girl. Do you? And tell me more.

My chatterer is tired and my pen is dry so for now, Honey, I will say goodbye.

Tell Aunt Catherine I liked her poems and give her my cheeriest greeting in case I don't get to write soon.

Remember, you sweet girl, that I love you with all my heart and want so much to come see you again and soon and always, to love you to hold you close and hug tight, and get practiced kissing you again, and have no end of fun cuddling with you,

All my love, Darling,

Dean

PS Did I tell you about the negatives in my last letter? If not you can get a blown up print made for you. That was when we got back from China the first time and the Bombardier caught me preparing for summer again.

19 January 1945, India

Dearest Sweetheart,

I have been going to write you dozens of letters but I keep remembering maybe I just wrote one, but now it must be time again and so it is. Guess I'm just thinking of you most of the time, Honey, which isn't all bad at all but it makes me lonesome.

We have lots of nice music on our radio too, which I like but that, too, makes me remember too many wonderful things that are not possible just now. I've heard "The Very Thought of You" several times. I think I heard it before I left but am not sure. I like it anyhow and lots more that would be nice to dance too, and just sit and listen to, and better to be making love to you by.

Your letters are not censored, Honey, at least none so far. I imagine it would be an impossible job anyhow censoring all the outgoing mail.

I saw a good show last night. It was "Music in Manhattan." It was good but affected me like some do. I know I sure did miss your company and remembered as if I need a reminder, that I love you ever so much, and with all my heart. No one, Honey, could ever be to me like you are always.

How is Junior? Still kicking, but not too hard? I guess it won't be too long before we'll be knowing what's been cooking since Lincoln Park!!!

I guess I'll have to write dozens of letters ahead so you can be reading them when you are in the Hospital. What shall I tell you, a story, Honey? I can tell you a true story. And that is that you are the most wonderful sweetheart and beautiful wife I ever had and I sure do miss you, Honey, and all the wonderful good times we had together.

I'm still in the Hospital. I broke the first cast so have a new one which is about ready to walk on. I sure do hate to use crutches while the cast is drying, so maybe I'll not break this one. I might even get out in a couple of weeks, I hope. Goodbye for now you sweet Girl so this catches the mail.

All my Love and Kisses,

Dean

22 January 1945, India

My Dearest Sweetheart,

Hello you sweet beautiful woman. Be happy, Honey, because just now I'm really happy with you and hope I can put into words all the wonderful things I'd love to tell you tonight.

Your #15 V-mail letter came today and it made me all smiles. I am still missing 11 & 14 tho, but I am still hoping for them. Maybe they took a "slow boat, no convoy."

I've been reading a good book today, and I read all of it, a big thick one too. It is "Leave Her to Heaven" by Ben Ames Williams. I think it was excellent, that's why I read it all without stopping.

It was very interesting and mostly made me think of you and all the wonderful things you are.

Darling, you are the only and always most beautiful woman in my life. My inspiration and ambitions seem all to spring from being with you and planning our life together. Having you, first to go thru the Temple with to start our life together in a beautiful endowment, and then having you for a companion and beautiful lover has been what brought out the best I've known. The thrilling memories of our love together of having you, so beautiful and sweet, to be all mine in those most sacred and intimate hours we had together have been completely satisfying. My dreams and plans for the future seem to be centered on bringing all those things to pass again, only never again to be broken by our separation.

For the present, I am so happy for us, that we have a baby coming. I guess it happens to some on every day, but that never decreases a mite, the wonderful things, the blessings it means to us and I want you to know, Darling, that even now, and because of that, I love you even more than I ever thought possible. I love everything about you, all your physical perfections, your wonderful personality, and because we just belong so much to each other. I don't think it will be different ever, tho everything isn't always roses, but working together, facing problems and troubles together, will always bring us closer and to better understanding of each other.

Honey, I'm so happy about you tonight, I hope all this sentimental chatter doesn't make you sad, but I am in a sentimental mood, and feel like talking hours and hours to you.

I am being interrupted at times for some good hot chocolate and fruit cake. It's good too, we have a sort of small kitchen here in the ward, which comes in handy. The Red Cross makes ice cream once in a while and that tastes very nice.

As you see I'm still in the hospital but enjoying it slightly. When I'm writing you a nice letter, or reading, or listening to all the good music on the radio the time goes fast. I heard Hit Parade the last two weeks. We have lots of waltzes and classical music to relax and listen to. It's really nice. Right now I hear "Let Me Love You Tonight." It was on Hit Parade too.

Goodnight, you Sweet Peach Blossom. I'll be dreaming of kissing your sweet lips.

All my love,

Dean

Chapter 9

Another Wonderful Letter

23 January 1945, India

Good evening, Honey,

Just received another wonderful letter from you which made me very happy. It was #14. I don't know why the mixup, except very little mail has come in the last few days. #11 is still coming I think and lots more too, I hope. Your V-mail takes just as long as the others and are "thinner" too, Honey, so I guess you know what to write, only once in a while would be nice to check on the service.

I'm still awful happy with you, Honey, like I wrote yesterday (insert: day before).

Have been reading quite a bit more today on books and prayers. It's all interesting when I get started and find what I like.

Also the Red Cross has a work shop (along with a lot of other things) where I was this afternoon, learning how to make fly fish hooks. It's fun too and interesting, how to make bugs and flies out of feathers and hair and thread. I hope I learn the art because it's fun and not too hard. Maybe I can catch some big fish when I get home again.

Let's go camping, Honey, off in the hills with sleeping bags and cots and all the good camping outfit we will have. (Or shall we both sleep in one sleeping bag?) It sure would be chummy and fun with you, you hot wonderful woman. Maybe we could even take time to fish and take some pictures too.

That's what I want to do, Honey, when we are together again, when we can arrange it with Junior. I know it will be a honeymoon for me, because we never did finish ours yet, did we, Honey? I do love you lots, Darling, just more and more all the time, and I guess you know that's lots!

I still want you to know that I'm really happy and pleased that we are going to have a baby, Honey. (Maybe I've been reading too many funny little books about "I'm going to be a Father.") If everything was just what we wanted I would still prefer March. Maybe we should have waited a month like you wanted, but then we wouldn't have had the nice Park would we?

Dean has trouble with his pen and writes the following, speaking to the pen:

#©!*&% (Censored!) "Now, don't let that happen again!"... That is what I think of my pen, must be the ink.

Now to continue, don't let Junior hear any of those bad words.

Anyhow I'm sure happy still and always about you and us. Darling, I really hope you don't have too much trouble. Please write me all the details tho, about what happens.

I'm glad tho, that you'll be flat and all beautiful and smooth and soft and sweet when I come to see you again. I'll bet you'll be just as good as new only better and hot and eager too, with all the experience you have had.

Darling, you are just the most wonderful, beautiful wife I could ever want, and it's just you and all of you I want, and can have too, can't I?

Sure hope I can get out of this hospital in a few days. I'll have to see about sending you some more money, but I'll hurt you if you don't save some of it. No more shoes, no more dresses and no nice new house if you don't! You'll just have to live on love I guess. I know we have plenty for each other.

I have a nice nurse to scratch my back, but not like you, Honey. She's nice and takes good care of us but more like a mother. She has grey hair and wears glasses and isn't beautiful like you, Honey. It is nice to get my back scratched sometimes, but I always think of a beautiful, wonderful Peach Blossom who scratches my back the best way, and is ready to be kissed mad, and makes hot love with me when we like.

I'll write you dozens more right quick, Honey.

You are always my best Sweetheart and I'll be yours.

Dean

From the pages of the Hellbird Herald:

(the 462nd's own newsletter)

Meet Miss Aedes Aegypti—She'll Heat You!

"Men have the skin I love to touch," said Miss Aedes Aegypti, in an interview. "There is something about their smooth texture that I can't resist. They get in my blood."

Miss Aegypti is the latest of the femmes fatale to visit this island. More familiarly known as Ada to her intimates, her picture is a familiar one in the four corners of the earth. Despite her fame, Ada is still the same shy girl that she used to be when she was just another mosquito in the larvae stage. Some of her better-known productions are, "Ten Nights in a Hospital Bed," and "Buzz Bomb on the Left Flank."

"I can safely say that more men get heated up over me than any other woman in the world," she said, with a coy flick of her left wing. "Miss Anopheles is strictly second rate," she continued, referring to her well-known rival. "She is fickle, and ofttimes travels long distances, changing from one man to another. Besides, Dengue is much nicer than Malaria.

"I am the faithful type," Ada added, displaying her well-shaped legs, all ten of them. "When I pick a man, I stick close to him, never let him out of my sight. Not only that," she shyly remarked, "but my children will be there too. Yes, I plan to have many children, and I know that all of them will be as popular as their mother."

Ada has been having a rather difficult time lately. "I can't understand it," she remarked, "but the United States Army doesn't seem to want me around. Every time I'm ready to get settled they dispossess me. It must be that the Yanks are women-haters.

"Why only the other day," Ada went on, "I was getting cozy in the bottom of a helmet which had just the right amount of water. And a wonderful blonde hunk of man lived in that tent too. I had it planned to spend the evening with him when someone came along and spilled that nice water out. It was all I could do to get away. I tried to find some other place to stay, but there was none. No flower pots, no rain buckets, nothing for me to settle down in. So I had to leave that blonde behemoth," she sighed, "and he would have been so interesting!"

If Enlisted Men Could Pull Inspections on Officers' Tents.

(An imaginary scene.)

Enter Pfc. Baggybottoms and Pvt. Loweyeque, into the tent of Major Seeyess for the purpose of inspection.

Major S: Attention! (All five officers snap to their feet.)

Pfc. B: (Approaches one of the rigid men.) You were a little slow getting up, Lieutenant. Just where did you get your training?

Lt R: Why, sir, in Miami Beach OCS.

Pfc. B: Hmmm that explains it. (Turns to others.) At ease. (Starts to walk about, his clear eye sweeping the tent—the first thing to sweep it in many a day.) Disgraceful!

Pvt. L: Disgraceful! (Both enlisted men beat the beds and a cloud of dust rises.)

Pfc. B: Who is the OIC (Officer in charge) of this tent?

Major S: I am afraid I am, sir. (Hangs his head.)

Pfc. B: Major Seeyess, is this a way to live? Look under that bed. (The Major looks under the bed.) Look at the shelves. (The Major looks at the shelves.) It is dirty, filthy, isn't it?

Major S: Yes, sir.

Pfc. B: Furthermore, major, do you think we put up diagrams on how to fix your tent on the bulletin board just to fill up space? (Silence.) Well, do you?

Major S: No, sir.

Pfc. B: The diagram distinctly shows that the bed should be four inches from the wall at one end and four inches from the foot locker at the other end. (He points.) Your bed is more than six inches from either side.

Major S: But my bed is smaller than regulation size...

Pfc. B: (Roars.) That makes no difference! (Turns to Pvt. L.) Take these men's names. We will show them we mean what we say.

Pvt. L: Okay.

Pfc. B: (Turns to Major.) I'm afraid there will be a bit of extra duty in store for all of you–each of you will pull an extra tour of duty as OD (Officer of the Day) starting Monday.

All Five: (In unison.) No—no, not that!

Pfc. B: Let's get over to Captain Rackemoff's tent–he should be easy pickin's. (Exit amid anguished cries.)

(Curtain.)
Sgt. Eugene Boyo

24 January 1945: Land of the Rising Sun

It was a war begun as a fight for oil and ended by the lack of it.

—The Asahi Shimbun

God was on the side of the nation that had the oil.

—Professor Wakimura

Japan participated in the Feudal Age longer than most. The trappings and influence of feudalism kept appearing in Japanese social and governmental life until the total surrender caused by World War II. In Japan's feudal system of conquest, glory, and honor, the samurai warrior and his castle were the center of society. He was the keeper and defender of all. First and foremost, that meant he sheltered and protected the community's rice. The price of his protection and a family's portion of rice was absolute loyalty.

These warlords held regional influence, but in the early 1600s, some 250 of them joined in confederation (some willingly, some by subjugation), and nationalism rather than regionalism began to emerge.

In that process a national identity took shape, one that embraced the value of hierarchy, a centralized authority, and collective responsibility. Collective responsibility put the good of the order above individual good. With that mindset, a system of social classes emerged.

Not a fluid, mobile society, encouraging individual accomplishment and ambition, but rather a caste system that honored social stability and function. Social castes were hereditary and fixed, be they warriors, peasants, artisans, merchants, or, of course, the bottom of every such system—the outcasts.

Outcasts were fixed by fate to their place. That was the only legacy they had to give to their children. Virtue and honor were gained not by wealth or upward mobility, but rather by perfecting one's ability to fill his or her role. Social stability and morality were greatly honored.

This national alliance, known as the Tokugawa regime, moved the newly-minted nation to effectively close its borders to outsiders. They wanted no part of the colonization they saw in China and Southeast Asia by the Europeans. They also wanted to maintain the purity of their social order, denying outside social ideals like personal freedom, ambition, and advancement of self from detracting from social order.

The Japanese realized colonization was best avoided by imperialism, or becoming the colonizer. That required modernization, industrialization, economic development, and a very strong military.

Several groups of "players" emerged to drive the nation's transition. The remnants of the samurai lusted for the modern weaponry and what could be accomplished with it; the "mega" merchants liked the idea of manufacturing the weaponry and not depending on suppliers from abroad; bureaucrats championed central control for an orderly society (which the military folks felt very comfortable with, as long as it didn't control them).

Japanese daily life was very constrained. The caste system prevented social movement, but travel was also highly regulated by way of highway checkpoints. Families were required to register and were monitored. Trade was controlled by feudal guilds, and rules and regulations governed daily life for all society. Personal freedom and initiative had no place. Perfecting the social good, stability, and order, were valued over self-freedom. Society was characterized by discipline and regulation.

Fierce, even radical nationalism emerged, including complete disdain for their "inferior" neighbors—the Koreans and Chinese. The belief in the divine origins of the Japanese people and their emperor, held together the race for modernization. The science and knowledge of the West were aggressively sought but their social thoughts about personal freedom disdained.

Medicine, commerce and industrialization, science technology, and the military were all modernized. The ruling social order began to resemble the European monarchies with courts and nobility. One distinction was that the emperor was not just some run-of-the-mill emperor—he was descended from the gods.

From the sixth century onward it was accepted that the emperor was descended from the *kami* (gods), was in contact with them, and often inspired by them.

This didn't make him a god himself, but rather imposed on him the obligation of carrying out certain rituals and devotions in order to ensure that the kami looked after Japan properly and ensured its prosperity.

The notion that the emperor was in contact with the gods, and often inspired by them, fit well with the inbred passion for social order. One need not take charge of events with the emperor in place. Virtue and honor came from living one's role well. The emperor would do his job, just as citizens would do their jobs, and all would be well. The people only needed to follow his lead.

One other thing survived the transition to nationalism—*bushido.* Bushido was the code of the samurai warrior. It was heavily influenced at different times by Buddhism and Confucianism, and emphasized the warrior spirit, military skills, and fearlessness in the face of an enemy. But it also emphasized frugality, kindness, honesty, and care for one's family members, particularly one's elders. The salient points of bushido were embraced as the moral code of the Japanese people.

When Japanese citizens became soldiers they took bushido with them. From the earliest engagements with Japanese ground forces, the Allied soldiers realized that they were fighting men with a different mindset, men without fear, who fought fiercely and thought naught of personal safety. These were men who would not surrender.

The Japanese feared death just as much as the Western people, but they feared the death of their nation more than they feared individual death. They considered that the death most to be dreaded would be submission to the yoke of the Muscovite. It was patriotism, pure and true, which made the Japanese die gallantly. Moreover, they had an old maxim that "a man lives only one lifetime, but his name shall live forever." They believed that to die on the battlefield for a righteous cause and for the emperor was the noblest death a man could have. (Hadley)

A young female resident of the invaded Okinawa explained her willingness to die rather than be captured. "We had a strict imperial education, so being taken prisoner was the same as being a traitor. We were taught to prefer suicide to becoming a captive."

Captured Japanese soldiers were often listed as KIA (Killed in Action) to spare families back home the shame and dishonor of capture.

As one American officer put it, "Every nation said its soldiers would fight to the last man. Only the Japanese did it."

26 January 1945, India

Good Morning, Honey,

It is evening here but that shouldn't matter, as at this particular time it should be morning there, and also when the mailman comes around too. (I will have him deliver a kiss next time).

I'll bet you're a little fatty now but I like fatties like you, especially like you, Honey, and I like you especially all the time anyhow.

Shall we get married sometime soon, Honey? I feel all in the mood for a honeymoon with you now, or anytime.

I am glad you would like to go horseback riding because I've just decided that is what I'm going to do the next chance I get, and I would like you to learn too. Maybe I could teach you a few things, I used to ride rough horses, remember?

This is sure getting monotonous just wearing out one shoe at a time. Do you want to borrow the other? I think my left leg is getting shorter too for some reason. Maybe I can walk on side hills better now. The cast makes it because it is about 2" high, but I'll get back in shape.

My mailman just came with your Christmas letter, so I am sure tickled. Your letters are never out of date with me, Honey, and I caught up lots of news.

Goodnight you Sweet Peach Blossom, I will be dreaming of kissing your sweet lips, in the only kiss we know so well, complete and blending us into one.

All my love,

Dean

27 January 1945: Japan's Military

The Japanese military fashioned an amazing transformation during the final decades of the 1800s. The army made themselves over in the image of one of the world's best armies, the Prussians. Major Jacob Meckel dragged the army out of the the feudal warlord mindset into modern warfare. He had very motivated students.

Not to be outdone, the Imperial Navy sought out the British and picked their brains clean about how a modern navy should look and operate.

From the beginning, the military, while announcing loyalty to the emperor, sought freedom from any civilian control. In 1878 the Imperial Japanese Army established the office of Army General Staff, modeled after the Prussian General Staff. The Imperial Navy soon followed with the Imperial Japanese Navy General Staff.

These general staff offices were responsible for the planning and execution of military operations, and reported directly to the emperor. As the chiefs of the general staff were not cabinet ministers, they did not report to the prime minister of Japan, and were thus completely independent of any civilian oversight or control.

In fifty years, Japan modernized itself and took its place as one of the world's five superpowers—along with Britain, France, the US, and Italy—at the Paris Peace Conference that ended World War I, and in the newly formed League of Nations.

The independence of the military had unintended consequences. The military made decisions that were in their own self-interest and not necessarily in the best interest of the nation. Without civilian oversight, the military became more and more radicalized. When the outcome of the war was no longer in doubt, the military refused to surrender, holding out for a negotiated settlement, and inflicting tremendous suffering upon the people of Japan.

Illustrating how radicalized the military became after World War I, the Japanese were lauded around the world, receiving several awards for their humane treatment of POWs during the conflict. After World War II, a few decades later, they would receive no such awards, but would be prosecuted as war criminals, with many being hung for their treatment of POWs.

28 January 1945, India

Good Morning Sweet Girl,

Aren't you glad I am in the mood to write you a nice letter this Sunday morning? And I am too, as you well see. #17 came yesterday and I sure was happy about it. Maybe #16 will come today. It's nice to keep me confused all the time.

I think I'll even go to church today, Honey. I can get a pass to get out for a few hours so that's what I will do for a pleasant change.

Boy! What have all you and your girl friends been doing? I'll bet I can guess since there sure are a lot of fatties (pregnant women) in your crowd. That seems like quite a record with so many babies all at once in such a few girls. Maybe they all like what you like lots of Honey, and I know what it is.

It's too bad abut Maureen, but it seems to be the best ending for their story. Seems like she would have taken time to know him better tho, maybe she did.

When is Junior due, Honey? Still Feb 15, or later, or has the doctor made up your mind for you? I know I sure would like to know before two weeks later. You should be able to send a cable in just a couple of days tho with the regular address.

What did the man at Mutual tell you about marriage? It's time I was learning, you know, so you tell me Honey what you think I should know.

Sounds like Junior should have plenty of fresh pants for a while. Do you have any of the paper variety yet? That might be good to use once in a while, might save lots of work.

There is always lots of good music on our radio, before noon even. And the news is good these days too, I guess you know.

Honey, I'll bet you wouldn't have a lot of trouble staying awake long enough to scratch my back even if you were sleepy. I'd feel bad if I couldn't wake you up enough to ever enjoy loving your nice back rubs. What do you think? Don't tell me, just show me when I come to your house again.

Goodbye Honey and I love you an awful lot all this week,

Dean

28 January 1945, India

Hello you Sweet Girl,

I guess you see I am writing you two letters all in one day, but it's just because I want to and still have lots of chatter for you, Honey.

Your other letter #16 came today like I thought and every single one of them makes me lots happier than before.

I'm sure glad you have your watch fixed so it keeps good time. We should have had it done long ago tho, which we know now. Maybe when nice watches are being made you'll get a better one.

Honey, please don't go feeling bad and having cramps any more. I sure don't want things like that happening to my sweet little girl. I'm glad to hear that it didn't last long and you are feeling fine and eager as of last letter.

How is your money doing, Honey? Do you have any left from the payday before or some in the post office? You better tell me where it's going if you are going to need more. How is the doctor and hospital bill doing or being paid for? I wish you would tell me how it's all making out. You can sure have all that's needed so long as we have it but as you know we're not buying that house or the new car very fast.

Guess what I did today, so I will tell you. I went to church today and we had a fine little meeting. With about 10 officers, I think I even learned something, too. Only I wish I could have some more good books on the subject. Maybe I'll get around to reading lots more of them sometime.

I've sure been feeling good and full of energy the last few days. It's nasty to be tied down with only one good foot to run on. I get around but I can't run so good. Anyway the weather is getting like spring here and I guess you know what a wonderful time of year spring is. And maybe you know what kind of energy comes along in the spring to feel so good but lonesome without you. I can remember all the romancing good times we had in the spring, Honey. Do you know that you are the only nice woman I mean to love in the spring or any other time for that matter. I couldn't have found as swell a wife anywhere even if it had taken years, because darling it just had to be you. It's good I found you first too. Don't you think?

"Let me Love You Tonight" and I mean that especially for you, Honey. That's getting very popular these days. I sure would like to be dancing with you at the Coconut Grove this evening. Maybe even we'll go to the Hotel Utah next time and have a big romance and flirt with you. Could I take you home then, and kiss you on the steps and then go tuck you in bed right after you tucked me in bed. Did you want a fireman? Well, here I am, Honey.

Goodnight, Darling,

Dean

Chapter 10

Some Big Sheets of Paper

1 February 1945, India

Dearest little Sweetheart,

Guess now I can write you a nice long letter now that I have some some big sheets of paper and that is good because I sure do have dozens of things to tell you. You are sure making me happy these days with your nice letters. I received a very extra special beautiful Valentine today from my favorite Sweetheart at the same time with the letter too. Thank you, Honey for it, too. I wish I could find a nice Valentine for you, but a big fat letter is about the best I can get. I hope you like it. I think I could tell you dozens of nice things right in your ear right now that would make you even happier than a Valentine.

Honey, maybe I got all excited about the money matters in some of my last letters. I want you to know that every little thing is OK now and I know you are taking very good care of things for us. I am lucky to have such a smart girl taking care of things for me too. So now you can know that I'm not worrying about any little thing anymore and when you are doing what you think is good for us, that is fine with me.

I am still glad, of course, that you put the money in the bank and didn't need it. There will be more going there too. I can send money direct to the bank thru the finance department without it costing me anything so maybe instead of buying money orders, that is what I will do. Will let you know about what goes on so you can keep the little book up to date tho.

And here is a money order for you for $50 as you have probably already seen. If you need it to pay the dentist that would be a good bill to be paid. But if the dentist is paid you can put it in the Post Office.

Do you have any money in the Post Office now? And if you need it for something else, it will be a Valentine present from me to you, Honey. I wish I could be around to buy you lots of nice presents, like I like to do.

Sounds like you are having too nice of weather there, but almost any weather there I would like. Remember the nice kind of weather we had a year ago Christmas and New Years to keep me there with you those extra days? The days have been nice and sunny here and plenty warm so I've been getting some good suntan but no burns. It's fun running around in pajama bottoms all the time too, only today it's real cool and making like rain.

As you have seen, I got out of here on pass for a while today to get paid and get the money order. Sure is nice to have all this money around. Still have quite a bit from last month after sending you the money order and buying $100 bond. Has the bond come yet, Honey? I think you should be getting it about this time.

There are several of the fellows here that were in Clovis. Some you know too, but probably I shouldn't say who. Jackson is at a base near here. I didn't see him but saw someone who did. Maybe I will get to see him some of these days, and I will let you know. Two of the pilots that were at Hobbs too are here, Simpson and Smith. Don't know if you remember or not. Some others that were at Clovis are missing, several that I know.

Honey, I hope you are still feeling fine these days. It's about time (when this gets there) that there will be big excitement at our house, I'll bet. I wish so much that I could be there with you, Honey, but I'll be thinking about you just about all the time and just trying to get home as soon as possible, altho it's a little early to be thinking about that now.

I'll be telling you that you have all my love, Honey, and my prayers with you, Honey, for everything to be going alright. I just hope you don't have to stay in the hospital as long as I have been.

I keep hoping that I'll get out of this cast any day but can't tell just when. Anyhow I want my foot to get back into good walking shape before I go testing it.

Honey, I really am missing you these days and I love you more and more all the time. Maybe we should get married some time soon, I know you would be the most wonderful little wife that I could ever have. Maybe even better than you have been these last almost two years. I guess we'll just have to have about 50 years of honeymoon to catch up on all the wonderful loving we've been missing, but how could we catch up and still be up to date? Do you think we could?

I do know that I wouldn't have a bit of trouble doing you the most possible good right now that would make you the happiest and sleepiest beautiful woman that I ever made love to, and that's only you, Darling.

It just started to rain so I can have wonderful dreams of you tonight, Darling.

Goodnight,

Dean

2 February 1945: Reo Goes to War

At the moment of dawn, lit by the symbolism of the rising sun taking new life, two women took up stations facing each other at the entrance to the home of Reo Kiyoshi. They became frozen, static sentinels, unfazed by the comings and goings of family and friends. Their presence announced that a new warrior would soon join the cause, and commanded all to shower respect and honor on this home.

They wore the uniform of the Japan National Defense Women's Association, a traditional kimono covered by a gray apron and a white sash over their right shoulder announcing their affiliation with the Shitamachi Chapter. They were elegant, stunning in their beauty, perfectly made up, and wearing smiles that would attract any soldier to follow them. They were here to lead Reo and his family and friends to the train station so he could report to the navy flight training and the war.

Yesterday, family and close friends had gathered until the house nearly bulged. What a day it had been. From midday into the late evening, those close to Reo and his parents celebrated and took their pleasure. It was a gathering befitting a samurai. Reo could claim that title only by geneology.

Costumes came out of hiding, unworn for years, to further the reveling—music, food, family speeches, and sake in abundance to honor the young future pilot.

The feast had been grand. Servings of fish, rice, meats, and vegetables that had not sat on a table of the Kiyoshi home since 1938, were there for all to partake of.

Reo had been showered with well wishes. "Be safe."

"We know you will be a good soldier."

"Your service honors us."

The children of the neighborhood were everywhere and caught up in the spirit of celebration. Their lessons in school were preparing them to also take this important step when their age allowed. Military service was not sacrifice, military service was glory. They were the children of a sacred nation, chosen by the gods to lead the world. To help the emperor achieve the goals of the gods was the greatest destiny possible.

Three older uniformed gentlemen approached the address of the Kiyoshis. They were members of the Veteran's Association, their khaki uniforms adorned with medals announcing their service, and their soft caps detailing their unit of service. Their faces were weathered and scarred by war, but there shone in their eyes the pride of unfailing duty and service to the emperor. Their arrival signaled the beginning of the procession to the train station.

3 February 1945, India

Dearest Peach Blossom:

I guess you know I'm sure happy with you about now, as is always the case with me. Your latest nice letter came and the bank envelope too at the same time. And thank you, Honey, even if I am in no hurry to use them now.

One thing I should mention while I am thinking about it, those envelopes could have been sent first class just as well since there is no big hurry. I think all first class mail goes by air across the ocean, so when you have any thing to send besides 'Sugar Reports' just send them regular mail. It may save you a couple of stamps. If you haven't sent the log book yet, first class mail should get it here just about as soon. Just so long as I get your swell letters in a hurry that's what I like, Honey.

I'll bet one of these letters pretty soon catches you in the hospital, Honey, so I guess I'll have to write lots of long nice letters to you to keep you company while you're there. Would that be different from what I've been writing tho?

I got checked out of the hospital today. I guess they got tired of me, or thought I was going nuts because I had entirely too much energy to be kept there. Anyhow I was always running around somewhere, and usually faster than I should so out I went. I still have the cast on tho, and was told I could wear it for two more weeks. It has been making my ankle sore the last couple of days, so maybe I'll do less walking.

Don't know where all the money comes from, maybe it's because I don't spend it here, and that's a good thing too, I guess. Anyhow I sent another $100 to the bank today and bought a $50 war bond. I don't know how long it will take for the money to get to the bank, you can let me know. I sent it thru the finance dept. So it didn't cost anything. If it's too slow tho, I'll be sending it to you to take care of. I might even increase your allotment, Honey, for Junior and you'll have to pay more tithing too, I'll let you know how much. It's sure fun anyhow keeping track of everything.

I'm glad you could find a nice baby buggy. It sure will save a lot of carrying and be nice to have too for other reasons.

Boy, I sure do have more business for you to take care of for us don't we? Anyhow I've been thinking, but still only thinking, of selling the car. You might keep that in mind if anybody asks you. It should be fixed up first anyhow and in a few months it may still be worth about as much as we paid for it. If you get any offers let me know, Honey. Of course it all depends on how soon I get home, or how the chances look and how the war goes. If gas rationing is off before I get back, the car probably will be worth lots more, and it might be a lot more valuable to someone to use than it is sitting around so much. Just let me know what cooks and if anybody offers $700 or more like it is let them have it quick.

Here I go chattering and chattering but I sure do have lots to tell you, Honey, and right now I love you millions and dozens even.

We have a new mess hall here now, it just opened a few days ago. It is quite a bit like Clovis, at least the system. It is an improvement anyhow. Before, we had a squadron mess for the officers and now all the base officers eat there. Lots more company now anyhow.

Oh, I just remembered to tell you the big news, Johnsons are expecting. Seems Hilda wasn't sure for a long time but now, everything's in order. Maybe you can find out everything if you write her.

Maybe I will go to church tomorrow like a good kid, like I did last Sunday. At least I'm a good kid tonight and writing you a nice long letter. Fine Saturday night!!!

Honey, I sure hope you are feeling good these days. Would you like a nice ride in an airplane to hurry things along? I'm still wishing I could be around where you are to keep your morale up just right. You sure did always keep mine good that way. I know that I sure do love you lots these days and I'm thinking about you mostly all the time too. I guess you know that you are my favorite wife these days and my sweetheart too. I'm a lucky guy I guess, that I could make passionate love to you by mail to get married by. I like your love lots closer than mail tho, Honey, and I guess you know how close. So close your nice skin rubs my skin. Oh what I said!! But that's nothing to what you did, you sweet woman. And besides I'd like to be kissing you for hours with the kind of kisses we have been practicing for these years, Honey. I sure am missing your sweet delicious lips to kiss and so many other kissable places that you like too, don't you?

You'd be so nice to cuddle with hours and hours, would you go to sleep in my arms, Honey? I'll bet not for a long time until you had enjoyed and thrilled to some tender and passionate caresses, and gave me all of your wonderful love making and more and more too.

I hope the censors ears burn if he reads this only I don't imagine anyone will.

Anyhow that isn't all I think about you, Darling, but enough to keep you happy, I'll bet.

Peaches, you have all my love and prayers for you to be getting along swell and not have any trouble of any kind.

> Goodnight my dream girl,
>
> Dean

8 February 1945: The End of Matterhorn

The futility of Operation Matterhorn finally came to an end on 8 February 1945, when the 770th flew its last mission out of India and China. The China-Burma-India Theater would continue the war effort, just without the benefit of B-29s. Crews wouldn't miss the Himalayas; of the 1,057 days that Allies were flying the Hump, six hundred planes and a thousand airmen were lost. (Sears)

With new bases in the Mariana Islands, the 58th Heavy Bomber Wing was moving to become part of the newly formed XXI Bomber Command led by General Curtis LeMay, based in Guam.

Ground crews left India 23 February for the five-week transport by ship. The trip reportedly had two high points—navy chow, which was noticeable better than the army fare, and the three-day furlough spent in Australia. Many a soldier lost his heart there, some several times.

India, 9 February 1945

Good morning Honey,

What is new and exciting at your house these days? I bet I could guess at least when this letter gets there.

Everything is fine here, I'm even sitting out in the sunshine writing to you. It's nice and warm, just right in fact. Yesterday three letters came all at once for me from my favorite woman #21, 22, 23. It sure was nice to get all the good news at once. I might even consider letting you be my all time sweetheart if you want.

I wish I could have been at your shower to carry all the things home. Sounds like Junior is all fixed up for a while with that you have been buying. I'm glad you got a baby buggy too, I guess they are just about a necessity for times like these.

I guess you are getting to be my regular business manager, taking care of everything. I'm glad to hear the car has been taken care of and every other little thing.

The insurance shouldn't be due on it for a while, or is it in February? I can't remember that far back. So long as it's taken care of, everything will be fine.

Honey, I see now that you have been taking good care of our money.

And now that you have told me where it goes I'm happy. Guess I'll have to send you some more yet to pay the dentist. Anyhow your payday will be bigger in April. It takes quite a while to get those changes made but now it's done as of April. You will have lots more money. I hope you can put $50 of it away tho. You had better or I'll beat you some more, of course the way you like. Anyway that should keep you all fixed up just right and I'll be saving some more to go on a honeymoon with. I'll bet you will like that too.

The sun got so warm for me so I'm back in my room to continue writing you pages and pages more. If I can think of all the things I want to.

I got a letter from my old buddy Joe. He is still in Italy with something like 68 missions, that was Dec. 15, and he was a Captain too. Boy I feel good, flying the great Superfortress. His missions are not nearly so long as ours, but still he has been busy. He said Dode (his wife) is OK and working, I think.

I guess I don't live right, Honey. Do you think so? Right now I sure do feel sore all over, we had shots (vaccinations) yesterday, four kinds all at once and now me with a sore arm and miserable all over. It's not very bad tho and I'm sure to recover sometime.

I'm getting around good otherwise with my cast still on. It still doesn't bother except just to be a nuisance, and not very nice to sleep with. It is supposed to come off next week so when you get this, I'll be running around good as new. I sure am getting eager to go fly again. Not to war of course, but just to be flying again.

Honey, I sure would like to be there enjoying some of your nice snow. Might even throw snowballs at you. But would lots rather be enjoying some of you, lots and lots in fact, and I know I would. I wish I could be around to take care of you when you need lots of taking care of. Here, you are having all the trouble getting us a family and I'm just waiting for it to happen. I still am praying for you, Honey, and you have all my love to be with you.

I'm still all in love with you, Honey, and like every wonderful thing about you.

Let's get married, Honey, when I come back to see you.

Goodbye you sweet Peach Blossom,

Dean

10 February 1945: Gold Turns to Silver

On 10 February 1945, 2nd Lt. Dean Harold Sherman became 1st Lt. Dean Harold Sherman. It wasn't a normal military promotion ceremony. Dean was still serving time in the Piardoba base hospital, trying to get a broken foot to heal. He was notified by orders issued by XXI Bomber Command, and with the orders were a set of silver bars to replace the gold bars worn by 2nd lieutenants.

Airplane commanders were supposed to be of the rank of captain or higher. Young officers like Dean, moving up through the ranks, needed time in-grade to meet ranking requirements. Dean had completed the time in-grade for 1st lieutenants on 6 February. He had been promoted to airplane commander status on 8 October 1944.

The difference between First Luey and 2nd Luey was a big deal. Second Lueys were at the bottom of the officer pecking order, and vulnerable to the whims of superior officers. Nowhere was it more obvious than for new arrivals in India and the Marianas. Second lieutenants, flying new B-29s, proud as could be of their brand-new flying machines, were immediately called into headquarters when they arrived from the States and relieved of their new B-29 by an officer of superior rank. The new young pilots were given the privilege of flying the squadron junkers.

Each squadron carried more crews than planes. That allowed planes to stay in the air when crews needed to rest. It also created a pecking order that allowed the highest-ranking officers to pick the plane they wanted to be flying.

It didn't hurt one bit that the change in rank included a significant raise in pay for Dean and Connie. They would spend quite a few letters figuring out what to do with their new income.

Honoring the efforts to not give any information that would benefit the enemy, Dean conveyed to Connie his promotion with the phrase "Gold Turned to Silver."

16 February 1945, India

Good Morning, Peaches,

I sure am doing good today and I sure hope you are too, Honey. I'll be walking the floor for you every night like I did last night for you. Does it help?

I'm highly impatient now because I think maybe I'll get my cast off today and I'm really eager to find out. I'll let you know too, but I'll hurry and write you this letter for now.

The log book came in just about airmail time, Honey, and thank you very much. It's big enough too and will keep track of plenty of hours.

And guess what else, a swell box of candy came from my favorite woman yesterday. It was in really fine shape too, not mashed a bit. The chocolates are perfect and my favorite kind, Honey. The Seafoam ran together a little bit which was probably from the heat but it sure does taste good. Most everybody liked it too, except they didn't get much, I'm saving it a bit.

I have a big package ready to send to you, which I'll get off today. There are lots of things in it which you'll see, mostly things of mine tho. My blouse is in it which the rats chewed up. If you can take it to a tailor's to see if it can be fixed I'd appreciate it, but I'll probably get a new one when I get back. There are some coins, two rings and my coon skin hat I got in China and some chop sticks and another pillow case, which is for my mother.

Honey, you can have the bracelet and beads and I'll consider the star as a sapphire ring, but not just yet, but you can look at it. It's pretty. But mainly the bracelet is a present from me to you, Honey, for some of my love for you which I sure do lots.

I have the money situation straightened out now too. Our tithing will be $41.70 and Junior won't get us any more, I found out, but still that's a lot.

Oh, I must tell you tho "Gold Turned to Silver." Peaches, I sure do love you lots these days, in fact you are my favorite Sweetheart all this week.

Tell me all what's new!! All my love and kisses,

Dean

18 February 1945: A Son Is Born

Except for a new presidential decree, Marvin Sherman would have spent his life celebrating his birthday on 17 February. During World War II, President Roosevelt declared what was called "War Time." Observed year-round, it was an effort to "save daylight" and provide standard time across the United States. Marvin entered the world at 12:05 a.m. "War Time," on 18 February 1945. Before or after the war he would have been born at 11:05 p.m. on the 17th. Marv could then rightfully claim that President Roosevelt cost him a day of his life.

Connie had started "nesting" a week earlier. Baby clothes were folded and refolded, organized and reorganized. Her bedroom furniture was arranged and rearranged.

Her energy returned, and the burdens of her pregnancy felt suspended for the final days. Momma and Mammy, veterans of childbirth, recognized her nesting behaviors and let Connie know that the time was close. Of course, the calendar and the doctor indicated the same, but the feelings her body was generating assured her as nothing else could.

Contractions had been part of her life for a month. They felt like muscles getting exercised for the big event. On the morning of the 17th, the contractions didn't feel like practice any more. When her water broke at noon, the car drove out of the driveway, destination—hospital.

The hospital was full of doctors and nurses who knew what to do, so nineteen-year-old Connie was in good hands. She had never done this, but they did it every day, sometimes many times a day. Of course, the contractions receded after arriving at the hospital, like Marvin had changed his mind about entering the world.

That signaled a walking caravan. Connie, Momma, and Mammy occupied the hall of the hospital, walking from the front of the maternity ward to the opposite end of the hospital. To help pass the time, much conversation was made about the coming child's name. It was up for discussion. Dean had made his preferences known, and Connie had several favorites, but she wanted to see the baby before she made a choice.

On their twelfth lap, the maternity ward doors flew open and two nurses announced, "We are ready for you, Mrs. Sherman," and escorted Connie away.

A mere twelve hours later, near 4 a.m., Connie, mounted on a gurney, came out of the doors with a small baby, Marvin Carl Sherman, wrapped in a blue blanket and wearing a blue knit stocking cap.

Momma waited for the Western Union office to open at six a.m. and sent Dean word that he had a fine son.

Completely unaware of the events in Salt Lake City this day, Dean composed the following letter:

18 February 1945, India

Good Evening Peaches:

Hello sweet girl, I sure have been thinking of you lots these days and wishing so much that I could be around to take care of you, and be holding your nice soft hands and giving you lots of moral support, and see your pretty face and look in your eyes and without saying a word, tell you millions of wonderful things that you mean to me. You do too, Honey, mean so many wonderful things to me. All the wonderful things a beautiful girl can be and my best companion ever, along with being the sweetest wife any guy ever could love. Those are just a few of the things, Darling, which make me love you more every day.

Whenever I hear nice soft music, I think of you. And when the sun comes up so bright and fresh in the morning, I'm reminded of you. When I take a short walk in the moonlight I have the pleasantest memories of you and all the wonderful times we have spent together. Darling, those things mean all the world to me, and I keep thinking of the something new that has been added to us, and the blessings that have been ours continuously all being added up to make the future all ahead of us better to live for and more to be desired. I guess you know from these things that I am ever so glad I married you, altho it never could have been any different because we were just meant for each other. All the incidents and happenings that brought us together, tho they may seem like accidents, seem to me to have just been part of a plan that's been so plain that we just couldn't see it. I just keep getting more and more in love with you all the time too, Honey.

I got out of my cast the other day when I told you I was going to try. I even walk good too. Of course I had to take it easy for a few days, and my foot is a little weak after not using it for over a month, but it hasn't hurt a bit and now I'm doing almost good as new. With a few more days of taking it easy I'll be back working again and happy at it too.

I think I forgot to tell you, but in the package there is an ivory doll. That is for us to keep, Honey. Of course you can put it on the piano if you think it's safe but it will be in our house some day and you can keep it for that.

This package may be a little slower coming than the last but you can see, and let me know when it gets there. Maybe sometime you can send the pillow slip to my mother's but no hurry cause I may have some more things before too long, I hope.

We are still having fun once in a while making ourselves ice cream. We have a freezer and can still buy an ice cream mix and when we can get ice we have a big time and crank out some ice cream. It's good too, but the powdered mix isn't to compare with the home made variety. We have fun making it anyhow. We have it figured out now so it only takes about a half hour to freeze.

I hope I can get flying pretty soon. I'm eager to get the L-5 and get me some more flying time. This setting on the ground so long doesn't make me happy at all, but as I said, I imagine I'll be working again in a few days.

I'm sure eager to hear the big news from your house, Honey, and I want you to know that I'm happy with you and what we did and I love you for it too, Darling. You will always be my favorite sweetheart, Honey, because I love you ever so much and will be dreaming of all your wonderful charms until I can show you just what I mean.

Goodnight Peach Blossom,

Dean

Chapter 11

Getting Eager

India, 20 February 1945

My Dearest Peaches:

I sure was happy this evening when I received two wonderful letters from you. They always make me happy, Honey and I'm glad you like what I write you. I always have hundreds of things to tell you, only hope I don't have to put too much of it on paper. I guess you know I'd much rather be telling you personally.

I'm sure getting eager to hear all the news from your house. I'll bet it's all good too. I guess I thought too late that you could have let the Red Cross let me know what is cooking much quicker than you could send a cable. They have a good system that way and if there is ever anything that you want me to know in a hurry that would be a good way.

I want you to know that I'm feeling good these days, in fact I have just too much energy for my own good.

I'm back in the hospital but it's nothing very bad. It's still the same thing. I did get my cast off like I told you and walked around good for a couple of days. I had an x-ray taken when the cast was removed only it took about 4 days before the doc looked at it good. The bone was in place OK but it hadn't healed much. There is still a separation in the fracture so now I'm back. I have another cast on now.

Walking on it didn't break it loose again but they are going to move me to another hospital so now, I don't know what's cookin'. I don't want you to worry. The only thing is that I'm wasting a lot of time. Anyhow something good might happen yet and I'm thinking about that. It will be a few days before I leave here for the other hospital so I'll be writing you more before then.

The dateline on that clipping I sent you about the tiger wasn't any where near here, I don't think. I was just letting you know about the tiger. There aren't any right close, so far as I know.

I have been listening to lots of beautiful music this evening, lots of beautiful popular and classical pieces. It's sure nice, like music from home.

Honey, I would like for you to be nursing me. That sweet loving care you could give me would be just what I need and like too. I'll bet you sure would be a fresh nurse but with you, I would like that. Maybe lots of your good food and fresh milk would do me lots of good too.

Maybe even some of your good milk shakes would do me good too, but what would Junior do? Honey, I sure would like to be making nice love to you now and always, and I will too before too long, I bet.

For now, I'll say goodnight to you Peaches, you wonderful sweet little girl that I love millions.

Dean

24 February 1945: The Cable

Dean Sherman was hunkered down in the far corner of the balcony of the Piardoba field hospital day room, bent over letters received and empty paper waiting for his written words. He was composing for Connie with an intimacy like she was across the desk from him. The commotion below him did not penetrate his world.

"Cable for Lt. Dean Sherman," called the courier, making his way through the obstacle course of healing men populating the day room.

"Sherman, I think that guy is looking for you," offered the only other occupant of the balcony landing.

Dean jolted out of his concentration. He was on cable watch and had been expecting big news for days. "Up here, up here," he stammered, beyond hearing for the courier.

"Cable for Lt. Dean Sherman."

Another futile "Up here," and Dean moved toward the object of his expectations as quickly as a man with a broken foot and cast could manage. He had seen enough cables delivered in the hospital to know where to intercept the courier on his return lap.

Encumbered as he was, he still missed him.

"I'm Sherman," he hollered to the back of the courier. "I'm a new dad, you know."

"Congratulations, sir. Please sign here, sir." Of course the courier had not known he was a father, but was happy for Dean nonetheless. His mission accomplished, the messenger disappeared among the sick and wounded to deliver his next message.

Dean was left to wrestle with the envelope. He tried to open it, but in his excitement, his fingers didn't work very well.

My kid is going to have his first birthday before I get this open!

> **TO: LT. DEAN SHERMAN**
> **MESSAGE: YOU HAVE A SON, MARVIN CARL**
> **SHERMAN. DON'T WORRY, MOTHER AND**
> **CHILD IN GOOD HEALTH. ALL IS WELL.**
> **SIGNED: MOMMA**

His eyes searched the sparse message for more information.

What day was he born?

How much did he weigh?

Just what does "all is well" mean?

There was nothing more to know, no matter how many times he re-read the Western Union message.

"You have a son, Marvin Carl Sherman." *What happened to Larry Max?* "Don't worry, Mother and child in good health. All is well."

The emotions that go through a first-time father surged through Dean's being. Gratitude, and some newly minted instinctive emotions that only fathers know, rose up out of his gut and manifested as tears.

But, but... Dean sniffled, joyous but unsettled; he knew far less than he wanted to know about this new son.

Misjudging the delivery speed of Western Union, when he wrote to Connie he assumed the birth had been the day before he received the cable.

25 February 1945, India

My Dearest Peach Blossom:

I heard about all the big excitement at your house, last night, Honey. I received the cable your mother sent. It didn't have any date on it tho so I'm still waiting for your latest letters. Darling Connie, I want you to know that I am the happiest guy anywhere and I love you because you are the most wonderful wife I could ever know.

I just hope and pray that you are getting along just right and are happy too, these days. Thank you for a boy, Honey. I guess you know we are the luckiest people and I know it too.

I wish so much that I could see you right now and help out your morale. I know that would sure do me lots of good and I'll bet you too.

I do hope so much that you didn't have too much trouble, Honey, and wish there could be some way I could help.

I will be writing you dozens of nice letters to keep you company tho until I can come chatter with you. I don't want you to be worrying about writing any letters when you don't feel so good because I know that you will have lots more to do than I have these days.

I wasn't worried about you, even if I was thinking of you all the time, until you mother sent the cable and said not to worry. Now that's just what I am doing until I hear something more.

I'm still here in the hospital but will move to another one tomorrow. I'll have another address then but until you get it, this one will be forwarded OK. I'm not having a bit of trouble except walking on this cast still and getting powerful eager to fly.

I'll let this short letter do for now, Darling, and write you lots more right soon now. I love you Honey, more and more everyday, and you'll see just what I mean, maybe when we go parking at Yellowstone sometime.

> All my love and kisses,
>
> Dean

27 Feb 1945: Senninbari

Kigi Kiyoshi slipped out of her home into a fog driven up the Simuda River delta by onshore flow via Tokyo Bay, a game Mother Nature played when the sun left the sky in the Land of the Rising Sun. The vapors erased the landscape except for the edges of her path. Knowing well enough the course of her journey, landmarks that morning were not necessary.

This day, designated by the calendar, was set apart for distributing rationed commodities by the Community Council. She would be overseeing the process. Her council would be giving to the Neighborhood Associations what would in turn be given to nearly three thousand families, food that would be dinner in the days ahead. But that would happen later. Now she could work on Reo's *senninbari*.

The urgency of finishing the senninbari weighed heavily on her. She had but weeks until he finished his flight training and she was only halfway to one thousand stitches. Her responsibilities would keep her long after dark, but now she had precious time to seek others to add a stitch of protection for her son.

The shrine was already bustling with many starting their day in darkness. Some came to worship or for the honoring of ancestors, but the vast majority of this reverent mass were there for stitching—gathering stitches of protection, protection that could be obtained no other way. Mothers, wives, and daughters gathered stitches of protection for their loved ones.

The magic of the senninbari comes from the freely given sewing of one thousand well-wishers, one thousand women aware of what a mother or wife or daughter sacrifices when their loved one answers the call of the war. The weight of this vast collection of empathy and goodwill causes a gravity that pulls protection to surround the wearer, shielding him from harm.

She had chosen a six-inch by thirty-six-inch white cotton cloth and red stitching for her gift of protection to her oldest son. The ends were to be adorned with six-inch strands of a chord tied in the knots associated with safety and courage. The center of the scarf depicted a prowling tiger, a use of symbolism encouraging his safe return to his family. Just as tigers wander far from home but return safely, it was hoped Reo would also.

Each woman that approached Kigi to add but one stitch asked graciously about her son, thanking her for her gift to the emperor, and leaving their most heartfelt well-wishes for his safe return. All were grateful for the blessing of sharing their loved one with the emperor for the benefit of their sacred land.

28 February 1945, India

Dearest Peaches,

Good morning, Honey, here's to let you know that my thoughts are with you still as always, and hoping you are well and happy. Seems like you should probably be home now with M.C. Altho I haven't had any letters as yet since February 5.

I am at another hospital now which you probably see from the address and it is in Calcutta. I have been hoping I could find out something to tell you but so far nothing has been done altho the Doc said that they would get around to give me some attention today. My foot still hasn't bothered any and I'm expecting I might go back to work pretty soon. This is a little early tho to be saying anything for sure.

This all seems kind of silly to me the way these medics are doing but best I relax and wait to find out something for sure. I know I don't feel like anything is wrong with me. If they keep me around much longer, I'll be getting sick in the head.

Here it is nearly March already and I'm wondering where the time goes. It sure has been flying by for me for some reason and I hope it continues that way.

It would be payday today but since I didn't do any flying I won't have much coming and don't need it anyhow. Your payday will come along OK anyhow, Honey.

I just can't quite realize that we have a boy now, Darling. Of course I believe it but it doesn't quite seem real. I'll sure be glad when I can see you and Marvin Carl.

That is the right name isn't it, Honey?

Haven't seen much of the city yet but from here can see lots of palm trees and other kinds of pretty ones too. And a small lake, and even green grass. The Indians are really an arrogant and independent lot of characters. I'll tell you more some time.

Now I'll tell you that I love you, Darling, more than I can put into words, and when you're taking good care of Marvin Carl give him my love too. Goodbye for now, Darling.

Love and kisses,

Dean

2 March 1945, Calcutta, India

My Dearest Sweetheart:

Just thinking of you as usual tonight, Honey, and wish so much that I could be with you and tell you the hundred things I would like to tonight. I'm thinking what a wonderful wife you are and I'm a lucky guy for having you. Darling, you are my inspiration for things good and my pleasantest thoughts all the time. I keep hoping everything is all right where you are these days, and want you to know that you always have all my love to be with you.

So far no mail has caught up with me since I moved, but it should be coming soon now, maybe tomorrow. I'm sure curious to hear all about Junior and every little detail. So far nothing but the telegram which came February 24.

Honey, I do hope so much that everything is all right with you and you are recovering in a hurry and feeling fine these days. Is Marvin Carl as good looking a baby as I think he should be? If he takes after you, Darling, there could be none nicer. Maybe if he is like me when I was his size he's fine too. My mother used to say I was the prettiest baby she had, but as you can plainly see, I have long out grown that.

How do you like this kind of chatter, Honey? It is nearly as fast as the other way and besides I have plenty of time as well as lots of chatter for you this evening.

Boy do I get around! From bad to worse tho, it seems. Today again I have another cast on my foot. It doesn't have a walker on it either so I'm well tied down. I wish I had you to nurse me, or me to nurse you. Any how I'll probably get a walker put on tomorrow I hope so I can get around again. The doctor got around to looking at the last x-ray but I still can't find out much. He said it wasn't healing much, altho it is in place and doesn't hurt even when I walked on it without the cast. Boy I wish I knew what was going on around here. I'm getting powerful tired of doing nothing, I don't mind saying. Don't have any idea yet how long I'll have to wear this cast but when I can walk on it the time will go a lot faster and might be able to see some of the town.

Would very much like to do a little shopping while I am here, I think I could find a lot of nice things for you, Honey. I sure would like to try, because I guess you know I like to buy nice things for you.

Honey I'm sure glad I married you when I did. I'll be ever so glad when we can play like married kids again and I can make lots of love to you, Honey, like we like. I sure have lots of what you like too, and all of you. Sweet woman is what I love forever and ever.

I'll dream of you, Sweetheart,

Dean

3 March 1945: Enter Curtis LeMay

"This outfit has been getting a lot of publicity without having really accomplished a hell-of-a-lot in bombing results," General Curtis E. LeMay said on his arrival to command the XX Air Corps. He had directed bomber command in Europe and built a sterling reputation. He would make sure the the outfit started getting results.

Changes were dictated by results. High-altitude, daylight, precision bombardment raids against critical industrial nodes just did not bring the desired results. LeMay was about to switch to low-altitude, day or night, incendiary attacks against Japanese urban areas.

Several factors made this new strategy work. The land mass and the topography of Japan mandated that manufacturing be concentrated into about a dozen cities, half of which produced two-thirds of the industrial output. Housing was concentrated around manufacturing centers and so tightly placed that roof areas approached 50 percent of ground area.

Supporters of the change (and propagandists) argued that the Japanese defense industry was partially a cottage industry. While large assembly plants existed, some parts (justifiers said up to 90 percent) were created in homes and shops throughout the residential areas surrounding the plant. While strategists originally rejected the idea of bombing civilian populations in favor of "industrial nodes," it was argued the civilian populations, by way of the cottage-nature of their manufacturing, *were* the industrial nodes.

The notion of the existence of an extensive cottage industry was debunked after the war. It simply did not exist. But justification was needed, justification for the inhumanity of it, political rhetoric that almost made firebombing people with napalm seem necessary.

A more honest assessment, pragmatic, if inhumane, built the case for bombing urban areas because workers were a raw material of the war industries. These workers were concentrated in Japan's six most-populated cities—Tokyo, Osaka, Yokohama, Kawasaki, Nagoya, and Kobe. It was estimated that destroying 70 percent of the housing and their inhabitants in these cities would decrease Japan's industrial output by 15 percent, a cold, hard fact of war. The results for the Japanese would create infernos that burned not only homes and shops, but also their citizens.

Japanese cities were especially vulnerable to firebombing. Captain Thomas D. White of the Air Corps Tactical School noted: "Large sections of Japanese cities are built of flimsy and highly-flammable materials. The earthquake disaster of 1924 bears witness to the fearful destruction that may be inflicted by incendiary bombs."

Even Japanese Admiral Isoruku Yamamoto had pointed out this vulnerability. "Cities made of wood and paper would burn easily. The army talks big, but if war comes and there were large-scale air-raids, there is no telling what would happen." (Gorman)

While Tokyo's fire departments were among Japan's best, they were not ready for what would be falling out of the sky upon them. Departments were not integrated, and narrow, ambling streets contributed to the problems. Some provisions were made for fire protection by neighborhood fire committees that placed many large containers of water for fire suppression within the neighborhoods. However, their fire suppression tactics involved oversize squirt guns and bucket brigades.

In the end it became a no-brainer for LeMay. High-altitude pinpoint bombing was not working. The war-material-producing industries and workers were clearly interspersed within the civilian population and the cities were highly susceptible to fire. He did recognize the implications of his orders, saying, "If we lose the war, we will be tried as war criminals." (Gorman)

The conversion to incendiary bombing for the crews that flew the B-29s was a game changer. Although Japanese homeland defenses at this point in the war were nominal, the change in strategy put the crews in harm's way. They no longer had the strategic advantage of flying at elevations beyond the capabilities of the defenders.

It also introduced the reality of moral dilemma to flight crews. Vernon Garner, B-29 pilot, said, "Of course we thought about the civilians, but we were hoping and praying and wishing that they would surrender and save their lives and our lives. But they started it at Pearl Harbor, so we had to keep it going. We were told to put it out of our minds, that we were doing a job, a nasty job, a job that we didn't like to do, but a job that we were called to do, sworn to do."

Ground fortifications for the Japanese homeland were never really in the game plan. The war they envisioned would happen far off, a naval war, quite limited in nature, a war that allowed them to control the natural resources they had captured. The defense plan was based on the safety of their remote island location and nature's cloud cover of protection. For a while, that strategy worked well. In the beginning, there were no bombers that could reach the homeland. Doolittle's raid in 1942, while an incredible morale boost for America, was a mere twenty-second mosquito annoyance, not a real sustainable threat.

Clouds were Mother Nature's contribution to the war and not a bomber's friend. Time and again, clouds erased possible "bombing days" over Japan, no matter what location raids originated from.

Fighter planes and pilots for home defense were a luxury the

Japanese could not afford. They were losing talented pilots in combat faster than replacements could be trained. The job fell to pilots of inexperience, flying gimpy planes that probably should not have been in the air. Add to that, if their assignment was to stop B-29s, they were being asked to do an impossible job.

The kamikaze approach was taken frequently, without good alternatives within the poorly prepared pilot's skill set. Flying into the attacking Superfortresses downed at least one plane. Kamikaze planes were stripped of weapons and non-essentials (even landing gear on some) to make them fly faster.

Special Attack Units were formed to train *soldiers of the divine wind*. While many of the kamikaze were intended for use against naval forces, they were also employed as part of the defense against B-29s. Soldiers were taught to not waste their lives; if conditions did not allow for success they were to return for a new assignment. There was, however a limit to this instruction. One fellow returned nine times without finding a suitable target. He was shot before he could be assigned a tenth mission.

At one point, LeMay wanted to up the payload of incendiary bombs by removing the gunnery from the B-29s. Crews pushed back. They didn't feel that expendable and the experiment ended quickly.

One fault with the gunnery was that flying in large sorties of hundreds of B-29s, in low-altitude formations engulfed in clouds, resulted in "friendly fire" incidents. A .50 caliber bullet leaves a rather distinctive hole, and the only fifties in the air were mounted on Superforts. There wasn't much doubt about cause on returning damaged ships with holes only fifties could inflict. No one felt the need to help the enemy out in that way.

All of these factors, and as we shall see, many others, led to the results of our story. A contorted collaboration of strategy, machines, egos, weather, and reactions to war, put Lt. Dean Sherman and his crew over Nagoya, Japan, as part of a low-flying bombing formation on 14 May 1945. He was flying an airplane very susceptible to engine fires. It did not end well for him.

4 March 1945, Calcutta, India

Good Evening Sweet Woman,

I'll have you know that I received two of your wonderful letters today and that is why I'm extra special happy right now. I'm glad that some mail is getting here since I moved too, so maybe I'll hear all about Marvin Carl one of these days soon. I guess he will be almost a whole month old by the time you get this and I'll very likely hear all of the details before then.

Honey, your perfume smells like a strange woman, that maybe I knew once and had an exciting affair with and I guess you know (knowing me) that that is pretty nice and exciting. I sure do like it because it is just like I would like for you to smell. And I guess you know what it will do to me, when there is a real live sweet woman wearing it and she is in my arms and willing. It reminds me of you, Honey, and I have lots of exciting thoughts about you, too.

Here it is another beautiful Sunday and me doing practically nothing about it. Of course this new cast I have on isn't made for walking yet, but it's a couple of days overdue and so tomorrow I'll get it fixed.

Seems like this should be a very good day there for blessing babies since this should be fast Sunday. Be sure and tell me what goes on around there along those lines, Honey. Maybe it is a little early but if baby didn't come the right month we have some other things taken care of in the right month.

When we start thinking about a next time, we'll make sure of the right month if it still matters.

Come oil my back, Honey, and see the good suntan I have. It's one of the best, of course I have only a couple hours a day to keep it in shape when I take the bother. It isn't much bother because I just go out the door to the sun porch and as I am on the third floor which is the top floor, it is very convenient. The view looks a lot like LA with palm trees and grass and stucco buildings in this section.

Do you have any of the War Bonds yet? Seems like two should be there by now. I still have the receipts anyhow. I'm glad to hear you have the money situation well in hand. I guess there are lots of bills about this time to take care of. I think you are a smart woman to be keeping things under control anyhow, Honey.

You are the sweetest most beautiful woman who ever made love to me. I'm lucky to have you, Darling, all mine forever to plan for, and think about, and when we are together to do all the things we have to accomplish together in a lifetime. I know it will always be a pleasure when we are always on our honeymoon together. It will be lots of fun thinking about and building our house too, Honey.

All my love and kisses,

Dean

7 March 1945, Calcutta, India

Good Morning Peaches,

Have some more of your swell letters to answer so here's a try. The birthday card came too and thank you, Honey. I liked the verse and it seemed to say a lot in a few words. I have your letters up to Feb. 15. They were forwarded from the 11th.

I'm getting powerful eager to hear just when Marvin Carl arrived, but see it must be 15th or 16th. I would like to know how much he weighed too, but imagine I'll find out in a couple of days when some more letters get here.

I hope you are feeling fine today, Honey, like I am. I'm quite happy since I've been reading your letters and love you always all day today and that will still be up to date when you read this.

The doctor said today that I could wear this cast for three weeks which makes til about 23 of March. I don't know what will happen but maybe I'll get to fly again. I think I would like that lots, at least I'm in the mood now and am just about every day.

The cast is fixed now so I can walk on it and that makes me happy because I don't have to use crutches any more.

I think I would even like to ride a bicycle right now so you see I'm full of energy and eager.

I would like to be eager with you these days, Honey, because I love you more and more. Let's go riding and park in a nice secluded spot. I'll bring my air mattress to keep the cold ground and sticks from interfering with our work.

Be good to Junior, Honey, and tell me what's doing. All my love for the sweetest wife in the world and our son.

Dean

Chapter 12

The Ice Breaker

It might have been better for me to die quickly than to see such a terrible thing. If the people up there in the B-29s were really human beings like us, I'd have liked to drag them out of their planes and make them witness it too.

—Kokomo Tekkie

THE CLOSING HOURS of 9 March came, in Tokyo, with a penetrating, raw cold that sank into the lowlands of the Shitamachi district, expedited by a raging north wind of Siberian origins.

Riku's jacket was no match for the elements, and he shivered his way to complete his chores as daylight was giving out. An aching in his hands and fingers from the frigid wind made them reluctant to help.

The neighborhood streets surrounding him were empty, and except for the rumbling of the wind, quiet. Curfew hour was close, and the frozen, relentless wind had enforced its observance and emptied the streets. It was Friday, normally a time of preparation for Shitamachi's market day.

Saturday was the day the artisans and craftsmen that inhabit the neighborhood made their living as the rest of Tokyo came searching through their wares. The streets should still be bustling with preparations right up until the edge of curfew tonight, but many had left final preparations for early in the morning in hopes of promised better weather.

Riku was still on the streets because he was the neighborhood "ice buster." He carried a small bag with a pick, a meager assortment of hammers, and a hatchet. He was charged with keeping the neighborhood fire-defense water reservoirs ice-free, so that their contents would be readily available to the home defenders' waterguns and fire brigade buckets.

This ice was decidedly thicker that night; his pointed miner's pick did not faze it, leaving only a small white scar around the pick's imprint. Raising up the two-pound hammer, Riku smashed the frozen lid, using every muscle a twelve-year-old can muster to induce cracks. Two more enthusiastic swings ruptured the frozen membrane, reducing it to bobbing chunks and then he easily evacuated the ice from the barrel.

Job done.

He maintained ten of the reservoirs. His Neighborhood Fire Captain father frequently reminded him it was a great honor to be asked at such a young age to provide such an important service. Riku stared at his throbbing hands, opening and closing his fingers as if to see if they were still working. All in all, right now, on this surreal night, they did not feel very honored.

Last barrel done, Riku surged with relief, put the wind at his back and bounded effortlessly down the street, accepting for a moment that while he traveled in this direction, the wind could be his ally.

The Kyoshi family now lived in the dark. Mandatory blackouts were in place to save electricity and to hide the cities of Japan from the enemy.

As Riku attacked his front door open, only the dim light of a few strategic candles, replacement lighting, outlined the contents of his home.

The boy did not bother to shed his jacket, for there was no coal for heating, only enough to cook the meager plate of boiled kidney beans and small rice ball his mother set before him.

"Hurry and finish eating and climb into bed. It will be warmer there," his mother advised.

"Finish eating" never took long these days; there just wasn't much to eat. The rationing started in late 1940s, sugar first, and then rice. By 1942, food in general was under some sort of rationing and in short supply. Kigi helped supervise the distribution of rationed items and was keenly aware of the shortages and the suffering of citizens.

"It is our part to do for the war effort," she would explain to Riku, a principle he embraced much more easily on a full stomach than when he went hungry.

Tonight, he dutifully followed her instructions, as he always did, and slid into bed fully clothed. His cold bed was not an immediate warming sanctuary. Riku pulled his covers over his head, curled into a ball, and slipped his hands between his thighs in search of warmth as his body shivered. The wind was pounding the side of their house and the noise of things that shouldn't be flying about colliding with the house kept startling him, making sleep slow in coming.

Meanwhile in Guam

Six flying-hours south of the shivering Riku, 334 B-29s were lining up on runways on Saipan, Tinian, and Guam, destination: the Shitamachi urban area of Tokyo.

Destination, Riku's home.

Air Corps General Curtis LeMay briefed pilots, bragging that they were going "to deliver the biggest firecracker the Japanese had ever seen." The firecracker was built using two thousand tons of incendiary bombs, two thousand tons of fire. (Craven)

The wind that blew through Riku's jacket would be tailor-made for the bombers, blowing away smoke and debris, giving their bombardiers clear view of the urban landscape below. It also aided the resultant inferno by acting as a giant bellows that forced air into the waiting mouth of the flames. Tightly built buildings of wood and paper burn very well when gasoline is poured on them, especially when the combustion is force-fed the life-enhancing element of oxygen.

This attack would mark a change in America's bombing strategy. Bombing raids had begun about six months before. They were occasional in the beginning, but when Iwo Jima fell in late February, they began to be most regular. The raids had been focused on military targets, airplane factories, or strategic inventory (oil tanks and such), attacks that the Allied Army labelled as strategic bombing.

Daytime raids, conducted at 30,000 feet, avoided urban areas. They also didn't produce much in the way of results. A 500-pounder dropped from five or six miles up, aimed at a well-defined target would ride the jet stream winds to unintended destinations. Napalm, on the other hand, dropped over a broad urban target, from 12,000 feet, could not help but hit something and start a fire that probably would also burn something else. This was a perfect outcome, in a general's mind.

The cruel reality was that civilian workers were just like aluminum or rubber, or TNT, an ingredient in the creation of the armaments of war. Reduce any one of the ingredients and Japan's war effort would be hampered. Strategic bombing of military targets was not destroying the Japanese war machine fast enough. When the generals learned they could "disrupt" the workforce by dropping firebombs on their homes urban areas became the target of choice for B-29s.

The Japanese were unprepared for this change in strategy. They had no expectations of nighttime firebombing raids on nonmilitary targets. The B-29s would meet no fighter resistance, and ground defenses, although heavy at times, were antiquated and inaccurate and thereby virtually ineffective. This war wasn't supposed to come to Japan's shores. No one in Japan saw the need of upgrading and modernizing anti aircraft defenses. The Pacific Ocean *was* their anti-aircraft defense.

The inhumanity of the attack stunned honorable Japanese warriors. This apparently indiscriminate bombing of innocent, peaceable, urban, civilian sites that might or might not surround military sites was inconceivable within the bushido moral code.

Major Ito would plead at his Yokohama War Crimes trial that public opinion of the Japanese people "was too bitter to put into words." Most had lost family or friends to the *Birds from Hell,* and they did not hide their loathing. They considered the airmen that inhabited the birds as *kichiku bei-ei,* "the demonic beasts." (Yokohama)

B-29ers who had the unfortunate opportunity to interact with Japanese citizens outside of their airplanes after crash landing, felt the brunt of it.

And in Calcutta

Lt. Dean Happy Sherman was prisoner of a hospital bed in Calcutta, India, considering the question, "Can boredom be fatal?"

On his right foot was a cast that would not go away. His appendage with a small broken bone, proved to not be good at knitting. He had been in one hospital or another since 12 January, mobile enough to hobble around, but not well enough to drop the cast and be returned to service.

And where would that be anyway? *Stars and Stripes* was full of reporting about the Mariana Islands, a mere six hours' flying time from the Japanese Islands. Now that Iwo Jima had fallen into Allied hands, it felt like the big push was on. It was only a matter of time until every B-29 at the army's disposal would be flying out of the Marianas, not Dean's current posting of India and China.

Any gathering of GIs created scuttlebutt, it was automatic, but a hospital full of servicemen, with nothing to do but lie around and work on healing, had to be the most fertile land anywhere for creating scuttlebutt. Dean's temporary home was no different; rumors flew among the grounded airmen.

The war will be over in a month.

MacArthur has already secretly landed on Okinawa.

Yesterday, Japanese farmers went on strike.

The Hellbirds and all other B-29s have already left India for Guam.

There was no end to it. Rumor upon rumor, many defied logic but were gobbled up and accepted as truth by a hospital full of men with time on their hands, time and an oversized desire for it to all be over so they could go home.

There were nuggets of fact amidst the fabrications. Generals were finally giving up on the CBI Operation Matterhorn, a noble effort, but killed by logistics. The last combat mission of the 770th was 8

February. Still, there were far more unknowns than knowns in the wards of healing.

Dean had his own unknowns. He was a father, this he knew, but precious little else. The eighteen-word cable he'd received announced Marvin Carl Sherman's birth, but he wondered *When was the baby born? How much did he weigh? How is Connie doing?* These were still mysteries to him and the army mail system was of no help solving them.

9 March 1945

My Dearest Sweetheart:

Your swell 'Sugar Report' of 16 Feb. came today and now I'm more curious than ever to know just when Junior arrived. Maybe the cable I got made better time than I expected. Of course, I should be knowing by now except the letters are delayed because they have to be forwarded, but it seems like it has to be in the next letter.

Darling, I am still hoping you are doing fine and feeling good and mean again about now. I know I sure do love you Sweet gal and miss you more than than I should say.

I have hours of chatter for you this evening, that is why I'm writing a bit smaller than usual, but I imagine you can read it all.

I'm still doing fine these days, running around (just around the hospital) with more energy and getting highly disgusted with having to be doing nothing. I haven't heard anything new about what I'm doing here, just that I have about 2 more weeks to wear this cast before my foot will be healed or another one will be put back on. That would be a sad state of affairs, in a way, but in another way it might be the best. It does seem like lots of trouble for just a wee small bone in my foot.

I got a Red Cross tour yesterday to see some of the sights of Calcutta. We didn't get to see a great deal, but a few of the more notable places. Saw some of the most magnificent and beautiful places as well as the most humble.

This is one of the Hindu Temples. It is notable mostly for the manner in which it is built with quite an abundance of gold and jewel inlaid work. It's hard to describe much of it but I'll tell you sometime.

We saw also a Rajah palace, a private home the size of ZCMI and decorated with sculpture and painting into the millions.

The Hindus burn their dead and we also saw that, burning ghats it is called. It takes a strong stomach and a hard heart to see, almost. In a city this size there is always plenty of business. It's done in a walled enclosure but just shallow pits in the ground and the bodies covered with wood. Best I wait for a more vivid description.

It is hard to imagine what a person could see here. Seems there are only the very rich and the very poor. There are the sights to see of course but so much filth, disease and hardship also that it is hardly a place to enjoy.

Remind me to tell you more sometime because I rather hope you never see any of it.

I might get to go shopping one of these days and spend all my money. That should be quite an expedition and I'll tell you more then.

Maybe I'll be writing some V-mail because it may be the only mail going by air and I want you to know what's cooking.

A Lt. Wisner from my squadron has been here in the hospital and he is on his way home now. He may write you when he gets there so you can be expecting to hear.

How I would like to be seeing you now, Darling, and chatter hours with you, and tell you also that you are the most wonderful beautiful wife I could ever ask for and I love you darling, for all eternity, through that long journey we love together to keep you company in our work ambitions and love without end.

My kisses for you and wishes for Junior,

Dean

10 March 1945: The Firestorm

"Riku, get up! Get up now!" His father's voice, but not his usual voice.

"What time is it?" The house was shaking. "Are we having an earthquake?"

"No earthquakes, we have to get to the shelter! The *Beasts* have come."

"B-sans!" shrieked Riku, as he ejected himself from bed.

They had practiced for this moment many, many times. The

Community Association had been holding regular air-raid and fire drills, sometimes twice a day. All citizens knew their part, what to gather, where to go, and what was expected of them.

The result of the many practice air-raids was an orderly beginning to a night that would soon disintegrate and career through its given hours without any semblance of order.

Hastily, the already fully dressed Riku grabbed the first aid bag he was responsible for and his air-raid hood, and slipped around his neck the samurai coin his grandfather had fashioned for him. He believed the medallion transformed him into a samurai, courageous and powerful, a special defender of *Nippon*, ready for any challenge.

He ducked out the front door into a challenge no one on earth had ever had to face. His neighborhood, his world, was in commotion, a commotion only war can create—a commotion of sound created by a raging wind, air-raid sirens, roaring B-29s, the human-made wailing and cries of the citizens, the percussion of firebombs hitting earth and exploding, and the noise of a fire growing around him with the intent of devouring him.

There was a visual commotion of napalm bombs exploding like grand fireworks in every direction, a smoke that burned the eyes and encouraged gagging, searchlights cutting up the sky, and a growing panic that was becoming visible to the naked eye.

The Kyoshi shelter, chiseled into the earth under their front sidewalk, had been built in response to a national order the year before. It was a modest eight feet long and five feet wide, with enough headroom to stand comfortably. A two-foot-wide bench was situated on the north wall and far end. The shelter was reinforced by bamboo poles, a product in abundant supply to the watergun maker, and a building material on no one's rationing list. Takana was so proud of his craftsmanship, he offered it as a model for other would-be shelter builders in the neighborhood.

Riku could not help looking up toward the growl of 8,800 horsepower of a B-29 making its way through the clouds and smoke to find a place to deposit its load of destruction.

Searchlights were roaming the sky, the eyes for ground defenders.

With a quick tempo, the lights moved, hoping to reveal and isolate a target. When a B-san was caught by a light, neighboring search lights joined in—two, three, four—the B-san's aluminum skin collected the searcher's sharp blue light and reflected it back to the city.

The lights inflicted no harm on the Superforts, and the ground gunners could not either. Unfazed, undeterred, bomb bay after bomb bay opened and the napalm stormed out like a swarm of monster killer hornets on a mission, intentionally racing to some sweet dessert on the ground.

Before Riku could reach the shelter's hatch door his father was holding open, another B-san demanded his attention, and another as he slid under his father's arm into the shelter already protecting his mother.

"Mother, the sky is full of B-sans."

Takana secured the shelter doors, subduing the noisy clamor of turbulence for Kigi and Riku.

The quiet helped their hope.

"Maybe we are safe here," Kigi offered.

Takana dodged his way through flying, burning debris to the assembly area for the neighborhood firefighters. He found only the lonely water barrels standing on duty. No citizens had yet answered the call. Hindered by a rising panic ignited by the flames, their well-practiced duty to stand and defend their homes was challenged by what they were witnessing. The growing inferno seemed far more powerful than they had been led to expect.

Peculiarly, the Korean man-servant appeared first. The stand-in, the displaced slave, the nonperson, answered his master's duty obligation first. The significance was not lost on Takana; he rewarded him with an unusual bow of respect.

Other citizens began to emerge from billowing shadows in the neighborhood. They came in a shock-induced trance of wonderment, produced by the spectacle of what was happening to their homes and shops. Some came in nightclothes covered by fire jackets, some half-dressed as if interrupted, and some fully uniformed and meticulously groomed. All wore the mandatory air-raid hood that surrounded very troubled faces. They had practiced fighting a red blanket with a target hung on the side of a house. They were now being asked to fight the fiercest fire they would ever see.

Takana bowed most graciously as each new would-be firefighter arrived, this while shouting rapid-fire orders into the night, "Form up, waterguns, form up!"

The sound of his voice fought to survive, challenged by the growling B-sans, the roaring fire and wind, and the Home Defense sirens screaming from every direction. The vociferous cacophony surrounding all of them swallowed up his words. Panic sought to dislodge their well-practiced duty to defend their individual homes.

"Form up!"

"Waterguns, form up!"

A handful of citizens armed with bamboo firefighting brooms were the first to advance on the fires. They were cut short in their advance by a broiling heat that burned away their eyebrows and blistered their lips. The brooms themselves burst into flames. Disheartened, the first line of defense fell back.

They turned to Takana. "What shall we do?"

"Get your waterguns."

"Waterguns, form up!" he directed and continued to shout.

"Form up, form up."

Takana raised his watergun over his head, waving it like a rally flag to emphasize his order. The visual aid cemented the message and out of the disorganization the formation emerged, guns were dipped, water drawn.

"The Hooper's shop, the Hooper's shop," Takana ordered; it presented the nearest target of fire. The two-story shop/home with a full, wide, covered porch was half engulfed in flames. A small cyclone of fire danced in the flames.

The watergun formation shifted in response. "AYH!" they screamed in unison as they discharged their guns and...and, nothing. The water seemed to be enjoyed by the inferno. No flames were diminished, no fire outpost disappeared; the blaze was unhindered and continued to eat away at their neighbor's shop.

"Aim at the porch roof," Takana directed.

Once more they dipped, drew, and cried, as they discharged their guns focusing on the porch roof. The brazen fire relished their attack and exploded onto the building's upper roof, defying their puny efforts.

Only Takana drew water a third time.

The bucket brigade fared no better. No one could approach the Hooper's shop close enough to heave the bucket's water on the flames. The fierce heat singed hair and wilted, then melted, their belief and resolve. Everyone had been trained to believe that waterguns, bucket relays, and fighting spirit could quench the fires ignited by bombs.

This night, against fires built by napalm, it was simply not so.

They had taken their stand against the fire monster. The evaporating stream from the barrel of his watergun convinced Takana of the futility of their efforts and the reality of their danger.

"We must evacuate. Go and save your families!" he ordered.

Riku had moved to the end of the shelter; the end bench was suitable for sleeping for a boy his size. There was a little more room these days with his twin sisters living at his uncle's home to the south.

Before sleep could take him his father again was calling him, this time shaking him, "Come! We must leave. We will die if we stay here."

Mail Call

That magic moment of hope...

A hospital ward full of soldiers stood around some buck private who completely held everyone's attention, calling out names, handing out mail. Names called out, like Rencowski, Meyers, and Rasmuson were met with whoops and "over heres" and the lucky ones disappeared to their bunks with their treasures. The convention quickly shrank until Dean and a few others, the uncalled, groaned at the private's consolation, "Maybe tomorrow."

Another day of no mail. Dean's only defense for the melancholy was to write.

10 March 1945

My Darling Wife:

It is raining this evening, the soft steady patter on green grass and new leaves, the quiet beating on the roof which is so plain and musical when I stop to listen. There is the distant rumble of thunder to keep interrupting my dream castles and thots of you, my Sweet. I can imagine you, remember plainly as I, what those memories of times past bring to my mind. The sweet freshness of rain-cleansed spring air, stormy weather it is and was, but to us, eager and young in our romance looked forward eagerly to have each other's company in that quiet, dark solitude where we could escape interruptions, and enjoy each other, enlighten each other on that mystery of love.

Where could one find a more fantastic surroundings to plant and nourish that spark that has grown, brought us together and made us as one, Darling. It has grown and is still doing so, Darling. My love for you, started in such beautiful happy surroundings, has been nourished aplenty by your beauty, gracefulness and charm of personality. Darling, I know that you are the most wonderful wife, sweetheart and companion for our life's work, that I can hardly even fully describe. I am continually thankful to Our Heavenly Father for our blessings. I know you are also, Darling Connie, and for that reason I believe they will continue.

My regrets, Darling, to have to change kinds of paper in the middle of my sentimental chatter, but now I have changed the subject, I will not go back for now. Maybe you can keep this first page to read when you miss getting a letter some day.

Marvin Carl is a rather long name for a little guy so let me know if you have a nick-name or should we use just the first? Perhaps I'll make a decision myself when I get to know him, which I surely hope may be soon.

Still I have received no new news since before Junior arrived. Maybe tomorrow will bring some. At least I keep hoping, and anyhow the time seems to go fast, even when I do think of you so much and that is just what I do, do, Peaches.

For you I like Peach Blossom, like it was to begin with, remember? Your sparkling eyes, and soft smooth skin like petals of peach blossoms, and a sweet feminine smell that was yours without added perfume. That

[172]

is why you are Peach Blossom, Darling, and you will always be just that to me. The beautiful girl, the wonderful passionate lover, a wonderful delicious bed warmer and my favorite sweetheart always.

I still have heard nothing new about me. I have about 10 days yet to wear this cast. Probably until they take another x-ray I won't be able to find out anything. My foot never hurts anyhow and I walk around plenty. Yesterday I went uptown again, on my own, on a pass. I didn't buy anything but looked around just a little bit in the main part of town. I did see a show, "None but the Lonely Heart." It was pretty good. I think when I go again I'll buy a few things to send you, some of the riches and jewels from the Far East.

The wind is blowing my paper away so for now, Darling Connie, Goodnight.

Kisses as you like,

Dean

Chapter 13

The Beautiful Terror

WHEN RIKU CLIMBED out of the shelter, the growth of the fire stunned him. Fires were closer, bigger, and he could feel, hotter. His young eyes were mesmerized by the spectacle—the glow of the firestorm, the shooting sparks, and flying, burning debris were, in their destructive way, beautiful.

His father offered another vision. "Our lives are in danger! We must run! Come push with us."

Riku moved between his father and mother to grab hold of the handle of the cart Takana had loaded. It was from his father's shop, a cart Riku had pushed many times, shuffling blank bamboo sections in the process of becoming waterguns. It made only short journeys in the shop, on a very smooth surface, but now it ventured into rough cobbled streets strewn with fire debris and discarded possessions.

Fire training emphasized that the path to safety was always behind a fire. Therefore, to survive, one should run toward the fire. But as the trio turned to face the fire, a wall of evacuees, being chased out of their burning homes, clogged the street. There would be no swimming upstream in the face of what was coming at them.

And what was coming at them was being driven by panic, the wretched fear that rises when one comes face-to-face with a horrible death.

"The fire is coming!"

"We are all going to die!"

Words spoken in screams. Words delivered with delirious hysteria.

"Run! Run for your life!"

"If you stay here you will die!"

Takana had lived a deliberate, intentional, disciplined life. Even in the midst of this surreal, stampede-driven scene of certain destruction, his logic did not desert him.

"We must go west to the Kuramae Bridge."

His objective was to cross the Sumida River. He reasoned that the vast area around Yokoamicho Park would be an oasis without fire.

They fell in behind a mother and son holding hands, shuffling along in a slow-motion jog, rocking to and fro with each step, each with oversize backpacks, and weighted down with large travel bags. They wore grim faces, not acknowledging the presence of others, only staring straight ahead as if the destruction that engulfed them was not happening if not witnessed.

Many chose, somewhat logically, to run to dark spots on the skyline, areas not burning, which worked unless the fire, driven by wind, passed them, or a B-san lusted for the same dark area they were seeking and shot out its fire ahead of them.

The street was a river of humanity trying to make its way somewhere else. Riku crashed into another refugee, Yasou, his tank-battle adversary with whom he had seen his very first B-san, the first *sliver of brightness*. The B-san then seemed so beautiful, pulling its magnificent white tail across the sky, so beautiful and so harmless.

They gave each other a nod, a wide-eyed acknowledgment full of unsaid things. Yasou and his father pulled ahead of them, not burdened by having to maneuver a cart around obstacles, and disappeared out of Riku's life.

10 March 1945, Calcutta

Dearest Peach Blossom:

I was all happy and scared and excited when three of your wonderful letters came today all at once. I guess you know I'm all happiness too, that you are doing fine now, if you did have a tough time before. Your letters were Feb. 19, 25, & 27. They caught me pretty well up to date at least for the mail service and now I can write you a dozen more maybe, I know I think about enough things, like how wonderful you are and how much I love you, and how fluttery and excited I get when you tell me about Marvin. I guess you know, Honey, I sure do like all that chatter.

You must be up and running around lots these days, by now, but be careful, Honey, and I guess you are. How many stitches did the doctor take? I hope you are all healed up and well again now. And I know you want to be as much as I. I'm glad you told me all the little details even if it does scare me sometimes but I do want to know.

You should be gaining some weight again by now. I hope your appetite is holding out good with you feeding two wonderful kids that I love with all my heart.

You should have received the V-mail long before this and maybe I'll write another one today. I'll see and you'll find out. Anyhow remember not to sell the car anyhow, something may be cooking, and I'll tell you as soon as I find out.

Honey, I'm willing for you to have a new checkered suit, when I get paid I might even send you the money, except that not flying costs me $100 a month, but I can get it if I fly before three months, which I will. Our tithing is $41.70, Honey, and payday comes to $417. I guess I told you that Marvin doesn't make us any more but that is alright. He makes lots of other nice things for us. Your payday for March (April 5-10) should be $250. So let me know if it is. Could be the record didn't go thru if it's the same so that is why you should tell me quick.

Happy Birthday, Sweetheart, and this is for a birthday card which I couldn't find, and besides I think you would like a long line of chatter especially because I love you so much, Darling, more than I can put in words, but still you are the most wonderful wife ever, and my sweetheart always.

I did look for you a birthday card yesterday when I went on a small shopping spree in town. I had a pass all afternoon and evening. I spent most of my time in a market, it is a whole block of small markets and stalls mostly under one roof, when almost everything imaginable is sold. Novelties, small hardware, jewelry of all and any description, dry goods, clothes, cloth, groceries, meats, candy, and on and on. Anyhow I was practically lost most of the time but fun. Ted was with me (he, Solomon and Orr were down on pass.) I didn't buy much but had a great sport arguing and bartering (they don't know hardly a fixed price but get all they can) and buying little. And then chasing off a hundred or so small boys wanting to carry my packages in baskets.

I did buy a silver plaited cocktail set, of what good I don't know but it looks good. And some pillow cases embroidered with silver thread, of the Taj Mahal. I'll send them when I can, but will probably get some more things first.

Also I ate uptown at a place called American Kitchens. They serve mostly American and Chinese food. I had the best (and first) fried prawns. They were really delicious and a whole plateful. They are like shrimps only not like the mealy canned ones we get there at home.

Let's go on a big date, Honey, and have a big delicious dinner even better than Jeans in LA. And dancing to beautiful music and lots of romancing. That's one of our dreams that will come true, Darling.

I have another week about to wear this cast before I find out what cooks. I'll let you know in a hurry how things are.

And let me know how every little thing is too, with you and Marvin. I sure would like to splash water with him if you would give me a bath too. I'm eager to get a picture of him when you get a chance.

I'll stop this chatter for now Darling Connie, but not for long. You have all my love, Honey, for you and Marvin Carl, only maybe two different brands like is good for both of you.

Please hurry and get good and well and fixed up, Honey, for all of us. Because I love you dozens all week.

Love and kisses,

Dean

10 March 1945, V-mail

My Dearest Peach Blossom,

Your newsy 'Sugar Report' of 21 Feb came today, Honey. I'm so happy and thankful that you are alright, Darling. I wish so much that I could have been with you, could have eased your pain and burden in any way possible and wish still that I could be with you, and see Marvin too.

Sure would like to see what goes on with him, watch him eat and be jealous. Be careful, Darling, and take just enough of the right exercises to get slim and cuddly again altho you will always be that.

I'll bet your house is crowded these days with diapers and bottles. Remember not to get Junior the mumps and I hope Dale is over them. Get Marvin Carl inoculated for diphtheria and those other things when he is old enough.

Tell me how this V-mail does for time, Honey. I just decided NOT to sell the car, Honey, at least until I tell you again.

For now Goodnight Darling and sweet dreams and remember I love you ever so much and more always.

Love and kisses,

Dean

Even the twelve-year-old Riku could discern the futility surrounding him. People were desperately trying to carry with them prized possessions, collected without the benefit of time and reason. Citizens loaded themselves with strange choices—futons, so they could finish their night's sleep, a pot of rice, because they would be hungry in the morning. One woman and her son were decorated with wooden clogs. They had been warned by national defense that walking on the aftermath of an attack required something other than rubber soled shoes.

The escaping hordes were burdened beyond what surviving would allow. As they raced away from death, their luggage and other possessions would catch fire and be left in the streets, obstacles to those coming behind, and more fuel for the fire.

A bicycle, ridden by a man in a tweed suit and wearing a panama hat, pulled alongside them and passed. The rider expertly weaved his way through the mayhem, his eyes fastened on the street and the many fast-appearing obstacles ahead of him. Riku was transfixed by this thing so unlike the others, such an out-of-place sojourner. In another moment in time, he might have been a suitor off to visit his beloved on a pleasant day in the park. Tonight, he was the suitor of survival. The bike's back wheel caught fire and instantly flattened, but the rider rode on, undeterred.

The inhabitants pushed carts, strapped goods to themselves, and dragged bags too heavy or cumbersome to carry. The fire demanded all of it. Bicycle tires burned; luggage collected embers that, fanned by the wind, became more outposts of the fire. Backpacks caught fire without the knowledge of the humans wearing them. Survival, at least the chance of it, required everything of them.

Some of the B-29s were dropping lava bombs, a concoction of magnesium coated by asphalt chemicals. Upon encountering the earth, they exploded, sending burning white-hot embers twenty-five feet in every direction, sticking to whatever they encountered. The napalm bombs were jellied gasoline, and exploded as one would suspect—as if someone "threw gasoline on a fire."

The B-29s bombing individually, not by formation, were ordered to search for black or dark spots where there was no fire. Riku, his family, and all the other desperate souls on the ground, were trying to do the same thing. Time and again, both those above and below came into the same dark neighborhoods just before they became infernos.

The Pathfinders, the initial B-29s, dropped their bombs to form a great X over the district. Three miles wide at the top, the legs of the X stretched for five miles. It marked the "spot" of a million inhabitants, who, by morning, would all be homeless. Bombardiers had orders to make the X a rectangle. They flew to any area not burning and "lit it up."

Many citizens kept running into impassable walls of fire, and had to make the choice again of what direction to run. The simple choice of right or left determined survival.

The first smoldering body they encountered brought them to a stop. A mother and daughter, perhaps, their bodies already ravaged by the heat and fire, clothes and hair gone; identification by normal means would soon be impossible. Their wagon's contents, showered by sparks and encouraged by wind and the stoppage, broke into flames.

Kigi looked at Takana. "We have no choice." Without saying more, they pushed the cart down the length of the bodies, abandoning it near other leavings at the side of the road, and began to run, hand in hand.

At the second intersection they came to, an inconceivable blast of wind came, unobstructed, down the street, and blew people off their feet. Fortunately, Takana was downwind, and he formed an anchor for his family. A woman and her child, torn from each other by the wind and flattened to the ground, began rolling before the wind and disappeared down the side street.

Takana's hope of safety at the Sumida River's Kuramae Bridge presented no such thing. The Sumida, hundreds of yards wide, formed the western boundary of the Shitamachi district. The bridge, because of the events of the night, had become the confluence of two great rivers of people, each side convinced that safety was on the other side. The masses pushed against each other, clogging the way with possessions and bodies. Two firetrucks, on their way to fire that was everywhere, were immobile in the middle of the bridge, adding to the blockade. The press of humanity made movement impossible, and families began to collapse in heaps, seeking protection, piles of parents trying to save their children by shielding them with their own bodies.

Rescuers, in following days, would come to stacks of humans six or seven or eight deep. Each layer had its own ecology—only charred death on the top layers, a couple layers of intact, clothed corpses, then, often, the surprise of life below.

The streets in every direction were littered with the burning possessions gained from a lifetime of effort, and often beside them lay the lifeless, charred, naked bodies of the human beings that had gathered them.

Downed electrical lines lay alongside and across the road, some still crackling with electrons looking for a destination. They raised the degree of difficulty of passage by their presence.

Smoke created darkness where flames were not. Breathing felt dangerous. The family covered their mouths and doused themselves with the water from bins of the neighborhood fire defense. It was laughable that their plan had been to form a bucket brigade of neighbors to extinguish the fires from this kind of bombing—it would have been like pissing on a forest fire in hopes of putting it out.

There had been, in the beginning, the sound of fire equipment, a professional effort to battle the flames, to resist the conflagration. It collapsed as the fire equipment burned and the heat drove firefighters to become traffic directors, blind traffic directors as the pathway to safety became indiscernible.

Riku's father dipped his steel pot helmet in one neighborhood bin and doused everyone. Soaked to the skin when they left the bin, they were completely dry in a hundred yards.

Once the kindling temperature for backpacks was reached, they seemed to spontaneously catch fire. One exploded on the woman in front of them. Fellow refugees alerted her and she threw it to the ground and ran on, unaware that the clothes on her back were also burning. Takana shouted to stop her, but words didn't travel very far and she disappeared into the darkness ahead of them, lit up like a human torch, running until she started to stagger and fall, becoming a broiling landmark they would pass by shortly.

Riku was puzzled by the first arm he saw lying on the ground. Bloodied at the shoulder socket but perfect below, there was no clue as to where its body might be. Soon, body parts were common, seemingly everywhere. Direct hits on humans by the bombs resulted in instant dismemberment—an arm here, a head there, some half bodies, none with clothes. The fire had made them naked and was turning them into roasted specimens that would soon be but partial human charcoal mannequins.

The Kuramae Bridge crossing impossible, Takana turned south and then east along the rail tracks near Asakusabashi Rail Station. They desperately held hands, Riku in the middle, afraid that even the separation of a few inches could be permanent. Possibly the parallel canal would be a safe haven.

Riku reached the canal first, and with a mighty leap, mounted the canal's wall, intent on jumping in. Takana grabbed at his coat and pulled him back. Mystified as to why his father stopped his leap to life, Riku turned to his father, who was staring into the canal. Riku's eyes followed his father's—there, below them, was a canal full of death; expired bodies covered the water's surface, life no longer in any of them.

At morning's change of tide, they would all magically disappear and become beached by the next tide change, on tidewaters of the surrounding bay.

His father dragged him away from the grotesque scene and toward the railway tracks. Their new ambition was Akihabara Station and the main train lines heading north and south, with Uneo Station and its surrounding park being their latest hope.

Wherever room permitted on main streets, body-size trenches had been cut into the shoulder areas to act as simple, personal emergency bomb shelters. Many, near exhaustion, fell into them. Some survived there, while an equal number died, roasted by the intense heat of the hellfire.

Neighborhood Associations had also constructed some larger roadside shelters along city streets. One, by the canal, was a magnet to those fleeing the carnage. The road was now so clogged that some could not cross to safety; they died where they stood. Some could cross the road but not gain entry to the already full shelter; those poor souls either jumped in the canal to their death or crawled under the base of the bridge where they also succumbed to the heat.

They came upon a family of four, furiously trying to put out the fire on their children's heads. Air-raid hoods, tied tight so as not to be lost in the wind, were homemade shields against the bombs. It had become mandatory for citizens to have one with them when out and about in the community. They were made of cotton fabric and looked very much like the old leather American football helmets. The tops and sides were stuffed with cotton and the hoods were tied tightly under the chin.

These air-raid hoods, made in homes across Japan, symbolized the naivety of the Japan Home Defense leaders. Designed to protect against concussion and flying debris, no one had considered their effectiveness against napalm. At the kindling temperatures of this conflagration, or simply by the wind that blew life into the sparks that landed in their hoods, they created human torches.

The parents' hands were so burned they could no longer manage the knots. Takana, the firefighter, threw his heavy coat over the children's heads and smothered the flames, while Kigi cut the ties with her special issue Neighborhood Association knife. The parents grabbed their char-headed children with their badly burned hands and quickly disappeared in the opposite direction of the Kiyoshis' travel.

Battered but alive, the Kiyoshis turned north at the intersection of train lines. The northern path of the multiple lines was an inviting tunnel of darkness. The chosen route of several lines formed an unintentionally large firebreak, wide enough for safe passage. The right-of-way led them out of the giant bomber-created X, now turned rectangle, into relief from the fire and its heat.

After several hundred yards, they ran into another impassable wall of humanity—citizens, victims turned into survivors, perhaps a hundred thousand of them, standing or sitting in familial clusters.

The Kiyoshis collapsed, having no strength left. They were surrounded by people like themselves—dazed, exhausted survivors, people with black faces, wide, white eyes without eyebrows, red, blistered lips, singed hair, wearing scorched clothing, and showing burns on any exposed skin.

These were people in a collective, silent, state of shock. They had lost every worldly possession and had only escaped with life itself. And on this horrible night, they were the lucky ones. This convention of the living didn't look very different from the nonliving; they looked more like ghosts than human beings.

Somewhere near five a.m. the demons stopped flying over them and the B-29s turned south toward their home bases. The winds that fed the fire followed after them, and calm descended with an almost disturbing silence.

Fires were dying for lack of fuel. There was nothing left to burn, only smoldering that produced an unbearable stench, the odor of tens of thousands of burned human bodies.

As the moment of dawn approached, the eastern horizon glowed its warning of the coming sun. The dawn glow lingered, postponing the appearance of the light-giver. It was coming, but so slowly that it appeared to be in its own struggle, fighting to take back the sky. Yellowed by the horror of the night, the sun's edge finally broke the dark, the new morning's light giving testimony to the destruction that had befallen them. Shitamachi now existed only as streets and sidewalks, the buildings, with few exceptions, gone, reduced to modest piles of ash.

The sun had power over the citizens. As it rose, so did they, as if the sun were connected to them, and like marionettes, they could be drawn to their feet by the connection. They rose in spite of their exhaustion, their injuries, their losses, and their pain, to face the great glowing orb.

Silence was amplified throughout the smoldering remnants of Shitamachi. There was no sound of mourning or wailing, or expressions of pain, or tears of loss. These survivors had been driven far past that to unthinkable depths of shock and trauma by the events of the night.

They simply stood and faced the sun. It was rising methodically, but rising, returning to take its place in the sky.

Nippon was their nation's name—Land of the Rising Sun, "the place of the sun's origin."

This symbol of their nation fought for the sky to present to its citizens another day. They fought to stand in reverence, affirming their national devotion, affirming they also would rise again.

Riku reached for his necklace, his very own reminder of his unique part of the nation. It was not around his neck. The night had stolen it from him.

Riku's father placed his hand on his shoulder. "I am sending you to your uncle's to be with your sisters."

"But, I don't…"

His father interrupted, "We will not discuss it. I will put you on a train tomorrow. You will be safe in Hiroshima."

————

As the B-29s turned for home, tail gunners could see the night's work for 150 miles.

The new tactics caught the fire department by surprise just as they did the military defense. The flames destroyed 95 fire engines and killed 125 firemen. Police records show that 267,171 buildings were destroyed—about one-fourth of the total in Tokyo—and that 1,008,005 persons were rendered homeless. The official toll of casualties listed 83,793 dead (later estimates would rise to 115,000). It was twenty-five days before all the dead had been removed from the ruins. Many found safety in the firebreaks, rivers, and canals, but in some of the smaller canals, the water was actually boiling from the intense heat.

The Home Affairs ministry reported: "People were unable to escape. They were found later piled upon the bridges, roads, and in the canals, eighty thousand dead and twice that many injured. We were instructed to report on actual conditions. Most of us were unable to do this because of horrifying conditions beyond imagination."

The Great Fire of London burned a mere 13,200 buildings. The 1812 Fire of Moscow burned 38,000 buildings. In the Great Chicago Fire of 1871, Mrs. O'Leary's cow purportedly burned a paltry 17,450 buildings, while in the Great San Francisco Earthquake and Fire of 1906, the 21,188 burning buildings were mere campfires compared to General LeMay's 2000 tons of fire.

Even the Hiroshima and Nagasaki atomic bomb drops would not touch the loss of life and property of the night of 10 March 1945. (Craven)

Chapter 14

Sugar Reports

16 March 1945, Calcutta, India

Good evening, Honey:

I'm right in the mood to write you maybe a short bit of chatter this evening but we'll see where it ends. I love you more and more these days, Honey, and I love Marvin too and you can tell him because I don't want him reading my 'Sugar Reports' to you. I'm really so happy that we have him and March didn't matter a bit either, and I'd probably be just as happy if he had been a girl but I'm more happy this way, I guess.

I just read all your latest letters over again and I like them dozens, and get excited and happy and scared a bit all over again. I really like all the chatter you write me, Honey, and am glad when you tell me all the details about everything. I hope you are getting around good these days and giving Marvin a bath every day.

Happy Easter, Honey, and since there are no nice cards available, I'll write you this happy chatter and you can give Easter Greetings to your Mother for me too. She sure has been good to us kids and probably is doing lots of work taking care of Marvin for us, being lots of help anyhow.

I'll bet the censor's ears get warm when he reads the chatter you get. Maybe I'd better watch what I say. The Base Censor checks the officers' mail once in a while. I think it's a good idea anyhow. Gotta keep the military secrets secret.

There is no news around here, at least abut my foot. As I said, I'll probably find out something next week early and I'll be telling you. I know

I sure would like to go fly again. It's nice and hot today as it has been most of the time About 100 degrees and damp too so it's not so good.

I still run around plenty, mostly on the hospital grounds and have a long afternoon nap. There are lots of crows and kites around to feed. I get scraps from the mess hall. The kites circle overhead and I toss stuff into the air to them and they catch it on the fly. Lots of fun to get about 50 of them around. It's quite a scramble, and the crows catch what falls to the ground. We have quite a show.

Think I'll get a pass tomorrow and go to town, maybe I can buy something new and get into lots of mischief, you'll hear what goes.

Have been reading lots of good books these days, some historical novels and other novels. It's good use of the time anyhow and fun.

Better say goodbye now, Darling, and tell you that I love you ever so much, I have wonderful dreams of you too, you sweet woman. Be good to you and Marvin, Honey.

My love and kisses,

Dean

17 March 1945: Tinian

The Mariana Islands are an arc of twenty-two volcanic islands stretching from Guam northward into the Philippine Sea. Two of these islands, Tinian and Saipan (five miles away), were, along with Guam, the coveted potential airport islands. Tinian and Saipan were about 135 miles north of Guam, the home base of the XXI Bomber Command. The North Field on Tinian held the distinction of being the largest and busiest airport in the world for a short time as America tried to bomb Japan into submission.

The thirty-eight square miles that was Tinian was first invaded 23 July 1944, thirty-eight days after the invasion of Saipan. After ten days of difficult fighting, it was declared secure, not free of Japanese soldiers, but secure enough for navy Seabees to start building and lengthening runways. Japanese soldiers would hold out through the end of the war, often stealing army supplies to obtain food and posing a threat of attack. Popular swimming beaches were patrolled by MP guards for protection from Japanese holdouts still fighting the war.

The first B-29 attacks on the Japanese mainland from the islands (as witnessed by Riku) occurred 23 and 24 November 1944. This was about the time Dean and his crew were flying to India to take part in the ill-fated Operation Matterhorn.

The climate in the Marianas was constant, with year-round high temperatures hovering between 87°F–90°F. The low temperatures were likewise moderate, ranging from 73°F–75°F. Sandy beaches were soldier-magnets for tanning and swimming. Warm ocean waters with an abundance of exotic fish made snorkeling seem like swimming in a fish tank.

Located 1,500 miles from Tokyo, the islands made bombing the Japanese homeland easy-peasy compared to the Matterhorn effort. Deep-sea harbors made supply direct and immediate. In India, supply came into the coastal area and had to be transported on trains that were not reliable and roads that did not exist.

Japan had acquired the Marianas by first taking possession of them and then legalizing it as part of the Treaty of Versailles that ended World War I. The islands were previously held by Germany, who had purchased them from the fading Spanish empire in 1898. The islands served as an outlier of protection for Japanese holdings in New Guinea, Borneo, the Philippines, Thailand, China, and Korea, as well as protection for the Homeland.

Tinian became the world's largest air installation on its meagre thirty-eight square miles. One airport was constructed for North Field. The Americans literally chipped the eleven miles of runway and taxi areas out of the coral earth. West Field, home to Dean's 58th Bombardment Wing, was a converted Japanese airfield. The two parallel runways were repaired and doubled in length. The Tinians of today continue to use it as part of their international airport.

Nearly as important as the acquisition of Tinian was the capture of Iwo Jima. Iwo lay on the flight line to Japan out of Tinian and was strategically placed about halfway. It became a haven for return flights that otherwise would have had to ditch. Over 2,400 B-29s would find refuge there for emergency landings.

Running out of fuel was a huge problem over such a long flight. Head winds, fuel leaks, combat damage, and the need to climb to high altitudes (especially when fully loaded with fuel) all could compromise miles per gallon. Iwo was that lifesaving gas station everyone needs once in a while.

With the Iwo safety net, fuel levels were reduced enough that extra bomb tonnage could be loaded in the bomb bays. Four thousand extra pounds of bombs per plane, for a sortie of 300 planes, meant 600 more tons of incendiaries could be unloaded on Japan.

Having Iwo also meant that fighter escorts could now accompany B-29 formations and offer added protection against enemy aircraft and ground defenses. P-51s, under the direction of Brigadier General Moore, provided a definite boost to B-29 crew morale.

The taking of Iwo also compromised the Japanese defenses. From Iwo the Japanese had launched raids on Tinian, Guam, and Saipan, wreaking havoc on Allied efforts.

The addition of a base on Iwo also helped dramatically with the accuracy of weather prediction on the Japanese homeland. Meteorologists had a much more complete picture to help them develop forecasts. Bombing missions became much more effective with improved forecasting, and the avoidance of bombing in bad weather saved planes.

Operation Detachment, as the campaign to take Iwo was called, lasted a little over a month. In some of the fiercest fighting of the Pacific war, 6,821 marines lost their lives while over 21,000 Japanese died. While mourning the loss of marines, air crews had deep gratitude for the many airmen saved because of their sacrifice.

The value of the safety net was shown even before the island had been taken. With heavy fighting still underway, on 4 March, B-29 *Dinah Might*, piloted by Lt. Ray Malo, dangerously low on fuel, was faced with ditching in the ocean or landing on the still-contested and dangerously short runway on Iwo Jima. B-29s like runways in the 8,000-foot range. This one was half of that.

Disobeying orders, Malo chose the runway, stopping just short of the runway's end under mortar and artillery fire. Scrambling the plane around, the crew loaded a couple thousand gallons of fuel by hand and took off.

They were dodging enemy fire all the way.

18 March 1945, Calcutta, India

My Favorite Sweetheart:

Evening, Honey, and 1/12 anniversary to Marvin too! Tell him for me will you, Darling, and I'll tell you that I love you dozens and miss you very much these days, Sweet woman. I hope you are doing good and feeling fine these days. Wish I could see you to keep up your morale like I think it should be.

I'm very glad Marvin was born on Sunday, aren't you? It doesn't mater especially but since it happened that ways, I am happy.

I went to Sunday School today only it was the Protestant service in the chapel here and very dry and incomplete it seemed, but was a change anyhow.

Also, I went to town this afternoon. Most of the stores were closed so didn't buy much of anything. Rode a rickshaw around some, and had some ice cream as well as some more delicious fried prawns. You will have to have some of them sometime when we find the right restaurant. These that I had were really good and I think you would like them too.

I did buy a couple of water color pictures that should be nice if I can get them home in good shape. I was surprised that they were so cheap as they were. That is funny about some things being cheap here and other things are really expensive.

Jewelry is really expensive here if one can get a good quality. The workmanship doesn't compare to that done on jewelry in the states.

I'm still feeling fine and full of energy these days and running around lots as you see. I guess the cast will come off in two or three days for another xray of my foot. It will all depend on how it is, as to what happens of course. But from the past progress, I suppose I'll get another plaster put right back on. We'll see anyhow. Even what happens, I'll probably have some big news. I hope so anyhow, and I'll hurry and tell you.

Honey, I love you dozens still and know that you are the most wonderful and beautiful sweetheart I ever knew. I like all your nice hair and sweet kisses and nice chatter and your wonderful loving, and I love you more and more always.

I'll write you more chatter right away and I'll be hoping for more swell letters tomorrow.

All my love to a wonderful wife and our son,

Dean.

Joining the Caterpillar Club

Everyone understands the process of metamorphosis, the means by which a caterpillar, a landlocked, developing, immature (larval) stage creature, turns into a butterfly that navigates the air as it flies above the earth.

The opposite of that process is a creature that flies about above the earth being changed into a creature that walks upon the earth—like a crew member of a B-29 forced to abandon ship and float down to earth by using a parachute. That is exactly why membership in the Caterpillar Club required jumping out of an airplane. The war created a huge number of new members to the club, a club no one but paratroopers was all that excited about joining.

Soldiers were drafted and trained to fly planes, not jump out of them. Training in the use of parachutes was never a very high priority. The need for airmen flying and bombing was so great that some sacrifices were accepted in the training process. After all, how tough is it to step out of a door and pull a cord?

In fairness, there was a ten-minute training film detailing the whole process that everyone was exposed to. It always ended in the army training way—"Any questions?"

For those unlucky enough to find themselves in a parachute for the first time, falling out of the sky over Burma or China or Japan, there were indeed, suddenly a lot of questions.

21 March 1945, Calcutta

Favorite Woman:

This evening I have two shoes on, Honey! And I can walk around pretty good too, considering that my arch is a little weak still. The break does hurt a little now for the first time in ten weeks for some reason, but not much. This morning when I got the cast off and had an xray taken, I thought I would get another cast put on but the doctor looked at the pictures and so I only got taped up a bit. While waiting I gave my foot and leg a bath and it sure did feel good. Of course, it needed it slightly too.

I saw the xray too and it didn't look so good to me. There was quite a crack showing but the bone is in the right position OK. I think something will have to be done, maybe only time, tho. But it will take some more days because no one is in a hurry here except me. Anyhow it feels good to be able to wiggle my foot and ankle around and I don't have to sleep with a big plaster cast.

I had to read your last letter again because no new mail has come through for a few days. But I love you dozens, Honey, no end in fact. You are the sweetest little dream girl I ever knew, and beautiful too, and sweet to me which I like lots. And best of all you are the most wonderful wife in the world and all mine too. That is what is wonderful, only it couldn't be any different.

I hope you are feeling in top shape these days, Honey, and feeling in the mood to buy nice pretty dresses. I sure like to see you in nice new dresses because you sure do make them all look swell. I guess you know too, that I like for you to have lots of pretty dresses and nice things, all we can afford. When payday comes, I'll see what can be done about it.

How is Marvin doing now? I'm sure anxious to hear about every little detail and know if he is treating you right. I want more than anything to see him and the sooner the better.

I hope you can pay the doctors without drawing all your money from the Post Office. It will be nice to keep all the money possible saved up so we can start housekeeping some day soon when I come to live with you. I guess this letter should get there about April payday so let me know in a flash if you get the raise like you should.

I guess you got the V-mail and remember not to sell our car. If possible I would like for you to get it fixed tho when you have the money to spare. I'll send you some for that too when I get it. I know it takes lots to buy all the things needed for Marvin and you too to get all fixed up. Your mother must be getting lots of work being nurse for you and Marvin. I hope you are paying some for your keep and I guess you do. Tell me.

I have been reading lots to keep the time going fast. It goes rather slow tho when I'm waiting for your letters, which get messed up around here somewhere close, anyhow I know that you write lots, Honey, and I sure do like all your loving 'Sugar Reports.'

Have you heard if George's offspring has arrived yet? It should be soon now, at least.

Darling, I sure do miss you these days. I have lots of day dreams and pleasant thoughts about you, too. I love you, Honey, ever so much. We'll see to it that we never get separated again like this because I like you too good. I think we can arrange things so you will be going where I go, and we'll be working together at whatever our life work leads us to. That certainly is a pleasant thought and, to have you with me always to work with and for, and to play with and make love to.

Darling, you are all those things for me, my inspiration and helper and the lovingest woman ever. I like you to chatter with always and especially on a warm summer evening, listening to beautiful music and with you close and sweet and see the sparkle in your pretty eyes and to feel lots of soft smooth skin, oh what we would talk about, that's why you are the wonderful wife you are to me, Darling, and that is why I love you so much. Goodnight for now, Darling Connie.

Love and kisses,

Dean

Chapter 15

Almost Sent Home

24 March 1945, Calcutta, India

Darling Connie:

I'm glad you liked your roses, Honey, and very glad you got some from me. I've been thinking that you will get lots of flowers from me when I'm around to deliver them to you myself, and chocolate too, like you used to get. Do you remember way back when?

I'm sure glad that I got some mail today, which is the first in a week. Today seven letters came, which will give me lots to do to answer them. Only one, 4 March came from you but I don't imagine it will be long before more come.

I'm sure glad you are feeling good and better now, Honey. You can gain some weight if you want to, because I'll like it, and I like your stomach flat too, only a little round to blow bubbles on. I guess you know. And dozens more, too.

I guess you will have to get Marvin a suntan if he's getting pale these days, and I'm happy and quite proud that he is a good looking kid. And ever so happy that he is ours, Honey. I sure want to see him soon as possible too.

I just remembered something that I have been going to tell you for days now. And that is to tell you to get some neat's foot oil for you alligator purse. I think the goat skin lining was cracking a little when I sent it. A little neat's foot oil applied with cotton would just fix it up right and wouldn't dirty anything either. You should be able to get some at a shoe repair shop or maybe ZCMI in their shoe polish department. I want you to be able to use the purse without it coming apart and that should fix it up. It would be nice if I could get you shoes to match.

I was in town again this afternoon on pass. I didn't buy much, just a couple more pictures because it seems more stores are closed Saturday afternoon than Sunday. Maybe next Wednesday I'll have a big time. I think I'll send the pictures pretty soon. I believe I can roll them and send them OK. A couple of them are beautiful even if they are watercolors and cheap.

I had a very good steak today, and quite a rarity around here. The Hindus don't eat meat at all. I imagine that it had come from Australia and it was really good anyhow.

I did a little so-called window shopping. I saw one of the world's largest star sapphires, it weighed 133 carats and was almost like a small egg. Saw also a very beautiful blue star sapphire and it was just about perfect. Lots of sapphires are mined in Celon. I would like to buy one but even here they are very high. Saw a $2000 ruby too.

I haven't forgotten your mother, Honey, but probably have neglected too long. I know she sure has been doing us lots of good, and is busy with you and Marvin, too. Do you have any new idea what she might like? It's hard to pick out things, at least hard for me, but I'll let you know what goes in the next box, which will be pretty soon now.

There are lots of places where I'd rather buy things to send home. As I've probably said before most things made here are pretty crude and would be practically worthless at home except for the fact that they are made in India and right now that doesn't mean too much to me.

Our tithing should be $41.70 in February, Honey. Maybe I forgot to tell you. I'm getting all messed up in the money situation as I'm not getting any flying pay, and for some reason I am supposed to pay back what I drew in January. I will be able to get it back for three months when I get my flying time in tho so it's just saving, but it makes a mess of things for a while. It amounts to $100 a month so you see, it has me quite concerned.

Honey, let's go on a big date this Saturday night! How would you like to go dancing after a nice dinner and a lot of things that you know about after the dancing? I think it would be a wonderful idea because I'm in just the mood and have lots of energy these days.

My foot feels pretty good too and walks OK but gets a little sore once in a while. Don't know how much longer I'll be here but I hope not too long. The doctors still don't tell us anything.

I love you, Honey, dozens today, and you are my favorite wonderful woman always,

Love and kisses, Sweetheart,

Dean

25 March 1945: Airplane 9966

A brand-new B-29, with the serial number 44-69966, landed at West Field, Tinian Island of the Marianas on this day. It was fresh from a Modification Center. Built by Boeing, it would be pressed into combat after an overhaul and combat shakedowns.

As she would be called in pilot shorthand, "9966" would be assigned to the Sherman crew when they arrived at Tinian on 30 April 1945.

On the 7th, 9th, and 12th of May, Dean and the crew took her out on "shakedown" flights of three to five hours. The gunnery and bombing systems were checked out in real time and this new version of *Peaches*, as Dean named her, was pronounced ready for combat.

25 March 1945, Calcutta, India

Good evening, Honey:

I'm glad my letters make you happy, Honey, just like yours do for me. Another one of yours came today, mailed 8 March. I like your chatter too, Honey, because I love you dozens and dozens. You're just the Sweet woman that I dream about when I'm in the mood for some nice pleasant things. I don't have to dream, tho, that you are the sweetest girl I know, and the most wonderful wife ever. I'm sure happy with you tonight, Honey, about lots of little things, mostly everything. I sure would like some of your delicious kisses this evening. Our special brand, that makes for hours of fun and wonderful thrills. I'd like to comb your soft pretty hair even for

[196]

about an hour. Would you like that, Honey? I sure would. It would even be fun cheating Marvin some, of course not really cheating him, but getting what he gets only better and more fun. Does it tickle when Marvin nurses, Honey? I guess I better stop chattering this way and not be saying what I'm thinking and I'll bet you are too.

How are you doing these days, Honey? You should be about recovered from what Marvin did, and ready to go shopping for pretty new Easter clothes. I would like to go with you to buy your Easter suit. I'd probably be sorry but I'd still like it. I'm willing for you to buy the clothes you want, Honey, only more than anything, I'd like to see them on you.

I had another pass today. We get them three times a week. I got some good food and that was about all as I didn't stay long.

I did buy you some perfume and cologne, which I'll send pretty soon. I don't know if it's good or not. It did smell pretty good, but I'll let you decide when you get it. If it isn't good just don't use it because I sure do like your good smell without perfume. I sure do get ideas about you tho, when I smell that Risque. I guess you know we can afford to keep you in good smelling perfume. I just keep loving you more, Honey, when you always look so pretty and smell good too. Of course clothes and perfume can't do all that but with those things and you too, it makes a wonderful combination. And then I guess you know you are most wonderful of all in just that soft smooth skin with nothing in the way to cover it up, that's extra special times of course.

How much is your doctor bill, Honey? I guess it should be paid by now, I hope your money is holding out to pay the doctor and buy you some nice new clothes too. You better be saving some tho, Honey, or I will cut your allowance when I get home.

What is Mack's address? Maybe I'd get an idea where he is if I knew that.

I like the name you mentioned too, Honey (Larry Max), we'll save that for a while tho.

Went to church again today, a Protestant service and I think I'll quit. I have lots of time to read the Book of Mormon, which I do, and let some of my buddies read the tracts I have.

The rest of the crew hasn't been doing much of anything since I've been away. They did go on one mission a while back with another pilot. Ted has been doing a little flying.

Haven't heard anything new about my foot. I'm giving it plenty of exercise anyhow and seeing the town. Maybe I'll find out something tomorrow, I hope so anyhow.

I'm sure in the mood to make hours of love to you tonight, Honey. No end of energy!! Boy! I'll bet you'd be scared!! But I could coax you until you weren't scared anymore, I'll bet. I think I could tickle you even on the ribs and blow dozens of fun bubbles and have hours of kisses like we like. Better watch what I say but I'll show you what I mean sometime.

What is the name of the Army Hospital at Brigham City? Or is that where it is? Anyhow I have been curious as to the name of the place.

Better tell you good night for now, Darling. I want you to know that I love you with all my heart and I love Marvin Carl too.

Keep sweet Connie, all my love and kisses,

Dean

26 March 1945: The Sad Love Story of Ed Gentry

Most all soldiers have a girl back home. Some are the pretend kind, some the best-friend kind, and some the serious kind. Corporal Ed Gentry, of Nashville, Tennessee, by all appearances had one of the most serious of kinds, the sure-thing kind that would wait for him, that would be there for him no matter what.

He had grown up next to Heloise. They had promised themselves to each other when they were ten years old. Studying to be an architect with his father, Ed had even drawn blueprints for their dream house to be built on the family compound overlooking the Cumberland River. There would be plenty of bedrooms for little Eds and Heloises.

On 13 December 1941, six days after the Japanese attack on Pearl Harbor, he presented himself at Fort Oglethorpe, Georgia, to enlist in the Army of the United States of America. The night before, he had dropped to one knee and presented Heloise with an engagement ring, which she enthusiastically accepted.

He tended to be a loner, and the crew decided he was "off with Heloise" when he sequestered himself. Her letters tended to be written every day although he would get them in gobs and bunches via the army Postal Service.

Ed never wavered in his love, devotion, and commitment to Heloise. He talked of her incessantly, showed anyone who would look her picture, and was known to the crew as "one lovesick puppy."

It was beyond doubt that she would wait for him, the war would end, and they would live happily ever after.

Then he got his letter. His "Dear John" letter.

The letter was six pages long, full of happy memories and encouragement, with no hint of what was to come. The last paragraph casually mentioned, "I was married last week but my husband won't mind you writing to me occasionally. He's a sailor and very broadminded."

He did not find that invitation all that comforting.

News of Ed's Dear John spread throughout the China-Burma-India Theater. About two months after his getting the letter, a copy of *Yank Magazine* showed up. It mentioned Ed Gentry without naming him. Sergeant Ed Cunningham, upon hearing Ed's story through the GI grapevine, had felt moved to write a very tongue-in-cheek article.

Jilted G.I.s in India Organize First Brush-Off Club

AT A US BOMBER BASE, INDIA—For the first time in military history, the mournful hearts have organized. The Brush-Off Club is the result, in this land of sahibs and saris; as usual, it is strictly GI.

Composed of the guys whose gals back home have decided "a few years is too long to wait," the club has only one purpose—to band together for mutual sympathy. They meet weekly to exchange condolences and cry in their beer while telling each other the mournful story of how "she wouldn't wait."

The club has a "chief crier," a "chief sweater" and a "chief consoler." Initiation fee is one broken heart or a reasonable facsimile thereof.

Applicants must be able to answer appropriately the following questions:

1. Has she written lately?

2. Do her letters say she misses you, and is willing to wait no matter how long?

3. Does she reminisce about the "grand times we had together, and the fun we'll have when you come back?"

4. Does she mention casually the fellows she is dating now?

Membership in the club is divided between "active members" and "just sweating members"—the latter being guys who can't believe that no news is good news.

Members are required to give each other the needle; i.e., full sympathy for all active members, encourage "hopeful waiting" in the just sweating members. Bylaws state: "As we are all in the same transport," we must provide willing shoulders to cry upon, and join fervently in all wailing and weeping.

One of the newest members of the club was unanimously voted to charter membership because of the particular circumstances of his case. He recently got a six-page letter from his fiancée back in Tennessee. In the last paragraph she casually mentioned, "I was married last week but my husband won't mind you writing to me occasionally. He's a sailor and very broadminded."

This G.I., so magnanimously scorned, is now regarded as fine club presidential timber.

27 March 1945, Calcutta

Dearest Peaches:

Good evening Honey! I'm sure missing you lots these days and thinking of you much too much for peace of mind. I guess I'll just have to dream of you, Sweet woman, which I do without coaxing, and like it, too.

I would sure like a picture of you sometime soon, taken in all your new Easter clothes. I would even like a studio picture, size about like this envelope (4x6) or there abouts. Someday when you are feeling good and eager when you are in town why don't you have one taken. And then you can save your camera film to take pictures of Marvin and you too, which I would like very much.

It's still, and getting more hot here every day. It hasn't bothered me much yet tho, maybe because I haven't been working, but it's too hot for comfort anyhow.

The Colonel was thru today. I don't know what his verdict was but anyhow I should be getting out pretty soon. There's nothing wrong with me anymore and I'm eager to go. I can walk about good as new now.

The time is going slower these days. Tomorrow is pass day so that will make the time go with lots of excitement. I'll tell you what goes on then.

I have dozens of chatter for you tonight, Honey, but this is the end of this stationery, so I will write you lots more chatter right away, and be looking for your sweet letters.

Harry James is giving out now and getting me. But I'm always in a loving mood for you, Darling Connie, and it makes me especially lonesome for you tonight. But there will be more beautiful moons and spring weather to enjoy with you on our long honeymoon. I like stormy spring weather better tho, I think, and love you dozens always.

You and Marvin have my prayers, Darling, write lots, sweet wife,

All my love and kisses,

Dean

PS Harry James plays "Sleepy Lagoon"

29 March 1945, Calcutta, India

Dearest Peaches:

This is certainly a beautiful evening to be writing you a letter, Honey. A nice big moon and warm spring breeze. Guess what I started thinking about right away? Your nice long letter #39, came today, Honey. I sure did like it too. There are two written ahead of it to come yet tho. Maybe they will be here tomorrow, I hope anyhow they sure do keep me happy and in love with you, Peaches.

I'm sure glad to hear that you are getting around and walking in the snow storms. I guess you are buying lots of nice Easter clothes and stuff, and I don't mind, even, Honey. Let me come give Marvin a bath, Honey, I'd like to do that but you can change the diapers!

I guess you see by the address that you can start using the old address again. I think I will be back there again in a few days and I'll like that. The doctor is going to let me go, so he says. I'll let you know about every little detail when it happens, but probably I'll write you another time from here.

Honey, you can pay all the tithing. I think I told you that we will get all our money and this payday I'll get two months flying pay so I can send some home even for you.

I'll tell you tho how much we get for everything. Base pay and longevity is $183.33. Overseas pay is $16.67 and flying pay half of the total or $100. Rations makes $42 and quarters allowance is $75 so you can add all that up ($417.00) and know until it changes again for the better. More money and more fun, and you better save some, Honey, for that double sleeping bag, but I guess we are doing pretty good.

I have a package fixed, ready to mail to you. I've about decided that there is not much worth sending home, except souvenirs. Hope you have the other package by now and hope it wasn't robbed. Anyhow this package has a couple of pillow covers, a cocktail service, a table cloth and some perfume for you. The table cloth is for your mother, Honey. I would like for you to keep one of the pillow covers for my mother and you can have the other. I think I'll buy you a nice star sapphire and deliver it sometime. That sounds like a fine idea to me. Do you like opals? There are lots of them here that I could buy. Maybe I will sometime, they would make you nice rings or ear rings.

I think that May would be a very good time to have Marvin blessed. That should be nice warm weather so he doesn't catch cold. I know March was too early now, for several reasons.

I guess you know now that my mother likes the letters she gets from you. She mentions the fact to me every once in a while that you have written.

Let's get married, Honey, when I come to see you again and don't waste any time either. Do you think we could make it as quick as last time? I know I love you dozens more if possible. At least I know hundreds more wonderful things about you now, and you've been getting prettier every day since I married you and you have lots more experience too, and that counts lots, only it's fun getting the experience.

I told a strange flirting woman that you thought we should get married for Junior's sake, when I get back, so you better not change your mind that should shock her enough. And I love you just plenty to get married to you for life, Honey.

I should be back flying B-29s when you get this, so write to me there, Honey.

I love you sweet woman with all my heart and like all your beautiful good looks and soft skin and nice chatter and your experience too.

All my love to a wonderful wife and son,

Dean

1 April Fools 1945: Cannibals

"Hey, I sure am glad we aren't in Burma," drawled Ben Prichard.

"Why's that, Ben?" asked Jerry Johnson.

"Well, I don't mind going to war with the Japs, but I don't want anything to do with cannibals."

"What are you talking about?"

"Well, it says here in the new *Survival Guide* that Burma and New Guinea have cannibals. I am just glad we aren't in Burma."

"Read me what it says."

"It is right here under 'Don't Fear the Jungle: With few exceptions jungle natives will be friendly if you make a friendly approach to them. DON'T TRY TO BULLY THEM. The exceptions include certain areas in Burma and Western New Guinea where there are cannibals.' I'm just glad we aren't going anywhere near there."

"Hey, dope, do you have any idea what CBI stands for? The B is for Burma."

"Well, at least we don't have to fly there."

"Uh, remember the mission to Rangoon?"

"Yeah, what of it?"

"Well, Rangoon is the capital of Burma. You were flying over Burma and its cannibals for about five hours."

That revelation silenced Ben. Totally. He didn't say anything to anyone for *two days*. He finally visited the chaplain.

"Chaplain, I know this sounds crazy, but I just found out we have been flying over cannibals. The first thing I can remember being afraid of was cannibals. My grandpa told me a story when I was just a little feller of how he was captured by cannibals an' barely escaped from being eaten. I had dreams about it and became afraid that I would someday be dinner for some cannibal family. It was fine back home, no cannibals, but here we are flying over them on a routine basis."

The good chaplain, a wise and experienced man, much older than Ben, listened intently, occasionally nodding and uttering an *mmm* or *I see* to convey his compassion.

In reality, Ben's fear level stunned the chaplain, a life-long pastor. He had heard a lot of stories, helped a lot people with their fears, but never had he met someone this afraid of anything, let alone of being eaten by cannibals.

For the moment he had no answer for Ben and invited him back the next day.

When they met again, the chaplain sat Ben down and explained that he had done some research. In the early days of the war, some crews had crashed and were captured by the cannibals.

Ben winced at that news; it was not what he wanted to hear.

The chaplain calmed him. "There is good news, Ben. Those cannibals did have a feast on some of the airmen. However, they decided they did not like "white meat." The meat had a foul taste to it. After the feast, almost all of the tribe got very sick. The white meat was immediately blamed and word has spread to all of the cannibal tribes not to bother to try the white meat. Now the tribes ignore the airmen and leave them alone."

Ben was very relieved with this news, and his concerns left him. He thanked the chaplain profusely and went about the rest of the war completely unaware that not a word of the chaplain's story was true.

2 April 1945, Calcutta

Hello Sweet Girl:

I'm really happy with you now since a nice letter just came and in good time too. Mailed March 21st. That is about the best time yet. And I like them all dozens too, Honey. I sure do love you today you sweet woman, because you are the best letter writer I know and the most wonderful wife in the world.

There are still two of your letters missing, #37 & 38. That must be when you got the last package I sent. I hope you told me everything got there OK, the rings and beads and stuff. Do you like the Ivory doll, Honey? I want you to like it mostly, or we can give it away.

I can get Aunt Catherine an ivory doll like she likes. You can tell her it will cost around ten dollars or more tho. I'll let you know what happens. I sure wish I knew what to get for your mother. Maybe I should name something and you tell me what she would like. I sent the table cloth already, which I told you about but it wasn't much altho probably more expensive than at home.

Some of the things I can get are, ivory carvings, animals as well as people, like elephants and stuff: the same in sandal wood which smells like incense all the time. Silverware, like vases, possibly cream and pitcher sets, and lots of cloth goods. The cloth is a great variety wool cashmere table cloths, yard goods of lots of kinds, mostly not much good but some of it OK. There maybe lots of more things that if I see I'll let you know. I know in Africa I could get some beautiful all leather purses but they are higher here. Would you or someone like a snakeskin purse? If I'm forgetting too many people, Honey, let me know and let them know I'm not exactly on a world hopping tour. Of course it's nice to send souvenirs and I like to do it but there's an end you know.

Since this is Dale's birthday tell him Happy Birthday for me, Honey. Maybe I should have written him, but you tell him I remembered anyhow. And I hope you had a happy birthday too, Honey. I love you millions when you are 20.

I'm so glad Marvin is growing nice these days, but he better smile once in a while like he appreciates all those nice things he is getting. Have you tried keeping him awake earlier in the night a little. I suppose he sleeps most of the time, but if you kept him awake a while before you go to bed, even in the day time, maybe he would like sleeping thru the wee hours better. I hope things get straightened so you sleep good, Honey.

I don't know if I should tell you now but since I've started I will do it. Maybe you won't be so disappointed now. When I just came to this hospital I heard that I might be sent home. The flight surgeon and others at the squadron said I would and even people here seemed to think so from some of my records I've seen, but they have changed their minds. And any day now I should be back working. I wouldn't want you to be too sad, Honey, and it's better that you didn't expect me. I was hoping in a way, but probably would have had to come right back over here, so a few more months with some flying time will fix me up so when I come see you, I'll stay. Naturally I'd like to see you and Marvin, more than anything but when I do I sure don't want to be worrying about coming back over here again.

Anyhow my foot is doing fine now and I'm ready to go. I went swimming at an English Country Club yesterday and enjoyed it. They have a beautiful golf course too, which I'd like to play on. It is certainly a beautiful place for India and surprised me no end.

I wish I could have seen you Easter, all dressed beautiful like you always do. Hope you had lots of nice weather to enjoy it. I remember a wonderful Easter with you, Honey. That's when I thought you were most beautiful but I was wrong, you have been getting prettier and nicer every day since. We'll have lots of Easters to have fun together yet. The main thing tho is to remember what Easter stands for. That way it means many more extra special things for us, darling. I'm sure eager to hear if you got your checkered suit for Easter. I want you to send me a picture right away as soon as you get one.

We'll have lots of wonderful times, spring, summer, and always to have fun together, Honey, taking lots of pictures and making all our plans and dreams come true. We sure do have lots too, don't we? I wish it didn't seem so far away, but maybe it won't be. I'll keep praying it won't be so long.

I love you millions, sweet beautiful girl. You are my favorite wonderful passionate wife for always.

> All my love and kisses,
>
> Dean

3 April 1945 V-mail letter, Calcutta, India

Morning Honey:

Your beautiful 'Sugar Report' of 11 March came this morning to make me very happy. It took only 12 days longer than the one 20 March but it sure tickled me as much anyhow. I'm glad to hear that the package arrived with every little thing too.

I mailed you another letter this morning so you can find out just how long and the difference for each kind.

Sure seems like it takes a long time to get anything done here, especially paperwork. I still hope I get out of here pretty quick but here patience is a great virtue. I'll have another pass tomorrow anyhow and spend all my money, that is, if I get paid by that time.

I guess you know that I'm just as proud of Marvin as anyone else and love him dozens too. I love you dozens too, Honey, because you are the beautiful, wonderful sweetheart always for me. I'll make you plenty of excitement one of these days.

> All my love and kisses,
>
> Dean

8 April 1945, Calcutta, India

Good Evening Sweet Girl:

Your latest letter of 26 Mar sure did buck up my moral today, Honey. It was almost a week too since the last one came. That makes quite a while it seems, at least here with not much to do but I like every one that comes anyhow.

Here's a small money order for you, Honey, to do most anything with, that needs done, like flowers for you and your mother on Mother's day next month, and a help for your checkered Easter Suit. This is about all I can spare this time. Guess I've been buying too many foolish things in town. I still want you to be saving all possible, and I guess you do.

As I was saying, I spent too much last Wednesday in the city just after I got paid. I bought an ivory doll and a few stones for some nice jewelry for you someday. I got two star sapphires, some opals and some white sapphires, which I may send or maybe bring myself sometime. I wish you would price some small opals per carat about the size of a regular pencil and a fat first grade pencil. If you would like some opal ear rings and a dinner ring to match, I have just what we can fix you up with.

If you price some opal, let me know. The ivory doll isn't quite as nice as the other one but you can see when I send it and if Catherine likes it, that will be fine. If she is eager to pay for it, you can charge her $8.50 for it.

Honey, I sure like all your chatter about Marvin and I'm happy that he's growing bigger and orneryer every day. I hope he knows about the days and nights now, so you can get some sleep. I sure am eager to see him, but can never tell just when that will be.

As you can see, I'm still in the hospital but ready to go anytime. It looks like it takes longer to get the paper work done to get out than to get cured, anyhow you can still write to the 770 Bomb Sq.

I wouldn't know how Peach Blossom is these days, but I imagine, still flying. Hope that I can get my flying time in one of these days soon.

I'll bet you would never guess what I did today so I'll tell you. I played 18 holes of golf and fun too. I wish you could have been along for the walk and to keep me company and for lots of people to whistle at including me, because I love you dozens always.

I played at the same English Country Club called Tallygunge Club. They have a very good golf course but lots tougher than Clovis. There are dozens of sand traps, small lakes, a river and big trees to get in the way, which they did for me. I put only two balls in the water, which the small boys get out for a small fee like 2 annas (4 cents) or there abouts. Anyhow it was fun and I did pretty good for a beginner again.

And then I had a swim again which was nice. It's a tough life these Calcutta Commandos have.

Honey, I sure get lonesome for you most all the time. I miss your wonderful kisses and loving that we had so much fun practicing on. You are the most wonderful sweetheart I ever knew. Let's get married right away, Honey, and go on a long honeymoon in Yellowstone, and just fish and make love and if you don't like it we won't even fish. WOW!!

Wish I was around to buy you dozens of flowers and candy, these nice spring days. Boy I'll bet I could convince you how much I love you sweet woman and have fun dancing and romancing.

Love and kisses always,

Dean

Chapter 16

The Exchanged Letters

13 APRIL 1945, Dean left Calcutta and returned to his unit in Piardoba. What he found was much different than what he had left. B-29 ground crews had shipped out for the Mariana Islands on 23 February. The last mission of the 770th was flown 8 February 1945. All that was left for him and his crew was to "get out of Dodge," too. On the 29th, they flew to the China forward base of Luliang, and then on to Tinian in the Mariana Islands on the 30th of April.

(Editor's note: In the following series of letters, Dean and Connie respond to each other's letters, so they appear not in date-order but in the order they are mentioned.)

13 April 1945

Dearest Connie:

Good Evening Honey! I've been reading your letters again to make me happy again and as usual, I sure like all your chatter and hope it isn't too long before more of it catches up to me.

I got back to the Squadron today after fighting the Calcutta wars. I'm glad to be back too, only sometimes I think I shouldn't have been in such a hurry. It was nice there, being able to go swimming and golfing once in a while but it's good that I'm not an orphan anymore too.

I guess I'll get my flying time in this month but anyhow there doesn't seem to be much of a rush. Might even fly the L-5 tomorrow.

There's a nice breeze this evening to help cool things down. It's a pleasant change too, because it's getting pretty hot these days here. Sure would like a nice swim.

Honey, I'm very glad you weigh 132 and I hope you do still when this gets there. If you exercise good to get the weight in the right places, I'll be very happy. I'll have you know that I love you dozens all the time, Honey, all of you.

It sure sounds interesting to hear your chatter about Marvin these days. I guess you know I would like to tickle him and make him laugh, maybe I'd even laugh especially at being with you, Honey.

The Px is having a sale on some ivory dolls so maybe I'll buy another one, because I think they are pretty nice. And if I can get one cheap it should be a good deal. I might even send you another small package someday soon.

Sweet woman, I love you dozens these days and miss you entirely too much. The time is going fast tho and we'll just be looking forward to that glorious time when we can be together again. I know we'll have a wonderful time together doing all the things we have to do, building our life together. Honey, I love you ever so much always,

Hours of love and kisses,

Dean

PS Honey, I've decided you can sell the car now if you want to and get the opportunity. You might let it be known around or even put an ad in the paper if that would help. I think it's worth about $650. Altho if you get an offer of $600 that would take it away. I believe that is above the ceiling price or something, anyhow you can let me know. None of my tools go with it tho, just the jack, pump and tire tools. Let me know what goes, Honey, and what you think. If we do sell it, I think this would be the best time of year.

If you think we should have a car, probably you should have some work done to it and it should do us good for quite a while, at least until good new ones are made.

21 April 1945, India

Good Morning Honey:

I guess its been days and days now that I haven't written you any loving letters, but I'll try to catch you up now, and anyway, I've been thinking of you most of the time, only not just in the mood to write. Also I haven't received any letters from you since I left the hospital. I sure hope they catch up pretty quick and then you should be writing here again by now.

I haven't been very busy here, still I flew a training mission and on engineering flight to get some flying time and a trip in the L-5 like I told you I was going to do. It makes me happy to get flying again too.

Darling, I have been missing you so much these days, and very lonesome at times, which I try not to think about. You are always my favorite sweetheart and most wonderful wife in the world. It certainly is hard tho for us to be separated so long. I guess you know only too well, and sometimes I wonder if all those wonderful things that have happened to us are really true. And then I know they are and there will soon be millions more of those wonderful experiences that we have shared.

Here is a picture that was taken one of the Sundays that I went to church. I just got it today and had almost forgotten. One fellow, in the center, you may remember, was at Hobbs, I believe, and maybe Clovis, he is from Chicago. If you look close you can see my bare toes sticking out of the cast I was wearing at the time.

Honey, I'm sure eager for a picture of Marvin and you too and your new flashy Easter clothes. I have a good idea how pretty you look, like you always do when you get dressed to go partying (a dancing or slumber party).

I sent you another package a couple days ago. There wasn't much in this one tho. Just two ivory dolls and a Ghurka knife. I think I've spent enough money on foolish things around here, so maybe it's save some for a change. If Catherine wants the big doll it is $15 so maybe you had better only show her one, depending on which one you like. As you see they are rather expensive even here.

I'll quit this chatter for now, Honey, and write you dozens of long sweet letters when I get yours. I love you Darling with all my heart and soul.

Love and kisses (no end!)

Dean

[211]

(Editor's Note: This is the beginning of the appearance of Connie's letters to Dean. It is actually the fiftieth letter she had written Dean, but was the first that was returned to sender, undeliverable because he was MIA. The following two letters were written on the same day that the couple prepared for their second anniversary.)

23 April 1945: The Anniversary Letters

#50: 23 April 1945 (Monday)

Dear Wonderful Husband,

Guess what got left to my house today? It was an interesting box from you, Honey, that caused lots of fun and excitement. Honey, everything is so beautiful and I'm so happy with it all. I do like the scarf and pillow slip (I have already decided which one I want). They are so pretty and unusual. And the cocktail service is really a beauty.

It will sure be nice when I can show them off in our house someday, Honey. And the perfume smells all wonderful and exciting! I sure do like it too, Honey! We sure do like the same smells!

Honey, Momma is so happy with her luncheon set too. She had better be careful, else I'll steal it from her. That wouldn't be a very nice thing for sure to do though, so I'll be a good girl. I will like using the shopping bag too.

I think I will be sending your mother the two pillow slips, one of these days soon. I bet she will be very happy to receive them.

Momma just appeared on the scene and said to tell you thank you for her luncheon set. She thinks you have very good taste in picking things out and she is very tickled. She was down to Grammys this evening and guess what, Honey? Grammy said that she would be willing to pay you for a set, similar to Momma's. So if it's ever convenient for you, I would like you to make her happy by sending a table cloth or something. Maybe I wouldn't charge her for it though, Honey. She and Grandpa were so nice about letting us use their garage last winter. (The car is kept home again these days.) If you find something, let me know your opinion about the cost. I was just thinking though when you are back to your base, maybe you can't go shopping very easy. Anyway, let me know, Honey.

I now have a black and white checkered suit that I bought last Friday. It's awful cute and nice and I even like it. The jacket to it is bolero style. I bought it with the money order you sent me. And there is still lots left to buy Mother's Day flowers with!

My long lost period made its reappearance yesterday afternoon. It's acting different than ever before. I didn't even have the cramps when it started. I had a backache though (which I never have had before at a time like this.) I wonder if it is going to be that way all the time now or if it is just for this first time. Bet I will be finding out! I will be keeping a close record about every little thing so that we will know what goes on when you come see me.

It's getting awful late now so best I get some sleep while I have the chance. Goodnight, Honey, I love you. Hundreds of torrid kisses,

Peaches

PS Hello from Marvin to Daddy! I found the newspapers very, very interesting.

23 April 1945, India

Dearest Peaches:

Some mail caught up to me today so I'm very extra special happy with you this evening and for dozens of other reasons, which I hope I can remember to tell you. All your loving chatter sure does me lots of good all the time, you sweet girl.

It would be nice if this could get there in time but probably not, but anyhow "Happy Anniversary," Honey. I wish I could be around to bring you lots of nice flowers and candy and make you extra special happy on our anniversary like I would like to do. I love you maybe even twice as much as ever if possible and because you are my favorite sweetheart and most wonderful wife. I'm very glad I married you April last, two years ago. I'll let you know just how happy you have made me and how much I like it first chance I get.

Sounds like Marvin is getting out of hand but you should find a remedy for the geyser (just hold the diaper a few seconds longer). I know I would sure like to see him. Is he growing as fast as he should, Honey? Some people here have been giving me a bad time and I just wasn't sure about what goes on. Naturally, I think he is just right by what you say, but I get kidded a bit. Sounds to me like he's doing fine anyhow. How long does it usually take babies to double their weight?

I'm glad you had him blessed on Easter, Honey. And I wish I could have been there too. Anyhow I'd like a copy of the Blessing sometime when you get one.

I'm sure happy you are feeling lots improved and full of energy these days. Be sure and take your exercises like the doctors ordered, because we want you fixed up good as new. I know a very good way to make good use of your energy too; maybe we'll try it some time (that "maybe" was a silly way to put it, wasn't it).

This is really a wonderful night here to be writing you long loving chatter, we're having a nice spring rain about now, and I guess you know what that does for me, and somebody is playing a phonograph, a beautiful piece called "Stormy Weather." That is a long time favorite with me. If you can, Honey, get the record as played by Raymond Scott. His is the best version yet.

This beautiful rain started out in a big dust storm with thunder and lightning. My bed is on the back porch and I had to move it in, and not only that but the rain blew clear in the room under the porch. Lots of fun. But it is nice sleeping outside anyhow, in fact the only place one can sleep on the hot nights. The rain really makes it cool and nice too, these days.

Speaking of buying records, I think I have a good idea thought up for our home someday. We are going to have plenty of our favorite music all the time anyhow. It will be a record player or maybe even a juke box so we just punch the numbers, for hours of the kind of music, popular, symphonic and sleepy time music just when we are in the mood for it. And even music to make love to you by. It will take loads of records but it won't cost more than a good radio and we will have what we want when we want it. I'll tell you more detail sometime. I think it's a very good idea, when it's worked out.

Everything is going quiet here these days, I haven't been too busy. My foot still feels good as new, and I can even run on it so I guess it's all fixed up. Sometimes I can feel the place where it was broken tho, but no pain.

I think I saw the show "Meet Me in St. Louis," in Calcutta a couple of weeks ago, or did I tell you already? I liked it a lot too.

I'm glad you still weigh 130, Honey. I think I'll even like it lots. I'll tell you when I see you. It won't hurt any if you gain two more ponds even, but that is about right.

I'm still not sure whether we should sell the car or not. Anyhow it needs fixed and in case you've forgotten, new rings, valve ground, gear shift tightened up and we hope that is all. If you get a good offer sometime it's okay to sell it. The way things look tho, I might be home before many new ones are being built, but when new ones are being built, ours won't be much of a trade in. Let me know what you think, Honey.

Sweet girl, I love you dozens this evening like always. I miss you much too much for comfort, but I guess I can get by OK until we can be together again and start our life right again. We'll have so many things to do and to catch up on, I guess you know. It will be wonderful being with you and Marvin and making our life like it should be. Beautiful woman, I love you more and more and I'm glad I married you, Honey. Good night for now, Peach Blossom.

Love and kisses always,

Dean

#52: 30 April 1945

Dear Wonderful Husband,

Hello, Honey! I sure do love you hundreds and millions this beautiful sunny spring afternoon that is our second wedding anniversary. It really doesn't seem like that much time has gone by since we were married. I'm awful happy that we got married, Honey. Let's do it again some time for Marvin's sake! Wonderful

Dean, I feel honored more than I can say, that a man such as you wanted me for his wife. And oh, how I do love you!

I just got home from town a little while ago. I left a roll of film to be developed that Dale took of Marvin and me yesterday afternoon I am just hoping and hoping that they turn out good, especially with the big shortage of films these days. I sure do want you to get a good picture of Marvin.

I don't think I told you about the rolls of film you sent to be developed. They all turned out blanks much to my unhappiness. I bet you had really taken some nice pictures too.

I bought me a nice white purse and belt in town today and a pair of low white non-ration play shoes. I like them all too even.

Last Saturday I saw a pretty good show. It was "Salty O'Rourke" with Alan Ladd and Gail Russel.

Guess what I did yesterday, Honey? I even went to Sunday School for once. I quite enjoyed it all too, even.

Then Momma and Grandpa came down to dinner. After that we all went for a nice ride up a couple of canyons in our car. I decided that it would be nice to go for a good ride before the car gets sold and so we did. It was such a beautiful day too, besides. Marvin sure enjoyed the ride!

Momma says thanks for the Mother's Day card. She sure does like it.

I called up a used car dealer and found out the ceiling price for a car like ours. It is $655. When I take the car in, I will find out just how near the ceiling price it is worth. If it comes close I will be happy. I would just as soon sell it no matter what we get for it. Whatever it is, it will be more than we can get later. I will tell you what happens whenever it does happen.

I have the two pillow slips all ready to send to your Mother. I will mail them next time I go to town.

Goodness, Honey, I have to get ready to go to a wedding shower now, so I'll have to close and say goodbye.

All my most torrid loving,

Connie

PS Marvin sends all his love too, to a wonderful Daddy.

#53: 3 May 1945

Good Afternoon, Honey,

You would never guess what I'm doing right this minute, besides writing this letter to you! I'm having myself a sun bath in my white shorts! It's lots of fun too and it's sure a beautiful day for such things. Come do it with me, Honey! I would like that.

I have some big news from Montana to tell you, Honey. Ruth and Bill have another baby girl. Her name is Alberta Mary and she was born 28 April at 3:40 a.m. At St. Joseph's Hospital. And she weighed 6 lbs. 7 onz. It looks as if they didn't get their boy. I hope they are awful happy anyway and they probably are too.

This morning I got the most super nice letter from you, Honey, written 23 April. I was awful excited when I saw it in the mailbox and then more so when I read it. I sure do like the way you build up my morale, Honey!

Marvin is growing in the most super way possible. Last Thursday (May 1) I took him to the Doctor. He weighed 12 lbs. 7 onz. The Doctor wants to check him in a month or six weeks.

Last time I measured Marvin (about a month ago) he was 24 inches long. It might have been 24½ but I think it was 24.

I told you a while ago that he had slept through his two o'clock feeding for the first time. Well, that was the only time it happened until the night of 30 April, at which time he slept through the night and he has been doing it ever since. So, I really get some nice sleep between his 10 o'clock and 6 feedings. I'm not a bit sorry about it either. And goodness he does like his orange juice and his bath. This past few days he tries to lift himself up when he takes ahold of someone's fingers and further more he does right good at it too! He sure does like to sit up. He takes 5 ounces of milk each feeding and sometimes 6 ounces. He gets 6 drops of cod liver oil in his 10 am bottle now.

Well, Honey, my period lasted 9 days. It was all together different from start to finish than it has ever been before.

Here are a couple of pictures that were taken last Sunday. Marvin was 10 weeks old. What do you think of our little son, Honey?

I sure had a big time at the Bridal Shower I went to last Monday. It was for our cousin Shirley, do you remember who she is? Anyway she got married yesterday. As I said I had lots of fun at the shower. We made her a Bride's Book. I had to make up the pages for the "First Night." Boy I really did the job up right! I wonder if you would be shocked at me if you could see what I did. I don't think you would be shocked at anything I might do though, I bet!!

Honey, you don't have to wonder whether we should sell the car or not anymore now. Cause guess what? It's all sold and the cash is in the bank. I didn't sell it to a car dealer after all. I sold it to one of Aunt Fern's friends, Charles Barrington. He paid the ceiling price, $655 for it and cash too! I sold it this morning. I hope that is all satisfactory to you, Honey. I just hope we don't regret the move when you come to see me again. Anyway we won't have to wonder anymore what to do and I'm satisfied with the price. It's the highest we could possible get for it these days.

That makes our bank balance $865.

Guess what I bought in town today? I bet you could never guess so I will tell you. I bought myself the nicest dress. I am trying to decide just what color it is, so I can tell you. As near as I can come to it, it is rose with black stripes. It is very striking and I like it. I hope you do too.

I was also to the dentist today. Next week my bridge will be all ready to put in my mouth. I'll be awful happy when I'm fixed up with it.

I hope I haven't forgotten anything I wanted to tell you. If I have I'll write you another letter right quick.

I mailed the pillow slips to your mother today.

Best I go in and get Marvin's formula made now.

> *I love you millions,*
>
> *Connie*

26 April 1945, India

Dearest Peaches:

Greetings sweet Woman! I guess you see I'm in the right mood again to write you a letter and I'm hoping it turns out good.

I'm just getting over a nasty mood and I'll tell you what caused it. It's just a little thing but I'll tell you anyhow. I just moved a poker game out of my room because I wanted to read and write a letter, they didn't like it. The fellow in the next room brought his table in here and invited anyone interested to play cards in my room, his room being next to mine and quite as good so far as I can tell. They played all afternoon, so when they went to supper, I swept out the pile of trash; cigar and cigarette butts and moved the table out and when they came back they weren't happy. But I don't mind and they are now going strong in the next room.

This is nothing important and goes on regularly somewhere around, but just something to write about. Maybe I'll quit wasting paper on such idle chatter, cause there's dozens of things I'd rather tell you, Honey.

The book came today that you sent, Honey, "The Way to Perfection." I'm sure glad it got here and thank you, Honey, for sending it. I will take time out one of these first days and read it. It should be very good to use some of the time we're having for leisure.

It looks like the monsoons have started. Of course it isn't my idea of what the monsoons would be. We had a big dust storm this afternoon and a wee small rain afterward. It looks like it might rain some more tonight tho.

I heard "You Belong to My Heart" for the first time yesterday. Maybe it wasn't a good version but it didn't impress me. Maybe if I hear it again, I will like it better. I know I sure would like to hear you play it, Honey, and dozens of other pieces that you play nice.

I'm hoping for more mail from you right soon now. I haven't had a letter from my mother in 9 days. Looks like you must not have changed addresses when I first told you or maybe your letters caught a slow boat, I'll see!

Here is the last of the CBI (China, Burma, India area of operations) as you can plainly see and I guess it's a good time for a change.

I know I'll be much happier when I can save the paper to write to strange characters and tell you all the idle chatter that comes to my mind.

Honey, I sure love you this evening like usual. It really makes me happy to think about you being my beautiful wonderful wife and us having a nice son. There are so many blessings that we have that it's hard to put all the things I feel into words, but I do know that I love you, Darling, with all my heart and soul. Seems so wonderful for pleasant memories from the past and plans for the future that we get along together so good. But then, how would we do any different together, Honey? I like you too good all the time for arguments or even disagreements. Guess it's because you are so beautiful and lovely always, and I guess you know I like beautiful girls, especially young ones like you, Honey, that are so nice to me all the time.

I'm so eager to see Marvin and you so we can teach him like good kids, and make love to you like big kids having lots of fun. More chatter later, Honey,

Love and kisses always,

Dean

#54: 7 May 1945

Hello Honey,

I am loving you today, like always, Honey, and am missing you millions. I received another of those best of "sugar reports" from you this morning (written April 26) so that helps the situation out lots.

Guess what Dorothy and George have got that was born on our anniversary? They have a baby boy! His name is George Edward. That is all the info on the situation that was on the announcement. I'm sure happy that they got a boy like they wanted, too. I wonder how many years it will be before George gets the good news. It almost seems like years when waiting for that kind of news to reach Daddy.

I also got a letter from your Mother this morning. She said that Marjorie has a baby girl born May 1.

Today turned out to be pay day too, besides.

I'm happy to hear that "The Way to Perfection" finally caught

up to you. I was beginning to wonder about it.

Honey, I have been wondering if you have sent more money to the bank than has gotten there so far. You will recall that you sent me a $100 money order that I put in the bank. Then you sent another $100 through the Finance Department that arrived alright. Have you sent any more than that? If you have you had better check and see where it is. If no more has been sent then everything is fine.

Honey, our lilacs are in full bloom now. And oh, they smell so delicious. We have bouquets of them all through the house and so both inside and out everything smells nice like lilacs.

Up to now I have been mixing doing Marvin's washing with writing this letter. I'm all finished with the wash now though. I really don't mind doing Marvin's washing especially when I have a washer to use. I am awful glad I don't have to use a bath tub for the purpose. Then, I would like to hang every little thing out on the clothes line, because on nice warm sunny days like now, I can have myself a good sun bath while I work. That's what I did today.

Last Friday evening Marvin stepped out into society! I took him to Shirley's Wedding reception. He was the best little boy too. I think he must have enjoyed himself. Among other things (of course) Shirley got 9 beautiful blankets. It all started me to thinking that maybe some time if I happen to see a nice blanket or two, that maybe I should make a purchase. No doubt we'll need a new blanket someday.

This is sure a delicious chocolate milk shake that I am eating.

I had a big time the other day cutting the back lawn. I wore my sun suit for a sun bath. Honest, Honey, I'm just so eager to get myself a beautiful suntan! I'll try not to get sunburned though.

Yesterday I was, without a doubt, the nicest girl. I went to Sunday School again even. And I liked it again too.

I found out definitely that Marvin is 24 inches long and not 24½. I bet he won't be 24 for very long though. Honey I really don't know how old a baby is supposed to be when they double their weight. I will tell you when I find out. I have been letting down on my piano playing lately, best I get practiced up again.

By now, wonderful man, I know that you are the grandest, best husband that I love in the whole world. None could ever be better, Honey.

> Thousands of my passion, Honey

> Peaches

9 May 1945—V-mail letter

Dearest man, Dean:

The latest package you sent me arrived today, Honey. That is an awful nice Ivory Doll to add to our collection of beautiful souvenirs that you are buying. I guessed that the smallest doll was for Aunt Catherine so she now has it. Did I guess right? Is that a hunting knife you sent, Honey? Or if not what is it called? It is sure nice and fancy. You probably have written a letter about these things, but I haven't received it yet if you did. I like the things a lot, Honey, and Aunt Catherine is happy too.

Come sleep in the dining room with me tonight, Honey. The floor in my bedroom is being varnished, so Marvin and I are parked in the dining room. I think tomorrow we can move back into our room. This evening after Primary, I went to my flower shop and ordered Mamma's and my corsages for Mother's Day, from you, sweet boy. For Momma I ordered pink roses and white carnations, and for me I ordered red roses and white carnations.

Honey, I can see me getting tanned already. This morning I had a nice sun bath while looking at my latest issue of "Harpers Bazaar" that came today.

I heard over the radio this evening that tonight is Waltz Night at the Coconut Grove. This being Wednesday, I can't quite figure it out. I'll have to look into the matter so will know all about it when you come see me.

I'm all run out of stationery, and this is the end of this V-mail, as you can fairly see, OK. I will just simply have to close for now. Good night, Honey. I love you millions, wonderful man,

> Connie

27 April 1945, India

Dearest Peaches:

Good Evening, you wonderful woman that I love millions always. Honey, I sure did get a thrilling 'sugar report' from you, today written 7 April.

Darling, your letters sure do me lots of good and make me happy and in love with you more and more all the time. And a bit lonesome for you most always too, which it's better that I don't think about while things are this way. But I can dream anyhow, lots of wonderful dreams and memories, of the sweetest most beautiful wife in the world, and the wonderful hot times we always had like extra special ones like when I came to see you from Victorville and then at Arrowhead!! And at Lincoln's Park and dozens more too. Honey, it hardly seems possible how anyone could be such a wonderful lover as you always are and I like you that way too. There will be years more of lots of fun times for us. Let's go to Yellowstone, Honey, and set a new record for long time hot love making.

Boy, I'll fix your spare energy some day, we hope soon. I guess you know I'm the guy who can, too. And you are the only one to do me good, Honey!

Sounds like the doctor bill is very cheap. I thought it would be lots more than that, but anyhow I guess its enough and I'm glad it will be paid quick without drawing any money from the PO. I think maybe I'll be able to send some more home after the next payday. Things are getting back to normal, at least not moving around to mess things up and I'll stop buying silly junk here or I have already. I hope the packages I sent are coming along by now.

I sure would like to go buy you some pretty new dresses these days. Because I guess you know I like to see you all dressed pretty in new clothes. Please don't buy anymore than you need now, Honey, and when I come see you we'll have a big party in a formal even.

Does Marvin's hair curl nice all by itself, Honey? I sure would like to see him, might even tease him a bit and I could tickle you too, dozens.

Might even start a fire, kissing your sweet lips and neck, that would take hours to put out. I could easily do both tonight Darling, Peach Blossom.

Goodnight, All my love and kisses,

Dean

#56: 11 May 1945

Good Morning Honey,

How do you like my new stationery, Honey? I think it is rather nice. It's fun to have a different kind to write your "Sugar Reports" to you sweet boy.

Honey, I really am convinced that you are my most handsome wonderful man. I was just so awful happy yesterday when the letter came with the picture in. It seems so good to have a good recent photo of you. Besides the letter with the picture in, I received my latest letter from you written 27 April. They made me all happiness, Honey, and I sure do love you.

Yesterday in Walgreens I really did find a prize. And that is a roll of film for the camera. I'm just awful happy about it. That will make for more pictures that can be taken and then sent to you. And that is definitely good, Right? Right!

Marvin and I were back in my bedroom last night for sleeping. It's nice in there now. I have it arranged so that the door can be opened for summer.

For quite some time now pretty colors have been causing Marvin dozens of excitement. It's so fun to watch him. His hands fly around in the air, his eyes just about pop out, the bubble stream from his mouth, and he tries his darnedest to get a hold of what is presently exciting him. Besides all that he grunts and snorts, talks and laughs.

If his rompers aren't fastened between his legs, he quite often has them all pulled up chewing on them.

In the vicinity of 8 o'clock every morning I hear big business going on in a certain little baby's bed. Those grunts really give the whole thing up. I am glad his bowel movements are so regular. I hope they continue to be.

Honey, Devon just called me and said for me to drop by the office at 1:00 pm and Bob would put my bridge in for me. I think I will get ready now, and do a little shopping first. I will be back.

As you see I am back again. I have my new tooth in too. You will have to come and see it sometime! My dentist bill is all paid too and that is really something considering how much it was. I got rid of $78 all at once without any trouble at all. (Nice? Well not very.) Anyway I paid it all from my newest payday and I didn't draw any money from the Post Office which is good. And I am definitely glad I don't owe the man anything.

When I got home, Lorraine was here to see me with her baby. So we had a nice visit then.

Aunt Catherine is paying for her ivory doll on the installment plan. She made the first payment yesterday, it was $2.50. She is definitely happy with her statue too.

It sounds good to hear that you are flying again these days.

I'm glad to know what kind of knife that is that you sent. I wish I knew if I was pronouncing it correctly though. I guess you can tell me sometime.

Honey, I wouldn't call all the nice things you have been sending me junk. I'm very happy with every little thing. Maybe you have just about bought enough though.

Yes, Honey, Marvin's hair curls really nice all by itself. I'm sure glad too. He has it all worn off of the back and sides of his head. I hope he stops wiggling long enough one of these days so that it will grow in again.

He sure doesn't like his "comfort." He never has liked it very much. I'm glad of that too.

Last night I did something I haven't done for a long time. I went to chorus practice at the ward. I'm going to sing with the chorus Sunday for Mother's Day.

Today a book that I ordered from the Literary Guild got here. It is "Captain from Castile." I hope it is as good as I think it will be.

Well I am back again, Honey. Momma and I took Marvin for a nice buggy ride. We mostly went over to the Bishop's so that I could get our tithing paid. Marvin definitely liked going for the ride too. After a while he was sound asleep. The little stand by the park is open again so we had a hamburger and milk shake before coming home. It was good too.

Honey, I'm all in the mood to go dancing and romancing with you tonight! Wouldn't it be glorious if we could only be able to? It will be so perfectly wonderful whenever we can do all we would like to do together again. And then for a thrilling night of hot love making!!

Goodnight Dean,

Connie

Chapter 17

Letters Back and Forth

V-mail—3 May 1945

Dearest Peaches;

Have had several nice letters from you just recently, Honey, and liked them very much. As you see I'll try and V-mail once more until I get time to write you another.

Have flown a couple more times lately to help on the flying time.

Have been busy the last few days making house. We now live in tents and I've been trying to build some furniture to help make it livable.

Have been swimming several times too, the last few days, and have been enjoying the swim fins lots. Even better than Long Beach. With water goggles I can see dozens of kinds of fish too. Will you see if you can find some water goggles for me, Honey, at ZCMI or a sporting store. If you do find some don't send them until I let you know. Paper running short but my love for you is growing every day, Honey.

Love and kisses, Always,

Dean

(The reason Dean needed swim fins and was building furniture was he had reached his new posting. He would now be flying out of the Mariana Islands and more specifically West Field on the island of Tinian.)

#58: 16 May 1945

Good evening Sweet Boy:

I'm sure full of hundreds of energy these days, Honey. I like feeling this way too. I just wish you were here so that I could put some of it to wonderful exciting use. Oh! So perfectly glorious, thrilling fun. It was wasn't it? It will be, won't it, again some day soon?

Honey, last Sunday afternoon we took some more pictures. And naturally I'm hoping for the best results. I'm patiently waiting for them to be developed. I'll send any and all good quality results to you immediately, Honey. And I sure do hope that you have received the other pictures that I sent by now.

Last Sunday being Mother's Day, Momma and I both went to Sunday School. Marvin came too. He was so cute and good the whole time too. In fact he was asleep most all the time. Mammy went to Sunday school with us too.

Besides Sunday school, I went to church. Dale tended Marvin while I was to church. I sang in Sunday school and church in the girls chorus. I liked doing it too.

After church lots of the family came to our house to talk and eat sherbet and cake.

Momma and I really did enjoy our corsages too, Honey. Thank you dozens for giving them to us.

And guess what, Honey? I stopped chewing gum completely. I have two reasons for doing so. First of all, gum just plain isn't good for your teeth and second gum sticks to plastic teeth like I have one of now. So, that is the whole story in brief.

Bout a week or so ago the paper "Super Fort" got here. I have been enjoying it till now.

I had more fun last night. Aunt Fern and I went to see "Sudan."

It was pretty good too. At least I was in the mood for that sort of thing at the time. When we got out of the show the rain was just pouring down. So we raced down Main street 60 per to get to the car. We just got soaked too! And it was fun!

This afternoon in Primary prayer meeting, I had to do lots of business. I gave the prayer, gave a talk, called the roll and read the minutes. It was a pretty good talk that I thought up too.

Your nice little V-mail of 3 May came yesterday. I'll see about getting you some water goggles, Honey, like you said to.

There doesn't seem to be any Neats Foot oil in town. I'm sure that won't do my purse any good.

Honey, I have on some very nice pajamas now and I'm completely ready for bed. Come be with me, Honey, so we can have hours of hot love making together.

Marvin sure does get excited when he sees the pajamas I have on. It's the pretty pink and white stripes that he likes so well.

Honey, you wonderful, torrid, handsome man that I married. I love you with all my heart and soul for time and all eternity. Oh, what you did to me with your most perfect, glorius love techniques! And you sure do know what makes for love thrills and excitement.

> Goodnight, Dean, I'm all yours forever
>
> Peaches
>
> *xxxxxxxxxx*

7 May 1945: VE Day

On this day, 7 May 1945, Germany surrendered, ending the war in Europe. America's fighting forces could now fully be brought to bear on Japan.

7 May 1945

Dearest Peaches:

Good evening, Sweet woman! Just about this time of day I sure do miss you, Honey. And get to thinking about all the wonderful things you mean to me. You are my favorite beautiful sweetheart always, Honey, and

I love you dozens, all the time.

I just read your latest letter over again on account of because none have come for a few days. I imagine it's the mail situation like always tho. I sure do like your 'Sugar Reports,' because it always makes me happy to hear from you.

I'm glad Marvin has his days and nights straight now so you can get lots more sleep. I guess he should have lots of things well under control now. It still seems not quite real, Honey, when I think about us having a son. I know it's very wonderful in all ways, but maybe me not seeing him makes it hard to realize sometimes. But it gives me a thrill always, to think that I married such a wonderful woman, in every respect, as you Darling, and that we belong to each other for all eternity. I know it will be wonderful when we can enjoy all those wonderful things together.

Hope the packages have come by now that I sent. I guess you'll let me know anyhow. It looks like I wont be able to get you a snakeskin purse, Honey, but I would like to if there's a chance sometime.

Have you heard of George's baby yet? It must have arrived before this.

Honey, I sure am eager to get some pictures of you and Marvin and especially you, Sweet Girl. I have two rolls of film yet if it isn't spoiled so maybe some of these first days I'll take a picture and see what happens.

The theater is just next door with a new show every night for free so maybe I'll be going now.

Goodnight my most wonderful wife and remember that I love you with all my heart and soul forever, kisses,

Dean

xxxxxxxxxx

#59: 19 May 1945

Evening Honey,

Goodness, Honey, just look at all the pictures you found in this letter! They are the ones that were taken 13 May, Mother's Day when Marvin was 12 weeks old.

Yesterday I got an awful nice letter from you, sweet boy (written 7 May.)

Honey, please hurry and get a picture of yourself with the films you said you have. I would like that lots, Honey.

Yesterday when Marvin was three months old, he weighed 14 lbs. 2 onz. and was 25 inches long. He sure enough is growing!

Thursday evening I went to Lincoln Junior High's Spring Concert with Mammy, Aunt Fern and Catherine. It was quite fun too. Barbara played in the orchestra.

Gosh, Honey, I haven't been able to take any sun baths since I last told you. It has been too cool for such things. It has been raining and hailing and has been cloudy most of the time. I don't mind the nice rain though. I have an awful cute new swim suit, Honey, that I bought yesterday. It is lots nicer than the other sun suit I bought once. So now, I want some nice warm sunny days to wear it. It can be worn as a swim suit too.

It is Sunday now and it is about 6:30 pm. I didn't go to Sunday school this morning and I'm not in the mood for church either, so I guess I'll stay home. Am I a bad girl?

Mammy and Aunt Fern were here for dinner.

I have been doing quite a bit of scripture reading today. I have to read a certain amount each month for Primary. I suppose it is really all for the best, for sure to read it all, I bet!

Honey, I say goodbye for now. Remember I love you millions for always.

> *All my best love and kisses,*
>
> *Peaches*
>
> *xxxxxxxxxx*

9 May 1945

Good evening Sweet Woman:

I have been reading lots of your letters over again and getting lots of new love out of them, since no new ones have come since I wrote the last letter. Sometimes I even find something new that I missed, but I hope the mail situation improves because I like to get all the latest from you, Honey.

I've even been part way busy these last few days, which I'll tell you about.

I've had lots of fun swimming everyday and using my swim fins; maybe I'll even get my money's worth before they fall apart. I borrowed a pair of water goggles a few times and things under the water look just like an aquarium with fish even, and they are nice for diving. I get lots of sun tan that way, too. And now I'm like a good Indian. I haven't even gotten sun burned since the time on the way over. I've been out in the sun as much as four hours too.

We have been short of lights in our tents but I traded for a good lantern, which is like a gasoline lantern but burns kerosene. It works nice too, and in the evenings when I get in a loving mood and thinking of you, I can do just like I'm doing now, writing you a letter, favorite woman.

I've been flying some training missions too, to keep things running as they should. It is just like the flights we used to make back at Clovis. It helps too, to be doing something to make the time go faster, which I like for it to do. We can even get a good radio station on the plane radio, so I heard the news and some nice music today for the first time in several days.

When we can hear a radio we get all the latest news just as soon as there, maybe even better at times, and it's good news the last couple of days, like the war being half over, and much over half, in time. We may even get some help and that is good, with things already under control here.

I have been reading the book you sent and learning lots of new things and wonderful for us, Honey. We have lots of things to do together yet to make our life complete and accomplish what we have to do on this earth. Darling, I'm so happy always that we had the privilege of going thru the Temple together.

Honey, I'm so happy about you too, that you are my favorite beautiful woman all the time. I guess you know you are the prettiest morale builder that I know, and I love you with all my heart, Honey. I love you for all the wonderful things you are, like a most wonderful wife, and the most wonderful lover ever, Honey.

Best I say goodnight for now, Honey, and all my love to you Sweetheart and Marvin.

Dean

PS I don't mind if you wear the star sapphire.

xxxxxxxxxx

11 May 1945

Dearest Peaches,

I guess you see I have the idea and time both together today, so you are about to get a letter.

Right now before I forget, I want to tell you to be watching for some more money. Yesterday I sent you some money thru the finance office and the same amount to the bank which is $50. So, Honey. When you get another government check for $50, you can go see the bank and get the little book up to date as they should get the money at the same time.

I don't know what you will be needing to buy this time, Honey, but you will take care of it, I know. Has the dentist been paid yet? And then there is the car to be fixed, still. I think it might be a good idea for us to keep the car, but I'm waiting to hear what you think about it. We might even go thru Yellowstone again like about the time we did last year. This isn't a promise but it's a good idea and I'm praying that it might come true, Honey. Those are the kind of things I've been thinking of lots lately.

I've heard somebody's optimistic idea, who should know, and that is that our job should be about at an end here in three months. I think I'll wait and see, because that isn't very long. I don't want you to get all excited, Honey, but I'll tell you what's cooking that I know about. This is hardly a rumor either, as it was given to us rather officially.

That way, I might even see Marvin before he goes to school! I sure would like to see him, Honey, and see what was cookin' when I saw you last. I still love you millions, Honey, from the wonderful things you did last time we were together.

I've still been busy swimming mostly every day and having great sport of it. The water doesn't even get in my nose or mouth much anymore to give me trouble.

We're going to have a small flower garden by our tent too. I got a few seeds from Lt. Dechert that he got somewhere and planted them around. Honey, I would like for you to get a collection of flower seeds, some big warm climate variety and send them. Regular mail would get here about as soon, too. I'd like to plant a few flowers in my spare moments. The watermelon seeds haven't come yet. My foot locker should come most any day now, I hope.

It would sure be nice if some mail would catch up. None has come for about 12 days now. That makes a nasty mess, because I sure like to get your 'Sugar Reports' sweet woman. I'd even like to know how Marvin is doing but I know he is doing just fine with all the best care he is getting.

I hope you still like being Primary secretary and that it doesn't keep you too busy, Honey. I think it's a good idea tho for you to be doing what you can along that line. Only I wish I could be taking you to church and be bringing you home again afterward, too.

We have been having lots of nice rains lately too. In fact almost every night. One night we just about got flooded out. It rained very hard and we had a big wind, too. Almost everybody got out in the middle of the night to pound down the tent pegs. Lots of fun and wet too. Last night we had a rain almost all night. It was nice tho, with not much wind. It made very wonderful sleeping and dreaming weather, Honey.

Always the nicest dreams are about you, you beautiful sweet woman. I don't have to dream tho to know how pretty you are, Honey, or that you are the most wonderful wife in the world for me. I'm so glad, Peaches, that I married you and that we belong together forever. Oh, you sweet girl, I love you so much, and much more than I can put into words, but I'll let you know just how much that is when I can come see you again, and cuddle with you for hours, and make love to you just like you like to our heart's content, and everything else content too.

Goodbye for now, my wonderful Peaches,

Dean

xxxxxxxxxx

#60: 23 May 1945

Hello Dearest Dean,

It is just nice today for a sun bath, so, I'm out in the back yard in my sun suit. It seems nice again to sit outside and enjoy the warm sun.

Two of your super wonderful letters have just recently arrived. I am all happiness and in love with you hundreds because of them, Honey (written 9 May and 11 May).

I suppose that some time ago you got the news that I had sold the car. I do hope that it wasn't a mistake and that you are happy. So you see, we can't very well get it fixed up soon.

You also should have heard by now that the dentist has been paid.

Honey, nothing could be more perfect for us than to go through Yellowstone next fall. It would be so wonderful. Please don't worry about me getting all excited at the prospects of seeing you, and then getting disappointed if you can't come then. I have about reached point where I expect things when they happen. I think you know just what I mean, Honey. So, Honey, I would like you to tell all that cooks that you are allowed to tell and I'll get as happy as I dare to. It will be a glorious day for us, sweet boy, when we can be reunited again. I love you, Honey, and Marvin sends his love too.

Good news that foot locker of your is certainly taking forever and a day to get to you. I was surprised to hear that it hadn't arrived yet. I'll see if I can remember to send you some flower seeds, Honey.

Wonderful man, that son of yours and mine just keeps getting the cutest yet, always and every day.

I will be watching for the money you sent too, Honey. I like to go get the bank book all fixed up and have our account grow.

The latest issue of the National Geographic came yesterday. It had a real good map of China in it too. It's a real big one that separates from the magazine. I enjoyed looking at it. You know how much we like to look at maps.

My period started Monday (21st) it came 2 days late. That's close though for me. The flow is quite heavy again too. The doctor said that was natural for about six months or so, so, I guess it is alright for now. I didn't especially have any cramps either just an odd feeling that is about all gone now.

I thought I had some more things to tell you, but I sure can't think of them now. So, I'll stop puzzling and say Goodbye, Honey.

I love you always,

Peaches

xxxxxxxxxx

Enclosed in this letter, Connie sent Dean two packets of flower seeds that he had requested in his 11 May letter: "The Wonder Packet—nearly 7 times 7 wonders of the flower world." The packets were labeled "Mandeville *Triple-tested* Flower Seeds." They cost five cents each.

(This is Dean's last letter.)

13 May 1945—Sunday, Mother's Day.

Dearest Peaches:

Happy Mother's day greetings, Honey. I know I sure would like to come give you my personal greetings, Honey, and I think it would be much better than on paper, too. That's mainly because I love you so much, Honey. I know I sure do love you lots all the time, everyday.

I guess you know I like to write you long letters but since none have come from you or anyone else for two weeks now, I'm kinda short of chatter today. So when I finish I'll go for a swim and some more suntan. I know, how would you like to come with me to get the suntan, and I would like for you to, Honey.

I even took a couple of pictures yesterday and when I finish the roll, I'll send you the negatives. I think I'll do it pretty soon even, so you can have some pictures. I hope you send me some pretty soon too, Honey because I'm eager to see my favorite beautiful woman again and I want to see Marvin, too.

I've been making like Mrs. Flannigan the washer woman, doing my own laundry. It's great sport, I guess you know, but I don't like it. Everybody else does the same around here, or wears it dirty. I think that last is the easiest way. I know it sure would be nice if we could just send it to the laundry or even let the "bearer" do it. ("Bearers" are the Indian house boys that we don't have any more.)

There sure is a lot of nice things coming over the radio these days, like wonderful music, and the latest news, too. My radio hasn't come yet so we hear it mostly while flying. One of the best programs that comes over the Armed Forces Radio is "Intermezzo." It is a program of classical and symphonies.

Honey, I've heard rumors and good ones even that I might get to be a captain, supposedly in a couple of months. I'm not holding my breath but it sounds good anyhow. I know there is a possibility anyhow because all the airplane commanders are supposed to be captains, again. You don't need to worry about it tho, Honey, until I tell you something has been done.

I saw Capt. Child yesterday too. I hope you remember him from Clovis. He is looking good. I didn't get to talk to him tho.

It sure would be nice if some mail would come so I could answer all your letters, because I like to be hearing from you regularly I guess you know. I'd even like to hear more about Marvin, too, and some pictures even.

Did you know I've sent $525 home since I've been here? And since there's no place to spend it III probably send you some more, Honey. I hope you are putting some of yours away too.

Better stop my chatter now, you sweetest Peach Blossom and just tell you that I love you ever so much because you are the most wonderful wife, and beautiful sweetheart, and hot lover even, for me.

Love and kisses, no end!

Dean

xxxxxxxxxx

14 May 1945: A Rather Odd Mood

(This letter was written the night Dean was shot down, a day after he had written his last letter.)

#57: 14 May 1945

My most wonderful man,

I'm in a rather odd mood tonight, Honey, and it is most all about you and Marvin and me. I have been trying to decide whether or not I would write to you tonight most all evening. I wanted to, but I didn't know if I could express my feelings as I would want to, and, as I feel them. As you can see, Honey, I have made up my mind to try. How well I succeed remains to be seen.

When I heard the news tonight that President Heber J Grant

[237]

had died this evening, it started me to thinking about some certain things. I thought of what a grand reward he will get for the great good works he did upon this earth and how happy he must be to have passed through this life so successfully. Then I thought what work yet lays ahead of him. It all seems so deep. Some beautiful thrilling church music was played over the radio in President Grant's memory. It got me all sentimental.

Then I was thinking of Marvin and wondering just what a great man he had been before coming into our care, Honey. I wondered what his talents were. To have a Daddy such as you here on this earth, Honey, he would have to have been great, kind and good, even as you were, and you still are. Honey, I'm really just beginning to realize what a great responsibility we have in teaching and caring for Marvin. We just have to do it to the very best of our ability. I know you have lots of ability, Honey, and I hope I have.

And Honey, I have just been wondering and thinking about lots of other similar things, like what our relationship was in the world before this. Do you suppose we knew one another? Honey, I think we must of because we were so meant for each other here.

Honey, that sweet little baby of ours is growing and growing. He's really getting to be quite the little chubby boy. And this evening he measured 25 inches long. I most always call him Marvin. Now and again I have to call him "Shorty Pants" though.

I keep thinking how perfect, like Heaven it would be if you were with me Honey, so you could see Marvin each day and watch him play and grow and eat and sleep and cry too. If I think too much about it, I get awful sad so I try not to let that happen. I try to think what a grand happy time we will all have some day.

Honey, I have been trying to think just how it would be to see you again. To play, work, laugh with you, to make passionate love with you and do just everything we used to do and dozens more besides.

I have a hard time getting the picture in my mind, the past seems like such a thrilling dream of love and happiness. I wonder if it all really happened, but then I know it did. And Oh! Honey, *how I do love you now and forever and ever ever after with all my heart and soul. Honey, I just can't express how deep my love for you is. It's an impossibility. I love you always.*

Good night my husband,

Peaches

xxxxxxxxxx

HEADQUARTERS XXI BOMBER COMMAND
APO 234

Field Order No. 75 TACTICAL MISSION REPORT   Mission 174
   Target: Northern Nagoya Urban Area
   14 May 1945
   Mission: Field Order 75, Headquarters XXI Bomber Command. Directed
to the 58th, 73rd, 313th, and 314th Bombardment Wings to take part in an
incendiary attack on the northern Nagoya urban area.

Importance of Target

The area of Nagoya selected for this incendiary attack lies in the northern
part of the city just below the Shonai River, in the vicinity of the Nagoya
Castle and to the castle's east and south.

In addition to being one of the most densely populated portions of the
city, the overall target area includes the Mitsubishi Aircraft Company Engine
Works, the Mitsubishi Electric Company (the Chug Branch), the Nagoya
Arsenal, and a number of smaller plants converted to war production.

The mission was planned so that an average of more than 225 tons of
incendiary clusters per square mile of the target area would be dropped.

In planning this mission as an incendiary daylight attack, primary consideration was given to the smoke from fires resulting from the bombing by
the first formation over the target.

Altitude: 16,000–18,000 feet
Initial Point: 3511N–13606E
Length of Run: 47 miles
Time of Run: 9 minutes

Chapter 18

Mission 174

14 May 1945: Mission 174

Missions were born in the minds of strategists and the highest-ranking generals in the War Department, sequestered safe from harm's way in Washington D.C. It was left to lower-ranking generals to implement the missions, utilizing the everyday soldiers, the grunts of the war. On 13 May 1945, the XXI Bomber Command, based in Guam, led by General Curtis LeMay, implemented Mission 174 under Field Order No. 75.

Some 524 B-29s, drawn from the 58th, 73rd, 313th, and 314th Bombardment Wings from Guam, Tinian, and Saipan, were ordered to take part in an incendiary attack on the Nagoya urban area.

At the rallying point, the 524 B-29s compressed into thirty-seven formations of three or more planes, and spent one hour and twenty minutes firebombing the urban area to the south and east of Nagoya Castle. Nagoya had 210 heavy anti-aircraft positions in and around the city. About half would be in range of the attackers and intent on stopping their intrusion.

Nagoya's air defenses included twenty-five twin-engine fighters and fifty-five single-engine attack planes. They mounted some two hundred seventy-five attacks on the Americans. Eighteen Japanese planes were declared destroyed with another sixteen listed as probable. The Superforts would claim another thirty as damaged. (HQ XXI)

There would be losses: eleven planes would not return. The B-29 commanded by Lt. Dean Sherman was downed by a Japanese Nick fighter early in the bombing run, and B-29 70017 was brought down by ground defenses directly over Nagoya. Nine other B-29s were lost due to mechanical problems or running out of fuel. Thirty-five airmen would die. Thirty-two would be rescued from the sea by the US Navy, utilizing six submarines and three surface vessels positioned along the attack route.

Nagoya merited the bombing attack by being the fourth largest city in Japan, and a critical part of aircraft production for the war effort. One-fourth of the city's million-and-a-half citizens made a living making airplanes.

For Lt. Dean Sherman and the Hellbirds of the 462nd, recently of India, this was the third mission staged from the Marianas and their home base of West Field on Tinian.

Mission takeoff was a spectacle. The planes mimicked an expedition of marching ants leaving home. One by one, single file, they went, the next taking the place of the antecedent. They were very, very noisy marching ants.

The engines of the thirty-six Hellbirds called to the mission had a cumulative 316,800 horsepower. The engines dominated the sound waves, no other intonation audible as the Twentyniners sought the air. Deafening, thunderous, and roaring—all fail to describe the noise level of that moment.

"9966 to tower, requesting taxiway access."

"Good morning 9966, you are number ten. Proceed down taxiway Alpha. Hold short behind 6671."

"Proceeding down taxiway Alpha, holding short behind 6671."

Peaches throttled forward on a 90-degree turn onto Alpha taxiway, moving one hundred yards to the tail of 6671, assuming her place in the parade, nudging forward every minute or so as a B-29 left the runway. Inside her belly, the crew worked the remaining checklist items.

Working a checklist had a calming effect on a crew contemplating a mission. Practicing a routine occupied the mind and left no room for "what if" questions. Just focus, focus on the checklist, not on the fact that in six hours or so Japan would be throwing flak and bullets at you with no good intent.

"More clouds than predicted," navigator Orr observed.

Radioman Johnson offered the explanation, "That cold front, predicted in the flight briefing, turned out to be a warm front and is kicking up a ton of clouds."

Miller felt compelled to note, "Those weathermen are all officers aren't they, Johnson?"

"Yes. Yes they are, Sergeant." The Corporalies, smiling and chuckling, were ardent believers that officers were responsible for all screwups in war. The officers were left to shake their heads.

"Careful, Miller—those stripes on your arm are removable," Lt. Reynolds warned, in feigned sternness.

"Yes, sir!" snapped off Miller, in his best trainee-to-drill sergeant voice.

It would take nearly an hour to get all thirty-six Hellbirds in the air. The runway was two miles long, liftoff occurred at speeds over 195 miles per hour, optimally attained by the midpoint. At the clear indication of a B-29 being airborne (meaning its wheels were a few feet off the ground), the green light flashed on the tower, indicating that the next in line should begin takeoff.

When the process was working, there was a B-29 gaining altitude at the end of the runway, one separating from the concrete at midway, and one starting takeoff at the beginning of the runway. It was not unheard of for breakdowns to be pushed off the end of the runway unceremoniously to allow for everyone to get airborne. By the end of the war, the scrap aluminum at the runway terminus was considerable and would take years to clear and recycle, creating a Tinian cottage industry.

Even under the best of conditions, with everyone getting off smartly in an hour's time, they would be scattered over hundreds of miles en route to Nagoya. Pilots would organize themselves and compress the strike force at a set of coordinates known as the rallying point, and move in small groups to the initial point of the bombing run.

Many miles of the journey were flown over safe territory, with no possibility of enemy attack. But once in proximity to Japan and its air defenses, there was safety in numbers. Each plane benefited by being surrounded by "friendlies," especially friendlies with .50 caliber guns.

Dean pulled around the corner at the end of Alpha and put his nose onto Runway 2.

"9966, you're up next. Go on green."

"Going on green."

The green light, mounted on a makeshift tower at West Field Runway 2, gave permission to start takeoff. Everyone in the front end of the plane was fixated on it.

"Green light!" called out Reynolds.

Engineer Miller checked his board, "All lights are green."

Dean's left hand moved the RPM controls forward, forcing life into the engines and creating a surge toward takeoff. *Peach Blossom* was in good form this morning, rarin' to go, he judged. This new version of *Peach Blossom* was going out on its second mission, the first with the Sherman crew.

They had not flown a real-life mission together for months—a few training flights, but no missions. There was some rust; not a major issue or anything anyone worried about. They had other more important concerns, like holding up their end of the deal—doing their job as well as it could be done, and holding trust that everyone else in the plane was doing the same thing.

"Crew Integration" manifested in physical ways, such as in the successful flying of the Superfort, but also in emotional ways. Trust was a big part of that—trust that was built on missions, trust that was built in the face of enemy guns, or passing through a storm in the Himalayas, or completing a mission they should never have been able to complete. Everyone contributed to the crew's emotional collective, and all, in turn, fed off of it.

In her allotted couple of minutes, 9966 cleared the end of Runway 2, intent on chasing the tail ends of the B-29s in front of them.

"Let's hold her at 4,000 feet," Dean announced. He and Reynolds were at the controls but he wanted everyone to know the game plan.

"Orders are for flight speed of 195 to 203 miles per hour. Let's hold her at 200 on the nose."

Flying low was good; it saved on fuel. Not trying to take the fully loaded B-29 up to 20,000 or 25,000 feet made a significant difference in fuel consumption. Running out of fuel and mechanical problems dominated plane failures. Far more were lost running out of fuel than to enemy fighters or ground defenses. That was the blessing of the taking of Iwo Jima. Literally halfway to Japan, and essentially on the flight line from the Marianas, planes with fuel trouble or mechanical issues had a safety-net airstrip.

Taking Iwo cost the lives of 6,821 American soldiers in fierce fighting that went on for five weeks. Airman, on the way to Japan or on the return trip home, tipped their caps as they passed by, honoring them, thanking them, and remembering them. They did not know them by name, but respected them, felt a kinship with them, and sorrowed for the sacrifice they were called to make.

Flying "on the deck" at 4,000 to 7,000 feet also had the advantage of visibility. Clouds were not a pilot's friend. Coming back from a mission to Omura they had been caught in a very tall stack of clouds that had greatly reduced their visibility. There is a vulnerability in the doldrums of six or so hours of monotonous straight-line flight. About two hours from home, a frantic right gunner Labadie came on the radio shouting, "Take her down! Take her down!"

Dean, without questioning, pushed the yoke forward as hard as he could and the nose dropped. Within seconds, a B-29 passed over close enough to write "Kilroy was here" on her belly.

"Auto-pilot bastards!" said an unforgiving Reynolds, as the offender passed over them.

"Thanks, Labadie."

Everyone had too much adrenaline flowing after that episode and spent the rest of the flight on watch for other wayward B-29s. From then on, given the chance, the crew always voted for staying out of the clouds.

The rallying point for Mission 174 was at land's end on the east side of Ise Bay. The bay acts as the mouth of the Kiso Three Rivers, located very near Nagoya. Covering 671 square miles, it intrudes into the gut of Japan on its eastern shore, one-third of the way from Osaka to Tokyo.

A half an hour from land's end, Dean began easing *Peaches* up to 17,000 feet, the established rallying elevation. The next-up lead plane was easy to recognize, circling the rallying point, his nose landing gear down, inviting arrivals to "follow me!"

Dean eased 9966 into the formation off the leader's starboard wing (number 2 position), a few hundred feet above and behind him.

Dean offered up an introduction. "This is *Peach Blossom*, piloted by Lt. Dean Sherman; 9966 reporting for duty."

"Welcome, Sherman. Happy to have you. This is Group Leader Harrison. Good luck and Godspeed. We will move out when we have collected ten or twelve planes."

Planes were arriving at the rallying point in numbers, Harrison dutifully greeting each one, and within minutes a gaggle of twelve was created. Harrison came back on the radio. "Okay, gentlemen, please follow me."

And with the precision that a flying skein of Canada geese would be proud of, the group came out of their circling pattern and headed for the initial point of the attack.

Radio chatter was coming in from planes ahead of them; Dean judged a quarter of the 500-plane formation had already dropped their bombs. Resistance from enemy aircraft was uneven, at times aggressive, while at others times the defenders seemed lackadaisical.

The batch of defenders that met the group Harrison was leading seemed to be the ones who wanted to win a medal. A half-dozen Nicks came hard and close, closing to within fifty yards. Their .30 caliber guns were no match for the .50s on the Superfort, but this was the air force of the kamikaze—caliber be damned, they were coming!

Japanese tactics included basically four defensive measures. Some fighters were equipped with special machine guns, aimed upward, that could attack the high-flying B-29s from below. Others became bombers. Once the generals started bombing urban areas at much lower altitudes, flying above the formations and dropping phosphorus bombs to ignite fires on the B-29s worked surprisingly well. Most of the fighters used a conventional head-on approach in concert with other pilots that would attack the flanks. Their .30 caliber machine guns had to get close, very close, to be effective.

The remaining attack option was the kamikaze approach, directly ramming a B-29 to disable it. The Japanese used it more often than the Americans could understand.

Passing over Osaka, still seven or eight minutes from the initial point of the bombing run, it started.

Manson and Labadie called it out simultaneously—"Fighters at three o'clock, level."

Enemy fire began to come in from a Japanese Nick. Manson turned everything *Peach Blossom* had at the Nick, as did several other B-29s in the formation.

The Nick was about to lose this battle, but not before Dean felt the subtle penetration of *Peaches*'s skin by a burst from the enemy's guns. He checked his engines. "Miller, are we okay?"

"So far, so good," replied the man who watched all the gauges.

Boy, that was close, thought Dean, unaware a slight wisp of smoke was trailing from number three.

"Labadie, Labadie, buddy, talk to me!" Howell was frantic. "Labadie is hit, sir!"

"Tend to him, Johnson. Everyone else okay?"

Howell reported for the other gunners, "The rest of us are okay."

"Gentry, how are things back there?"

"All good here, sir."

Dean strained to look behind himself, visually checking his upfront crewmates. "You guys all right?"

Nods and yeses answered him all around.

Johnson navigated the tunnel with an urgency new to him. He was not going to play cards or take a nap—a wounded comrade needed him. He fell out of the tunnel hatch and grabbed the compartment's first aid kit before he even looked at Labadie.

When he did look, he knew his comrade was in trouble.

Labadie was slumping, his head against the blister, his body arched and held in place by his safety harness. Johnson rightly judged him already unconscious, and there was a shocking amount of blood seeping through his flight suit. Johnson followed his training and looked for a pulse, pressing two fingers to Labadie's neck. His search became frantic but was unsuccessful.

Jerry had gone to B-29 medic training, and he had instructed at the school for a time, but he had never worked on a badly wounded human. He had never worked on a badly wounded friend.

Trying to process the realization that Labadie no longer had a pulse, he stepped back and raised his eyes slowly to the gunner's blister. It framed a cyclone engine on fire.

"Fire on three!" Johnson shouted.

This was an "oh, shit!" moment. Everyone knew what that meant.

They had all been on board when Dean and Miller miraculously nursed in a B-29 with an engine fire back home in training. That produced the grand champion of all ass-chewings, not just for Dean, but for the whole crew, the point being that a crew is more important than a plane. If your B-29 has an engine fire, *abandon ship*!

Dean flipped the fuel switch to number three off, turned the fire suppression selector to number three, and activated the system.

"What do you see, Jerry?"

"The fire is smaller, but I can still see flames."

Dean turned off the ignition and feathered the prop. And as a last-ditch effort, he flipped on the second suppression system. He was the man of faith on the crew, but everyone was praying, and those who could see had eyes glued on number three. They would have to be incredibly lucky for the fire to be out.

The visible flames disappeared.

Their chances improved with every second that the flames were unseen. Seconds felt like minutes—it went on long enough that breath returned—and they were beginning to feel like they had dodged a bullet.

"Sir, Labadie is dead," reported Johnson.

"Johnson, give me another visual on number three," commanded Dean.

Jerry was frozen by what he saw.

Dean came on again. "Where is that engine report, Jerry?"

"The fire is back, sir. Number three is still on fire!"

"Mayday, Mayday, Mayday! This is 9966. We have fire on number three."

Group Leader Harrison came on. "Break off and turn back, Sherman; 5329, fall out and 'buddy' 9966."

Dean nosed left on a gently turning arc. No need to put extra stress on that wing.

"Solomon, jettison the payload," ordered Dean.

The bombadier shortened his protocols. "Bomb doors opening," and a few seconds later, "Bombs away."

The radiomen reported without request, "Bomb bays clear."

"Leave them open, Norm. We will be using them in a minute," instructed Dean.

As directed, 5329, commanded by Captain Charlie Wolfe, was mimicking Dean's route. "I am with you, 9966—we are on your starboard side and 100 yards behind you. Time is 23:37. Air speed, 235 miles per hour; we are at 14,000 feet."

"Thanks, Charlie. Can you give me a visual?"

"You're definitely on fire, buddy. Flames are extending about thirty feet. You're losing about 200 feet per minute."

Wolfe did his own housekeeping and ordered his bombardier to sever their load. The bombs fell harmlessly into the waiting bay, the incendiaries exploding on impact and being quenched by the sea as quickly as they hit.

Ditching

Without orders, navigator Orr supplied radioman Prichard with the plane's position and heading, and "Prich" got on the horn.

"Air Sea Rescue, this is 9966. Sea Rescue, this is 9966."

"Roger, 9966. This is Air Sea Rescue."

"Rescue, we have a fire on engine number three."

"Give us your location and heading, 9966."

"We are on a heading of 160 degrees mag. We are just beyond the rallying point."

"We are on it. We will pick you up. We are sixty miles off of land's end. Just clear the bay and we will find you."

Dean came on, "We will need a little luck to clear the bay."

Rescue submarines could only penetrate so far into the bay. Japanese defenses had laid protective submarine nets and fortifications, forming a line that the rescue subs could not cross.

Wolfe came on the radio. "It is 23:39. Your fire is looking serious."

A minute later, at 23:40, stringers of fire were reaching the plane's tail section and debris was falling from the engine. "Sherman, prepare to abandon ship. It looks like you're dead meat."

"I am going to hold out as long as possible."

Dean knew the fire was a fight he could not win. It would have a catastrophic effect; the wing would simply fail and fold. But if he could clear the bay...and then there was the other "but"—if he waited too long there was no getting out!

"Abandon ship, men!" He gave the order, but did not move from the commander's seat.

Engine number three was mounted just beyond the landing-gear well. The well gave a protected area for the fire to grow and plenty of rubber, oil, and aviation fuel to feed on. The temperature rose quickly to become uncomfortable in the gunner's compartment.

The Corporalies prepared to abandon ship, and surrounded their lifeless comrade, Labadie. They wanted him to get up and go with them.

Gentry came out of the back tunnel, shouting, "What the hell are you doing? Sherman said abandon ship. We gotta get out of here!"

Without hesitating, he strode to the side hatch, pulled its release, let the door go, and disappeared out of the plane.

At 23:41, Wolfe and his crew witnessed Gentry's escape and felt some relief, but when no one else showed, he got on the horn again. "Sherman, it is *past* time to get out of there!"

"I hear you, 5329. We are thinking about it."

Johnson moved to the open escape door and took command of the gunners. "Come on, guys, we gotta go."

The gunners lined up behind Johnson and followed his exit.

Manson paused before his expired friend, Labadie, grabbed his dog tags from his neck, said, "Goodbye, my friend," and became the last of the backend crew to throw themselves out of the plane.

Dean was calculating the distance to the rescue sub against the diminishing control he felt in the yoke.

Orr had been furiously calculating line of travel and distance.

"Can we make it to the open sea, Bob?"

"We are still at least twelve minutes away."

Dean could feel the fire was winning over the controls of the plane.

"We don't have twelve minutes. Let's get out, men."

"Ted, lower the landing gears." He gave his orders in a calm, train-ing-mission voice.

And with the pull on a lever, *Peaches*'s floor opened up, revealing the route of escape.

His men started moving away from their stations to the open front landing gear. Forming a line with military order befitting their training, one by one the men silently fell into Japan, sent off with a "good luck" and pat on the back from Dean.

He was the last to step off. Approaching the nose well, checking his body's connections to his parachute, he planted his toes at the edge of the escape portal, teetering for a moment. Gazing at the blue water that filled the opening, he took in an oversize breath, executed a slow-motion forward fall, rolled onto his back, and fell into Japan.

It was his first time flying outside of an airplane.

His right hand, without conscious direction, searched for the rip cord handle mounted on his left side. His vigorous pull plainly ex-pressed his intentions. Immediately, a meticulously stored package of silk began to fulfill the purpose of its existence as it caught wind and snapped into shape, swinging his feet up over his head, rocking him like a pendulum before his feet could get oriented and point in the right direction.

Wind was rushing up from below him, contrary to his expectation that his forward momentum from flying at more than two hundred miles an hour would project him into a headwind.

He was falling into silence—startling silence—disturbed only by the flapping of his chute, the rattling of tethered equipment he was about to need very badly, and the rapidly diminishing roar of *Peaches*'s three remaining cyclones. The quiet became semi-serene, and yet he reached for his .45 to be sure he had not lost it.

His lips began mumbling a prayer—a prayer for his wife, a prayer for the son he had not met, a prayer that someday they would be together and embrace in the love he felt for them, a prayer for safety of the crew, and a prayer for his life.

Amused, he noticed that even in this position, this extraordinary setting, he bowed his head and closed his eyes to pray, just as he had been taught, a way of showing reverence when addressing God, he was told.

Just what is it God doesn't want us to see when we pray?

His abandoned *Peach Blossom* was moving toward the horizon, with visible flames and smoking badly, engaged in a slow-motion journey to the waiting sea. Following the B-29 script, the wing carrying number three folded like a closing book. The nose of the plane dropped, and she twisted herself down to the inevitable.

The bay accepted her like a pond might accept a child's thrown pebble, the sixty-five tons of her displacing water in every direction, hollowing out a place for herself in her new home. She hesitated for but a moment and lurched below the surface, welcomed by the great waters to her final resting place away from bullets and flak, fires, mechanicals, and the dangers of being 30,000 feet in the sky.

At 23:43, Wolfe miscounted and reported eight more chutes. In reality, a total of ten crewmen came out, while Labadie would join *Peach Blossom* at the bottom of Ise Bay. The plane was covering around three hundred forty feet per second; the three or so minutes it took for everyone to abandon ship meant the crew would be spread out over eleven-and-a-half miles. Dean was at the end of the arc of parachutists.

Knowing he was around 10,000 feet meant it would take about ten minutes to get down. And like the airplane commander that he was, he began to make a checklist of what he needed to do for himself and his crew.

Can I see my crew?

Is the enemy aware of us?

Are we sitting ducks in these parachutes?

Have we survived only to drown?

Dean could clearly see one chute near to him and maybe two others in the distance.

The airplane commander without an airplane did a pull-up on the chute cords, positioning himself into the sitting position on his seat pack, the part of the pilot's chair that came out of the plane attached to him. That pack contained his survival gear and life raft, stuff he definitely didn't want to get separated from in the water.

The order of things was important. If he inflated the "Mae West" before slipping out of his chute shoulder straps, the escape would be a struggle. He knew his uniform would remain buoyant for a time and he would not go very far below the surface at splashdown. His biggest worry was the chute itself falling onto and trapping him. With little or no wind, that felt likely.

One thing he knew he didn't need anymore was his auxiliary chute, mounted across his stomach. He grabbed the release and let it go.

He grimaced as the water came up to meet him.

I am about to be baptized in Japan.

As the water accepted his body, ignoring the shock of the cold, he unsnapped and slipped out of the chute straps. Pulling the double cords to inflate the Mae West, he felt himself elevate in the water, his head making a pimple-like bump in the chute.

This is a lot colder than the ocean at Tinian.

Dean was a great swimmer; he loved swimming, in fact. But he had never worn a flight suit and combat boots, or been suspended in a parachute when he went swimming.

The chute settled over him, sticking to the water like flypaper. He raised one arm, creating space under the nylon trap for himself, and semi-swam to the edge, careful not to let go of the chute strap connected to his life raft. It felt like it would take less effort to swim across the whole bay in a swimsuit and fins.

Gaining the edge, the chute slid down his extended arm and off his shoulder. Time to reel in the rubber raft at the end of the chute strap.

The raft was stowed in a case inside another case. The outer covering had to be peeled away completely, the inner only opened. Once the CO_2 cord was pulled, the raft came out of its cocoon and popped onto the surface. All of this he accomplished while treading water. The Mae West that had annoyed him most of his flying career, the Mae West he had complainingly dragged around for years, suddenly felt like his best friend.

Having the raft and being in the raft were two different things. Dean knew to mount from the tail of the raft, so he grabbed the tubes forming the sides to force it under him as he pulled himself onto his deliverance. The tail of the raft rolled up under his chest, creating a barricade his body could not get over. He reached farther up the tubes and pulled harder, trying to submerge as much of the raft as possible, and again the barricade rolled up under him. A third attempt had the same ending.

Then, a tender mercy—a remembrance from the training video came to him: one arm on the side tube, the other hand on the end of the raft, and level up by kicking your feet. With the next lunge, he easily mounted what would be his new home for the next two hours.

So far, so good.

Dean turned his attention to paddling toward the nearest downed parachute, a couple of hundred yards away. As he closed in, he recognized it was Manson.

"Hey, sir! We made it, sir!" exclaimed Manson, implying that he was not sure that he would. He rose up to salute in a shock-induced piece of logic.

"At ease, Corporal." Saluting protocol did not seem very important right now.

"Carl, are we close to anyone else?"

"Not that I can see, sir."

Chapter 19

Landings and Capture

WHILE THE FATALLY WOUNDED B-29 known as 9966 was making a desperate but futile attempt to clear the submarine barricades in Ise Bay, the Home Front warriors below fixated on the spectacle of the flaming Superfort, its demise at once a cause for celebration and a call to action.

While there had been this obvious victory over the birds from hell, the demonic beasts inside must still be dealt with.

Fishermen and sailors in the bay, as well as farmers, laborers, soldiers, women, and children from the surrounding shore rallied from dozens of miles.

"Intruders! Intruders are among us."

"The beasts are in their parachutes!"

The falling airmen, the cause of so much death and suffering among them, must be captured. Sailors and soldiers came with guns, farmers with machetes, rakes, and hoes—any instrument that might be converted to a useful weapon in defending the homeland from these demons. Others came with kitchen knives and clubs of various sizes. Some brought sharpened bamboo, homemade spears especially stockpiled for the coming invasion.

Thus, the Home Front warriors rose up, transformed. They were no longer citizens, but now defenders, called to go on the attack, called to be the emperor's humble shields.

They came, driven by a hatred-filled rage, sourced in the helplessness and horror of lighted gasoline being poured upon them. B-29s brought the firebombs that consumed everything.

Everything.

Not just the factories, not just strategic targets of the supporting agencies of the war effort, but peaceful places—homes, schools, shrines, and hospitals. And with the burning and destruction of the buildings, peaceable people, the relatives and friends that lived and worked in them, were also consumed in an abominable, fiery conflagration.

What kind of nonhumans could do such things?

They did not deserve to live.

Orr and Miller

It was a hollering conversation, conducted thousands of feet in the air over enemy territory, by two novice parachutists.

"Hey, is that you, Miller?"

"Yeah, is that you, Lt. Orr?"

"Yes. How are you doing?"

"Except for the fact I am about to be swimming in the ocean in enemy territory, pretty good. How are you, sir?"

"I'm okay. Nothing is broken yet. Once we get on our rafts, let's connect."

"Will do, sir."

Japanese Navy Patrol Boat 19 was a Shokai Maru–class gunboat which was actually a powerful tugboat not equipped to tow anything. She tended to the waters of Ise Bay, escorting and patrolling. She was captained by a proud, curious man with a history.

He had once captained destroyers in part of the fleet under the command of his older brother, an admiral—a disgraced admiral that failed in his assignment to protect aircraft carriers at the naval Battle of the Coral Sea. The admiral was ordered to commit suicide for the failure. This captain was only demoted. Suicide would have been more honorable.

Short in stature, carrying a stern look, and manifesting an unyielding sense of his duty, he took extreme pride in his ship and its performance, and was most anxious to recover some stature by way of meritorious service.

At the sighting of 9966 going down, Captain Yonemaru immediately ordered a course in the direction of the damaged B-29 north of his position. He intended to cross perpendicular to the flight line of the damaged plane in the hope of finding survivors for capture.

The captain's pride was severely stung by his treatment by the navy, but it was the army that he hated. The Japanese Army and Navy had always been competitors, but as the navy was collapsing under humiliating defeats at Midway and the Coral Sea, the army adopted a superior attitude toward the "disgraced" navy.

With the formation of the Tokai Army District in and around Nagoya, which also happened to be Yonemaru's home port, conflicts began to arise. The district was created late in the war to strengthen home defenses and prepare for what would surely be an Allied invasion. More than once, the officers of Tokai made public statements embarrassing to navy personnel and signaled out Yonemaru in particular.

So, when orders were disseminated by Tokai that all captured Americans should be turned over to Tokai District Army offices, Yonemaru's response was not easily translated, but approximated "like hell."

Patrol Boat 19 arrived at Orr and Miller after they had been in the water for a little less than an hour. With no English-speakers in his crew, Yonemaru struggled to communicate with his new captives, but he did have a plan for them. He would not report the capture, and kept Orr and Miller off the deck and out of sight.

He set a patrol course that would take him roughly two days to complete, allowing him to dock under the cover of darkness. He saw to it that Miller and Orr were put on a train bound for a navy prison near Tokyo. That decision saved their lives, barely. The prison camp they were sent to was Ofuna, made famous in the story of Louis Zamperini in the book and movie *Unbroken*.

Ofuna was a secret camp of interrogation; the International Red Cross never was aware of its existence. Prisoners thought to have vital intelligence were sent there to have it extracted from them by any means necessary. B-29ers were of special interest to intelligence gatherers, the B-sans being a relatively new threat. Now that they were bombing the homeland, any shred of information about their operation was deemed valuable.

Breaking prisoners was their specialty.

Prisoners were shaved and stripped, and solitary confinement was the norm. Speaking with other inmates was not allowed and carried severe punishments, usually in the form of beatings. Food rations were minimal. Prisoners were forced to exercise or stand at attention, and deprived of sleep.

Living in squalor and on dimming hope, there were beatings for talking, beatings for moving too slowly, beatings for the entertainment of the guards, or beatings for no reason at all.

Ofuna held the distinction of producing a record thirty Japanese guards and officers convicted as war criminals after the war's end. They got their reward for their conduct. Miller and Orr got to go home.

Reynolds

2nd Lt. Ted C. Reynolds was injured in the process of bailing out. He came down in a forest in Ando-mura, breaking a leg in the process. He was found hanging from a tree by woodsmen. After cutting him down the woodsmen loaded him into a rather ancient wood cart and pulled him five miles to the local military police, the Kempeitai.

Ted was the only crew member that would receive medical attention. The military police had a doctor assigned to them who was an essential part of "interviewing" the unfortunates who were arrested. Ted's leg was broken badly enough that it was deemed prudent to send him to the hospital adjoining the Tokyo Military Prison.

From there, after having his leg set, he was sent to convalesce at the prison in Shibuya, near the west end of Tokyo. There were sixty-some other B-29 aviators imprisoned there. The sprawling facility housed Japanese criminal civilians, military deserters (which were mostly conscripted Koreans), and starting in early May, Americans from captured B-29 crews. The total population of the prison was nearing four hundred.

On 25 May, the neighboring area and the prison were hit by B-29s in an incendiary raid. The wooden prison was a willing participant in the firestorm the raid created. Guards worked furiously to move the three hundred non-Americans to underground shelters prepared for such an event.

They did not bother moving the Americans. Prison guards thought it only appropriate that the Americans experience being on the other end of napalm.

A half-dozen of the airmen did manage to escape their cells, but were quickly rounded up by the Kempeitai and beheaded as prison escapees.

Sherman and Manson

Yoturo Yokkachi, an undersized, hardened-yet-tender soul, threw a length of line to an airman bobbing in a raft beside his fishing boat—an American airman, an enemy airman. He noted gold bars that identified the rescued man as an officer, and when the airman pulled himself onto the boat, his left hand revealed a plain gold band that announced he was married. The second man rescued had two stripes on his sleeve. An enlisted man, Yoturo deduced.

Everyone was wary. Dean and Manson had heard stories of attacks on downed fliers, and the captain lived in a culture that labeled them as demonic beasts.

What do you say to a demonic beast, to someone who might want to kill you, especially when there are no words to communicate? No one spoke or understood the other's language.

Dean handed the captain his .45 and asked Manson to do the same. The captain ordered one of his sailors to bring dry clothes, and led the airmen to a heater to help stop their shivering. Words were spoken through looks, by gazing into the eyes of the other. Food was brought (fish, naturally), and a comfortable level of trust was established.

Yokkachi was a man of some influence on the docks. His father, and his father before him, and as far back as had been recorded, were all fishermen. They were also leaders for many generations in the *kabunakama* guild, the trade association of fishermen in and around Ise Bay.

So when Yokkachi and his captives pulled into his slip in Nagoya, then populated with many agitated citizens, his command to let the prisoners be was obeyed.

[259]

The captain led Dean and Manson up the long dock, through a jeering crowd who were disappointed that they could not do harm to the fliers, and turned them over to the local police outpost.

The local police followed the orders of Tokai Army Headquarters, and shortly, Dean and Manson were in custody within eyesight of the smoldering castle their comrades had nearly leveled in Mission 174.

Solomon and Gentry

Solomon and Gentry, along with Reynolds, were the only crewmen that made it to land on their own. They came down near each other just offshore, and pretty quickly got themselves onto dry land. Their original idea was to make for the forest, a few hundred yards above the shore, and hide out while they figured out their next move. Locals had a better plan, and they were surrounded by a tight circle of Japanese citizens three or four people deep.

There was much yelling and threatening in a language Solomon and Gentry did not understand. Lt. Solomon took the lead and put his pistol on the ground and raised his hands, Gentry following suit. The citizens were not armed with military grade weapons, but their clubs and spears (and one especially animated fellow wielding a machete) established who was in charge.

The circle moved onto a road and traveled about two miles, all the while taunting and threatening the airmen. They were rescued by an army officer in a Japanese jeep, out looking for "the demons from the plane."

Solomon and Gentry gladly got in the jeep, and within the hour were the first of the crew imprisoned in the Tokai Army's stockade.

Johnson, Howell and Prichard

The remaining three survivors, all landing in the water, were picked up individually by fishermen. It was really quite the honor to capture an enemy, especially one of the demons from the B-sans, so, as the boats came into the docks, there was much celebrating, bragging, and posturing.

Local police had now been stationed at the docks to immediately gather up any of the captured. Without delay, the Americans were delivered to the Tokai Army District Headquarters.

The Fellows from 0017

The other plane downed by the enemy on this raid, B-29 44-70017, was brought down by flak as she finished her bombing run. The ship absorbed two direct hits: one exploded at engine number two and the other hit the plane's fuselage just in front of the bomb bays. Accompanying crews spotted the fire coming out of number two engine. The direct hits caused her to fall off to the left, and she dropped what was judged to be 3,000 feet.

The plane then leveled off and flew a level course for about fifteen seconds, and then fell off on the left wing again. Immediately the plane broke apart, forming two flaming pieces.

Bodies came out of the plane segments, falling into the city. One came down on the awning of the Hori-Sangyo Company, one at the Kodama fire station, and a third at a middle school. These poor souls were dead before falling from the plane's separated sections, their identities never accurately established. The Japanese buried them in Empukuji Temple Cemetery in Shinfukaji-cho, Nishi-ku.

Four airmen went down with the ship and were obliterated in the crash.

Four were able to parachute out of the plane—2nd Lieutenant Elton Kime, 2nd Lieutenant Keith Carrier, Corporal George Granziadel Jr., and Corporal Joseph Shelton. They were all gathered up and delivered to Tokia Army Headquarters.

Lt. Kime, bombardier, was the only survivor of the upfront crew. That second hit killed everyone in the front end but Kime, who was protected. Being the bombardier, he sat below the main floor, so the blast blew over him, blowing out most of the glass nose of the plane. When the plane leveled off, he was able to gain his feet and began looking for a way out. The front wheel wells were not an option because of fire, but the plane made the decision for him as it fell off to the left for the second time and he was somehow thrown clear of the plane, out the hole where the glass nose had been.

The guys who came out the back end of the falling ship were radar-man Lt. Carrier and gunners Granziadel and Shelton. The gunners were the only two parachutists observed from that point of demarkation. Carrier came out so late the smoke from the bombing had engulfed the falling B-29, and he was not recorded as seen by witness planes. (Yokohama)

These four avoided the dread of a water landing by virtue of being over the city. They came out at such low altitude that their time in the chutes was brief. It was long enough, however, that each was met by several policemen or soldiers, along with a large crowd of citizens, many now homeless because of the raid. Many now homeless and *all* angry.

"Let us beat them!"

"No! Let us kill them!"

The Americans could not understand any Japanese words, but got the gist of the hostile intent. They welcomed the soldiers taking them into custody.

These four became the first B-29 prisoners to occupy the Tokei army's stockade. They would serve as the official greeters as the crew from 9966 came in.

The Prison

The stockade, built into Tokai Army Headquarters, was a compact dormitory-style prison. Its main function, prior to the arrival of any Americans, was the detention of Japanese military deserters, none of which were of Japanese lineage; they were Koreans or Chinese or Mongolians conscripted into Japanese military service.

They lacked the blind loyalty and allegiance of Nippon natives who were schooled from birth in the concept of fealty to the emperor. Desertion would never enter a Japanese mind, but often appealed to the foreigners who were treated more like slaves than soldiers. Rank was almost impossible for them to attain, and their duties always seemed to be the most onerous and undesirable. Desertion seemed a worthy goal; being in prison could be no worse than being on active duty and cleaning latrines and other repugnant opportunities offered to the foreign soldiers.

When B-29ers began being taken into custody, the prison's function changed, deserters were removed, and a lockup for "Special Prisoners" was created. The stockade consisted of three cells, each with twelve futons arranged in bunkbed style. The lower bunks, three-inch tatami mats, lay flat on the concrete floor. Raised four feet above them were rope beds supporting their own tatami mats.

The injured or weakest men, often those last beaten by the guards, were assigned top bunks for ease of getting in and out of bed. As the starvation diet wore on, nearly everyone qualified for an upper bunk. Rising in the morning became a group effort, as the crew lent each other a helping hand to rise up to stand. A small, Japanese-style short-legged dining table occupied the center of the cell. About three feet by six, it was surrounded by six legless chairs with worn and frayed cloth cushions that no longer cushioned very well.

The comfort facility was a slit in the floor in the corner of the cell. A puzzling head-scratcher to the Americans, it was the Japanese way of toileting, privacy not provided.

Special Prisoners

B-29 crew members that were captured in Japan, after the strategy change away from strategic bombing of industrial areas to urban area incendiary bombing, were not looked upon as Prisoners of War (POWs). They were given the designation "Special Prisoners" and treated as war criminals.

The Japanese Parliament enacted the Enemy Airman Act after Doolittle's raid over Tokyo. The raiders dropped bombs that killed civilians and seemed unconnected to a military target.

In their defense, they were dangerously short on fuel, and felt an urgent need to get to the safety of free China. They didn't have the luxury of haggling over appropriate targets.

The language of the Act applied to all enemy airmen who raided the Japanese homeland or zones of military operations by bombing, strafing, and otherwise attacking civilians with the objective of cowing, intimidating, killing, maiming, or with the intent of destroying private property. Any enemy airmen accused of bombing urban and other nonmilitary targets were in danger of being sentenced to death, some with a trial or hearing, but most without.

Not having POW status, they were not given Geneva Convention POW treatment. War Crimes Trials estimate that Dean's crew of Special Prisoners received about 500 calories a day and lived in remarkably unsanitary conditions. Odd as it is that a starving person would develop dysentery, it was devastating, especially in the stockade conditions. The slit toilet became a disgusting landmark of out-of-control bowel movements. Walls, floor, and clothing became soiled but uncleaned. And the body, lacking any provision for cleaning it, became caked with fecal matter and then boils—painful, unattended, infected boils.

To make things worse, the lack of sanitation caused the meager rations they were supplied to become contaminated, causing blood to appear in the stool, abdominal pain, cramps, fever, and malaise.

After being on the receiving end of a visit by B-29s, the Japanese dreaded the "Birds from Hell." When strategic bombing attacks were abandoned for carpet incendiary attacks on Japanese urban areas, the destruction and devastation were beyond the power of words to convey. The Japanese recognized the change in strategy; they titled the destruction of noncombatant citizens and peaceful property "indiscriminate bombing."

They felt the B-29 prisoners deserved no quarter.

16 May 1945: Enter Major Ito

Major Nobuo Ito of the Japanese Imperial Army, one can suppose started his day on 16 May 1945 with little suspicion that he would be hung for his part in the sequence of events that were about to unfold. The end of the war was near. Hiroshima would be bombed with an atomic weapon in less than three months, yet for now, Ito was charged with determining the fate of the American airmen newly held in his detention center.

Ito was a lawyer by training and had entered military service early in 1939 at the age of thirty-six. Married, with one child, his career as an attorney was his reward for fourteen years of education, culminating at the Judicial Department of Nippon University. He began his professional life with a four-year engagement with the Home Ministry. He entered the service as a probational Judicial Officer in the army.

In February 1945 he was promoted to Judicial Officer, Judicial Judge, and Chief of the Detention Camp. In March, Ito was appointed Judge and Prosecutor of the Military Discipline Conference for the Thirteenth Area Army, or Tokai Army District, headquartered in Nagoya. The same army district that now held Lt. Dean Sherman and six members of his crew, following Mission 174.

In all, forty-four B-29 airmen would survive landing and being held prisoner within the Tokai Army District, but only six would survive the war.

Ito was a disciple of the Enemy Airman Act. He was quick to identify the bombing of urban areas as "indiscriminate bombing." He considered it a violation of the world's laws of war. Enemy participants were immediately relegated to Special Prisoner status and judged guilty of war crimes. Ito's punishment was certain—an Ito conviction meant death by the sword.

Before Ito was given charge of the Judicial Office for the Thirteenth Army District, six American airmen had been captured in the district, part of a small bombing raid on an aircraft industrial site near Nagoya. It was a strategic bombing mission conducted from 30,000 feet using conventional bombs. It was judged the airmen had not attacked civilians and a verdict rendered them prisoner of war status and not war criminals, and they were shipped to a POW Camp and survived the war.

The eleven men from the May 14th raid, made up of Dean's crew and the four from the 70017 out of Guam (Lt. Elton V. Kime, ranking officer), were not part of a strategic bombing mission. They were sent to Nagoya on Mission 174 to accomplish an incendiary attack on urban and industrial areas south and east of Nagoya Castle. To Ito, that meant indiscriminate bombing, a war crime that warranted the death penalty.

Ito would spend two months planning, arranging, and executing an elaborate trial for Dean and Kime's crews. Twenty-seven other airmen came into Major Ito's domain as the end of the war was closing in. There was no time for the pretense of a trial for them. That farce was skipped. The twenty-seven were simply executed without the benefit of one of Major Ito's trials.

He took his work very seriously and was intent on achieving the outcomes he sought for Special Prisoners. Certain of the trial's outcome, he was not hindered by honesty or matters of judicial integrity or even rule of law, for that matter. Major Ito had eleven graves neatly dug, and selected a squad of executioners, each skillful in the use of a sword, the day before the trial of Dean Sherman and his crewmates.

The Interpreter

An ambitious and studious linguist, Hiyung Pak became Toshio Aromoto the day he was drafted into the Japanese Army. All members of the Imperial Army, no matter their nationality, were required to have a Japanese name. He was able to shed that label in September of 1945. When released from the Army, he returned home to Pusan, Korea, and again became Hiyung Pak.

Pak had come to Japan in 1939 to study English at the Tokyo Foreign Language School. After three-and-a-half years of study, he could read, write, and speak English, along with Japanese and his native Korean. His graduation reward was a draft notice into the Japanese Imperial Army and his new Japanese name.

Pak would serve as the interpreter for the interrogations at Tokai Army Headquarters, for the trial and for the executions. His allegiance, notwithstanding his induction, was not to the Japanese. He later recalled:

> "I was longing for the liberation of our enslaved Korea. I welcomed the Allied prisoners, and very soon, I became their friend." (Yokohama)

At the Yokohama War Crimes Trials, Pak became a strong witness for the prosecution against the Japanese officers that once had subjugated him.

Major Ito's testimony at the trials indicated Ito "furthered examinations in an atmosphere of kindness." He even claimed to have offered the airmen tea and the right to smoke and move about freely during interrogations. Pak presented quite a different story, a description of prisoners weakened by malnutrition and dysentery struggling to stand for the interrogations. His account spoke of a four-foot bamboo stick and strikes across the backs of prisoners. He recounted that if Ito was not making the progress he wanted, was upset with a particular answer, or was angered by a captive's attitude, the stick found its way between the flier's legs. The weapon was then swung upward with great force until it met resistance, usually causing the Americans to collapse in a heap of pain.

Pak coached the airmen on how they should answer questions, especially around the issues of urban bombing. He counseled, "Prosecutor is very anxious to know whether or not you intended to bomb the residential area. If you state that your target was the residential area, you will surely be killed in compliance to the Japanese War Time laws. Be careful about your answers."

His testimony was "I tried to help them, but alas, my rank was only a private and my attempts did not succeed."

When Ito was pressed about the fliers' attitude on the stand at the trials he said, "They seemed to have an objection to the attack on Pearl Harbor by Japan." (Yokohama)

The Interrogations

The interrogations of the 9966 crew began immediately after their capture. The military, or secret police, the feared Kempeitai in the form of Captain Inagaki and his assistant Sergeant Matsui, took the first crack at the airmen. Hiyung Pak acted as interpreter. Sergeant Matsui came back by himself a few days later to complete the Kempeitai's investigation.

Major Ito then eagerly took over. He designated the court's anteroom as the site for the fliers' interrogations. Located a few yards and up a few steps from the prison cells, the anteroom was accessed by use of a long corridor that connected the prison to the central building, a long, busy corridor filled with people actively doing the business of a Headquarters Company.

In Dean's first interrogation with Inagaki, he was collected with Prichard and Howell and led up the stairs to the hallway. The captain, through the translations of Pak, invited Dean into the anteroom. The interpreter then turned his attention to Prichard and Howell, instructing them to wait in the hall for their turn. They were instructed to sit, legs folded under them, in the Japanese *seiza* style. The two soldiers guarding them stood on either side at attention, their rifles held crossing their chests.

While the interrogations inside the anteroom could be brutal, the two fellows exposed in the hallway weren't on a cakewalk.

The news did not haphazardly spread through the Headquarters offices. It came as if on the wind of a typhoon—"*Chichi bei-ei* in the hall!" The demonic beasts had arrived. Everyone in the city was aware of their capture, especially those within these office walls. Gossip full of details had been rehearsed incessantly about the new prisoners, the dialogues had morphed as gossip does, describing life-forms unlike humans, but more like malformed beasts.

Within minutes, hundreds of workers were rearranging their schedules, finding tasks and chores that would require them to visit or use the lower hallways of the building, the hallways where the beasts were, just to fulfill rabid curiosity, to see what manner of men had been trying to kill them and destroy their homes.

Male and female, they came, some more enraged than others but all happy to taunt these "demons from hell," kicking at them, spitting on them, and delivering choice Japanese "blessings," all performed and delivered with great animation in decidedly angry tones. The Americans, ignorant of the language, easily got the gist of the message.

Everyone in the building found some excuse to pass by.

When Major Ito took over conducting the interrogations, he

continued to use Pak as interpreter and enlisted two clerks for recording testimonies. He continued the practice of holding two prisoners in the hallway while the third was interrogated.

Questions at each of the interrogations were remarkably similar, and the questioner usually already knew the answer. Ito was interested in truthfulness. Asking the questions he knew the answers to helped establish that. But of far more importance was gauging the airman's sincerity and remorse, revealed by his attitude of submission.

Name, age, rank, job title, and hometown were the opening questions.

Where are you based?

How many planes are based there?

Who ordered you on this mission?

What route did you follow?

What were your instructions?

What was your target?

This is the question Pak cautioned as the most dangerous. "I knew this point was very important to Major Ito and cautioned the fliers to be careful with their answers." (Yokohama)

Ito had very specific rules for how testimony was to be recorded. He wanted his questions to be recorded verbatim. He reserved the right to summarize and edit the airmen's answers. He especially wanted all responses to the question, "What was your target in Nagoya?" to include the term "and adjacent area." When a soldier would respond they were intent on bombing industrial areas, Ito would have the scribes add "and adjacent areas." On the occasions that the recorders failed to add the phrase, Ito, in his own hand, added the words.

The fliers were required to sign the transcripts as a form of confession. Hiyung Pak testified at the War Crimes trials, "I was required to translate the statements to the prisoners and get them to sign the statements. When I did translate the statements to the fliers, Major Ito ordered me to omit the phrase 'and adjacent areas.' The airmen came away believing they were admitting to bombing industrial areas only."

Even after the war when Ito realized an investigation was imminent, he directed the clerks, if ever questioned, to indicate "the defendants had admitted indiscriminate bombing." (Yokohama)

Ito taught the captives with his bamboo switch that they should behave in a regretful, self-reflective manner about their crimes of indiscriminate bombing. They should avert their eyes and look down at all times. In the spirit of Japanese *hansei* (reflection), they should desire to confess and seek forgiveness in great humility and complete honesty to purify themselves of their crimes. The words of the confession were much less important than the amount of sincerity the prisoner displayed. Sincerity might allow for some small mercies although the true and noble warrior would expect none.

The perfect ending for Ito was a prisoner that would bravely follow the Bushido code of conduct and humbly accept the punishment meted out by the authorities to purify himself of his crimes.

None of Ito's expectations were normal skills or behavioral practices for American soldiers, a fact that infuriated him.

19 May 1945: New Friends

The crews from 9966 and 0017 filled eleven of the twelve beds in their cell in the Tokai Army stockade. In such close quarters there were no secrets. Really, at this point in their lives, facing what they were facing, no one felt the need to keep secrets or hide the embarrassing parts of their lives. In fact, long hours were spent recounting personal adventures.

The story of Ben Prichard stealing a police car became a group favorite. Ben was asked to repeat the anecdote often. Being a creative storyteller, he would embellish the story in some new way each time, always, *always* leaving his captive audience in stitches. One version had him picking up his friends and giving them a ride to school. Another claimed he used the police car to take his girl to prom. Another had the story end with him driving it into the river while being chased. No one minded that the versions were not true, they just enjoyed the diversion.

Lt. Kime, it turned out, was a college graduate and also the oldest man, at twenty-eight, in the group. He had matriculated at the University of Oklahoma, played on the football team, and had been lucky enough to marry one of the cheerleaders, Leta Leona Loudermilk. When Kime said her name in his Okie twang, Leta Leona, it sounded almost musical. Kime and Dean and Johnson engaged in more than one talk about the joy of marriage, and often shared their concerns for their wives, regrets of their bullheadedness, or the many things they wished they had done differently.

It also turned out Johnson was maybe a distant cousin to Joe Shelton. Both from Louisiana, they had spent their growing-up days a mere sixty miles apart. Joe had a rascal uncle that married and divorced seven times, and Jerry Johnson was pretty sure his aunt was one of his victims. It was hard to verify, though, as they were seven thousand miles from home and with no way to ask family to substantiate.

Manson generously educated Shelton and Granziadel (which to everyone's relief he reduced to Grahz) about the Corporalies, and invited them to join, not charter members, but welcomed as if they were. Sadly, the group's favorite pastime, the consumption of beer, was not possible. But that didn't stop the group from recounting their exploits—the drinking of humongous amounts of beer, deep-sea fishing expeditions on the way to India, or being scared shitless flying over the Hump.

They enjoyed remembering the movies they had seen together and never failed to bring up Evan Howell and *The Lady Takes a Chance* on their visit to Khartoum.

Chapter 20

War Criminal

#61: 27 May 1945

Good Evening Honey,

Friday I received your most wonderful "Sugar Report" that you wrote on Mother's Day. You can bet that it made me awful happy.

Honey, I will be so glad to get some pictures of you that you said you had just taken. I hope you hurried and took the rest of the roll so I can see too. I guess you know that I like to get the latest pictures of my most wonderful man.

Boy! You should be here to listen to all the beautiful music coming from the front porch. Dale and some of his boyfriends are out there harmonizing. Every now and again I hear the wolves a howling too. It is really quite the serenade as you can well imagine.

The flower seeds you wanted me to send will get mailed along with this letter tomorrow. I'm sending them airmail. I hope they get there alright and that you grow some nice flowers too besides. The mailman is going to wonder what goes on when noises come forth from the envelope.

That rumor about maybe getting to be a captain really sounds like a good one. I guess you know I'm hoping awful hard that it happens. I'll try not to hold my breath on the subject. I'll just wait and see if you have some good news later for me to get all happy about.

The mail situation doesn't sound so good with you. I do hope that you soon get all caught up on the latest news real fast.

It seems as if the wind has just now started blowing rather strong around in these here parts. No, Honey, I didn't know that you had sent $525 home. I can't imagine where it all is. Could be that some has just lately arrived at the bank. I'm going there tomorrow morning and see what goes on.

Yesterday the $50 government check arrived and so I'm going to put it in the bank tomorrow. Honey, I think that is the best way yet of sending money home. Maybe you should do it that way all the time.

Last night and today I have had an upset stomach and that isn't so good. I think it is feeling quite a bit better this evening though. I sure do hope so anyway. I told Momma this morning that if I didn't know different I'd think I was off for another summer of "baby troubles."

And so I didn't go to Sunday School nor church. I was down to Mammy's for a couple of hours this afternoon though.

I just lately received a letter from your mother and was surprised to hear that you might see George soon. It's got me rather puzzled, but I suppose one of these days you can tell me all about it, in person too!

Friday Aunt Fern went up to the capitol building to get her driver's license renewed. I went with her and while she was getting her business taken care of, I went and got Marvin's birth certificate. I have been wanting to get up there and get it for quite some time now and now I have done it.

If you can imagine it, Marvin is 26 inches long. I just measured him a couple of days ago. He likes to suck his thumb every now and again, too. He was really full of big long loud snores today. And Honey, that son of ours hasn't a bit of modesty! He sure enjoys running around without his diaper on.

And goodness how he does like to have his neck kissed. I wonder who he takes after? Could be you, could be me, mostly it could be both of us!

I bought him a nice little white sweater the other day and a pink light weight shawl for lots of use this spring and summer.

I've got a bit of news now that I think is going to surprise you. Aunt Fern is getting a divorce from Uncle Ken. It is turning out to be a complicated affair. I'll tell you more about it some time.

Wonderful man, if you don't hurry and come sleep with me and hundreds of other things I'm going to forget how thrilling and glorious it all was. But then I don't see how I could ever forget anything so perfectly heavenly as our past life together. I'm just all as eager to take up where we left off and have hours and years of grand, exciting, torrid love making and dozens of everything.

Yours for eternity, Peaches

Howdy Do from Marvin.

xxxxxxxxxx

Hap Halloran

In the closing year of the war, some 570 Allied airmen were captured on the Japanese mainland and in surrounding waters. According to the Japanese POW network, approximately half of them were executed, died of diseases, or were killed by friendly air-raids including the A-bomb in Hiroshima, and never returned to their homelands.

One such captive was 22-year-old Ray "Hap" Halloran. Trained as both a navigator and bombardier, he was part of the *Rover Boy Express* crew that was shot down while flying at 30,000 feet returning from a strategic bombing run over the Nakajima Aircraft Factory in Tokyo, 27 January 1945.

Personal accounts of the Special Prisoner experience in Japan are hard to find. The Japanese destroyed an astonishing amount of military records just prior to their surrender, leaving little record of what prison life was like from their point of view. Most American survivors found it difficult to talk about.

Halloran, however, wrote a detailed memoir entitled *Hap's War:*

The Incredible Survival Story of a P.O.W. Slated for Execution, chronicling his experience.

"For what seemed like a very long time, I wavered between life and death."

His captives forced him to sign several papers admitting that his B-29 indiscriminately bombed and killed civilians, and that he waived his Geneva Convention rights. The sentence for his crimes was death.

For 215 days (he was liberated 29 August 1945) he expected an execution that never came, surviving in what he called a living hell that was indescribably brutal and terrifying. Held mostly in solitary confinement or in cages he described as frigid and dark, his only reprieve was the severe beatings and interrogations by his captors.

Halloran subsisted on two or three small, bug-infested rice balls each day. There was never any medical treatment and his body became covered with running sores, lice, and fleas. Sleep was nearly impossible because of the bedbugs. He lost over one hundred pounds and was failing rapidly, both physically and mentally.

The American Ex-Prisoners of War organization describes a portion of his incarceration: "Hap was moved to Ueno Zoo in Tokyo where he was a prisoner in an animal cage, tied to the front bars in his lion cage so civilians could march by and view a B-29 flier. He was naked and black from lack of washing, with hair all over his face."

The ordeal took its toll. Halloran describes living on the very fringe of existence, losing buddies that either died or were killed, and struggling to maintain a will to live. In his own words, "It reached the point where I never thought I would survive and make it home. I prayed to God to help me live through another minute, then hour, then day. I'm not afraid to admit, I cried often in that cold, dark cage."

#62: 30 May 1945

Evening Wonderful Man,

Hello, Honey! This nice soft, cool, rainy evening. It is really the grandest weather for love and I'm all in the mood. Sweet boy, you aren't around to help me out. And make hours of torrid excitement for our liking and pleasure, so, I'll just be saving all my love for you, Honey, when you can come collect it in person. Oh! Glorious!

Honey, I got $17.70 back on the insurance I took out on the car last February. I think that is pretty good. The money is going to end up in the bank too one of these first days.

When I was to the bank on Monday to deposit the government check no other money had arrived yet. As I said before I think a government check to me is a real good way to send the money. A money order to me is another good way to send it too maybe, as long as the mail gets through.

I got a recent picture of Deanna in a letter from Ruth yesterday. I bet she is a cute little girl. Also Ruth sent Marvin a real nice pair of rompers that she knitted herself. She did very good work on them. She said she finished making them when she was in the hospital. The top is white and the bottom is blue.

Honey, I don't think I even told you that after Mavin was born I had a brown stripe down the center of my tummy. It seems to be fading out some now, though.

It's time for me to snuggle down comfortable in this bed of mine and see about getting some peaceful sleep, and to dream thrilling dreams about you, Honey. Good night. I love you, Dean.

Connie

xxxxxxxxxx

31 May 1945: The March Around the Breakfast Table

They were now seventeen days in. Dean studied his little flock as the days ticked by. Everyone seemed to be holding up, considering. Considering they had little food. Considering the beatings with Ito. Considering blow-out diarrhea episodes conducted in full view of everyone. Considering the uncertainty of being a Special Prisoner and being held by a culture they could not understand.

Dean and Solomon were the optimistic ones, half-full guys, but they had their opposites in the group—Kime and Prichard were the unofficial leaders of the despair movement. The others fell somewhere in between, vacillators, sometimes optimistic, sometimes not; sometimes with Dean, and sometimes with Kime.

Some of the crew were starting to be chased by depression. A starvation diet short-circuits the body's ability to function. The loss of physical strength and energy was obvious, but perhaps even more importantly, they were experiencing the deterioration of mental cognition, the onset of debilitating malaise, and the evaporation of will even to survive.

Being just seventeen days in, the symptoms were not yet serious. It was irritability mostly, and some apathy. And obsessing about food— talking about food, dreaming about food, staring at their food for hours, anticipating the eating of it. They had not yet, however, started to consider eating the crickets and other insects that shared their cell. But they would eventually cross that threshold.

The optimistic ones introduced storytelling hour. Most evenings they shared stories. It was an outgrowth of Prichard's "I stole a police car" anecdote and its many versions. Anyone that wished to speak was invited to tell a favorite story. Some were personal, some were true, and some were the stories their grandparents told them. Often, they told Bible stories, stories of faith and perseverance in the face of overwhelming challenges—David and Goliath stories, Daniel in the lion's den stories, stories about people facing impossible situations, like themselves.

Solomon came up with an exercise plan. He and his mother were great fans of the radio program called *Don McNeill's Breakfast Club*. It was part of their morning routine.

Every quarter of an hour, a rousing Sousa march called listeners to breakfast, the meal preceded by "The March Around the Breakfast Table."

The crew, lacking a marching band, created their own accompaniment by loudly la-la-la'ing *The Stars and Stripes Forever* as they shuffled around their little cell-room table. Initially the march was not confined to breakfast, but was conducted at 10 a.m. and 4 p.m. Later, in June and early July, the march was held only once a day, with some days skipped. Notably, the tempo and enthusiasm was greatly diminished, stolen by not enough food and constant beatings.

#63: 2 June 1945

Good Evening Honey,

Howdy Do, Sweet boy. I sure do love you millions tonight.

I received some big news tonight in the form of a birth announcement from the Samsons. They got the daughter they wanted. They named her Shirley Ann. She was born 29 May and weighed 7 lbs. and 3 onz. It's more fun hearing about what kind of baby everyone gets.

Aunt Fern is now a free woman. She was granted a divorce yesterday. In six months on December 1st it will be final. She is living down to Mammy's with Sharon and Gary. I sure do hope everything works out fine for her now and that she gets along good to Mammy's with the children there too.

Yesterday I saw "God is my Copilot." I was just awful lonesome to see something about airplanes so that is mostly why I went. I enjoyed the show too besides.

Honey, I think I am lonesome to live by an Army Camp with you. It would need to be an Army Camp though, cause anyplace with you would suit me fine.

Among other things today, I was busy painting Marvin's little chest of drawers. More fun too! I'm painting it white. I surprised myself too. I expected for sure that I should get my dress all painted up too, extra for free, but I didn't. Maybe I'll accomplish that next time. I hope not though.

It's time to do Marvin's final fixings for the night and give him his 10:00 bottle, so I'll be back real fast like when I finish.

Marvin is all cozy in bed now. The string of plastic red, yellow, and blue beads that I bought for him yesterday cause him more mass excitement. Gosh, Honey, he is getting to be so darn much fun now. He just tickles me.

I didn't wait till pay day to put the car insurance refund check in the bank. Instead I deposited it yesterday. It brought our account up to $932.70. Sounds good! Doesn't it.

In the letter I wrote your mother last night, I put a couple of snapshots of Mammy, Momma, Marvin, and myself. I had already

sent a picture of Marvin and myself to Ruth a while before.
I want you to know, Honey, that I love you with all my heart
and soul, now, always and forever. Goodnight Dean,

Peaches

xxxxxxxxxx

5 June 1945: Reo and B-29 9665

Attacking a Superfort might be compared to fighting a porcupine. You just want to be very careful. The Japanese prepared their homeland defenders in several techniques. Planes were stripped of guns and armor in hopes of gaining enough speed to compete with the B-29s; however, that left one offensive option, ramming. Entire units were prepared for that option. *Pilots of the divine wind* they were called, and by the more common name *kamikaze.*

When the Japanese realized their planes could not fly as high as the B-29s, weaponry that could fire straight up was installed on a number of their fighters. Some intercepters were outfitted for dropping phosphorous bombs from above, the propensity for B-29s to succumb to fires making that an effective option. After the Americans gave up on bombing from 32,000 feet for bombing at lower altitudes, that was attempted more and more often.

Reo's military training path led him to the Navy Flying School at Tsuchiura, a school with a proud history of turning out exceptional pilots. For Japan, the war was about gaining or protecting resources, and pilots themselves became a valued resource. The battles at Coral Sea and Midway cost the Imperial Navy 330 or so pilots, good pilots, experienced pilots.

By June of 1944, the Imperial Navy lost at least another 400 aircraft and pilots in the Battle of the Philippine Sea, these losses in part because the replacement pilots were quick-timed through training and lacked skills that could keep a pilot alive. With the implementation of *the divine wind* squadrons, nearly 4,000 more would be lost.

Keeping up with demand for new pilots changed the training

approach at Tsuchiura. During the latter half of the 1930s, admission was highly competitive and selective. In 1937, only seventy candidates were accepted and the ten-month training was so demanding that forty-five of them did not make it to graduation. Turning out twenty-five pilots a year for peace time may have been adequate, but at that rate of graduation, the battles at Coral Sea and Midway would have wiped out fourteen years of graduated pilots.

There were reasons for Tsuchiura's heavy cadet failure rate. Training was simply brutal. Brutal physically. Brutal emotionally. Brutal mentally.

One former student described it as a monstrously harsh, disciplined approach. Instructors delivered extensive beatings for the smallest infractions or lapses, often accompanied with the explanation: "I am not doing this because I do not like you, Candidate Kyshogi. It is because I want to make you a good pilot." (Sakai)

The good pilot speech was always accompanied by many swats on the buttocks with a piece of wood that could have served as a baseball bat. Not delivered lightly, but forcefully. The result was a pulverized bottom that reminded the candidate for a week not to make foolish mistakes.

The school had three disparate classes of students enrolled, ensigns who had completed training at the Naval Academy, non-commissioned officers already in the service, and boys like Reo, seeking to begin their military careers as student pilots.

Instructors took it upon themselves to bring the youngest candidates up to speed militarily with the midshipmen and non-coms. The process of fast maturation resulted in efforts to terrorize the youngest cadets. The hope was that a recruit would dare not disobey any order or doubt any authority and be programmed to immediately carry out any command.

Reo's ancestral connection and his upbringing in a samurai household prepared him for such a rigorous curriculum. It only served to grow his self-discipline.

The school was famous for its wrestling matches. Two random students were invited to the center of the mat to wrestle. The winner got to sit down, while the loser had to take on the next man up, and the next and the next until he won a match. The trainees that could not win a match washed out of training. The object of the lessons? A fighter pilot must be aggressive and tenacious. Always. (Sakai)

Reo graduated to advanced pilot training at the Training Air Division located at the Akeno Airfield in Mie-ken. There he furthered his training in a Kawasaki Type 5 fighter. Developed late in the war, they were a limited-edition plane, production cut short by B-29s. The Type 5 was a powerful, fast, and exceptionally nimble plane. It was not afraid of B-29s or their escorts, the P-51 Mustangs. It was in this single-seat fighter that Reo and his comrades flew to intercept B-29s on Mission 188 as they were attempting to return home after successfully bombing Kobe.

B-29 #44-69665 from the 468 Bomber Group, piloted by Airplane Commander Robert Arnold, fell under their guns. Mortally wounded, 9665 made a remarkably long, arcing flight of descent, slowly delivering its airmen as they abandoned ship before the B-29 crashed near the Jizoin Temple in Nabari-shi.

7 June 1945, News from the Outside

They came in a bunch around noon on 7 June. Six Americans from Mission 188, aircraft 9665, they had landed in the Omani forest area and avoided a water landing. Lieutenants Garmin, Wolf, and Polger, Sergeants McDonnell and Vreeland, and Corporal Mainiero were the half-dozen now entering the prison.

Their freedom on Japanese soil was short-lived. Within minutes of touching down and collapsing their parachutes, they found themselves surrounded by civil defense guards and local citizens. The citizens especially seemed belligerent. Everyone took a few hits with sticks or the occasional flying dirt clod or rock even though the civil defense men feigned protection. Resistance, to the Americans, didn't seem like a good idea.

All were then gathered in the Nabari police station and sent by train to Tokei Army District Headquarters by way of the Tsu Kempeitai. Of course, new rounds of interrogations were conducted at each stop along the way. (Fukubayashi)

New captives imprisoned in the stockade meant new reports and some gossip from the outside world. Other than Pak, it was the only window to world news they had.

As the "new" six filed into the stockade, the old-timers recognized the dazed look—part shock, part panic—common to new arrivals. They had worn it themselves three weeks before. The newbies were locked in with the Sherman crew, while a cell that had been used for storage was cleared out.

Sherman: "Who's ranking?"

Garmin: Stepping forward. "I am. Lt. Garmin, sir."

Sherman: "Are you the A/C [Airplane Commander]?"

Garmin: "Copilot. Captain Arnold was A/C. He didn't make it."

Sherman: "Any of your guys got any medical issues?"

Garmin: "McDonald; we think has busted-up ribs. He can't stop pukin'."

Sherman: Nodding to Jerry. "Johnson is our medic. He doesn't have many supplies, but he will take a look at him."

Polger: "Won't these guys have a doctor check him out?"

Sherman: "Well, we have been here three weeks and haven't seen one yet."

Wolf: "Three weeks here? You guys look pretty ragged, like you have been here longer than that."

Gentry: "He means we look like crap, sir."

Prichard: "Truth be told, Gentry, you never looked all that good in the first place."

Gentry: Suddenly angry. "Look who's talkin', butt-face."

Prichard: Moving toward Gentry. "You wanna make something of that, little man?"

Howell: "Hit him, Prichard! He has been asking for it all day."

Dean raised his hand in their direction ending the outburst. Imprisonment was wearing on them, and everyone's anger was near the surface.

Solomon: "Garmin, what can you tell us about how the war is going?"

Garmin: "We are running out of targets of any value. We have been mining harbors. Polger says he has heard we are out of napalm."

Polger: "The scuttlebutt of Japanese eminent surrender is dying down."

Prichard: "Pak tells us they are down to eating grass and dandelion salads topped off with insects."

Solomon: "They sure don't act like they are going to surrender."

Garmin: "I think MacArthur is going to get his way and be able to lead the greatest invasion in the history of the world."

Solomon: "His ego has no bounds."

Garmin: "Thinks he is God's anointed."

Polger: "There is something else—weird activity at Tinian's North Field. Hush-hush kind of stuff."

Garmin: "Yeah, fifteen or so B-29s that don't look like our B-29s. No gun turrets and they are practicing dropping huge, round bombs they call pumpkins."

Polger: "Can't get near the place. MPs make it pretty clear to stay away."

Sherman: "Maybe the brass has cooked up something special for the Japs."

Solomon: "That would be nice."

Sherman: "Are you guys out of Tinian?"

Garmin: "No, Guam. Nice and close to headquarters."

Sherman: "What is brewing with them?"

Garmin: "Now that Okinawa is winding down, MacArthur is starting to stage for the big one. There is talk of an invasion with a million casualties."

Solomon: "My God!"

Polger: "What is being in here like?"

Sherman: "Crowded, no food, no medical, sanitation is that slit in the floor in the corner. None of us have had a shower since we got here."

Solomon: "You get to have nice conversations with the major."

Garmin: "I think we met him. Short guy, thick glasses, doesn't speak English, likes being in charge, and seems very angry."

Solomon: "That's him."

Johnson: "Y'all get to talk with him and answer the same questions over and over and over. Keep your eyes on his bamboo walking stick."

Prichard: "My privates still ache from my last visit two days ago."

Manson: "Tell you what, I much prefer Ito's stick to sitting out in that hall."

Howell: "Me too! Some of those folks are nasty angry."

Johnson: "Especially the women. I don't understand a word they are saying, but I bet they can out-cuss any of us."

Howell: "I got kicked so many times yesterday my legs are black and blue."

Manson: "The spitters are my favorite."

Gentry: 'Yeah. Lordy, can those women spit."

Solomon: "You could almost call it a spit-bath."

Prichard: "How about the old one with the cane? She looks pretty harmless until she starts flailing with the cane."

Gentry: "I thought for sure she broke my arm last week."

Sherman: "Have you met Pak, the interpreter?"

Garmin: "Nobody spoke English when we came in."

Sherman: "Good guy. Korean. Hates the Japanese too."

Solomon: "He wants to be friends."

Garmin: "You trust him?"

Sherman: "Yes, he has proven himself. He coaches us on how to answer the major's questions and smuggles in what news he can."

Solomon: "Sometimes he tells us intel right in front of the major, who can't speak a word of English and is none the wiser."

Sherman: "I see a couple of you are married."

Polger: "Yeah. Me and Lt. Garmin."

Garmin: "How can we contact our wives to let them know we are alive?"

Sherman: "I don't know how you would do that."

Polger: "But, but...my wife is having our baby..."

Johnson: "Hey, man, Lt. Sherman and I are in the same boat."

Garmin: "Doesn't the Red Cross help with that stuff?"

Sherman: "The Red Cross, as near as we can tell, has no idea we even exist."

Polger: With indignation. "That's a violation of the Geneva Convention!"

Johnson: "The Geneva Convention doesn't apply to us."

Solomon: "Ito calls us Special Prisoners, war criminals."

Garmin: "That's horseshit!"

Solomon: "Yeah, but that is the way it is."

Prichard: "It's not like we can call the Red Cross and let them know we are here."

Sherman: "Ito insists B-29s firebomb 'noncombatant people' and 'peaceful property' instead of military sites."

Polger: With some anger. "Why don't they surrender? They have to know they are licked."

Prichard: "Pak says the major keeps quoting the bushido code—*suffering is the way to greatness.*"

Garmin: "Well, they are fixin' to be pretty damn great then."

(Survivors of Mission 188 were beheaded 14 July 1945, without trial, behind #2 Barracks of Tokai HQ) (Fukubayashi)

#64: 7 June 1945

Hello Honey,

I was sure hoping for a letter this morning, but none came. Maybe I'll have better luck next time. It will be two weeks tomorrow since I received your last letter. That's about the same story you told me in your last letter. So we both know how it is to not hear from the other for quite a little while, although I think you have had the worst luck along the line.

Honey, I sure do love you millions and dozens today like always and more even too! You're my most wonderful dream man, sweet boy.

Thursday I took Marvin up to the doctor, and Honey, everything is just perfect with him. I'm so happy because of that fact too. The doctor still wanted to know what I was feeding him to make him grow so fast. He weighs 15 lbs. 12 onz.

I found that babies are supposed to double their weight in six months. Marvin has doubled his weight and more even in just 3½ months. How is he doing, Honey? I think he's doing just grand. And he is 26 inches long. The doctor left his formula much the same because he is doing so well. He said that in about two weeks I could start giving Marvin a little cereal. I'm anxious to see how our cute little boy reacts to it. Doctor wants to see Marvin again in six weeks.

It seems as if Marvin has been slowly losing the hair he had when he was born. There is still some there but lots less than he had once upon a time. I hope it isn't too slow in growing back.

He enjoys sucking his thumb every now and again. I wonder if I should let him do it or try breaking him of the habit. What is your opinion? I have arguments for and against both sides of the question.

And Honey, Marvin is just so much fun! He laughs and chuckles, plays and talks. And sometimes his talk is all grumbles. Honey, how I wish you could be with us and see all the fun yourself.

As that is impossible right now I try not to think too much on the subject. I'd rather think of all the grand times in the future. Honey, Marvin can almost sit alone now. It will probably be a while yet till he really does, but he sure does good.

It has almost rained continually since I wrote your last letter. The weather seems more like March than June. It's all rather disgusting, because I want to take lots of sun baths as you know. I do enjoy listening to the rain when I get into bed though. It fills me full of beautiful dreams of you, you thrilling man that I love and want always.

There are lots of the prettiest roses in bloom now. In between rain storms this morning I picked quite a few for the house. They all smell and look very nice.

There is something new doing with Aunt Fern that I bet you will be interested in knowing. Tuesday evening she accepted a proposal of marriage from a certain flight Officer that will soon be on his way to India with the Ferry Command. He is known as Rusty. I don't remember his real name, as Rusty is only his nickname. His last name is Arnold. Aunt Fern met him back when she was 19. Tuesday was the first time they had seen each other in about 10 years. This all has to be kept very secret and from the Smiths. If that former husband of Aunt Fern ever found out about what's going on he could sure make a mess of everything. When the divorce is final then everyone can know about it. Aunt Fern is now 29 and Rusty is 35.

They, plus Mammy and Grandpa were here for dinner and to spend the evening last night. It was fun too.

I'm sure happy about Aunt Fern and Rusty. I hope that it all works out good for them.

I had the practice session at the piano this morning. It was lots of fun. The big piano playing desire came upon me after I had started playing some pieces for the people last night. And this morning I was still in the mood for that sort of thing. I wish I could get that way more often. Don't you?

I have had quite a bit of business to do for the Primary lately it

seems. The latest is to make up a nine month report for the Stake
secretary that I just found out about yesterday. I'll have to get it
done right away today. Worse luck! Why don't you come help me,
Honey? I would like that.

My goodness, Honey! Surprise—the sun just came out of hid-
ing. Just you wait and see though, it will be raining again in five
minutes!

I've been trying to find you a Father's Day card but I haven't
been able to find just the right one, so right now I say to you,
"Happy Father's Day, Honey!" Bye now, I love you, Dean,

Connie
xxxxxxxxxx

10 June 1945: A Conversation

"You awake, sir?" asked Evan Howell.

"Yeah, sleep isn't coming tonight," replied Dean.

"That was almost a feast tonight."

"I have never been a big fan of lima beans, but tonight they were incredibly delicious."

"How did Pak get them past the guards?"

"He wouldn't say, but I suspect he gave them a cupful too."

"Six raw lima beans! I swear it felt like Thanksgiving dinner."

"He took a big chance smuggling them in."

"Sir, do you think we will ever get to have a Thanksgiving dinner again? Will we ever get home?"

"I hope so, Evan, but I think that is in the hands of the Japanese, and God."

"Do you think God even knows we are here?"

"I am sure He does. I remind Him several times a day."

"It kinda feels like He has abandoned us."

"Why do you feel that?"

"Well, I am locked in here, starving and having my life threatened every day."

"Are you a believer, Evan?"

"I used to believe. My mom took me to church every Sunday. Now, after what we've seen and been through, I don't know."

"Did your father go with you?"

"Maybe Christmas and Easter. I think he believes, but he is a quiet believer."

"You're lucky, Evan. My dad isn't quiet about anything, especially his dislike for church people."

"But *you* believe, sir."

"Yes, I do believe. I met my wife while going to a new church. I liked both so much I married her and joined the church. What did you mean by 'used to believe'?"

"I dunno. Back home there are Methodists and Catholics and who knows how many others, all preaching you need Jesus, and you need to worship their way. Then we get to India and they think cows are sacred, and Bennie told me they believe in reincarnation. In China they pray to a statue of a large, fat man. The Japs believe the emperor is some kind of god. There seems to be a lot of versions of God."

"Indeed. What church did you go to back home?"

"Ma was an Episcopalian. Pa was raised Catholic but wasn't too proud of that, I guess, cuz he just went to the Episcopalian church with Ma and me when he went."

"Do you think the God you learned about in your Episcopalian church answers prayers?"

"Well, we are here, sir, and I prayed pretty hard that we wouldn't be."

"Yes, we are here, Evan. Yes, we are."

"So, do you think your God from your wife's church answers prayers?"

"Yes, I feel He does."

"How do you know that?"

"Just through my feelings. I feel something special telling me He is there and is aware of me and hears my prayers. That special feeling is a witness sent by Him, assuring me."

"I don't know."

"I think God always answers prayers, just some of the time the answer is not what we want to hear. Evan, His wisdom is different than ours;

[289]

He understands things we don't. That is the heart of faith, trusting in Him even though we want something different."

"But if there was a God, he wouldn't allow all this killing."

"God isn't killing people, people are killing people. The war is the choice of politicians and generals. God allows us to make our own choices. Some choices we make aren't very good. Sometimes they have horrible consequences. Sometimes a lot of innocent people get hurt."

"But what about us, dropping napalm on people? Isn't that like murder?"

"It is a horrible thing that we do. But it is because of the leaders of Japan making a bad choice, attacking Pearl Harbor, making this war, and refusing to surrender now. God is still in charge."

"I wish I could believe that."

"Use my faith until you get yours back."

"What do you mean?"

"Lean on my faith. I believe this life is only part of our existence. Whatever we have to suffer here will only prepare us for the next life. God says over four hundred times in the Bible, 'Be not afraid.' I am pretty sure He doesn't want us to be afraid no matter what we have to face. You know that Bible verse, 'Yea, though I walk through the valley of death, I shall fear no evil'?"

"Well, yeah. Is that where we are, sir? Is this the valley of our deaths?"

"Whatever we have to go through, He will help us bear it well."

"I really don't want to bear it well. I don't want to die here. I want to live out my life. I have never even kissed a girl, let alone made love to one. Shouldn't everyone get to do that before they die, sir?"

"That would only seem fair, but sometimes life isn't fair."

"This stopped being fair when we got shot down."

"Turn your fear over to Him. Let Him worry for you."

"I don't understand why you aren't angry. You have a child, don't you, sir?"

"Yes, a son—Marvin Carl. I hear he is quite a little man."

"Tell me about him."

"Not much I can tell. He is four months old, but I have never seen him, held him, or even seen a photograph. Some pictures were on the way to Tinian, but I didn't receive them before we left. And I haven't been able to get away to go get them."

"How do you do that?"

"How do I do what?"

"Make jokes. My brain doesn't see humor in anything here."

"It's easy. My middle name is Happy."

#65: 11 June 1945

My Most Thrilling Man,

Let me tell you first of all that I love you, Honey. And I sure do too, sweet boy.

Marvin is sitting on Momma's lap playing the piano and singing too, in a baby sort of a way. It sure sounds like fun.

Come help me eat all these cherries that I have to the side of me. Oh! So delicious they are! I was surprised to see them in the store, but of course, I was awful glad that I could get some.

Payday came on the eighth this time, like it usually does. I added $50 to the Post Office account then too. And that's good, as you know.

Honey, I was reading the rules and regulations in the front of our bank book and I found something out that maybe you don't know about, so I will tell you. It says that the bank may require notice in writing of withdrawals of all amounts represented in the book as follows: Amounts up to $100 thirty days notice and amounts up to $500 sixty days notice; on amounts up to $1000 ninety days notice; and amounts over $1000 one hundred and twenty days notice. I was just thinking it wouldn't be so good if we wanted to draw lots of money out all to once. Right? Right! And also I have decided to build up the Post Office account instead of putting part of payday in the bank like I was going to do. I'll still put any money you send in the bank though. Do you think that is a good idea?

I saw an awful good movie Friday. It was "Salome When She Danced." I'm going to go see it again tomorrow evening with Aunt

Fern. Maybe I'm foolish to go see it again, but anyway, I am going to do just that. Shucks, it was a super show, and anyway I like the pretty girl (Yvonne DeCarlo) that played the lead.

Marvin is all through at the piano now, and good news the whole front of his rompers is wet from all the excitement bubbles he blew. Oh! Honey! He's such a cute little boy. I'm going to take a few minutes off now and give him his orange juice.

I do do it!

Saturday, Marvin reached for and took a hold of a rattle for the first time. He's an old smarty. He also helps me hold his bottle and he will pull it out of his mouth and put it back at his pleasure.

You would never guess what I bought me so I will tell you right now. I bought a pair of good sun glasses for $7.50. I'm sorry now that I didn't believe you before when you told me that good sun glasses were the only kind to buy! I know now that you were absolutely right about the matter. The pair I have look real nice on me and feel grand on my eyes. I am happy with them in fact.

You will find out sometime just how many little things I am learning about that I should have done before to make us even happier. Maybe I am just growing up. You will see what I mean later, Honey, because I think it would be rather difficult to explain right now. I hope I'm not leaving you too puzzled on this matter.

I had a good time the other evening at a Mothers and Daughters banquet at the Ward. I will be very frank and say that food was only fair. The program was super though and the people lots of fun.

It rained all day yesterday, but today the sun has been warmly shining. I'm still thinking about and hoping for some nice sun baths.

Still no mail, Honey. I know that is either your letters caught a slow boat or you have been so busy that you couldn't write. I keep thinking, "Well, maybe tomorrow." One is bound to come sometime and soon, I hope, I hope!

Honey, do you still like me to wear dark nail polish? I hope. And once in a while I like to go to the other extreme and wear clear polish.

Wonderful husband, I hope with all my heart that every little thing is as it should be with you tonight and always.

I'm loving and wanting you with all my heart and soul, Dean.

My love forever,

Peaches

xxxxxxxxxx

Chapter 21

The Incident

#66: 14 June 1945

Howdy Do Honey,

Gosh! It sure is nice and comfortable sitting here in front of the fireplace with a warm fire burning in it. The stoker has been turned off so Momma and I decided that a fire would be just the thing, because it is a little too cool today for comfort. The sun is shining, but it doesn't give to with very much heat. That is an awful condition for June to be in.

Still no mail from you, Honey. I know it isn't your fault though, and I will be hundreds happy when a letter does come as you can well imagine. I bet something important is going on with you, Honey. Yesterday I received a letter from Dorothy. In it she said that George had written that he had been at Guam. Who knows, maybe you are still there.

Dorothy sent a picture of her and George taken last August. I was glad to get it and I enjoyed the letter too.

Today I received a letter from Ruth. Everyone is fine there.

Tuesday a high chair and swing were delivered for Marvin. The high chair is of light colored wood and has a blue lamb on the upper part of the back. It shouldn't be a long time till Marvin can make regular use of it. He really does enjoy his swing! It is on a stand and can be used outside as well as in. The swing can also be put up in a doorway (or arch.) And then, the straps and springs can be taken off and it can be used as an auto seat. Quite the deal, don't you think so too?

Marvin was having quite the big time this afternoon sitting in his swing looking at the fascinating fire. His eyes never left it.

Right now he is in the bedroom asleep, with the blanket pulled up over his face.

Honey, I bought us a new church book yesterday that I thought would be a good one to have in our library. The title of it is "Assorted Gems of Priceless Value." I also bought two Bible primers, one for the Old Testament and one for the New Testament. The will be just the thing for Marvin when he gets older.

Guess what I bought me, Honey? You can't guess? All right then, I will tell you. I bought me a "classy" new spring, summer, and autumn coat. It is a beautiful shade of gray. I really needed it and as always I hope you will like it on me. I bought a pair of navy blue shorts too. I think I'll stay away from town for awhile now so I won't spend any more money.

Starting yesterday Primary is from 10:30 to 11:30 am. It will be in the mornings the rest of this month and July too. There won't be any Primary during August and I'm glad too.

We are going to have strawberries and cream tonight. Want some? I know you would really have liked the strawberry short-cake we had last Sunday for dinner.

I'm listening to the most beautiful music on the radio, Honey. It all makes me think of you and how much I love you, wonderful handsome man.

My hottest love and kisses forever,

Peaches

xxxxxxxxxx

14 June 1945: An Anniversary No One Wanted

Ben Prichard knew how to do time. His youthful experiences with the law gave him a skill set no one else had. One of his first activities in their new home was to fashion a crude calendar.

Solomon: "What day does your calendar say it is, Ben?"

Prichard: "Thursday, 14 June, sir."

Solomon: "So, it has been a month since we were shot down."

Johnson: "Now there is an anniversary I did not want to have."

Gentry: "Not much to celebrate in that."

Howell: "Well, we are better off than Labadie."

Prichard: "Are we? I would rather die fast like him than slow in here."

Solomon: "Hey guys, don't start writing any obituaries yet. If we just hang on, the war has gotta be over soon."

Manson: "I have been hearing that since gunnery school."

Howell: "Wish I had a nickel for every time I have been told that."

Gentry: "I don't get it! We have beat the ever-lovin' crap out of them and their country, and they still won't surrender."

Prichard: "I wouldn't mind beatin' the crap out of that short, round guard."

Manson: "You mean Santa's Little Helper?"

Howell: "Why do we call him that?"

Prichard: "Cuz he looks like an angry little fat elf."

Johnson: "That little elf planted his rifle butt in my privates yesterday. I still can't stand up straight."

Prichard: "I hate all the guards here."

Gentry: "Pak is the only person who doesn't treat us like shit."

Howell: "What is that about?"

Solomon: "He hates the Japanese as much as we do—he's a Korean."

Howell: "How can you tell the difference?"

Solomon: "For one thing, by the way he treats us."

Manson: "Amen."

Howell: "What's he doing in the Japanese Army?"

Solomon: "He was here going to college and got drafted."

Gentry: "What? On a visa here and got drafted?"

Prichard: "Some country, Japan, drafting people from other countries."

Johnson: "He wants to come to the States and do more college."

Gentry: "Carrier told him his dad would help. He works at some university."

Solomon: "Would you be Pak's friend back home?"

Prichard: "Probably not. I don't think he would like my hometown."

Solomon: "Not many Orientals there?"

Prichard: "No slant-eyes allowed."

Howell: "I took a half-Chinese girl to a school dance."

Prichard: "She must have been hard up."

Manson: "There are plenty of Orientals in California, even Japs."

Solomon: "Aren't they all in internment camps?"

Manson: "Most of them, I think. I knew a family that got rounded up."

Gentry: "Can't trust them. They are all spies."

Prichard: "Pretty sure they have it better than we do."

Gentry: "Yeah, they probably have water to bathe in and food to eat."

Howell: "How about that breakfast this morning?"

Johnson: "Ha! That wasn't no breakfast. Smallest rice ball I have ever seen."

Gentry: "Yeah, about ten grains of rice stuck together. Couldn't even make it into two bites."

Prichard: "Let's make a rule not to talk about food."

Howell: "Yeah, it is better for me not to think about it."

Gentry: "I am so hungry, I ain't hungry anymore."

Howell: "I dreamt I got a package of Mom's chocolate chip cookies."

Johnson: "That was a dream for sure."

Manson: "You're hallucinating now!"

Gentry: "Your mom makes the world's best chocolate chip cookies!"

Howell: "Yeah. What wouldn't I give for one now."

Prichard: "Probably best you don't have it. We would beat you up and take it away from you."

Howell: "You would have a fight on your hands."

Prichard: "Well, it would break up the monotony."

Manson: "I am way too weak to fight. I can't even jerk off anymore."

Prichard: "Yeah, I haven't had a stiffy for weeks."

Solomon: "That is saltpeter, boys. Provided to you free of charge by Major Ito."

Johnson: "He is some kind of son of a bitch, ain't he?"

Solomon: "Indeed. But I think A/C [Dean] gets the worst of him."

Howell: "Like every day."

Prichard: "Ito's time will come."

Johnson: "I hope before ours does."

Manson: "Geez, Gentry, you readin' that letter again?"

Solomon: "You're gonna wear the paper out."

Howell: "I wish I had an old one to read."

Manson: "Man, I miss getting letters from home."

Howell: "Yeah, I miss them and I don't even have a girlfriend."

Johnson: "Where is the Red Cross when you need 'em?"

Prichard: "No Red Cross for you, Mister 'Special Prisoner.'"

Johnson: "Ito yells we are not POWs every once in a while."

Prichard: "I kinda enjoy pissing him off, so I ask if the Red Cross will be bringing our mail soon."

Johnson: "Does it work? Does it piss him off?"

Prichard: "Guaranteed explosions, man."

Solomon: "Shame on you for tormenting the bastard."

Prichard: "Yeah, I feel real bad about it."

Gentry: "Doesn't he get out the stick and wale on you?"

Prichard: "It's worth it. He's gonna beat the shit out of me anyway. I like getting beat on my terms."

Gentry: "There is a word for people like you."

Solomon: "That would be masochist."

Prichard could only smile, a celebration of his victories over the major.

#67: 17 June 1945

Hello Wonderful Man,

Happy Father's Day, Honey. If we could only be together for the occasion, you, Marvin and me, what fun we would have. Maybe we will have hundreds of better luck next year. Right now, today, this very minute, I want you to know that I love you with all my heart and soul forever and ever.

Marvin has been so cute and full of squeals, talk, growls, laughs and everything else this afternoon, lots of fun. Honey, he has worn a hole in the heel of one bootie and almost another hole in the other bootie. It is the last pair that fits him still. That is they almost fit him. In a couple more days they would have been too small, I bet. Anyway, so I put on him his first pair of white leather shoes with soft soles (size 1.) They look real cute on him too.

A week ago yesterday, Rusty left for Oregon to visit his parents. Then Thursday evening he was back again and he leaves tomorrow morning for Tennessee, from there he should be headed overseas.

Friday afternoon Rusty took Aunt Fern and me bowling. I enjoyed it very much too. The first game I bowled 133. That's pretty hot for me. The second game I didn't do so good though, I only bowled 68. Could be that I was getting a little tired. Lets us go bowling again sometime, Honey, I would sure like that.

Honey, last night I went to a dance at the Old Mill. I didn't want to go in the first place but I got talked into it. Momma and Daddy, Aunt Catherine, Uncle Warren, Aunt Phyllis, Uncle Walter, Aunt Fern and Rusty are who I went with. I tried to have a good time. For a while I was successful but it didn't last. As the evening advanced I got more lonesome for you and I was awful sad, Honey. You were on my mind continually, wonderful man, and Oh! How I did miss you and wish you were there with me to dance and romance with. The music was beautiful. I was afraid I would break out crying before we finally left. I had a hard time keeping my feelings to myself. Do I sound foolish or do you understand, Honey? You're the only one in the world to make me completely happy, thrilling Dean.

Tonight lots of relatives are coming to our house for ice cream and cake. Sounds good doesn't it?

Stanley Carter and his wife and baby are living together these days. He is wearing civilian clothes again, so I hear. I haven't seen him myself.

Honey, I'm afraid I have been losing weight lately. I wonder if

I am losing weight for the same reason I started losing my milk. I'll tell you about it sometime. Gosh Honey, we have got hundreds and dozens of things to talk about when we are together again. Won't it be wonderful though?

I think I will say Bye for now Dean. Again I say Happy Father's Day.

My most passionate love,

Connie

xxxxxxxxxx

18 June 45: The Incident

Morale of the Japanese people was being put to the test. In Nagoya alone, the B-29s had burned a huge section of the city, including their famous castle, to the ground. The castle, begun in the 1630s, had protected the city for hundreds of years. The inner and outer keys and other defenses could fend off any intruder. Any intruder except the mighty B-sans.

During the 14 May raid that Dean and his crew intended to participate in, tens of thousands in the city had been killed, hundreds of thousands left homeless, a story repeated across every major Japanese city. Two-thirds of the nation's merchant vessels, including the precious oil tankers, lay at the bottom of the ocean, put there by American submarines and airplanes.

The mining of waterways and harbors effectively stopped shipping and water transportation by the remaining vessels, not good for an island nation.

Food was becoming scarce to the point that for some, obtaining it became the focus of every day. People known for being gracious and kind-hearted became ruthless as they competed with others to feed their families. Stealing and dealing on the black market, unthinkable in pre-war times, became the norm. There developed a serious mistrust of strangers; citizens withdrew into their families.

Perhaps as serious a problem was that the food that was available, beans and other starches, became the mainstay of a diet that offered little nutritional value. The poor diet made an already challenging life even more difficult.

The citizens were asked to make sacrifice after sacrifice. People were asked to clear their kitchens of metal cutlery and replace it with ceramic utensils, so the metal could be melted down and used in the war effort.

Some sacrifices were easier than others. Part of the burden for the people of Nagoya and the surrounding areas was what had recently happened in Saipan and Guam. Their sons and husbands were part of Japan's Third Army Division, particularly the Eighteenth Regiment sent to defend Guam and Saipan in the Mariana Islands. They, of course, were unable to defend the islands from the Allied onslaught and most died there, their remains buried there or returned home in urns.

The natural result of these many issues was a population with a depleted state of morale.

When the B-29s turned their attention to smaller cities, the citizens of Japan began to feel that their personal safety was slipping away. No place was safe any longer.

Military people, especially army personnel, were accosted on the streets by citizens.

What are you doing to stop this?

Why can't you protect us?

The army was very sensitive to such questions. No one in the Japanese culture, civilian or military, wanted to be shamed for failing in their responsibilities. It was the social force that held Japan together in the face of horrific military losses.

The Holy Nation has not lost a war in 2,600 years! We cannot let it happen on our watch.

The Imperial Japanese Army organized the Thirteenth Army District in Nagoya late in the war, in preparation of the anticipated Allied invasion of their homeland. No man, woman, or child would be exempt from the defense of the "Holy Country."

The other army branch operating in Nagoya was Kempeitai, the military police, called by some the secret police. The Kempeitai, by nature of their tactics, established and maintained a healthy level of fear in the eyes of the people in both civilian and military populations.

Lt. Colonel Tamura, of the Kempeitai, hit upon a plan—a one-man public relations campaign to bolster the army's image in the eyes of the citizens. He was trying to address production numbers for military manufacturing that were down all over Japan. Tamara was convinced that if citizens could see captured fliers on display, a demonstration of the army's successful defense of the homeland, morale would rise and military production, in turn, would increase.

Tamura was aware of the recently captured six Americans from Mission 188. Major Okada, of the Tokai Army District Headquarters, was given charge of them and quickly took to their interrogations.

Lt. Colonel Tamura instructed his underling, Captain Narita, to obtain the detainees from Major Okada and take the six fliers on a "tour" of Nagoya for the evening. The fliers were herded into an open deuce-and-a-half and bound hand and foot. The six were less than two weeks into their lives as special prisoners. McDonald had stopped puking, his ribs no longer painful, but they were all hungry, sleep-deprived, and had not recovered from the deep state of shock caused by the circumstances they found themselves in.

And that was about to get worse.

The first stop was Yanagibashi. The captives were made to stand in the back of the truck, parked in the busiest pedestrian way. Within a few minutes, the attention of thousands had been gained.

"Citizens, citizens, your attention please! Gather round! See here the demonic beasts from the Jigoku No Tori. Please observe, citizens: they are but *men*! We need not fear them."

The crowd rose in derision. "Devils! They are not human!"

The crowd pressed against the truck, close bystanders reaching into the truck to grab at the airmen. The airmen had little defense, and huddled against one another, heads turned away from the developing mob. Two men started to climb into the truck for no good end, but guards held them back.

When the Japanese lieutenant felt his crowd was big enough and angry enough, he began his prepared speech.

"Look at them, citizens!"

The officer was interrupted by jeers and whistles from the crowd. "They are the very men who dared to raid our holy country, Japan. They raided even the Shrine of Ise and our Imperial Palace."

Again, the crowd's jeering stopped the speech. Verbal threats came from every direction, and objects started to fly, targeting the airmen.

"They killed many of our brothers, husbands, and fathers. They burned our homes. They committed many inhumane acts, but nevertheless, they don't seem to feel sorry about any of them. Indeed, they have committed unpardonable crimes against Japan."

"Give them to us! We will take care of them!" shouted someone in the crowd.

The officer stepped forward, arms raised, pushing the crowd back, afraid his precious cargo would not make the second stop of the tour.

"Citizens, to win the war we must increase production. If you can build one more plane a day than your quota, then we can gain revenge for the family and friends who have lost their lives to the bombs!"

The end of the speech was drowned out by the crowd.

The spectacle gained a massive crowd. Thousands had lost their lives in raids conducted by the B-29s. If members of the crowd hadn't lost a relative in the latest raids, they had lost one somewhere else to "the demons from hell."

"Let us beat them!"

"Yes! May we hit them?"

The lieutenant signaled permission, and three men swung up into the truck with the prisoners and began beating the Americans with their fists. The fliers tried to dodge their blows and protect themselves by shielding each other with their bodies, even pushing against the attackers. Nevertheless, several were soon bleeding profusely.

The tour then visited Nagoya Station. Here the Kempeitai had soldiers in civilian clothing. They circulated in the crowd during the speeches, inciting the crowd.

Several women began to wail, "We must have revenge on them!"

That proved to be a very good idea to the crowd, and a mass of humanity lunged toward the truck and several men were hoisted onto the vehicle and tried to beat the prisoners. Soldiers interceded and pushed back the civilians and ordered the truck to move out. The crowd sent a host of projectiles toward the truck as it pulled away.

At Jingu-Mae Station, the display and speeches were again repeated. According to War Crimes transcripts, nothing "out of the ordinary" happened there. (Yokohama)

The airmen were returned to Tokai Army Headquarters, offered no medical attention, and placed in their cells. They did not object to being locked up in their cells, away from the citizens of Japan.

#68: 20 June 1945

My Dearest Husband Dean,

I sure am wondering about you these days, Honey, especially ever since yesterday afternoon when I got a long distance telephone call. It was from Hilda Johnson in Birmingham. She had just received a telegram from the War Department saying that Jerry was missing in action since May 14th. She said she just had to call me and find out if I knew anything about anything. I sure hope it made her feel some better to talk to me. But now I really am wanting to know what is going on with you, Honey. I'm not a worrying though, till I get some bad news and I pray that that never happens, and I'm hoping so hard that it is all a mistake about Jerry. It's too bad Hilda had to hear something like that, now especially. She has been in the hospital five days with false labor pains. She expects the baby in four weeks.

Summer has really come to Salt Lake now. And I have been enjoying some nice sun baths the past few days.

Gosh, Honey, I had some of the most delicious cherries today. Even better than the other ones I had. Honey, we have a radio, phonograph combination in our house now. It's so nice to have it here too. Dale is buying it from Aunt Fern and I'm going to help him with a dollar here and there along the way. It's a Zenith Radio-

Phonograph. Besides it, Aunt Fern is including all her records and her record holding cabinet and the price is $150. It seems so good having it all here. There are some very good symphony pieces as well as popular ones.

It all makes me think of how wonderful it will be when we have our own radio-phonograph in our own home some day, with dozens and hundreds of records for our romancing and listening pleasure. I wonder how long we will have to wait for such a grand thing to happen? It will be wonderful beyond description, I know!

Honey, I am so all comfortable and cozy in bed right now. There is one thing wrong though, a certain handsome man is missing from my side.

Marvin is all happy and peacefully asleep. Honey, he looks just like a beautiful angel from Heaven. He had a bad cry for an hour before feeding time tonight, but he is most definitely over it all now. He is such a lovely intelligent baby boy!!!

I had to laugh at him this morning when he got his first taste of cereal (pablum). He swallowed it alright, but I have never seen such awful faces as he pulled during the process. After a while we fooled him though. I would give him some cereal and then Momma would hurry and put the bottle in his mouth. We got most of it down him and he couldn't make anymore funny faces! I mixed one teaspoon of pablum with some of his formula. He took about ¾ of it. I think he did right well for the first time, Honey.

I saw "Valley of Decision" last night starring Greer Garson and Gregory Peck. I enjoyed it much. Momma and Mammy went with me.

Gosh, Honey! I'm getting so sleepy I can hardly write anymore so I will be saying good night!

This long silence gives me awful funny feelings, Honey. I'm praying that all is right with you, Honey, and that I'll get a wonderful "sugar report" from you soon. Good night sweet boy, I love you millions,

Peaches

xxxxxxxxxx

[306]

22 June 1945: Tea with the Major

Ito's interrogation room was a compact, high-ceilinged accommodation, befitting a judge's anteroom. Windows near the top of the walls let in light but blocked prying eyes from within or without. Sparsely decorated, but business functional, it had a four-by-eight-foot table covered with maps of the Nagoya region near the front of the room. Three plush chairs, which interrogatees were absolutely never allowed to use, provided the backdrop for Ito's side of the table.

Prisoners were brought to face Ito at the table.

Dean, after six weeks of a nearly starvation diet, and just off a couple hours in the hallway enduring Japan's anger, found standing at the table and facing his questioner difficult. He supported himself using both hands on the table. He definitely knew the drill, and could anticipate or even recite the questions. This ordeal had been conducted nearly every day.

Ito was frustrated with the confrontations; the repetition had not produced the results he sought. Dean's weakness angered him, even though the major was unwilling to increase the prisoners' rations or provide medical assistance. But the greatest frustration for Ito was not getting the answers—or humility and sincerity—that an honorable person would provide.

American soldiers were beyond his understanding. Their type would never be allowed to participate in the Japanese military. They fell far short of samurai material. Their lack of discipline and honor, the peculiar, brash Yankee attitudes—all of it was baffling. But the major was a trained interrogator, a duty-bound soldier that persisted diligently, with, from what the Americans could observe, no results of consequence. This fact was baffling to them.

The interrogation began as every interrogation began.

"Where is your home base?"

"What areas did you intend to bomb in Nagoya?" Ito's words were translated by Pak.

"Industrial areas," Dean answered, raising his eyes to meet Ito's. Pak translated Dean's answer. Ito responded to the eye contact insubordination with a slap of his bamboo staff across Dean's supporting hands on the table.

"Be more specific."

Dean refused to avert his eyes. "We did not get to Nagoya. We bombed *nothing*," he replied, raising his voice in further defiance.

Ito moved around the table and delivered two more whacks across the back.

"I asked *where you intended* to bomb in Nagoya!"

"Industrial areas," repeated Dean with gritted teeth, knowing what was coming.

He wasn't wrong—another whack.

Use of a translator slowed testimony. Pak exchanged the translated words without emotion, methodically. Even with the delayed system of communication, Ito clearly sustained his anger.

"What industrial area?"

"The industrial area south and east of the main crossroads."

Ito slapped the table with his bamboo switch. "*There is no such place!*"

The bamboo again came against Dean's back, opening old wounds.

"Where did you intend to bomb?"

Still staring directly at Ito, Dean defiantly muttered, "The industrial area south and east of the main crossroads."

Ito unleashed an attack of lashings on Dean's back and finished with a mighty swing between his legs for good measure. The pain stole what strength Dean had left.

Ito, slobber leaking from the corner of his enraged mouth, slapped the map with his switch. "*Show me that area on this map!*"

Dean's legs collapsed under him. His face bounced off of the table on his way down. Enraged, Ito kicked at Dean on the floor.

The major judged him despicable, shameful, and unworthy to be a true warrior.

"Return him to his cell."

#69: 23 June 1945

Good Evening, Honey,

Howdy Do, Sweet Boy! I am loving you with all my heart and soul tonight. Boy! Wouldn't we have a hot time if you were here to take advantage of all my torrid wonderful feelings? Oh such thrilling happy times get to come for us! Gosh, Honey, our honeymoon will go on and on forever, always more perfect than before.

Gosh, Honey! Marvin is quite the little boy. Having such a wonderful Daddy as you he would have to be just like he is. You know, his name is somewhat longer than it used to be. His actions forced me to do it, so you may call him "Marvin Cute Flirt Complete Lack of Modesty Sherman." Isn't that a nice name for a cute pretty little baby boy whose Daddy is named "Man Boy Honey Dean Sherman," and whose momma is named "Woman Peaches Connie Constance Avilla Baldwin Sherman plus." Goodness! Such funny chatter! It's fun though, I bet! I bet!

Honey, Marvin has taken to growling and growling and growling some more. He sounds worse than a bear and dog together when he gets going. I haven't heard any snake noises yet though!

Excuse me, Honey! I just burped. I haven't been drinking either. I haven't had anything stronger than milk for a long time, except water that is.

I enjoyed eating lunch at the Hotel Utah Coffee Shop this afternoon. I was all in the mood for oysters, but due to the fact that they are out of season, I had to settle for some chicken.

Honey, I just like to play all the nice records on the new radiophonograph in our house. They are such nice instruments to have. I like to play the rumbas over and over again. Of course I don't carry it too far but I do love that rhythm! Let's learn to rumba real good when we have the chance next. I would sure like that lots, Honey!

Honey, how would you like for me to have a super beautiful nightgown? I was just thinking that maybe I would like one if I can find just the right one for me.

[Page four of this letter has Marvin's foot and hand outlined on the page with these notes.]

This is the thumb that he doesn't suck. These are the best out-lines Marvin could stand for. See the mess he started to make of the paper.

Honey, I'm eating a great big dish of vanilla ice cream with some delicious chocolate syrup poured over it.

Goodnight wonderful, handsome, torrid man, that I love hundreds of millions all the rest of this month even.

Peaches

xxxxxxxxx

26 June 1945: The Telegram from Washington

A military green US Army sedan, decorated with a singular large white star on its front doors, pulled onto Sherman Avenue in Salt Lake City, Utah. The driver was a soldier—in soldier-speak an MOS 345, Truck Driver Light, or in civilian-speak, a chauffeur. He carried a passenger of some import. This passenger was a captain, not a young captain, but one with a face weathered and sculpted by his service on the battlefields, his agonizing recovery from wounds, and not insignificantly, his present detail. Next to him on the seat was a box of telegrams, all scheduled for delivery that day. He fumbled through them, searching.

He did not ask for this awful duty, but consoled himself with "At least it is better than dodging bullets at the Front." His justification comforted his wife, but for him, it lost its strength whenever he had to retract the next telegram from his file box, or face a new widow and her children, or deliver his devastating news to a mother.

These particular automobiles were not vehicles of stealth; when they entered a neighborhood, detection was immediate. Seemingly everyone had radar that warned of the approaching messenger. The empty street provided a route for a parade with one entrant. The neighbors came out of their homes to gather and watch, holding their collective breath, all aware a soldier or sailor somewhere had been killed or was missing in action.

One of these vehicles was never good news.

The car slowed, the driver looking furiously for address numbers. Their arrival at 567 allowed him to pull to the curb.

The captain stepped out of the vehicle as he had done so many times before. His uniform was perfectly arranged, ready for any inspection. From his shiny double bars, polished brass buttons, and medals of special merit, to his shoes polished so well the toes could pass as mirrors, he personified what the army wanted its soldiers to look like.

Pausing to check the telegram he was about to deliver to Mrs. Dean Sherman, he nodded to affirm it was correct, and purposefully proceeded up the steps to the front door and rang. He stretched himself to his full height, let his shoulders migrate backward, and assumed the position of attention.

The opened door revealed three women standing shoulder to shoulder, arms around each other—a soldier's wife supported by her mother and grandmother, positioned on either side like bookends.

They all knew full well the purpose of the visit; it was expected. Hilda Johnson had received her telegram six days prior, and had called Connie hoping for answers. Connie had none, and had spent the last six days on the edge of terror.

"Mrs. Dean Sherman?" the uniform asked.

"Yes."

"I have been asked to inform you that your husband, 1st Lt. Dean Harold Sherman has been reported missing in action over Nagoya, Japan, as of 14 May 1945. On behalf of the Secretary of War, I wish to extend to you and your family my deepest sympathy."

The captain handed Connie the telegram, offered his salute of respect, and quickly returned to his army vehicle. He had many more stops to make.

The three women stalled in the doorway, pausing for assimilation, then retreated in lockstep to the waiting rocking chair of comfort, the chair where ordeals were dealt with. Connie collapsed into its waiting arms.

She found no contentment in the captain's message of condolences or his salute. Her face revealed her struggle as all of her worst fears began their onslaught, unabated. Her defenses had been destroyed. She could no longer avoid thinking about "what ifs" or pretend that Dean was okay. He was MIA. *Missing in action,* whatever that meant.

Her mother gently reached for the telegram in Connie's shaking hand and asked, "May I read it?"

Connie answered with a slow deliberate nod, her eyes fixed and staring at nothing in particular, and her mother read the telegram aloud:

> THE SECRETARY OF WAR DESIRES ME TO EXPRESS HIS DEEP REGRET THAT YOUR HUSBAND, FIRST LIEUTENANT DEAN HAROLD SHERMAN, HAS BEEN REPORTED MISSING IN ACTION SINCE 14 MAY OVER NAGOYA, JAPAN. IF FURTHER DETAILS OR OTHER INFORMATION ARE RECEIVED, YOU WILL BE PROMPTLY NOTIFIED.
>
> THE ADJUTANT GENERAL

There was no other information to answer her questions.

Chapter 22

The Trial

JAPANESE IMPERIAL ARMY SECRET ORDER: Execute all B-29 personnel.

11 July 1945

It was a hot, rainy July in Nagoya, Japan, the kind of day with more clouds than sun, temperatures pushing the mid-90s, and the ever-present humidity, a palpable weight endured by all, sapping strength and energy, pulling every movement toward slow motion. The showers would come with relief as they watered the earth, promoting a false sense of deliverance from the oppression, only revealing after the squall that the heaviness was compounded.

Through this stickiness, Korean native, Japanese soldier, and American fliers' friend, Hiyung Pak, crossed the parade grounds of the Tokai Army Headquarters, intent on visiting his friends in the stockade. The debris and destruction that Mission 174 had rained on the Nagoya Castle complex was nearly cleared away, an attempt to make things seem normal, an effort to inure citizens to the shame of the attack, as if the nation's disgrace could be gathered up, thrown in a trash bin, and dumped away; out of sight, out of mind.

The grounds were again immaculate, attended to by a bevy of sweepers, cleaners, and gardeners, but the collapsed shell of the once five-story castle was hard to hide. Since the early 1600s, this mighty fortress had defended the realm, and was symbolic of the power of its rulers. A citadel manned by warriors, the ultimate function was to keep and protect the rice, for the rice ultimately determined political power, created allegiances, and established loyalty.

Even as clans rose up and the political tides washed them away, replacing them with other families intent on ruling, the castle stood. And by standing, it established a continuity of society, a firm foundation growing and confirming the belief, "We are a sacred people; this is a holy land."

The massive five-story keep was protected by two very large golden *kinshachi*, tiger-headed dolphins, a male and female, mounted on the ridgeline of the roof. Kinshachi adorned most every castle in Japan, but these were the largest; they were Nagoya's not-so-subtle declaration of greatness, of superiority. The jumbo dragon-fish, made of gold, twice saved the realm from economic ruin. The sculptures had been lowered, melted down, reconstituted and hoisted again atop the Nagoya Castle, now a little less pure. The kinshachi were ancient reserves, cash cows that maintained economic stability.

However, the kinshachi's protective power was limited; they could not save the castle from B-29s and napalm.

Pak was intent on visiting his American friends to gauge their mood and encourage them. He had been ordered to interpret before the *Gunritsu*, a Military Tribunal hearing the case of eleven American B-29 special prisoners, the legal proceedings to be held in the Judicial Court section of the Tokai Army Headquarters building at the direction of Major Ito.

Pak had no illusions about how the day would go. Ito had shown him a document stamped "approved" a few days before. It established his authority to dispose of the prisoners.

Ito had given very specific instructions: "If the prisoners are asked about their target and they reply that they intended to bomb only an industrial area, it might cause some delay in the trial. Therefore, regardless of what they answer, you interpret the reply to the effect that they intended to bomb industrial and adjacent areas.

"The prisoners will be sentenced to death. However, when you interpret the sentence to the prisoners, use the term 'severe punishment' rather than 'death.'"

Pak understood.

The Judicial Courtroom of Tokai Army Headquarters was simply furnished, austere save for an elaborate oversized dais that served as the court's bench. A man's height above the floor, furnished with throne-sized chairs, and constructed with exotic dark woods, the judge's bench was enough to intimidate any candidate brought before them for justice. Justice, of course, being a relative term.

Facing the dais, a simple railing a dozen or so feet long, served as the witness stand where the accused were brought to stand for trial. At the arrival of 10:30, three men, wrapped in judicial robes, began to occupy the king-sized chairs of judgment. Major Matsuo, chief judge, led the entourage, taking the most prominent middle chair. He was flanked on his right by 1st Lt. Santo, and on his left by 1st Lt. Kataura to complete the triumvirate. On the right of the group sat the court recorder, diligently preparing his papers and machine for action. To the left of the judges stood the proud, confident prosecutor of the proceedings, Major Nobuo Ito.

Before them, just right of the witness stand, stood the anxious and somewhat fidgety Pak, known only to the court by his Japanese name, Toshio Aromoto, a translator with no one to translate to. The room was empty, other than half-a-dozen armed military police spread around the outside walls.

The trial began with Matsuo's rap of the gavel and the order, "Bring in the prisoners."

The sound of their shuffling feet preceded them.

The men who entered the room, blindfolded, hands bound, were by absolute definition the prisoners. American fliers all, B-29ers specifically, soldiers identified by uniforms, and yet they seemed to be impersonating human beings—emaciated, bony, cadaverous, peaked, shuffling shells barely able to stand, in spite of the "generous" double portion of breakfast rations they had received. They came to rest facing Pak, directly in front of the great bench of their judgment. Only then were the blindfolds removed.

Matsuo declared the proceeding open and through the interpreter he only knew as Private Aromoto, interviewed each of the eleven standing before him.

Name?

Rank?

Age?

Military occupation?

Nationality?

Birthplace?

Matsuo refrained from exploring the charges against the prisoners or what their individual part in the accusations might be. He turned the floor over to Major Ito for a statement of the charges.

"Leaving the airbase of Guam, eleven fliers came over the land of Japan and raided on 14 May, massacring a lot of noncombatant citizens, destroying a tremendous amount of peaceful property. This is absolutely unpardonable, and should duly be punished by court-martial. If they had the intention of bombing only the industrial areas, they would not have used only small incendiary bombs. Some of them claimed that their target was the northwest section of the main crossroads, but could not point it out on the map and in reality, it does not exist. Sherman's crew has insisted that they did not reach the city of Nagoya, but if they had not been shot down, they would have committed the same destruction and massacre as the rest of the planes of his formation did.

"They recognize that such acts are brutal and inhumane but seek to excuse themselves because it is a part of war. From the above statements we can see very plainly that they intended indiscriminate bombing to weaken the fighting spirit of the people.

"I investigated the case of Iwata [that crew of airmen were judged to be bombing military targets and were given POW status and survived the war], but I could find good reason to protect them. I think these men should be punished by the death penalty that our military law regulations so provide."

Pak cleaned up any of Ito's references to the death penalty as he reiterated Ito's charges to the Americans.

Major Matsuo invited Lt. Kataura to question the prisoners.

He asked only one question to no particular prisoner, "What is the public opinion in America in regard to urban area bombing?"

Lt. Kime spoke up, "I do not know anything about that."

Dean then asked, "Should we bear the whole responsibility, or only part, for the damage which has been caused by the United States Air Force?"

Upon hearing the translation, lead judge Matsuo jumped to his feet and shouted, "*Bakayaro!*" (imbecile).

Major Ito claimed the floor and said, "Prosecutor Ito hereby demands the death penalty."

The interpreter followed Ito's orders. "Prosecutor Ito demands that these eleven fliers shall receive severe punishment."

The judges stood and filed out of the courtroom to the judges' chambers. They did not deliberate, they simply returned to the courtroom a short time later.

Major Matsuo stood to deliver the joint verdict: "In accordance with the prosecution of Major Ito, the eleven fliers are sentenced to death."

The interpreter continued the ruse: "In accordance with the prosecution of Major Ito, the eleven fliers are sentenced to severe punishment."

Radioman Jerry Johnson asked, "What is meant by severe punishment?"

Pak addressed the judges with Johnson's translated question. No one responded. They busied themselves gathering papers and preparing to leave the courtroom.

Major Matsuo paused long enough to say, "I declare the trial over. Return the prisoners to their cells."

The blindfolds were again placed on each of the prisoners and they began the slow, shuffling migration back to their cells, not really sure of the punishment that had been mandated. (Yokohama)

12 July 1945: The Execution

The Americans B-29ers, held in Major Ito's prison, knew but didn't know what 12 July 1945 held in store for them. Aware that "severe punishment" was now in their future, the what, where, and when of that reality had yet to be revealed.

The events about to transpire that morning would determine that Dean Sherman and Jerry Johnson would never get to see or hold their children, that none of the others would ever marry or have families or lives beyond this day. Their friends would never again see or be with them. Future nieces and nephews would never know them. Mothers, fathers, and siblings would mourn them until the end of their days. The communal good and the accomplishment of their potentials and futures would go unrecorded, un-lived.

At 4:30 a.m. the guards came.

The rag-tag, feeble group of eleven fliers of Mission 174 were gathered, blindfolded, and had their hands tied behind their backs. They shuffled their way to waiting trucks with a destination of Obatagahara Rifle Range, a sprawling, remote location, away from the eyes of the world.

The site, now a modern residential subdivision bustling with residents, shows no sign of having been the location of acts such as executions. Today's citizens walk the streets, unaware of the secrets the earth below their feet holds, most unaware of the unspeakable things that were done here.

Part of the multi-vehicle entourage that traveled to the range was a cadre of preselected executionists, soldiers whose skill with the sword was renowned, recruited by Ito for the morning's work. There was also a vehicle full of laborers, more specifically grave diggers, who were returning to the site where they had prepared eleven graves, side by side with military precision, while the trial was being conducted.

The trucks entered the range under the permission and salute of the gate guards, guardians of entry as Dean Harold Sherman had been back in January of 1941 when he met Stanley Carter, who led him to Constance Avilla Baldwin. It was Connie and Marvin Carl, his baby son who he had never had the chance to meet, that occupied Dean's thoughts as he bumped along in the back of a truck headed for his end-of-life experience.

He felt an abundant serenity that ran counter to what he was about to face, a divine tender mercy, an intervention created by his faith and devotion to the promises he had made to his God and to Connie. His belief that his life on earth was but a paragraph in his eternal story, that the forever that followed his death would be full and rich and include his sweet Peaches and his son, Marvin Carl, provided the comfort and courage allowing him to endure the last few moments of his life without fear.

The trucks meandered through the rifle range, seeking the outermost reaches of the compound, and came to a stop beside a small lake about a hundred yards from eleven waiting graves.

Ito quickly organized the scene, his great moment having arrived, the moment he had been working and preparing relentlessly for these last two months. Perhaps he felt he was striking some sort of retaliatory blow on the nation's enemy with this sham of justice being carried out. Or perhaps he sought to glorify himself as one who punished the "Birds from Hell." His motives are lost to us. His well-practiced War Crimes testimony only reveals he believed he was carrying out orders.

The executioners were sent to the lake to await their turn. The grave diggers went into the forest above the graves, hidden from view until a grave needed to be quickly covered. Ito arranged the prisoners in a semicircle facing him. He had a declaration:

> "From now on, the execution of eleven fliers who raided Nagoya on 14 May and killed innocent noncombatants and destroyed peaceful property, will be done, and may God help you." (Yokohama)

Pak, taking advantage of Ito's ignorance of English, substituted his own statement for the translation. He had composed a special poem in tribute to his friends:

> "Poor Sherman, poor Gentry, and other brave warriors, in spite of all my efforts to save your lives, all of you were sentenced to death yesterday. Japanese military authority says you must be killed for your indiscriminate bombing, which killed lots of noncombatant citizens and destroyed a tremendous amount of peaceful property. Now, forget all, and rise with sure steps to the fountainhead of peace divine. Even though you will be killed here, your brave actions will be remembered forever by your people as heroic. May God help you!" (Yokohama)

And the death parade began. As a prisoner was called forward, he was led partway up the trail to a small table. There he would be offered a drink of water, a ritualistic attempt at honor and dignity.

The innocents then completed their walk to the grave sites, where they were compelled to kneel at the edge of their waiting pit tomb.

Toshiatsu Kataura would later testify: "I was the fifth in order, and was to behead First Lieutenant Sherman, who was the same rank as I. As everyone else had done, I first of all went to his side and bowed and prayed for his heavenly happiness; and drawing my sword with one stroke, 'Ya!' I severed his head. And once more, as I had done before, I bowed and washed my sword with water. I waited quietly by the lake until everything was finished." (Yokohama)

The macabre event continued until the number of fliers was exhausted. The perpetrators gathered and readied to return to headquarters.

Hiyung Pak recalled: "When the fliers were buried, it suddenly rained. I felt as if it were the mournful tears of the families of the fliers, and everyone present at the executions got drenched to the skin."

Major Ito was convicted at the trials and hung for the role he played.

Pak wrote to Lt. Carrier's family in 1948: "Now the Allied Commission is trying four Japanese officers who handled this case. I came to Tokyo from Korea as a live witness to testify to the commission every truth. And my mission is completed, but I may testify again, as the Japanese witnesses are not telling all the truth. I will fight out till last for the justice, because it is the last duty of mine to fulfill to the misfortunate eleven fliers."

Hoshino Yoshimi, also an excellent swordsman, and one of the men chosen by Ito to accomplish the day's work explained, "The man I executed was, indeed, a splendid soldier. It was because of the war that he met such a miserable fate, and because of my profound sympathy for him, I secretly made a mortuary tablet for him in our family Buddhist shrine and prayed for the repose of his soul."

At the War Crimes Trials, a witness to the executions revealed: "Even to the very end, none of the crew members showed the least fear, and truly I was deeply impressed by their splendid and soldierly attitude, which was such that I instructed the non-commissioned officers and others that they must consider it as a model." (Yokohama)

22 July 1945: The Divine Wind Carries Reo

The "divine wind"—the last, desperate hope of Japan.

Just as a typhoon of accepted divine origin had destroyed the invasion fleet of Kublai Khan in the thirteenth century, thereby saving the holy nation, it was hoped that somehow a decrepit collection of substandard planes, flown by young, under-trained pilots, would smite the vile Americans into disarray and submission; 3,800 of them gave their lives trying.

The kamikaze came into existence in October 1944 as the war was slipping away from the Empire. Japan had lost an incredible number of experienced pilots and planes. The skies and the seas were being dominated by the Allies.

The kamikaze represented a new attack weapon. They were essentially exploding missiles that had pilots guiding them. These weapons were more accurate than conventional bombing, and as a result caused more damage. Successfully sinking an Allied warship or downing a B-29 was a highly esteemed choice for those seeking to make what was described as a "body attack" on the enemy.

The aircraft of the divine wind were stripped of unessential equipment, armaments, and parachutes, and loaded with extra explosives. Once B-29 bombing missions changed from high-altitude strategic missions to low-altitude incendiary raids, they became vulnerable to the suicide attacks.

Japan's air forces were in tatters after the invasion of Okinawa. The Special Attack Units' planes were a collection of misfits—some planes were battle weary, some had missing parts but were still capable of flight, some were older planes, now obsolete except for kamikaze missions. The pilots were very young, teenagers mostly, and lightly trained, some with as few as thirty flying hours. Taking off, flying in formation, and diving were the only skills needed.

The standing orders were simple: when radar ordered a scramble, pilots had to get into the sky and find a target and complete their mission. There was some allowance for not finding a target and returning to base, but it was not something one should make a habit of.

Reo made preparations for what he knew would be his end.

Dear Father and Mother,

Are you well? I think of you often. My mind is full of my pleasant memories of your love and our lives together.

But the time for happy dreams is over. Soon, I will dive my plane into a B-san. I will cross the river into the other world, fighting in the defense of our emperor.

I ask your forgiveness for the difficulties I brought to you in my foolish childhood shortcomings and especially my lack of filial piety. I will never be able to repay you for the love you gave me from your hearts and the many kindnesses you have extended to me.

It is now, when we face the prospects of defeat or victory for the Empire, that I find myself completely committed to repay the emperor's grace with my life. This would be the greatest honor and accomplishment, the fulfillment of the greatest hope, for any military man.

Take care and be blessed with high spirits.

Reo

His Ki-45 was patiently waiting for him, tuned and ready. These Kawasaki designs struggled to find a niche in the war effort. Originally designed for bomber escort duty, they could not hold the initiative against P51s—they were too slow and not very nimble. The Divine Wind Unit gave them new life, albeit a short one, as interceptors of B-29s. Ki-45s had twin engines, with a larger fuselage and the ability to inflict much more damage than a single-engine fighter.

Gunnery had been stripped to lighten the load and increase airspeed. The backward-facing rear seat was removed, and the cavity filled with explosives. The plane was totally lacking in defensive weapons, which were of no use to the pilot who sought no defense. This plane had only one mission—ramming B-29s or attacking American naval ships.

Radar sounded the scramble. The day was ready for him. The sun was already hanging in the sky, the winds calm. Reo Kiyoshi reported for duty.

The final walk across the tarmac was purposeful; he did not linger or feel anything resembling foreboding or trepidation. His step was strong; he felt a newfound power within, the swelling pride and honor of serving his emperor in the most meaningful way possible.

He was celebrated by the ground crew assembled to line his path, giving and holding a deep bow as he passed, as if he himself was the sovereign.

He slid into his seat and pulled the canopy shut, buckled his harnesses, and carefully draped his senninbari over his shoulders for the last time. Lifting the shawl's protective ends, he kissed the gift of his mother and a thousand others.

Flight goggles adjusted, he turned his attention to his controls. Toggles were flipped, knobs turned, levers pulled, and the mighty twin engines brought to life.

The Ki-45s were known as *Toryu*, the Dragon Slayer. Today it would have a chance to live up to its name.

He answered the salute of the ground crew as he pulled to the edge of takeoff.

The launch flag dropped in front of him, the Dragon Slayer lunged. Reo bolted down the runway, pulling up hard into the sacred air above Japan searching for his B-29.

6 August 1945: Hiroshima

"Tell us again of our plans, Uncle," begged Mio and Mei.

"Please, Uncle. Please!"

Uncle sighed in feigned exasperation. He had lost track of how many times he had told them.

"Well, we will meet Takana and Kigi at the train station at 10:05 a.m."

"Why are we here, Uncle?" asked Mio.

"What time is it now, Uncle?" was Mei's question.

"I must visit the bank this morning. It is 8:05. We will go to the train station after the bank opens."

It was Sunday morning in Hiroshima, Japan, 6 August 1945. Summer was nearly worn out and so was the nation of Japan. Okinawa had fallen, nearly everything, especially food, was in short supply or unavailable. Millions of their sons, husbands, and fathers had come home from the war in urns; perhaps another million civilians had lost their lives. All citizens were being mobilized and were in training for the coming homeland invasion.

"Take at least one enemy soldier with you when you die," children and women were admonished as they trained in the martial arts with spears of bamboo. The Community Council had begun pushing an effort of making homemade hand grenades, furnishing tubes, gunpowder, and fuses for the planned all-out defense of the sacred Land of the Rising Sun. No one would be exempt from defending the homeland.

"After we meet our mother and papa, what will we do?"

Uncle's patience was growing a bit thin, but he loved his nieces. "We will go visit the zoo and have a wonderful lunch."

"What then? What then?"

"Ah, that I cannot tell you. You know that. That is the day's great, secret surprise, but I do promise you will like it."

Mio and Mei danced in giddy anticipation. The possibilities were intoxicating, and they giggled their way to the sidewalk in front of the steps to the bank and began playing hopscotch.

So, Riku, his sisters, and his uncle found themselves on the front steps of the Hiroshima Branch of the Sumitomo Bank, a few minutes after 8 a.m. With the bank opening less than half-an-hour away, they settled in for the wait on a very pleasant morning.

In the major cities of Japan, both industrial and urban areas had been firebombed down to the sidewalks by the B29s. The mining of Japanese harbors essentially stopped the nation's navigation. Public morale had fallen lower than anyone could have predicted, and the major indicator that things were not right, the unthinkable: the Japanese trains were not running on time.

There had begun to be murmurs suggesting reaching a negotiated settlement to end the hostilities, but the Allies were adamant in requiring unconditional surrender. That was a pill much too bitter for the Japanese to consider swallowing. The Land of the Rising Sun had not lost a war in 2,600 years, and the current generation wanted no part of failing in that way. It would be better to die defending the homeland than to be disgraced so.

But none of these things were on the mind of Riku and his twin sisters. For them, this was a day to be celebrated. Their mother and father were coming to visit them from Tokyo.

Riku divided his time between interfering in his sisters' hopscotch game and asking his uncle incessant questions about the stories he was reading in his newspaper.

"Is there good news of the war, Uncle?"

"Is there mention of Reo's unit?"

"What did you do in the First World War, Uncle?"

Uncle sank deeper into his newspaper, trying to disappear. Riku gave up easily; he knew when he was being ignored and moved his boredom into a search of the sky. To his surprise, there at the end of a huge white tail, Riku saw another "sliver of brightness."

"B-san!" he screamed.

Bouncing and pointing nearly directly above them, Riku announced, "Uncle! Uncle! A B-san!"

He had not seen one since he left Tokyo in March. The girls stopped their game and moved beside Riku, their eyes following his pointing finger.

It was their very first sighting of the dreaded B-san. "It is so small," said Mio.

"Because it flies so high, sister." Riku thought himself a B-san expert.

Uncle joined in the search of the skies, looking hard, but cut his exploration short. "No danger. There is but one." He returned to his place sitting on the front steps of the bank, reading his newspaper.

"Bombs have never been dropped here," he confidently assured the children.

Time then slipped a few gears to very slow motion. Riku thought he could see the bomb bays come open, reminding him of that terrible night in March back home. He saw the plane lurch hard to the left, signifying the bombing mission was complete. He could not judge at first what came out of the belly of the plane. But as the payload sped to earth, Riku soon could discern it was a huge, apparently round object, taller than a full-grown man. It was not like any bomb he had learned about in his military studies.

Riku cocked his head in wonderment, "What has B-san brought us this time?"

Riku would never know the answer.

He would never learn that the object's name was "Little Boy," that Little Boy had a handwritten message on it—"Greetings to the emperor from the men of the *Indianapolis*," that the B-san had a name, the *Enola Gay*, named for the mother of the pilot, that the bomb carried the equivalent of 12,500 tons of TNT, that he was watching the first atomic bomb ever dropped on humanity. He did not learn these things because when Little Boy got within 1,900 feet of the ground, a few feet from directly over the Sumitomo Bank, it exploded with a blinding white light and Riku, his sisters, and his uncle were instantly no more.

Riku never learned anything after that.

The only hint of their existence was a black stain where Uncle had been sitting, reading his newspaper, on the steps of Sumitomo Bank.

Chapter 23

A Visit from Lt. Sherman

AFTER THE WAR, the years, as the cliché says, slipped away for Connie and Marvin.

Like a cruise ship departing after an enchanting holiday on some Pacific island, Dean and their idyllic romance moved into the background of Connie's life. Just as, over time, the island grows ever smaller, harder to see, harder to remember, so it was with Dean.

Entertaining his recollection was complicated by the pain missing him caused; her only defense was to not bring Dean to her mind's stage. Besides, she had a child to raise, a life to live, and the necessity of making her way in the world alone.

The void caused her to struggle to feel complete.

For Marvin, Dean was the father he never knew. They never played catch or went camping or hunting or exploring like some fathers and sons do, like Dean would have wanted to do. Dean never held the baby Marvin, changed his diaper, or even simply saw him; he was even denied seeing the picture of his son that arrived in his mail a few days after he was shot down.

What Dean was denied, Marvin was also denied, and he missed the nurturing.

Several years after the war, Connie married a traveling salesman. He very much enjoyed traveling on the money she sent him. Eventually, she had had enough and the union was annulled.

Connie busied herself with local musical theater, singing in the

Mormon Tabernacle Choir, and holding down a full-time office job at Cudahy Packing Company.

A few years later she found another husband, a widower with a daughter, who proved more durable than her second husband and provided a sister for Marvin. Connie never wanted for suitors, but a suitor that measured up to Dean Happy Sherman never came across her path. Nevertheless, Frank Griffith was a good and decent man. He provided the needs of life and some stability for Marvin. Their marriage lasted forty-two years until he passed from this life. After that Connie was quite done with marrying.

Marvin struggled a bit with growing up, as half-orphans are prone to do. He developed an early fondness for alcohol, did not graduate from high school, instead enlisting in the army, possibly to just get away from the troubles he kept getting into in Salt Lake. He did possess enough self-awareness to realize he needed to find some discipline for his life. The army helped grow him up, and the GI Bill paid for the education he needed to become a Doctor of Veterinary Medicine.

After an appropriate amount of time from the passing of Frank, Connie redecorated the house. She brought out Dean's effects and placed them prominently—his flag, his medals, his pictures, their pictures, and mementos he had sent home from halfway around the world. These are the things she surrounded herself with in those final years of her life.

She brought out his letters and read them. She had kept every one.

The reading of Dean's letters was both comforting and troubling. Her love for him rekindled and she felt the special excitement they shared as young lovers again, but Connie also felt a loneliness that reminded her of leaving Dean for the final time on that train platform in 1944.

There were some regrets, self-condemnation, and crippling self-judgments. At the bottom of it all, beyond simply missing him, was the gnawing belief she had betrayed Dean by remarrying. They had married in the Temple she would reason, for time and all eternity. Their family was supposed to be forever, yet she entered relationships with other men. She hated that she could not live alone with his memory and keep her part of the eternal bargain. Her seeming lack of faith and commitment to her sacred vows with Dean pained her. The self-condemnation was staggering.

On a particularly difficult night, when Connie was especially not liking the person she had become, she had a visitor.

She felt his presence before she could see him. She heard him call her, "Peaches, Darling" before his vision came into view.

As surreal or impossible as this moment might seem to some, she was not afraid, and embraced, by way of her faith, the reality of her visitor.

She could only think to apologize and beg his forgiveness for her self- judged weakness. "Dean, I am so sorry…"

Dean raised his hand and stopped her. "There will be no such talk between us," he gently said.

"You have lived well; I have been watching. Dear one, we will be together again, to share our company without life's interruptions, to enlighten each other on the great mystery of love. As I told you in my letters, you are a most wonderful wife, sweetheart, and companion. In spite of the challenges we were called to face, I can assure you we will continue together in the eternities."

They conversed into the night, laughing, remembering, as if they had never been separated, as if the war had never happened, as if 9966 had never been shot down.

"When you left me, I know you couldn't help it, but the only way I could go on living was to put you out of my mind. I couldn't bear to think about you. It was too painful. Now that you are here, it is as if you had never gone." (Sherman)

Dean nodded his understanding.

They continued conversing, catching up on family, events, and especially Marvin, until sleep began to claim her. As she transitioned into slumber, he slipped away and she fell into what would be the most restful, glorious sleep she could remember.

From that evening forward, she had far less trouble being Connie Happy Sherman.

The End

From the Author

Dear Reader,

Thank you for taking the time to read *They Called Him Marvin*. If you enjoyed it, I would like to ask a favor. I am a self-publisher, therefore I don't have a Fifth Avenue marketing agency behind me. Several things you can do will help immensely. First, recommend the book to friends and family members. Second, write a short review on Goodreads or Amazon; this seems a small thing, but it will have an amazing effect.

If you have questions or comments you want to share with me personally, please visit our website, www.theycalledhimmarvin.com.

Thanks,

roger

Bibliography

Blankman, Candie L. 2011. *Forged By War: A Daughter Shaped by a WWII POW Story.* Friendswood, TX: Kae Creative Solutions.

British Broadcasting Corporation. 2009. *Divinity of the Emperor.* London. Accessed November 2015, http://www.bbc.co.uk/religion/religions/shinto/history/emperor_1.shtml#top.

Craven & Cate. 1983. *The Army Air Forces in World War II, Volume 5, The Pacific: Matterhorn to Nagasaki June 1944 to August 1945.* Washington, DC: Office of Air Force History. Wesley Frank Craven and James Lea Cate, editors.

Dorr, Robert F. 2012. *Mission Tokyo: The American Airmen Who Took the War to the Heart of Japan.* Minneapolis, MN: Zenith Press.

Fukubayashi, Toru. 2015. *POW Research Network Japan Activities,* Tokyo. Accessed May 2015, www.powresearch.jp/en/.

Gorman, Major Gerald S., USAF. 1999. *Endgame in the Pacific: Complexity, Strategy and the B-29.* Fort Leavenworth, Kansas: School of Advanced Military Studies, US Army Command and General Staff College, Second Term AY 98-99.

Hadley, Gregory. 2007. *Field of Spears: The Last Mission of the Jordon Crew.* United Kingdom: Paulownia Press Limited.

Hanley, Fiske II. 1997. *Accused American War Criminal.* Austin, TX: Eakin Press.

Haulman, Daniel. 1999. *Hitting Home: The Air Offensive Against Japan.* Colorado Springs: Air Force History and Museums Program.

Hellbird Herald, vol.1, no.5. 23 June 1945. 462nd Bombardment Group, Col. Alfred F. Kalberer, Commanding Officer. Accessed May 2017, http://www.462ndbombgroup.org/Portals/0/Documents/462nd-Hellbird-Herald-1945-06-23.pdf.

Hellbird Herald, vol.1, no.6. 30 June 1945. 462nd Bombardment Group, Col Alfred F. Kalberer Commanding Officer. Accessed May 2017, http://www.462ndbombgroup.org/Portals/0/Documents/462nd-Hellbird-Herald-1945-06-30.pdf.

Hideki, Tojo. 1941. *Tojo's Speech*, Tokyo. Accessed February 2020, http://www.bookmice.net/darkchilde/japan/tojo3.html.

HQ XXI Bomber Command. *Tactical Mission Report, Mission 174.* Accessed June 2016, https://www.scribd.com/document/61701912/21st-Bomber-Command-Tactical-Mission-Report-174-Ocr.

Landis, Mark. 2004. *The Fallen: A True Story of American POWs and Japanese Wartime Atrocities.* Hoboken, NJ: John Wiley and Sons.

Marshall, Chester, Ray "Hap" Halloran. 1998. *Hap's War: The Incredible Survival Story of a P.O.W. Slated for Execution.* Taiwan: Global Pr.

Mays, Terry M. 2016. *Matterhorn: The Operational History of the XX Bomber Command from India and China 1944–1945.* Atglen, PA: Schiffer Publishing, Ltd.

Morrison, Wilbur H. 2001. *Birds from Hell: History of the B-29.* Central Point, OR: Hellgate Press.

Robertson, Gordon Bennett Jr. 2016. *Bringing the Thunder: The Missions of a World War II B-29 Pilot in the Pacific.* Sequim, WA: Wide Awake Books.

Roosevelt, Franklin D. 1941. *Franklin Delano Roosevelt Speech* (New York Transcript). Library of Congress, Accessed July 2017, https://www.loc.gov/resource/afc1986022.afc1986022_ms2201/?st=text.

Sakai, Suburo. 1956. *Samurai! The Autobiography of Japan's World War II Flying Ace*. Great Britain: Amazon.

Sears, David. 2016. *The Hump: Death and Salvation on the Aluminum Trail*. Originally published in *World War Magazine*, Nov/Dec 2016. Accessed May 2019, https://www.historynet.com/salvation-hump-wwii.htm.

Sherman, Constance. 1986. *Sherman Family History*. Salt Lake City, Utah.

Spector, Ronald H. 1985. *Eagle Against the Sun: The American War with Japan*. New York: Vintage Books.

Spencer, Otha C. 1992. *Flying the Hump: Memories of an Air War*. College Station, TX: Texas A&M University Press.

Twentieth Air Force Association 2003. *Twentieth Air Force Association Newsletter*. Santa Barbara, CA. Accessed September 2018, http://www.20thaf.org/groups/20thorg.htm.

Yamishita, Hideo Samuel. 2005. *Leaves from an Autumn of Emergencies*. Honolulu: The University of Hawaii Press.

Yokohama War Crimes Trials. 1948. *Review of the Staff Judge Advocate*, Yokohama, Japan: Headquarters United States Eighth Army.